U0141315

GEPT
初級模擬試題
第1回
解答、翻譯與詳解

第 1 回解答

 聽力測驗解答

1. B	2. B	3. B	4. C	5. B
6. C	7. C	8. C	9. B	10. C
11. C	12. B	13. B	14. C	15. B
16. C	17. A	18. B	19. A	20. A
21. C	22. A	23. B	24. A	25. C
26. B	27. C	28. A	29. A	30. B

 閱讀測驗解答

1. C	2. B	3. B	4. C	5. A
6. C	7. B	8. A	9. D	10. D
11. C	12. C	13. B	14. D	15. C
16. C	17. B	18. D	19. A	20. A
21. B	22. D	23. A	24. B	25. D
26. C	27. A	28. D	29. A	30. C

第一部分 看圖辨義

__B__ 1. For Question Number 1,
　　 please look at the picture.

　　 What is the man doing?

　　 (A) He's sweeping the floor.

　　 (B) He's wiping the table.

　　 (C) He's holding a knife.

第一題，請看此圖片。

男子正在做什麼？

(A) 他在掃地。

(B) 他在擦桌子。

(C) 他拿著刀。

解析 男子看起來是在擦桌子 (wiping the table)，其他選項皆不正確，選 B。

__B__ 2. For Question Number 2,
　　 please look at the picture.
　　 Where are the women?

　　 (A) They are in the ocean.

　　 (B) They are at the lake.

　　 (C) They are at the beach.

第二題，請看此圖片。

這些女子在哪裡？

(A) 她們在海裡。

(B) 她們在湖邊。

(C) 她們在沙灘。

解析 「at + 地方」可表示「在 ____ 旁邊」例：at the lake（在湖邊），at the table（在餐桌邊）。女子們在湖邊慢跑，故選 B。

B 3. For Question Number 3,
please look at the picture.
How's the weather?

(A) He's holding an umbrella.

(B) Rainy and windy

(C) It's snowy.

第三題，請看此圖片。

天氣如何？

(A) 他拿著傘。

(B) 颱風下雨。

(C) 下雪。

解析 圖片中的人雖然拿著傘，但問題在問天氣狀況，因此選項 A 答非所問。選項 C 則和圖片不符，選 B。

C 4. For Question Number 4,
please look at the picture.

How does the boy feel?

(A) He's interested.

(B) He's excited.

(C) He's scared.

第四題，請看此圖片。

男孩覺得怎麼樣？

(A) 他很感興趣。

(B) 他很興奮。

(C) 他很害怕。

解析 圖片中的男孩被野狗圍繞，神色緊張害怕，C 選項最貼近圖片描述，其他選項不正確。

B 5. For Question Number 5,
      please look at the picture.
      What is the girl with long hair
      doing?

   (A) She's holding an ice cream
       cone.

   (B) She's looking for something.

   (C) She's at the supermarket.

第五題，請看此圖片。

長髮的女孩正在做什麼？

(A) 她拿著冰淇淋甜筒。

(B) 她在找東西。

(C) 她在超市。

解析 選項 A 為拿著冰淇淋甜筒的女孩，但她留短髮，選項 C 是女孩所在位置，只有
      選項 B 是正在進行的動作，選 B。

__C__ 6. Wow, I haven't seen you for days!

(A) I've been doing this for days.

(B) Yeah, I'll be leaving tomorrow.

(C) Sorry, I've been really busy lately.

哇，好幾天沒見到你了！

(A) 我已經做這件事好幾天了。

(B) 是的，我明天就離開。

(C) 對不起，我最近很忙。

解析 題目為現在完成式，表示一段時間沒見到對方。選項 A 答非所問，選項 B 告知未來的計畫，只有選項 C 回答了問題。

__C__ 7. How do you like the dish?

(A) I'm fine, thank you.

(B) Better late than never.

(C) It's great. What's it called?

你覺得這道菜怎麼樣？

(A) 我很好，謝謝。

(B) 遲到總比不到好。

(C) 很好吃。這叫什麼？

解析 "How do you like..." 常用來詢問喜歡某種事物的程度。選項 C 回答了問題，並延伸提問菜名，其他兩個選項答非所問，故選 C。

__C__ 8. Do you know the woman over there?

(A) Yes, she has curly hair.

(B) He's my friend from L.A.

(C) Oh, that's Ray's cousin, Tina.

你知道那邊的女子是誰嗎？

(A) 對，她頭髮捲捲的。

(B) 他是我洛杉磯來的朋友。

(C) 喔！那是雷的表妹，提娜。

解析 女子搭配的代名詞為 she，B 選項使用男生的代名詞 he 回答，故不正確。A 選項答非所問。

__B__ 9. Would you like some coffee?

(A) Yes, I work at a coffee shop.

(B) Sure, a coffee sounds great.

(C) Can you pass the cream, please?

你要喝點咖啡嗎？

(A) 對，我在咖啡館工作。

(B) 當然，喝杯咖啡聽起來不錯。

(C) 你能幫我拿奶精嗎？

解析 B 選項用 "...sounds great." 的句型來表示贊同對方的提議，最符合情境。其餘兩個選項答非所問。

__C__ 10. Mary, your friends are here!
  (A) My friends will arrive soon.
  (B) I'm too busy to answer the phone now.
  (C) Can you ask them to wait in the living room?

瑪莉，妳的朋友來了！
(A) 我朋友快到了。
(B) 我現在太忙，沒空接電話。
(C) 你可以請他們在客廳等一下嗎？

> **解析** 題目的「人 + be 動詞 + here」，有「到了」或是「來了」的意思。選項 C 的 ask 在這邊是請求的意思。請到訪的朋友在客廳稍等最符合情境，故選 C。

__C__ 11. Is this yours?
  (A) Sure, I'd love to.
  (B) I believe they're mine, too.
  (C) No, it's not. I think it belongs to May.

這是你的嗎？
(A) 好啊，我很樂意。
(B) 我也相信這些是我的。
(C) 不，不是。我想這是梅的。

> **解析** 「事物 + belong to + 人」可用來表示事物的歸屬，所以選 C。問句為單數，選項 B 回答用複數形 they're，句尾的 too 也和題意不合，因此錯誤。

__B__ 12. How will the weather be tomorrow?
  (A) It's been raining all week.
  (B) I don't know. I'll check later.
  (C) It was nice and dry. We enjoyed it.

明天天氣怎麼樣？
(A) 這一週都在下雨。
(B) 我不知道。我等等會查。
(C) 天氣很好，沒下雨。我們都玩得很開心。

> **解析** 問題為未來式，詢問隔天的天氣。選項 C 為過去式，說明過去的天氣。選項 A 用現在完成式，說明這週以來的天氣，兩者皆不正確。故選 B。

__B__ 13. Do you have time to talk later?

    (A) I have no idea what this is all about.

    (B) Yes. I'll call you when I get home.

    (C) No. We can talk about it tonight.

你等一下有時間說話嗎？

(A) 我不知道這是怎麼回事。

(B) 可以。我到家後打電話給你。

(C) 沒有。我們今晚可以討論這個問題。

解析 題目中沒有提及要討論的話題，因此選項 C 的代名詞 it 不知道是指什麼，語意不成立。選項 A 答非所問。只有 B 回答了問題。

__C__ 14. Did you visit Mr. Lee last week?

    (A) Yes, I'm going there next Monday.

    (B) I've known Mr. Lee for years.

    (C) Yes, I did. He took me to a fancy restaurant.

你上星期有去拜訪李先生嗎？

(A) 有，我下星期一要去。

(B) 我認識李先生好幾年了。

(C) 有，我有去。他帶我去一間高級餐廳。

解析 問題為過去式，詢問上週的行程，因此回答也要用過去式回答。三個選項中只有 C 是過去式，並且有回答到問題。

__B__ 15. Do you have a pet?

    (A) Sorry, I don't have a pen.

    (B) No, but I'd like to get one.

    (C) My favorite animal is the rabbit.

你有養寵物嗎？

(A) 不好意思，我沒有筆。

(B) 沒有，可是我想養一隻。

(C) 我最喜歡的動物是兔子。

解析 A 選項的 pen 和 pet 發音相像，要仔細聽尾音。B 選項中的 one 指的是 a pet。故選 B。

C 16. W: You don't look well. Are you all right?

M: Not really. I feel tired.

W: Let me take your temperature. Oh, you have a fever.

M: No wonder I feel so bad.

Question: What's wrong with the man?

女子：你看起來不太好。你沒事吧？

男子：不完全是，我覺得疲累。

女子：我幫你量一下體溫。哦，你發燒了。

男子：難怪我感覺這麼不舒服。

問題：男子怎麼了？

(A) He's injured.
(B) He's old.
(C) He's sick.

(A) 他受傷了。
(B) 他年紀大了。
(C) 他生病了。

解析 看對話得知男子生病 (sick) 而非受傷 (injured)，故選 C。

A 17. G: Mom, I'm home. I'm so hungry.

W: There's an apple pie on the table in the kitchen.

G: Wow! Did you bake it today?

W: I got it at the new bakery on the corner. I knew you'd want to try it.

Question: What did the woman do?

女孩：媽，我回來了。我好餓。

女子：廚房的桌上有蘋果派。

女孩：哇！是妳今天烤的嗎？

女子：我在街角新開的麵包店買的。我知道你會想嚐嚐看。

問題：女子做了什麼？

(A) Go to a bakery.
(B) Bake an apple pie.
(C) Open a shop on the corner.

(A) 去麵包店。
(B) 烤蘋果派。
(C) 在街角開一間店。

解析 got（取得）在這邊是購買的意思。女子的蘋果派是去新開的麵包店買的，故選 A。

B 18. W: I can't find my car keys anywhere.

M: Have you checked your desk?

W: Yes! And I also checked the pockets in my jacket. I saw them just five minutes ago.

M: How about your purse? Have you looked there yet?

Question: Where are the keys?

女子：我到處都找不到我的車鑰匙。

男子：你檢查過你的桌子了嗎？

女子：是的！我還檢查了我的外套口袋。五分鐘前我還有看到它們。

男子：那你的錢包呢？你去找過了嗎？

問題：鑰匙在哪裡？

(A) On the desk.

(B) We don't know.

(C) In the woman's purse.

(A) 在桌子上。

(B) 我們不知道。

(C) 在女子的錢包裡。

解析 對話中的男女還在找鑰匙，還沒找到，故選 B。

A 19. W: We're having a picnic next weekend and you're invited.

M: Great! How can I help prepare?

W: Can you drive me to the supermarket to shop for food?

M: I'd love to, but my car broke down.

W: That's all right. I can just take the bus.

Question: What did the man say?

女子：我們下週末要辦野餐，你被邀請了。

男子：太好了！我要怎麼幫忙準備呢？

女子：你能開車送我去超市買東西嗎？

男子：我很想去，但是我的車壞了。

女子：沒關係。我可以坐公車。

問題：男子說了什麼？

(A) He can't do what the woman asked him to do.

(B) He will buy some food at the supermarket.

(C) He feels bad that he wasn't invited to the picnic.

(A) 他不能做女子請他做的事。

(B) 他將在超市買一些食物。

(C) 他因為沒有被邀請參加野餐而感到難過

解析 "I'd love to, but..." 的句型常用來婉拒邀請，或是表達自己無法達成對方的要求，故選 A。

A 20. M: Hurry! The train is about to leave!

W: I can't go any faster! Oh no, there it goes!

M: Looks like you'll be late for your meeting.

W: I'd better tell Jason that I can't be there on time.

M: You should set your alarm clock for 7:30 next time.

Question: What happened to the woman?

男子：快點！火車馬上就要開了！

女子：我不能更快了！哦，不，它開走了！

男子：看來你開會要遲到了。

女子：我最好告訴傑森，我不能準時到場。

男子：你下次應該把鬧鐘調到 7:30。

問題：那位女子怎麼了？

(A) She missed her train.

(B) She missed her meeting.

(C) She didn't hear her alarm clock.

(A) 她錯過了火車。

(B) 她錯過了會議。

(C) 她沒聽到鬧鐘。

解析 女子說無法準時到場，表示沒有錯過整場會議。根據男子最後一句可得知女子的問題是鬧鐘時間調太晚，但沒有提到她沒聽到鬧鐘。對話中女子有提到火車開走了，故選 A。

C 21. W: Welcome to the cooking class. Today we're learning how to make an omelet.

M: What ingredients do we need?

W: Butter, eggs, mushrooms, and some salt. You can find them on the counter over there.

M: Great. I can't wait to get started.

W: Oh, and grab a bowl to mix your ingredients in.

Question: What will the man make?

女子：歡迎來到烹飪課。今天我們要學習怎麼做歐姆蛋。

男子：我們需要什麼材料？

女子：奶油、雞蛋、蘑菇，還有一些鹽。你可以在那邊的櫃台上找到它們。

男子：太好了。我等不及要馬上開始了。

女子：喔！還要拿一個碗來混合材料。

問題：這名男子要做什麼？

(A) A bowl.   (A) 一個碗。

(B) A counter.   (B) 一個櫃台。

(C) A kind of food.   (C) 一種食物。

解析 雖然 omelet 非常見英檢初級單字，但從準備的材料中的奶油、雞蛋、蘑菇、鹽可以判斷男子要做的東西是食物，所以 A 和 B 不正確，故選 C。

A 22. W: Can you do me a favor? I need to put this box on the top shelf.

M: Sure. But I need you to hold the ladder for me.

W: No problem. Be careful!

M: Wow, what's in it? It's quite heavy.

W: Some new glasses I just bought. We can use them when Robin visits next week. I don't really like our old ones.

Question: What will happen next week?

女子：你能幫我一個忙嗎？我需要把這個箱子放到最上面的架子上。

男子：當然可以，但我需要你幫我扶著梯子。

女子：沒問題。小心點！

男子：哇，這裡面是什麼？好重。

女子：我新買的一些玻璃杯。下週羅賓來訪時，我們可以用。我不太喜歡我們的舊玻璃杯。

問題：下週會發生什麼事？

(A) Someone will visit them.

(B) They will buy sunglasses.

(C) The man will help the woman.

(A) 有人會去他們家。

(B) 他們會買太陽眼鏡。

(C) 那位男子會幫助女子。

解析 女子在解釋新買玻璃杯的原因時提到羅賓將在下週來訪，故選 A。

B 23. M: Why is it so hot in here?

W: Sorry, the air conditioner is broken. Let me get you a fan.

M: Actually, I'll just take my order to go.

W: We're really sorry about that. Your noodles will be ready right away.

Question: Where is the man?

男子：這裡為什麼這麼熱？

女子：對不起，空調壞了。我幫你拿個電風扇。

男子：其實，我的點餐改成外帶好了。

女子：真的很抱歉。您點的麵馬上就做好了。

問題：男子在哪裡？

(A) In a taxi.

(B) At a restaurant.

(C) At a supermarket.

(A) 在計程車上。

(B) 在餐廳。

(C) 在超市。

解析 從男子的回應中的關鍵詞：order（點餐）和 to go（外帶）得知他在餐廳，選 B。

A 24. M: Have you seen Eddie by any chance?

W: His son has the flu, and he's taking him to see a doctor today.

M: That's too bad. We have an important meeting this afternoon, and he was supposed to give a presentation.

W: Is it too late to find someone else to give the presentation?

Question: Why isn't Eddie at work today?

男子：你有沒有看到艾迪？

女子：他兒子得了流感，他今天要帶他去看醫生。

男子：那太糟糕了。我們今天下午有一個重要的會議，他本來要上台報告。

女子：現在找別人來做報告還來得及嗎？

問題：為什麼艾迪今天沒來上班？

(A) He has to take care of his kid.

(B) He's busy preparing for a presentation.

(C) He's sick and has to stay home and rest.

(A) 他要照顧他的孩子。

(B) 他在忙著準備報告。

(C) 他生病了，必須在家休息。

解析 從女子第一句的回應得知艾迪要帶孩子去看醫生，故選 A。

C 25. M: Will I see you tomorrow night?

G: Yeah, my sister and I are going for sure. We're looking forward to the concert.

M: How are you going to get there? By bus or by taxi?

G: Actually, my mom is driving us. Do you need a ride?

M: Sure. That would be great.

Question: How will the man go to the concert?

男子：我明天晚上會見到你嗎？

女孩：是的，我和我妹妹肯定會去。我們很期待這場音樂會。

男子：你們打算怎麼去？坐公車還是坐計程車？

女孩：事實上，我媽媽會開車帶我們去。你需要搭便車嗎？

男子：是啊！可以的話就太好了。

問題：男子將怎麼去音樂會？

(A) By taxi.

(B) By bus.

(C) By car.

(A) 搭計程車。

(B) 搭公車。

(C) 坐汽車。

解析 關鍵詞：a ride（搭便車）。因為男子接受女孩的提議要搭女孩媽媽的便車，得知答案為 C。

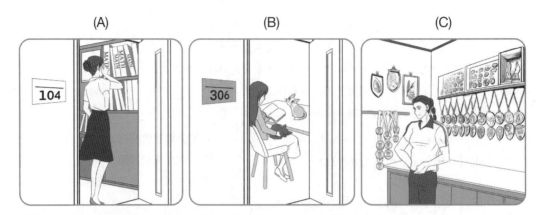

(A)   (B)   (C)

__B__ 26. For question number 26, please look at the three pictures.

Listen to the following announcement. Which is Penny Lin's office?

Attention, students: We have a new teacher starting work today. Her name is Penny Lin. Her office is room 306. She's been teaching English for 10 years. You can visit her whenever you have any questions regarding English. Also, you may be surprised by her two little pets. Let's all welcome her to our school!

第 26 題，請看三張圖片。

請聽以下聲明。林佩妮的辦公室是哪一間？

同學們請注意：學校今天來了位新老師。她叫林佩妮。她的辦公室在 306 教室。她教英語已經有 10 年的資歷了。各位對英語有任何問題，都可以去找她。此外，您可能會對她的兩隻小寵物感到驚訝。讓我們歡迎她！

解析 聽聲明可得知，新老師為女性，三個圖中的老師皆為女子。由於她的辦公室在 306 教室，因此可排除選項 A。另外有提到她有寵物 (pet)，所以選 B。

(A)   (B)   (C)

__C__ 27. For question number 27, please look at the three pictures.

Listen to the following talk. Which picture suits the description best?

Last week, we went to a park near Rosaline Lake. The weather was nice and sunny. Some people were jogging; others were biking. My family and I brought some snacks and fruit to the park to enjoy in the warm weather.

第 27 題，請看三張圖片。

請聽以下談話，哪張圖片最符合敘述？

上週我們去蘿絲林湖附近的公園。天氣很好，是晴天。有些人在慢跑，有些在騎腳踏車。我和我的家人帶了一些零食和水果去公園享受溫暖的天氣。

解析 天氣是晴天，所以排除選項 B。談話中沒有提到有人在遛狗，所以排除選項 A。選項 C 的人在野餐，最符合敘述，所以選 C。

(A)　　　　　(B)　　　　　(C)

__A__ 28. For question number 28, please look at the three pictures.

Listen to the following statement. Where would you probably hear it?

Our restaurant is getting busier and busier. We need to hire another cook. Right now, we have one chef and one cook, which just isn't enough. The customers always complain about our slow service.

第 28 題，請看三張圖片。

請聽下面這段話。你可能會在哪裡聽到它？

我們的餐廳越來越忙了。我們需要再聘一個廚師。現在，我們有一個主廚和一個廚師，根本不夠。客人總是抱怨我們服務太慢。

解析 從關鍵詞中的 chef（主廚）、cook（廚師）、和 our slow service（我們服務太慢）可以得知這是在餐廳廚房工作者的對話，所以選 A。

A 29. For question number 29, please look at the three pictures.

Listen to the following announcement. Who is missing?

Ladies and gentlemen: We've found a lost child, an eight-year-old boy wearing a T-shirt, shorts and a cap. He's about a hundred and thirty centimeters tall. If this is your child, please come to the Information counter on the first floor. Your child is waiting for you.

第 29 個問題,請看這三張圖片。

聽聽下面的廣播。誰走失了?

各位女士,各位先生:我們找到了一個走失的孩子,一個穿著 T 恤、短褲和帽子的八歲男孩。他大約有 130 公分高。如果這是您的孩子,請到一樓的服務台來。您的孩子正在等您。

解析 由廣播中衣著、年齡和性別的描述可以得知答案為 A 選項。

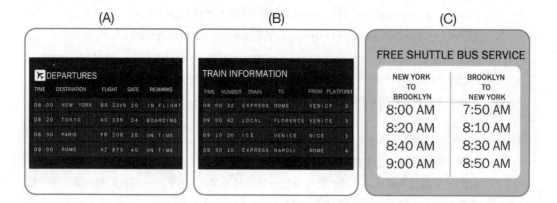

__B__ 30. For question number 30, please look at the three pictures.

Listen to the following announcement. Where would we hear the announcement?

The 8 AM express train from Venice to Rome is now approaching and will depart in five minutes. Passengers for the 8 AM express train, please go to platform 2 to board the train. The next train from Venice to Florence is delayed. We apologize for the inconvenience and thank you for your cooperation.

第 30 題，請看三張圖片。

聽聽下面的公告。我們會在哪裡聽到這則廣播？

早上 8 點從威尼斯到羅馬的特快列車現在正開進月台，將在 5 分鐘後發車。乘坐早上 8 點特快列車的乘客，請到 2 號月台上車。下一班從威尼斯到佛羅倫斯的列車誤點。造成不便非常抱歉，感謝您的合作。

解析 由關鍵詞 express train（特快列車）、platform（月台）、train（火車 / 列車）可以得知這段廣播是在火車站，只有選項 B 的時刻表上寫 train。

第一部分　詞彙

__C__ 1. There's been an accident. Can someone please call _____ ?
發生事故了，可以幫忙打電話叫救護車嗎？
(A) a clerk 店員　　　　　　(B) a medicine 藥物
(C) an ambulance 救護車　　(D) a businessman 商人

__B__ 2. Do you know how we can _____ the waterfall?
你知道我們怎麼能去到瀑布嗎？
(A) arrive to 抵達　　　　　(B) get to 到達
(C) reach to 抵達　　　　　(D) go on 繼續

__B__ 3. Preparing for tests and doing my homework _____ a lot of time.
準備考試和做我的回家作業佔用了很多時間。
(A) cost 花費　　　　　　　(B) take 佔用
(C) spend 花費　　　　　　(D) pay 支付

> **解析**　題目中的主詞為動名詞 preparing 和 doing，在描述花時間時，動詞需為選項 B 的 take。若句子的主詞是人，動詞才用 spend。

__C__ 4. To take a photo, simply push this _____ .
只要按下這個按鈕，就能拍照。
(A) cotton 棉　　　　　　　(B) curtain 窗簾
(C) button 按鈕　　　　　　(D) bottom 底部

__A__ 5. Mike is a good worker, so I don't think he missed the meeting _____ .
麥克是個優秀員工，所以我不覺得他是故意錯過會議。
(A) on purpose 故意地　　　(B) by accident 偶然地
(C) on time 準地　　　　　 (D) by mistake 錯誤地

__C__ 6. I haven't _____ Tina in three years.
我已經三年沒有收到來自提娜的消息了。
(A) heard of 聽說過　　　　(B) heard about 聽說
(C) heard from 收到消息　　(D) heard out 聽（某人）說完

解析 "heard of" 指聽說過某人的名字或事物，"heard about" 指聽到某人或某事的消息，"heard out" 指聽完某人的陳述或意見，但這三個片語皆無法表達 I 與汀娜的連結，也不符合句子的語境，只有 (C) heard from「收到消息」最合理。

__B__ 7. Robert Johnson is the only _____ I like in that movie.

羅伯特·約翰遜是我在那部電影中唯一喜歡的演員。

(A) player 球員   (B) actor 演員

(C) dentist 牙醫   (D) audience 觀眾

__A__ 8. What's a good store to buy _____ for my art class?

去哪一家店買美術課要的用品比較好呢？

(A) supplies 用品   (B) clothes 衣服

(C) snacks 零食   (D) paintings 畫作

__D__ 9. When you have too many choices, it can be hard to _____ .

當你有太多選擇時，作出決定可能會很難。

(A) express yourself 表達自己   (B) take your time 不急不徐

(C) forgive others 原諒別人   (D) make a decision 做出決定

__D__ 10. Learning new things is fun! _____ , it can be difficult sometimes.

學習新事物很有趣！另一方面來說，有時候也可能很困難。

(A) In the end 最後   (B) By the way 順帶一提

(C) On the one hand 一方面   (D) On the other hand 另一方面

解析 這兩句的主詞為 learning new things，第一句提到了一項優點（很有趣），第二句則是提到一項缺點（有時很困難），由於前後兩種觀點對立，所以中間應用可表示對立的片語連接，只有 on the other hand 符合。

第二部分　段落填空

共 8 題，包括二個段落，每個段落含四個空格。每格均有四個選項，請依照文意選出最適合的答案。

Questions 11-14

This morning, our neighbor, Ms. Green, saw Toby almost get ____(11)____ by a taxi when he was crossing the street. Toby was checking his phone and not paying attention to traffic. "Watch out!" Ms. Green shouted when she saw the taxi ____(12)____ toward him. ____(13)____ Fortunately, he only broke his phone. The situation ____(14)____ have been a lot worse. After being lectured by his parents and his teacher, Toby decided that he would never look at his phone while crossing the street again.

今天早上，我們的鄰居格林女士看到托比在穿越馬路時，幾乎被一輛計程車 (11) 撞到，托比正在看手機，沒有注意交通。「小心！」格林女士看到計程車朝著他 (12) 靠近時大喊。(13) 托比站住並且把手機摔到地上。幸運的是，他只摔壞了手機。情況 (14) 可能會更糟。在被他的父母和老師教訓以後，托比決定再也不會在過馬路時看手機了。

__C__ 11. (A) run around 四處跑　　　　　(B) run after 追趕
　　　　　(C) run over 被車撞　　　　　(D) run thorough 仔細檢查

__C__ 12. (A) reaching 抵達　　　　　　　(B) rolling 滾動
　　　　　(C) coming 靠近　　　　　　　(D) leaving 離開

__B__ 13. (A) Toby put his phone in his pocket. 托比把手機放進口袋裡。
　　　　　(B) Toby stopped and dropped his phone. 托比站住並且把手機摔到地上。
　　　　　(C) Toby walked and held his phone. 托比邊走邊拿著手機。
　　　　　(D) Toby smiled and waved to Ms. Green. 托比微笑著向格林女士招手。

__D__ 14. (A) will 將　　　　　　　　　　(B) should 應該
　　　　　(C) can 能夠　　　　　　　　　(D) could 可能

解析 由於本句的上一句是 Fortunately, he only broke his phone.（幸運的是，他只摔壞了手機。）這句後面出現了 have been a lot worse，表示「情況可能會更糟」，答案為 (D) could。

Questions 15-18

I have always loved the story of how my parents met. My dad was born and raised in London and has a great ____(15)____ in Turner's paintings. That's why 20 years ago, when a friend of his told him that there was a Turner exhibit in Berlin, he decided to go. ____(16)____ was that it is also the place where he would meet my mom. It happened after my dad saw the exhibit and ____(17)____ to go back to the hotel and have dinner. My mom was standing at the exit of the gallery, holding a map and looking lost. He walked up to her and ____(18)____ help. And the rest is history.

我一直很喜歡我父母相遇的故事。我爸爸在倫敦出生長大，對透納的畫作有極大的 (15) 興趣。這就是為什麼 20 年前，當他的一位朋友告訴他柏林有一個透納的展覽時，他決定前往。(16) 他沒想到，那也是他遇到我媽媽的地方。這是在我爸爸看完展覽後，(17) 即將要回飯店吃晚餐時發生的。我媽媽站在畫廊出口，手持地圖，一臉茫然。他走向她，(18) 提供幫助。其餘的故事就成了歷史。

__C__ 15. (A) fear 恐懼　　　(B) information 資訊
　　　　 (C) interest 興趣　　(D) knowledge 知識

__C__ 16. (A) When he didn't go 當他沒去
　　　　 (B) Why he didn't know 他為何不知道
　　　　 (C) What he didn't know 他沒想到
　　　　 (D) Where he didn't go 他沒去的地方

解析 空格後的句意為「那也是他遇到我媽媽的地方。」只有選項 C 和該句意符合，其他選項不合理。

__B__ 17. (A) pay attention 注意　　(B) was about 即將要
　　　　 (C) fell behind 落後　　　(D) found out 找出

__D__ 18. (A) asked for 要求　　　(B) sent for 派遣
　　　　 (C) went to 前往　　　　(D) offered to 提供

共 12 題，包括 4 個題組，每個題組含 1 至 2 篇短文，與數個相關的四選一的選擇題。請由試題上的選項中選出最適合的答案。

Questions 19-21

From	rubyfisher@tktech.edu.tw
To	phoebe@net.edu.tw
Subject	A favor

B *I* <u>U</u> ¶- ✐ A- T- ⇔ 🖾 🏷 ☰ ☰ ☰ ↺ ↻ </>

Dear Joseph:

Melinda told me that you're going to Tokyo next week. I wonder if you could do me a favor while you're there. Last month, I went there to visit my sister, Karen. I bought a lot of snacks, but there was no room in my luggage, so I had no choice but to leave them at my sister's place. Do you think you could find time to meet with my sister and get the snacks from her? If you think you can do this for me, I've included my sister's address in Tokyo and her contact information. Also, to thank you for doing this for me, I'll pick you up at the airport and treat you to dinner when you come back. Please let me know your decision.

Michael

Send

From   rubyfisher@tktech.edu.tw

To   phoebe@net.edu.tw

Subject   請幫個忙

B *I* U ¶▾ ✎ A▾ T▾ ⊖ 🖼 🏷 ☰ ☰ ☰ ↺ ↻ </>

親愛的約瑟夫：

梅琳達告訴我你下週將前往東京。我想知道在你那裡的時候，能否幫我一個忙。我上個月去那裡拜訪我姐姐凱倫。**(19) 我買了很多零食，但我的行李箱裡沒有空間了，所以我只好把它們留在我姐姐的住處。(20) 你覺得在那裡是否會有時間和我姐姐碰面，然後向她拿零食呢？**如果你覺得可以幫我這個忙，我已經將我姐姐在東京的地址和聯絡方式附上。另外，為了感謝你幫忙，我將於你回程時為你接機，並請你吃晚餐。請讓我知道你的決定。

麥可

傳送

Karen Wu

Phone number: +81(0)3-5228-8107

Address: 1-3 Kagurazaka,

Shinjuku-ku, Tokyo 162-8601,

Japan

P.S. She can only be reached in the daytime before five o'clock.

吳凱倫

電話號碼：+81(0)3-5228-8107

地址：**(21) 日本東京都**新宿神樂坂 1-3，郵遞區號 162-8601

附註：她只能在白天的下午五點前接聽電話。

A 19. What can we learn about Michael?

(A) He left something in Japan.

(B) His sister is always available.

(C) He didn't bring luggage on his trip.

(D) He wants to send something to his sister.

我們可以得知關於麥可的什麼事？

(A) 他在日本留下了某些東西。

(B) 他的姐姐總是有空。

(C) 他旅行時沒有帶行李。

(D) 他想寄東西給他姐姐。

解析 由電郵第三句可看出麥可把零食留在姐姐的住處。

A 20. What is the main reason that Michael wrote this e-mail?

(A) To ask Joseph to help him.

(B) To thank Joseph for helping him.

(C) To find time to meet with Karen.

(D) To apologize for not being careful.

麥可寫這封電子郵件的主要原因是什麼？

(A) 請約瑟夫幫他忙。

(B) 感謝約瑟夫幫忙他。

(C) 找時間與凱倫碰面。

(D) 為自己不夠小心道歉。

解析 由電郵第四句可看出麥可詢問約瑟夫在東京時，能否幫他把零食拿回來。

B 21. Which of the following is true?

(A) Karen's e-mail address is written on the note.

(B) Karen lives in Tokyo, Japan at present.

(C) Joseph has agreed to do Michael a favor.

(D) Michael offered to give Joseph some snacks.

以下哪一項正確？

(A) 凱倫的電子郵件地址寫在便條上。

(B) 凱倫目前住在日本東京。

(C) 約瑟夫已經同意幫忙麥可。

(D) 麥可提議給約瑟夫一些零食。

解析 從便條上的訊息可以看出正解為 (B) 麥可的姐姐凱倫住在日本東京，至於其他選項，(A) 便條上沒有凱倫的電子郵件地址，(C) 麥可目前只有詢問，電子郵件和便條中都沒有提及約瑟夫是否同意幫忙。(D) 麥可提議幫約瑟夫接機和請吃晚餐。

Questions 22-24

The Komodo dragon, also known as the Komodo monitor, is a species of lizard that can only be found in Indonesia. It is the largest lizard in the world, with some individuals reaching lengths of up to 10 feet and weighing over 150 pounds. They have strong jaws and sharp teeth, making them powerful **predators**. Their diet includes birds, snakes and even deer. Komodo Dragons are also skilled climbers and swimmers, and they can move quickly when they hunt for food.

Unfortunately, the number of Komodo Dragons is getting smaller because they are losing their homes and people are hunting them. To keep them safe, they are now a protected species. People are working hard to take care of them and make sure they survive. Indonesia even created the Komodo National Park to protect these amazing animals.

In short, the Komodo Dragon is a large lizard found only in Indonesia. They are both large and unique. It's important to protect them and their homes and tell others about why it's necessary to take care of them. This way, we can make sure they keep existing for a long time.

科莫多龍，也被稱為科莫多巨蜥，這種蜥蜴品種僅分布於印尼。牠是世界上最大的蜥蜴，某些巨蜥的長度可達 10 英尺，重量超過 150 磅。**(23) 牠們有強大的下顎和鋒利的牙齒，使牠們成為強大的掠食者。牠們的食物包括鳥、蛇、甚至鹿。**科莫多龍也很擅長攀爬和游泳，並能在捕獵食物時迅速移動。

很不幸地，科莫多龍的數量正在減少，這是因為牠們喪失棲息地，並且被人類獵捕。**(22) 為了保護牠們的安全，牠們現在為保育物種。人們正努力地照顧牠們，並確保牠們得以生存。(24) 印尼甚至創建了科莫多國家公園來保護這些驚人的動物。**

簡單來說，科莫多龍是一種棲息於印尼的大型蜥蜴。牠們體型既龐大又獨特。保護牠們和其棲息地是非常重要的，並要告訴世人牠們為何須要被照顧。這樣，我們就能確保牠們能長久存在。

__D__ 22. Which is true about Komodo Dragons?

    (A) They don't exist anymore.

    (B) Their size is still increasing.

    (C) They eat fruit and vegetables.

    (D) They aren't allowed to be hunted.

關於科莫多龍哪一點正確？

    (A) 牠們已經不存在了。

    (B) 牠們的體型仍在增長。

    (C) 牠們吃水果和蔬菜。

    (D) 牠們不允許被獵捕。

解析 可由第二段第二與第三句得知，因為棲息地被破壞和生存危機，所以他們現在是被保護的物種。選項 D 的意思與文意符合。

__A__ 23. What does the word "predator" mean?

    (A) An animal that eats other animals.

    (B) An animal that protects other animals.

    (C) A friendly animal that kids can play with.

    (D) An animal that is eaten by other animals.

"predator" 這個字的意思為何？

    (A) 一種會吃其他動物的動物。

    (B) 一種會保護其他動物的動物。

    (C) 一種可和小孩玩耍的友好動物。

    (D) 一種會被其他動物吃掉的動物。

解析 包含 predator 的句子中還提到科莫多龍有 strong jaws and sharp teeth，而且他們很有力量，推測是掠食所用。另外從下一句也可看出，牠們的食物包括 birds, snakes and even deer，可判斷牠們會吃其他動物，因此選項 A 最適合這些描述。

__B__ 24. Where would we likely find this article?

    (A) In a modern history book

    (B) On a national park website

    (C) In a magazine for pet owners

    (D) At the entrance to an aquarium

我們可能在哪裡找到這篇文章？

    (A) 在現代歷史書中

    (B) 在國家公園的網站上

    (C) 在給寵物主人的雜誌裡

    (D) 在水族館入口處

解析 全文並沒有提到關於現代史、寵物、或是水族的部分。而第二段的最後一句有提及現在有科莫多龍的國家公園，本文較偏向網站介紹文，因此選項 B 最符合。

Questions 25-27

Dear Gina,

How have you been lately? I came to visit my grandparents a few weeks ago and I've been staying with them since then.

My grandparents own a <u>hostel</u> in downtown Seoul. They're busy hosting travelers from all over the world every day. In the morning, I help my grandfather clean the rooms and common areas, and my grandma prepares breakfast for all the guests. In the afternoon, my grandfather takes travelers hiking in the mountains while my grandmother shows others around downtown Seoul.

All the guests here have a pleasant stay, and some of them even said they will definitely choose to stay at our hostel next time they visit Korea. This had been such a fantastic experience, and I hope you can come with me when I visit next year. You can even stay at the hostel for free!

Love,
Mindy

親愛的吉娜，

你最近好嗎？幾週前我來探望祖父母，從那時起我就和他們住在一起。

(25) 我的祖父母在首爾市中心擁有一家旅舍。他們每天忙著招待來自世界各地的旅客。(26) (27) 早上的時候，我幫助祖父打掃房間和公共區域，而祖母則為所有客人準備早餐。 到了下午，祖父會帶旅客登山健行，而祖母則帶另一些人在首爾市中心逛逛。

所有客人都在這裡住得很愉快，有些人甚至說下次來韓國時，一定會再選擇我們的旅舍住宿。這真的是個很棒的經驗，希望我明年拜訪的時候，你能和我一起來。你甚至可以免費住旅社！

愛你的，

敏迪

D 25. What is a "hostel"?

(A) a restaurant

(B) a school

(C) a store

(D) a hotel

"hostel" 的字意為何？

(A) 餐廳

(B) 學校

(C) 商店

(D) 飯店

解析 針對敏蒂在信件第二段中提到和祖父母的工作內容，由於內容包括接待遊客、打掃房間、為賓客準備早餐等，四個選項中字意最接近者為 (D) 飯店。

__C__ 26. What is Mindy doing in Korea?

(A) She opened a hostel with her grandparents in Seoul.

(B) She takes travelers to experience the beauty of Seoul.

(C) She is helping her grandparents with their business.

(D) She is inviting people from all over the world to visit.

敏迪在韓國做什麼？

(A) 她與祖父母在首爾開了一家旅舍。

(B) 她帶遊客去體驗首爾的美麗。

(C) 她正幫祖父母作生意。

(D) 她正邀請世界各地的人們拜訪。

解析 由第二段第三句 I help my grandfather... 得知，敏迪協助祖父母旅社事宜，因此選項 C 正確。

__A__ 27. Which is true about the story?

(A) Mindy helps keep the hostel tidy.

(B) Mindy is not in South Korea now.

(C) Mindy's grandmother enjoys hiking.

(D) Gina is going to visit Korea next year.

關於此故事，何者正確？

(A) 敏迪幫忙保持旅舍整潔。

(B) 敏迪現在不在韓國。

(C) 敏迪的祖母喜歡登山健行。

(D) 吉娜明年將去韓國作客。

解析 第二段第三句指出，敏迪在幫祖父做清潔工作，因此選項 A 正確。文末敏迪雖然有邀請吉娜來首爾，但無法確知吉娜明年是否將去韓國作客，選項 D 不能選。

Questions 28-30

Since my father had to go on a business trip to France, our family stayed in Paris for a week. While my dad was working during the day, my mother and I visited all the famous spots in Paris. We went to the Eiffel Tower, the famous Louvre Museum, and had a picnic at a beautiful park. It was so much fun. Although we don't speak French, the locals were so kind and offered help when we needed it. We also went to Galeries Lafayette Haussmann, where my mom bought a purse and some new clothes for me and my dad. After that, we met my dad at a French restaurant and had a nice dinner.

I spent the rest of my free time with my uncle Daniel, who moved to France two years ago. He took me to places that are rarely visited by tourists. He even took me to a restaurant where I tried escargots—snails—for the very first time! I had a great time with my uncle. I'll definitely come visit him again.

(29) **由於我爸爸需要去法國出差，所以我們家在巴黎待了一週。**爸爸白天工作的時候，我和媽媽參觀了巴黎所有著名的景點。我們去了艾菲爾鐵塔、著名的羅浮宮，並在美麗的公園野餐。真的非常好玩。雖然我們不會說法文，當地人卻非常友善，並在我們需要時提供幫助。(28) **我們還去了哈斯曼的老佛爺百貨公司，媽媽在那裡買了一個包包，也為我和爸爸買了些新衣服。**之後，我們在一家法國餐廳與爸爸會合，享用了一頓美味的晚餐。

我和丹尼爾叔叔共度了剩餘的空閒時間，他兩年前才搬到法國。他帶我去了一些遊客很少會去的地方。(30) **他還帶我去了一家餐廳，我在那裡初次嘗試了 escargots—也就是蝸牛！**我和叔叔玩得很愉快。我一定會再來拜訪他。

___D___ 28. What type of place is the Galeries Lafayette Haussmann?

(A) A museum

(B) A restaurant

(C) A supermarket

(D) A department store

哈斯曼的老佛爺百貨是什麼類型的地方？

(A) 博物館

(B) 餐廳

(C) 超市

(D) 百貨公司

解析 由第一段倒數第二句得知，媽媽在哈斯曼的老佛爺百貨買了包包和衣服，因此選項中最有可能賣這兩者的，就是選項 D 的百貨公司。

__A__ 29. Which of the following is true?

(A) The writer's father went to Paris for work.

(B) The writer's mother is able to speak French.

(C) The writer met Daniel for the first time in Paris.

(D) Daniel took the writer's parents to a restaurant.

下列何者正確？

(A) 作者的父親去巴黎出差。

(B) 作者的母親會說法語。

(C) 作者在巴黎初次見到丹尼爾。

(D) 丹尼爾帶作者的父母去餐廳。

解析 由第一段第一句得知，作者的父親要去巴黎出差，因此全家才在巴黎待了一週，選項 A 正確。第二段雖然有提到丹尼爾叔叔，但沒有提到是否為第一次見面，因此不能選 C。

__C__ 30. What is true about the trip?

(A) Daniel took the writer shopping.

(B) The people there all speak English.

(C) The writer tried a new kind of food.

(D) A guide took them to tourist spots in Paris.

關於這次旅行，哪一項正確？

(A) 丹尼爾帶作者去購物。

(B) 那裡的人都會說英語。

(C) 作者嘗試了一種新的食物。

(D) 一位導遊帶他們去了巴黎的旅遊景點。

解析 可由第二段第三句得知，丹尼爾有帶作者去餐廳嘗試蝸牛，這是作者第一次嘗試，因此選項 C 正確。文中並沒有提到丹尼爾帶作者購物，只有提到去觀光客較少的地方，因此選項 A 不符合。

GEPT
初級模擬試題
第 2 回
解答、翻譯與詳解

第 2 回解答

 聽力測驗解答

1. B	2. C	3. A	4. C	5. A
6. B	7. A	8. B	9. A	10. C
11. A	12. B	13. A	14. A	15. B
16. C	17. A	18. B	19. A	20. C
21. C	22. C	23. B	24. A	25. B
26. C	27. B	28. C	29. A	30. A

閱讀測驗解答

1. B	2. B	3. C	4. C	5. D
6. C	7. B	8. D	9. B	10. C
11. B	12. D	13. C	14. A	15. C
16. C	17. A	18. C	19. A	20. D
21. A	22. B	23. B	24. B	25. D
26. A	27. A	28. D	29. A	30. D

第一部分　看圖辨義

__B__ 1. For Question Number 1,
please look at the picture.
What likely happened to the boy?

(A) He lost his pet dog.

(B) He fell down and got dirty.

(C) He got locked outside.

第一題，請看此圖片。

男孩可能發生了什麼事情？

(A) 他的寵物狗不見了。

(B) 他跌倒，全身弄得髒兮兮。

(C) 他被反鎖在外面。

解析　圖片中沒有寵物狗不見或是被反鎖在外面的提示，只有選項 B 符合圖片描述，因此選 B。

__C__ 2. For Question Number 2, please
look at the picture.
What are the kids doing?

(A) They are playing soccer.

(B) They are walking home.

(C) They are skating.

第二題，請看此圖片。

這群孩子正在做什麼？

(A) 他們正在踢足球。

(B) 他們正在走路回家。

(C) 他們正在溜冰。

解析　圖片中的孩子看起來正在溜冰 (skating)，其他選項皆不正確，選 C。

_A_ 3. For Question Number 3, please look at the picture.

What is Tina probably doing?

(A) She is watching a movie with her parents.

(B) She is having a snack.

(C) She is chatting with her parents.

第三題，請看此圖片。

提娜可能正在做什麼？

(A) 她正在和她的爸媽看電影。

(B) 她正在吃零食。

(C) 她正在和她的爸媽聊天。

解析 圖片中提娜和爸媽往同方向看，手上沒有拿著零食或是在說話的樣子，因此只有選項 A 的看電影 (watching a movie) 符合圖片提示，故選 A。

_C_ 4. For Question Number 4, please look at the picture.

Where is the library?

(A) It's behind the school.

(B) It's between the post office and the movie theater.

(C) It's across from the school.

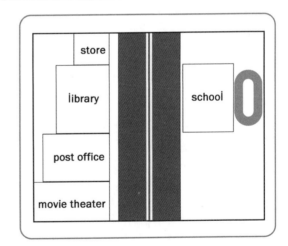

第四題，請看此圖片。

圖書館在哪裡？

(A) 在學校後面。

(B) 在郵局和電影院的中間。

(C) 在學校對面。

解析 由圖片所示，圖書館在學校的對面；商店 (store) 和郵局 (post office) 的中間。因此只有 C 選項正確。

A 5. For Question Number 5, please look at the picture.

Where are these people?

(A) They are in the mountains.

(B) They are near a lake.

(C) They are close to a castle.

第五題，請看此圖片。

這些人在哪裡？

(A) 他們在山上。

(B) 他們在湖附近。

(C) 他們在靠近一座城堡的地方。

解析　圖片中每個人都拿著登山杖，可以看得出來他們在山上，因此選 A。

__B__ 6. Do you mind if I borrow that pencil?
    (A) Of course. I don't mind.
    (B) No, I don't. Here!
    (C) Sorry, it's my pen.

你介意我跟你借一枝筆嗎？
(A) 當然。我不介意。
(B) 不，我不介意。這邊！
(C) 對不起，這是我的筆。

解析 回答 "Do you mind..." 的問題時，答案若為不介意，需使用否定句。選項 A 需改成 "Of course not." 才正確。選項 C 答非所問，故選 B。

__A__ 7. I don't remember seeing you around here.
    (A) Actually, I am new here. I'm Jason.
    (B) You're right. This is my home.
    (C) I forget, too. But it's a nice neighborhood.

我不記得在附近見過你。
(A) 其實我是新來的。我叫傑森。
(B) 你說對了。這是我家。
(C) 我也不記得。但這是個很好的社區。

解析 題目有「你是哪位？我好像沒有見過你。」的意思，因此只有選項 A 回答了問題。選項 B 和選項 C 皆答非所問。

__B__ 8. Why don't you join the school team?
    (A) I think I'll wait until they leave.
    (B) I am not sure if I have enough time to practice.
    (C) The school team has won a lot of games.

你為何不參加校隊呢？
(A) 我想我會等到他們離開。
(B) 我不確定有沒有足夠的時間參加練習。
(C) 校隊贏了很多場比賽。

解析 選項 A 答非所問，選項 C 沒有回答到問題。如果將 C 選項改為「校隊贏了很多比賽，所以對我來說壓力太大。」便可以選 C 選項，但此題沒有做出此連結，故仍選 B。

___A___ 9. Would you like to check out the house we just bought?

(A) I'd love to. It sounds amazing.

(B) I can't afford a house right now.

(C) I don't think anything is wrong with it.

你想來看看我們新買的房子嗎？

(A) 我很樂意。這提議太棒了！

(B) 我現在買不起房子。

(C) 我不認為這有任何問題。

解析 接受 "Would you like to..." 的邀請時，可以用 "I'd love to." 來表示自己樂意接受。故選 A。

___C___ 10. Look at this beautiful oil painting!

(A) Yes, it's a wonderful drawing.

(B) Pants like that must be expensive.

(C) I hear it was done by a famous artist.

看看這幅美麗的油畫！

(A) 是的，這是一幅很棒的圖畫。

(B) 那樣的褲子一定很貴。

(C) 聽說這是一位著名藝術家的作品。

解析 drawing 指的是由鉛筆、筆或是蠟筆所繪製的圖畫，因此不能拿來呼應題目中的 oil painting（油畫），因此選項 A 不正確。選項 B 的 pants 為「褲子」，答非所問，故選 C。

___A___ 11. My brother and I are planning a trip to the USA.

(A) Where to?

(B) I'd love to.

(C) Was it fun?

我哥哥和我正在規畫去美國的旅行。

(A) 去哪裡？

(B) 我很樂意。

(C) 好玩嗎？

解析 題目用現在進行式，表示旅行正在規畫當中，因此選項 C 不正確。另外題目只是平鋪直述最近在做的事情，沒有暗示邀約，因此選項 B 不成立。選 A。

B 12. What can I get you, sir?

    (A) Yes, can you help me?

    (B) Black coffee would be great.

    (C) I appreciate it.

先生，您要什麼？

(A) 是的，你能幫我嗎？

(B) 黑咖啡好了。

(C) 我很感激。

解析　在為人點餐時可以使用 "What can I get you?" 詢問。回答時除了 "..., please." （請給我…），"...would be good/great." 也是常用的句型。

A 13. We stayed at the same hotel as last year on our vacation. It was fun.

    (A) You mean the one on the coast?

    (B) How long will you stay at the hotel?

    (C) Having a vacation with you is a fun experience.

我們去年度假時也住同一間飯店。很好玩。

(A) 你是說海岸上的那間嗎？

(B) 你會在飯店住幾天？

(C) 和你一起度假是很好玩的經驗。

解析　選項 A 當中的 "the one" 指的就是飯店，有回應到題目的句子。其他兩個選項皆答非所問。

A 14. It's been raining for days.

    (A) I wonder when it's going to stop.

    (B) Really? Let's check the weather report.

    (C) Time to wash my clothes.

下雨下好多天了。

(A) 我在想什麼時候才會停。

(B) 真的嗎？我們來查一下氣象報告。

(C) 該洗衣服了。

解析　題目為現在完成進行式，表示從過去到現在持續下雨中，且有可能會持續下去。因此選項 A 最適合。

B 15. How often does the bus run?

    (A) In twenty minutes.

    (B) Every thirty minutes.

    (C) Tomorrow.

公車多久一班？

(A) 20 分鐘後。

(B) 每三十分鐘。

(C) 明天。

解析　"How often" 用來詢問事物發生的頻率，因此只有選項 B 有回答到問題。

C 16. M: Wow! You were pretty when you were young.

W: I'm not pretty now?

M: I mean you were prettier years ago.

W: Oh, OK. I think I need to take care of my skin now.

Question: What does the man say?

男子：哇！你年輕時很漂亮。

女子：我現在不漂亮了？

男子：我的意思是幾年前你更漂亮。

女子：哦，好吧。我想我需要開始保養我的皮膚了。

問題：男子說什麼？

(A) The woman is prettier now.

(B) The woman is quite old.

(C) The woman is not as pretty as before.

(A) 女子現在比較漂亮。

(B) 女子很老。

(C) 女子沒有以前漂亮。

解析 從男子的第二句回答得知，他覺得女子以前比較漂亮，也就是現在沒有以前漂亮的意思，故選 C。

A 17. M: Watch out! The dog is running toward us!

W: What should we do?

M: Get into the car!

W: Phew! That was close!

Question: What happened?

男子：小心！那隻狗正朝著我們跑過來！

女子：我們該怎麼辦？

男子：快進到車子裡！

女子：呼！真是好險！

問題：發生什麼事？

(A) They were chased by a dog.

(B) The woman ran after the dog.

(C) Their car hit a dog.

(A) 他們被狗追。

(B) 女子在追狗。

(C) 他們的車撞到狗。

解析 "running toward" 表示往自己的方向跑過來，由此可知他們是被狗追，選 A。

B　18. M: Can I take your order?

　　　W: Yes, I'd like fried chicken with rice.

　　　M: Anything to drink? We have great coffee here.

　　　W: Oh. Can I have tea instead of coffee?

　　　M: Sure. We have black tea, green tea, and milk tea. Which would you like?

　　　Question: Where are the speakers?

　　　男子：我能幫您點餐嗎？

　　　女子：當然。我想點炸雞和飯。

　　　男子：要飲料嗎？我們的咖啡很好喝。

　　　女子：喔！我可以點茶，不點咖啡嗎？

　　　男子：當然。我們有紅茶、綠茶和奶茶。您想要哪一種？

　　　問題：說話者在哪裡？

(A) At a tea shop.　　　　　　　　(A) 在茶店。

(B) At a restaurant.　　　　　　　(B) 在餐廳。

(C) At a friend's place.　　　　　(C) 在朋友家。

解析　女子點餐的內容有餐點和飲料，因此得知他們所在的地點在餐廳，選 B。

A　19. W: We're out of milk. Can you please get some on your way back?

　　　M: But I have to work late today. I have a lot of work to do.

　　　W: Oh, that's fine. I'll get some tomorrow morning.

　　　M: By the way, I'll be home around eight, so don't wait for me for dinner.

　　　Question: What is the man going to do?

　　　女子：牛奶沒了。你回家路上可以買一些回來嗎？

　　　男子：可是我今天要工作到很晚。我有很多工作要做。

　　　女子：喔！那沒關係。我明天早上再買。

　　　男子：對了，我八點左右到家，所以晚餐不用等我。

　　　問題：男子要做什麼？

(A) Stay at the office later than usual.

(B) Cook dinner for himself.

(C) Get some milk for his wife.

(A) 留在辦公室到比平時還晚。

(B) 自己煮晚餐。

(C) 幫他的太太買牛奶。

解析 由男子第一句話得知他需要加班,從他的第二句話可推斷他平時會在八點以前回家吃晚餐,綜合以上所述得知選項 A 為正解。

C 20. G: Mommy, there's something wrong with my leg.

W: Oh, no. Does it hurt?

G: Yes, it hurts when I walk.

W: OK. Stay here. Let me call your dad and ask him to take us to the hospital.

G: I don't think it's that serious. Let me just rest and see how I feel tomorrow.

Question: Which of the following is true?

女孩:媽媽,我的腿有點怪怪的。

女子:喔!糟糕。會痛嗎?

女孩:對,走路的時候會痛。

女子:好!妳在這邊不要動。我打電話給爸爸請他帶我們去醫院。

女孩:我不覺得有那麼嚴重。讓我休息一下,看看明天覺得怎麼樣再說。

問題:請問以下何者正確?

(A) The girl is going to the hospital.

(B) The mother is going to call her husband.

(C) The girl doesn't feel like seeing a doctor now.

(A) 女孩要去醫院。

(B) 媽媽要打電話給她的老公。

(C) 女孩現在不想要看醫生。

解析 從女子和女孩的最後一段對話可得知,女孩不希望媽媽打電話請爸爸載他們去看醫生,因此選項 C 為正解。

__C__ 21. M: Hello. Is Anna Wang there?

W: Yes, this is she. Who is this?

M: I'm from the post office. I have a package for you.

W: OK. One minute. I'll be right down.

Question: Who is the man?

男子：您好！請問王安娜在嗎？

女子：我就是。請問您哪位？

男子：我是郵局的人。有您的包裹。

女子：好的。請等我一下。我馬上下去。

問題：請問男子是誰？

(A) He's Anna's friend.

(B) He works at Anna's office.

(C) He's a mailman.

(A) 他是安娜的朋友。

(B) 他在安娜的辦公室工作。

(C) 他是郵差。

解析 郵差可以是 mailman 或是 postman，選項中的 mailman 和對話中的郵局（post office）比較難做聯想，請注意。

__C__ 22. W: I'm so bored. I don't know what to do.

M: So am I. How about going for a drive in my car?

W: Good idea. Where should we go?

M: We can drive to the beach and enjoy the sun.

W: Sounds nice. Let me go get my sunglasses and sunscreen.

Question: What are the people going to do?

女子：我好無聊。我不知道要做什麼。

男子：我也是。要不要坐我的車去兜風。

女子：好主意。我們該去哪裡好？

男子：我們可以去海邊，享受陽光。

女子：聽起來不錯。讓我去拿我的太陽眼鏡和防曬油。

問題：這兩個人要去做什麼？

(A) They are going to rent a car.

(B) They are going to buy sunglasses and sunscreen.

(C) They are going to spend time at the beach.

(A) 他們要去租車。

(B) 他們要去買太陽眼鏡和防曬油。

(C) 他們要去海邊打發時間。

解析 男子提到是坐他的車，因此選項 A 不正確。get 可以作為「買」或是「拿」。因為 "Let me..." 的關係在這邊可以判斷是「拿」，因此選項 B 不正確。選 C。

B 23. W: Hey, look what I found.

M: What is it?

W: I think it's a smart watch.

M: Who do you think it belongs to?

W: I think it's Lilian's. I saw her wearing something like this yesterday.

Question: What happened?

女子：嘿！看我找到了什麼？
男子：那是什麼？
女子：我想這是智慧型手錶。
男子：妳覺得這是誰的？
女子：我覺得是莉莉安的。我看到她昨天戴了類似的東西。
問題：發生什麼事？

(A) The woman forgot her smartphone.
(B) The woman found a missing watch.
(C) They bought a gift for Lilian.

(A) 女子忘了她的智慧型手機。
(B) 女子找到一支遺失的手錶。
(C) 他們買了一個禮物給莉莉安。

解析 「missing + 名詞」表示「被弄丟 / 被遺失的東西」。另外，也可以從關鍵字 "watch" 推測選項 B 為正解。

A 24. W: How may I help you?

M: I'm looking for a nice sweater.

W: What color do you want? And what size?

M: I wear a medium. And I'd like a black one.

Question: What is the man doing?

女子：我能幫您什麼嗎？

男子：我在找一件質感好的毛衣。

女子：你想要什麼顏色？多大尺寸？

男子：我穿 M 號，我想要黑色的。

問題：男子正在做什麼？

(A) He's shopping.	(A) 他在購物。
(B) He's ordering.	(B) 他在點餐。
(C) He's eating.	(C) 他在吃東西。

解析 對話中 "How may I help you?" 是服務人員待客時常用的句子。從男子提到的關鍵字 sweater（毛衣）可以得知男子正在購物。

___B___ 25. W: I don't think I can do this. It's just too difficult for me.

M: What's too difficult?

W: Look at this problem. I've been trying to solve it for twenty minutes and still can't figure out the answer.

M: Let me see. Hmm...I think we learned this last week. Let me get my notebook.

Question: Who are the speakers?

女子：我覺得我沒辦法做這題，對我來說太難了。

男子：什麼東西太難？

女子：看看這個題目。我已經解題解了二十分鐘，還是算不出答案。

男子：我看看。嗯…這是我們上週學過的內容。我去拿我的筆記。

問題：說話者是誰？

(A) They're husband and wife.	(A) 他們是夫妻。
(B) They're classmates.	(B) 他們是同學。
(C) They're nurses.	(C) 他們是護士。

解析 數學題常用的英文表達方式為 problem 而非 question 請注意。另外，男子最後一句提到這是上週學的內容，因此可以推測兩人關係為同學，選 B。

(A)   (B)   (C)

C 26. For question number 26, please look at the three pictures.

Listen to the following announcement. Which picture suits the description best?

Attention! There's been a car accident on 8th street, and it's caused a traffic jam on 7th, 8th, and 9th streets. Please avoid those streets if you're driving. If you need to go to the city center, taking the MRT would be a better choice.

第 26 題，請看三張圖片。

請聽以下廣播。哪張圖片最符合描述內容？

注意！第八街上發生一起車禍，造成第七、第八和第九街交通阻塞。開車時請避開這些路段。如果需要到市中心，改搭捷運會是較好的選擇。

解析 由關鍵字 "car accident" 可知這起意外是車對車的車禍，選項 A 是火車，可排除，因此選 C。

(A)   (B)   (C)

B 27. For question number 27, please look at the three pictures.

Listen to the following announcement. Which picture is the special meal?

Dear guests: We have a special meal on the menu tonight. You'll love this meal if you like beef. We have the best steak in town. And it comes with a salad, a piece of chocolate cake and a nice coffee. The price is just 20 dollars, and it's only available today.

第 27 題，請看三張圖片。

請聽以下廣播。哪張圖片是今天的特餐？

親愛的顧客：今晚的菜單上有一份特餐。喜歡牛肉的人將會非常喜愛這份餐。我們有全市最好的牛排。餐點附有沙拉、巧克力蛋糕、和精品咖啡。價格為 20 元，只限今天。

解析 由關鍵字 beef（牛肉）和 steak（牛排）可以得知答案為選項 B，另外該選項也有題目中提到的 salad（沙拉）、chocolate cake（巧克力蛋糕）和 coffee（咖啡），由此能更確認。

(A)　　　　　　　　(B)　　　　　　　　(C)

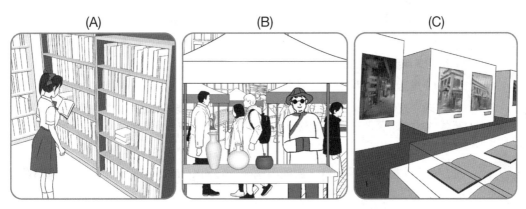

C 28. For question number 28, please look at the three pictures.

Listen to the following talk. Where is the talk probably given?

OK everyone, please come this way. Here you can see some photographs of Taiwan from seventy years ago. And on your right is a collection of Japanese books that was left in Taiwan. On the left, you can see some drawings of old streets of Taiwan that were done by local artists.

第 28 題，請看三張圖片。

請聽以下談話。這段話可能出現在哪個地點？

好的各位，請往這邊走。在這邊您可以看到台灣七十年前的照片。在您的右手邊是留在台灣的日本書籍。在您的左邊，可以看到台灣本土藝術家所繪製的台灣老街畫作。

解析 由關鍵字中的 photographs（照片）和 books（書）可以得知答案為選項 C。

(A)　　　　　　　　(B)　　　　　　　　(C)

__A__ 29. For question number 29, please look at the three pictures.

Listen to the following telephone message. Why can't Peggy go to school?

Ms. Jones? This is your student Peggy calling. I am afraid I can't go to school next Monday and Tuesday. My dad is sick and will be staying in the hospital for a few days and I'm the only one who can take care of him. Sorry for not being able to take the test next week.

第 29 題，請看三張圖片。

請聽以下電話留言。為什麼佩琪不能去上學？

瓊斯老師？這是您的學生佩琪來電。下週一和週二我可能沒辦法去學校上課。我的父親生病了，會住院幾天，只有我能照顧他。很抱歉沒辦法參加下週的考試。

解析 住院的英文動詞使用 stay，由關鍵詞組 "staying in the hospital" 可以得知正確答案為選項 A。

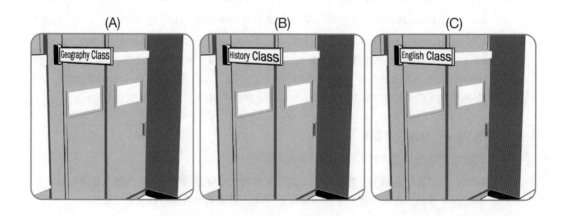

(A)　　　　　　　　(B)　　　　　　　　(C)

__A__ 30. For question number 30, please look at the three pictures.

Listen to the following talk. Where would we hear this talk?

We all know about countries like the U.S., the UK, Japan, and Korea. But do you really know where they are? I've drawn a world map here on the blackboard. You each have a card with the name of a different country on it. When I call your name, please put your card on the right place on the map.

第 30 題，請看三張圖片。

請聽以下談話。在哪裡可能會聽到這段話？

我們都知道像是美國、英國、日本、韓國等國家。但你真的知道它們在哪裡嗎？我在黑板上畫了世界地圖。你們每個人手上有一張卡片，上面有各國的國名。當我叫到你的名字時，請把卡片放到地圖上正確的位置。

解析 由關鍵字 map（地圖）可以知道這是地理課 (geography class) 上的談話，故選 A。

第一部分　詞彙

共 10 題，每個題目裡有一個空格。請從四個選項中選出一個最適合題意的字或詞作答。

__B__ 1. A: Do you know why Danny is being punished? B: Because he was being
_____ to Ms. Chen.

A: 你知道丹尼為什麼被處罰嗎？ B: 因為他對陳小姐很無禮。

(A) active 積極的　　　　　　　(B) impolite 無禮的

(C) negative 負面的　　　　　　(D) peaceful 和平的

__B__ 2. Can you pick up a _____ of bread on your way home?

你可以在回家的路上順道買一條麵包嗎？

(A) liter 公升　　　　　　　　　(B) loaf 條

(C) gram 公克　　　　　　　　　(D) foot 英尺

> **解析** 本題四個選項都是單位名詞，而 loaf 則為一整條麵包的單位，選項 B 正確。
> 若要描述單片的切片麵包、蛋糕、或披薩，則是用 "a piece of"，如 a piece
> of bread/cake/pizza。

__C__ 3. There's not _____ sugar left since Mandy used most of it yesterday.

糖沒有剩下很多，因為曼蒂昨天用掉了大部分。

(A) many 很多　　　　　　　　　(B) little 少量

(C) much 很多　　　　　　　　　(D) amount 數量

> **解析** 雖然選項 A 與 C 的意思都是「很多」，但選項 A 的 many 之後要加複數可數名
> 詞，而選項 C 的 much 後才可以加不可數名詞 sugar。little 和 amount 也是
> 跟不可數名詞連用，但語義不符。

__C__ 4. I am trying to _____ some weight because my doctor said I'm too thin.

我正在嘗試增加體重，因為我的醫生說我太瘦了。

(A) obtain 獲得　　　　　　　　(B) get 得到

(C) gain 增加　　　　　　　　　(D) decrease 減少

> **解析** 本題空格後接的是「體重」，適合搭配的字只有 gain 或 lose。而後半句提到現
> 在太瘦，由此推測應該是要增重，選項 C 最符合。選項 A 的 obtain 雖然意思
> 相近，但是後面通常會接「物品、資格、許可」。

___D___ 5. Rose's husband is taking her to a fancy restaurant, so she's going to wear a _____ dress.

蘿絲的先生要帶她去一家豪華餐廳，所以她打算穿一件正式的洋裝。

(A) casual 休閒的　　　　　(B) colorful 彩色的

(C) tight 緊身的　　　　　(D) formal 正式的

___C___ 6. The soup _____ sour, so I don't really like it.

這湯嚐起來是酸的，所以我不太喜歡它。

(A) sounds 聽起來　　　　(B) feels 感覺起來

(C) tastes 嚐起來　　　　(D) notices 注意到

___B___ 7. The office is on the twentieth floor! I'm not taking the _____ .

這間辦公室在二十樓！我可不打算走樓梯。

(A) boat 船　　　　　　　(B) stairs 樓梯

(C) elevator 電梯　　　　(D) bridge 橋

___D___ 8. Gina is such a _____ student. She spends a lot of time studying.

吉娜是如此勤奮的學生。她花很多時間唸書。

(A) humble 謙虛的　　　　(B) patient 有耐心的

(C) humorous 幽默的　　　(D) diligent 勤奮的

___B___ 9. My sister is interested in cooking and hopes that she can be a _____ one day.

我妹妹對烹飪很有興趣，而且她希望有一天能成為一名 _____。

(A) officer 長官　　　　　(B) chef 廚師

(C) director 導演　　　　(D) waiter 服務生

___C___ 10. We plan to plant some sunflowers in the _____ .

我們打算在庭院種一些向日葵。

(A) stage 舞台　　　　　(B) platform 月台

(C) yard 庭院　　　　　(D) library 圖書館

共 8 題，包括二個段落，每個段落含四個空格。每格均有四個選項，請依照文意選出最適合的答案。

Questions 11-14

The boy who moved into our neighborhood last month broke Ms. White's window with a baseball while he was playing ____(11)____ with a friend. Because he didn't want to ____(12)____ trouble, he ran away afterwards. However, the boy felt sorry for ____(13)____ , and later admitted that he was the one who broke the window. He also helped Ms. White fix the broken window, so she ____(14)____ him for his careless mistake.

上個月搬到我們這附近的男孩，在他和朋友玩 **(11) 接球**時，用棒球打破了白女士的窗戶。因為他不 **(12) 惹上麻煩**，所以之後就跑走了。然而，這個男孩對 **(13) 他之前做的事**感到抱歉，並且之後承認是他打破了窗戶。他還幫白女士修理破碎的窗戶，所以她 **(14) 原諒**了他的無心之過。

__B__ 11. (A) throw 丟球　　　　　　(B) catch 接球
　　　　(C) joke 開玩笑　　　　　(D) sport 運動

> **解析** 由空格前的 baseball 得知，男孩是玩跟棒球有關的運動，而 "play catch" 指「傳接球遊戲」，為常用說法，故選 B。

__D__ 12. (A) get on 搭乘　　　　　　(B) put on 穿上
　　　　(C) put off 延後　　　　　(D) get in 陷入

> **解析** 能和空格後 trouble 搭配的片語，以選項 D 的 get in 最適合，和 trouble 連用為「惹上麻煩」的意思。

__C__ 13. (A) how he did it 他做的方法

(B) what to do 該做什麼

(C) what he had done 他之前做的事

(D) who had done it 之前做的人

__A__ 14. (A) forgave 原諒　　　　　(B) forgot 忘記

(C) blamed 責怪　　　　　(D) praised 讚揚

Questions 15-18

A: Lisa still hasn't found her lost rabbit, _____(15)_____ ?

B: No, not yet. I hope someone will find it and return it to her soon.

A: I do, too. It was a birthday gift from her dad, so she must be really sad.

B: Oh, Mr. Chen. I _____(16)_____ him in ages. He must be busy with work.

A: Actually, Lisa has a younger brother living in Canada, so her dad travels back and forth a lot.

B: So her dad is over there now?

A: Yeah. I think he left for Canada last week. Lisa must be _____(17)_____ really upset about her lost rabbit. Maybe we could call her and cheer her up.

B: That's a great idea! I'm sure she'd love to _____(18)_____ us.

A: 莉莎還沒找到她走失的兔子，**(15) 她有嗎**？

B: 沒有，還沒。我希望有人能找到牠，並且儘快歸還給她。

A: 我也是。那是她爸爸送她的生日禮物，所以她一定很難過。

B: 哦，陳先生。我已經很久 **(16) 都沒看到**他了。他工作一定很忙。

A: 事實上，莉莎有一個弟弟住在加拿大，所以她爸爸常常來回奔波。

B: 所以她爸爸現在是在那邊嗎？

A: 是的。我想他上週前往加拿大去了。莉莎因為兔子走丟一定 **(17) 感到**非常難過。也許我們可以打電話給她，讓她開心起來。

B: 這個想法太棒了！我確定她會很想 **(18) 聽到我們的消息**。

_C_ 15. (A) does she 她是嗎　　　　　　(B) had she 她之前有嗎

　　　　(C) has she 她有嗎　　　　　　(D) didn't she 她沒有嗎

_C_ 16. (A) have seen 已經看到　　　　　(B) saw 看到了

　　　　(C) haven't seen 都沒看到　　　(D) didn't see 沒有看到

解析 空格後的「in ages」表示一段很長的時間，加上猜測陳先生忙於工作，所以可得知是很久沒有見到他了，因此選項 B 現在完成式的否定用法最符合。

_A_ 17. (A) feeling 感到　　　　　　　　(B) feel 感覺

　　　　(C) feels 感覺到　　　　　　　(D) felt 感受到

解析 由空格前的 must be 判斷，要填入可和原型 be 動詞搭配、表主動的選項來描述覺得傷心，因此選項 A 的現在分詞形式正確。

_C_ 18. (A) listen to 聽　　　　　　　　(B) contact to 聯絡

　　　　(C) hear about 聽到關於…的事　(D) didn't see 不再見到

第三部分 閱讀理解

共 12 題，包括 4 個題組，每個題組含 1 至 2 篇短文，與數個相關的四選一的選擇題。請由試題上的選項中選出最適合的答案。

Questions 19-21

Read the following department store directory.

FOURTH FLOOR	FURNITURE, BEDDING
THIRD FLOOR	MEN'S CLOTHING
SECOND FLOOR	WOMEN'S CLOTHING
FIRST FLOOR	SHOES, INFORMATION, LOST AND FOUND
BASEMENT	FOOD COURT, GROCERY STORE

請閱讀以下百貨公司樓層導覽。

(20) 四樓	(20) 家具、寢具
三樓	男裝
二樓	女裝
(19) 一樓	鞋類、服務台、(19) 失物招領
(21) 地下室	(21) 美食廣場、食品雜貨店

____A____ 19. Where should people go if they lose their wallet?

(A) The first floor

(B) The second floor

(C) The third floor

(D) The fourth floor

如果有人錢包不見了，應該去哪裡？

(A) 一樓

(B) 二樓

(C) 三樓

(D) 四樓

解析　若錢包不見，應該去失物招領櫃檯。依文中顯示是在一樓，因此選項 A 正確。

D 20. Mrs. Wilson wants to buy a coffee table for her living room. Where can she find it?

(A) The first floor
(B) The second floor
(C) The third floor
(D) The fourth floor

威爾遜太太想要為她的客廳買一張咖啡桌。她能在哪裡找到它？

(A) 一樓
(B) 二樓
(C) 三樓
(D) 四樓

解析 咖啡桌屬於家具，因此要去四樓買，選項 D 正確。

A 21. The Wilson family wants to have a meal at the department store. Where should they go?

(A) The basement
(B) The first floor
(C) The second floor
(D) The third floor.

威爾遜一家想要在百貨公司吃頓飯。他們應該去哪裡？

(A) 地下室
(B) 一樓
(C) 二樓
(D) 三樓

解析 依文章來判斷，這家百貨公司可吃飯的地方是美食廣場，位於地下室，因此選項 A 正確。

Wearing a seat belt is one of the best ways to protect yourself on the road. In fact, seat belts can greatly reduce the risk of death in a car crash. That's why it's important for everyone in the car, including the driver and passengers, to buckle up. Failure to do so is also illegal, and can result in a ticket.

However, many people still do not wear their seat belts, especially back seat passengers. We should keep our seat belt on at all times not because we might get a ticket, but because it is the most effective way to stay safe while in a car. The government is working to educate people about the importance of wearing seat belts. They hope that if people better understand the dangers of not buckling up, there will be less injuries and **fatalities**.

(23) 繫安全帶是在道路上保護自己的最佳方式之一。事實上，安全帶能大幅降低車禍死亡的風險。這就是為什麼車裡的每個人，包含駕駛和乘客，都需要繫上安全帶。未能這樣做也是非法的，並且會被開罰單。

然而，許多人仍然不繫安全帶，尤其是後座乘客。**(24) 我們應該隨時都將安全帶繫上，這並非因為我們可能會被開罰單，而是因為這是在車裡保持安全最有效的方式。**政府正在致力於教育民眾有關繫安全帶重要性的知識。**(22) 他們希望，如果人們能夠更理解不繫安全帶的危險，就會減少受傷和死亡的情況。**

__B__ 22. What does the word "fatalities" likely mean?
  (A) tickets
  (B) deaths
  (C) patients
  (D) accidents

"fatalities" 這個字最可能的意思為何？
  (A) 罰單
  (B) 死亡
  (C) 病患
  (D) 意外

解析 fatalities 這個字在文中的最後一句有提到，繫安全帶的用處為 "there will be less injuries and fatalities"。由此可得知，和傷害同一類別的為選項 B 的 fatality 死亡。選項 D 的 accident 不符合，是因為「意外」這個字的意思已經把「傷害」的層面包含在內，不需要再把兩個字分開提及。

B 23. What is the best title for this passage?
(A) *A Ticket to Save Your Life*
(B) *Buckle Up for Your Safety*
(C) *How to Avoid Car Accidents*
(D) *A Message from the Government*

這篇文章最適合的標題是什麼？
(A) 一張拯救你生命的罰單
(B) 為了你的安全請繫安全帶
(C) 如何避免車禍
(D) 來自政府的一則訊息

解析 本文從第一段第一行就開宗明義提到繫安全帶可以保護安全，第二段論述雖然提及不繫安全帶有被開罰單的危險，屬於文章細節，但主旨大意仍在強調安全帶對道路交通安全的重要性，因此選項 B 最符合。

B 24. According to the passage, which is true?
(A) Only the driver is required to put on a seatbelt.
(B) Not wearing a seatbelt while driving is against the law.
(C) Handing out tickets is the best way to prevent car crashes.
(D) The government is trying to reduce the number of accidents.

根據這篇文章，哪一項正確？
(A) 只有駕駛需要繫上安全帶。
(B) 行駛時不繫安全帶是違法的。
(C) 發放罰單是預防車禍的最佳方式。
(D) 政府正試圖減少事故的數量。

解析 可由第二段第二句得知，不繫安全帶會收到罰單，因此是違法的，選項 B 符合。第二段的前兩句有提到，後座乘客不繫安全帶也是會被開罰單。

The Grand Tour

You can:

- Stay at luxury hotels
- Enjoy delicious local foods
- Visit famous tourist spots
- Take the fastest train in the world
- Do all the shopping you like at fashionable department stores

Date: July 30 ~ August 5

Price: NT$ 20,000 / adult
        NT$ 18,000 / age 12 - 18
        NT$ 15,000 / age under 12
        (flights, hotels, and train tickets are included)

Call "Get Away" at 1123-6789

Check our website: http://www.getaway.com.tw for more information

** Print out this coupon for **20%** off **

豪華之旅

您可以：

- 住宿豪華酒店
- 享受美味在地食材
- 參觀著名景點
- (27) 搭乘世界上最快的火車
- 在時尚百貨盡情購物

日期：7 月 30 日至 8 月 5 日

價格：(26) 每位成人 台幣 20,000 元

12 至 18 歲 台幣 18,000 元

12 歲以下 台幣 15,000 元

(25)（包含機票、酒店和火車票。）

請撥打「度假」專線：1123-6789

請造訪我們的網站獲得更多資訊：http://www.getaway.com.tw

(26) ** 列印出示此優惠券，可享八折優惠 **

_D_ 25. The price does not include which of the following?

(A) hotels
(B) air travel
(C) train trips
(D) souvenirs

價格不包括下列哪一項？

(A) 飯店
(B) 飛機旅遊
(C) 火車旅行
(D) 紀念品

解析 第二段最後一句說明了旅費涵蓋的項目，並沒有包含選項 D 的紀念品。

_A_ 26. Mr. and Mrs. Chen have a daughter who is seven years old. They want to join the tour. How much will they have to pay if they use a coupon?

(A) NT $44,000
(B) NT $46,400
(C) NT $55,000
(D) NT $58,000

陳先生和陳太太有一個七歲的女兒。他們想參加這次的旅行。如果他們使用優惠券，需要支付多少錢？

(A) 台幣 44,000 元
(B) 台幣 46,400 元
(C) 台幣 55,000 元
(D) 台幣 58,000 元

解析 夫妻旅遊以兩位成人計價，七歲的女兒以 12 歲以下計算，共 55,000 元，加上文章最後一行提到優惠券的折扣是八折，因此最後需付 44,000 元，選項 A 正確。

_A_ 27. Which activity on the Grand Tour is a unique experience?

(A) A train ride
(B) A hotel stay
(C) A shopping trip
(D) A restaurant meal

豪華之旅中，哪一項活動是獨特的體驗？

(A) 火車之旅
(B) 飯店住宿
(C) 購物之旅
(D) 餐廳用餐

解析 題目中的 "unique"，可與介紹行程裡的 "take the fastest train in the world" 相對應：「世界最快」即是其他項目無可比擬的獨特，因此選項 A 正確。

Questions 28-30

Jimmy and I were best friends in high school. Both of us wanted to major in English in college and become English teachers. We used to do everything together and had many of the same hobbies and interests. However, something changed after the new transfer student joined our class. Jimmy didn't talk to me as often as he did before, and he spent more time with him than with me. I felt like I was being left out. I wasn't sure what to do, so I went to my teacher, Miss Ou, to talk about my problem. She told me it's very common for friends to become less close, even best friends. She said that I shouldn't take it personally. It was hard to hear that, but I knew that Miss Ou was right. I gave Jimmy some space, focusing on my own life instead. But I still believed one day we would find our way back to each other.

(30) 吉米和我在高中時是最好的朋友。我們都想在大學主修英文,然後當英文老師。以前我們每件事情總是都會一起做,還有許多相同的愛好和興趣。(28) 然而,自從一位新轉學生加入我們班後,有些事就變了。吉米不再像以前那樣常和我聊天,而且花更多時間與他相處而不是我。(29) 我感覺像是被排擠了。我不確定該怎麼辦,所以去找我的老師歐女士談我的困擾。她告訴我,(30) 朋友之間變得冷淡是很常見的問題,甚至最好的朋友也可能發生。她說我不應該把此事當作是對方在針對我。雖然聽到這些很難受,但我知道歐女士是對的。我給了吉米一些空間,也反過頭來專注在自己的生活。(29) (30) 但我仍然相信,有天我們會重拾當初的友誼。

___D___ 28. Why did the author and Jimmy's friendship change?
  (A) Because they didn't have any common interests.
  (B) Because the author wanted to focus on his own life.
  (C) Because the author transferred to a different school.
  (D) Because Jimmy spent more time with another student.

作者和吉米的友誼為何發生變化?
  (A) 因為他們沒有任何共同的興趣。
  (B) 因為作者想要專注在自己的生活上。
  (C) 因為作者轉學到了不同的學校。
  (D) 因為吉米花更多時間和另一位學生相處。

解析 由第四句和第五句得知,改變的原因是轉學生的加入,吉米花了更多時間和新學生相處,因此選項 D 正確。

第2回

__A__ 29. Which of the following is NOT true about Jimmy?

(A) He is best friends with the author.

(B) He shares interests with the author.

(C) He was good friends with the author.

(D) He goes to the same school as the author.

關於吉米，下列哪一個選項不正確？

(A) 他現在是作者最好的朋友。

(B) 他與作者有共同的興趣。

(C) 他曾是作者的好朋友。

(D) 他現在和作者就讀於同一所學校。

解析 由第六到八句，以及最後一句得知，老師點明了友誼有時候不會永遠如此緊密，而且作者希望最後能和吉米再恢復友誼，因此可推斷吉米與作者不再是最好的朋友了。選項 A 的「現在簡單式」表示兩人還是最好朋友的「事實」，與文意不符，因此選 A。

__D__ 30. What can we learn from the story?

(A) Making friends is important.

(B) Friendship is about forgiving.

(C) Teachers give the best advice.

(D) Friendship doesn't always last.

我們可以從這個故事中學到什麼？

(A) 交朋友很重要。

(B) 友誼和原諒有關。

(C) 老師會給出最好的建議。

(D) 友誼不會總是長久持續。

解析 整篇文章敘述作者和好友情誼的轉變，還有老師對作者的建議，最後以作者希望友情能恢復而結束。可由此得知本文是關於一段變淡的友誼，因此選項 D 正確。

GEPT
初級模擬試題
第3回
解答、翻譯與詳解

第 3 回解答

🔊 聽力測驗解答

1. C	2. A	3. C	4. B	5. C
6. C	7. B	8. A	9. A	10. A
11. B	12. B	13. A	14. A	15. C
16. C	17. A	18. A	19. A	20. A
21. A	22. C	23. C	24. B	25. A
26. A	27. C	28. A	29. C	30. A

閱讀測驗解答

1. D	2. B	3. A	4. A	5. B
6. A	7. A	8. A	9. C	10. B
11. D	12. D	13. C	14. B	15. C
16. A	17. B	18. B	19. A	20. B
21. A	22. D	23. B	24. C	25. A
26. B	27. B	28. C	29. A	30. A

第一部分　看圖辨義

___C___ 1. For Question Number 1, please look at the picture.
What does Joy spend the most time doing?

(A) Learning English

(B) Resting at home

(C) Practicing the piano.

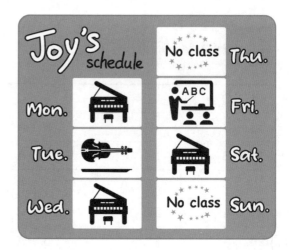

第一題，請看此圖片。

喬伊花最多時間做什麼事？

(A) 學英文。

(B) 在家休息。

(C) 練琴。

> **解析**　圖片中可以看到喬伊一週有三天時間在練琴，所以答案為 C 選項。

___A___ 2. For Question Number 2, please look at the picture.
What will probably happen next?

(A) The police will come.

(B) The men will drive to the police station.

(C) The men are going to park the car.

第二題，請看此圖片。

接下來可能會發生什麼事？

(A) 警察會來。

(B) 男子們會開車到警察局。

(C) 男子們會去停車。

> **解析**　從圖片中可以看到女子正在打電話叫警察，所以可以預測接下來警察會到現場，答案為 A。

__C__ 3. For Question Number 3, please look at the picture.
What did the boy likely do last night?

(A) He studied math.

(B) He went to bed early.

(C) He played video games.

第三題，請看此圖片。

男孩昨天晚上可能做了什麼？

(A) 讀數學。

(B) 提早就寢。

(C) 打電動。

解析 男孩在撰寫的考卷似乎是數學考卷，但這並非昨晚發生的事，另外圖片提示可以看到電動，因此選 C。

__B__ 4. For Question Number 4, please look at the picture.
What is the woman's job?

(A) She is a nurse.

(B) She is a reporter.

(C) She is an engineer.

第四題，請看此圖片。

這名女子的工作是什麼？

(A) 她是護理師。

(B) 她是記者。

(C) 她是工程師。

解析 從圖片中可以看出女子是記者，正在做新聞報導，因此答案選 B。

C 5. For Question Number 5, please look at the picture.

What is the man's problem?

(A) He isn't very hungry.

(B) The menu is written in Chinese.

(C) He doesn't understand English.

第五題,請看此圖片。

這名男子遇到的問題是什麼?

(A) 他不是很餓。

(B) 菜單是用中文寫的。

(C) 他不懂英文。

解析　男子手上拿的菜單上寫著 scallop（干貝），頭上很多問號,因此可以知道他因為看不懂英文菜單感到困擾。選 C。

__C__ 6. Excuse me, where is the restroom?

   (A) You can get it at the front desk.

   (B) Yes. Here's a towel.

   (C) It's next to the elevator.

不好意思，請問廁所在哪裡？
(A) 你可以在櫃檯取得。
(B) 好的。毛巾在這裡。
(C) 在電梯旁邊。

解析 廁所的常見說法有：toilet, bathroom 和題目中的 restroom。只有選項 C 針對題目回答，其餘兩選項皆答非所問，因此答案選 C。

__B__ 7. I don't think I can go jogging with you next week.

   (A) I don't think it's a good place to go.

   (B) How come?

   (C) This is a great department store.

我覺得我下星期不能跟你去慢跑了。
(A) 我不覺得那裡是個好地方。
(B) 為什麼？
(C) 這間百貨公司很好。

解析 "How come?" 和 "Why?" 的意思相同，用來詢問原因。選項 B 詢問不能一起慢跑的原因最能呼應題目，其餘兩選項皆不正確，因此選 B。

__A__ 8. I'm meeting up with my niece at that new pizza place next Sunday.

   (A) Cindy, right? I met her last summer. She's fun.

   (B) I'm a meat lover, especially beef and chicken.

   (C) You should see a doctor if you hurt your knee.

我和我的姪女下週日會在新的比薩餐廳見面。
(A) 是辛蒂，對嗎？我去年夏天認識她的。她很有趣。
(B) 我很愛吃肉，尤其是牛肉跟雞肉。
(C) 如果你膝蓋受傷了，應該去看醫生。

解析 選項 A 的 met 是 meet 的過去式，有初見面的意思。選項 A 接續對話，討論說話者的姪女，其餘兩個選項偏離主題，因此選 A。

<u>A</u> 9. How do I look in this shirt?
   (A) It looks great on you.
   (B) Thank you for the gift.
   (C) The shorts don't fit.

我穿這件襯衫看起來如何？
(A) 看起來很棒。
(B) 謝謝你的禮物。
(C) 短褲的尺寸不合適。

解析 選項 A 的 It 指的是題目中的 shirt 說明衣服適合某人穿時，可以用「It looks good/great/wonderful...on 人」的句型。因此選項 A 的回應最恰當。

<u>A</u> 10. When will the party begin?
   (A) At 6:00 PM next Saturday.
   (B) It's going to be at my place.
   (C) Vicky and I are going together.

派對什麼時候開始？
(A) 下週六晚上 6 點。
(B) 會在我家。
(C) 薇琪跟我會一起去。

解析 "When" 開頭的問句用來詢問時間，只有選項 A 回答了時間，其餘兩選項皆答非所問，因此選 A。

<u>B</u> 11. The final exam is only two weeks away.
   (A) It happens every two weeks.
   (B) We'd better start studying for it.
   (C) What was the test like?

再兩週就期末考了。
(A) 這件事每兩週發生一次。
(B) 我們最好開始準備了。
(C) 考試內容如何？

解析 選項 B 的 "We'd better..."（最好…）用來給予建議和忠告，最能呼應題目。選項 A 答非所問，選項 C 使用過去式不能用來討論未來要發生的考試，因此選 B。

<u>B</u> 12. Where did you take the photo?
   (A) I'm going to have a birthday party next week.
   (B) At the park next to the school.
   (C) I painted it in my art class.

你這張照片在哪裡拍的？
(A) 我下週要辦生日派對。
(B) 學校旁邊的公園。
(C) 我在美術課畫的。

解析 只有選項 B 針對提問回答了拍照的地點，其餘兩個選項皆答非所問，因此選 B。

__A__ 13. Oh, no! Ms. Fisher is mad at me.

(A) Why? What have you done?

(B) When did you go fishing?

(C) That's so sweet of him.

糟了！費雪老師在生我的氣。

(A) 為什麼？你做了什麼事？

(B) 你何時去釣魚？

(C) 他人真好。

解析 只有選項 A 針對老師生氣做後續的提問，其餘兩個選項和題目不能相呼應，因此選 A。

__A__ 14. I have no idea where we are.

(A) Neither do I. I think we're lost.

(B) 8:30 will be too late for us.

(C) But I know who they are.

我不知道我們在哪裡。

(A) 我也不知道。我想我們迷路了。

(B) 8:30 對我們來說太晚了。

(C) 但我知道他們是誰。

解析 迷路時英文常使用 "Where am I?" 或是 "Where are we?" 來表達。只有選項 A 是針對迷路做回應，因此選 A。

__C__ 15. Watching movies is a great way to learn English.

(A) Yes, that movie is great.

(B) Which movie theater should we go to?

(C) Yes. That's how I improve my English.

看電影是學英文很棒的方法。

(A) 是的，那部電影很棒。

(B) 我們應該去哪個電影院？

(C) 是的。我就是這樣讓我的英文進步的。

解析 "a great way to..." 常用來說明「做某事的好方法。」只有選項 C 針對主題：「學習英文的好方法」做出回應，因此選 C。

C 16. M: I like your new hairstyle.

W: Thank you. You don't think it's too short?

M: Not at all. You look better with short hair.

W: Thanks! I never thought I'd look good with short hair.

Question: How does the man feel?

男子：我喜歡妳的新髮型。

女子：謝謝。你不覺得太短了嗎？

男子：不會啊！妳留短髮比較好看。

女子：謝謝！我從來不覺得我留短髮會好看。

問題：男子覺得如何？

(A) He thinks the woman's hair is too short.

(B) He thinks the woman looks better with long hair.

(C) He thinks the woman looks good with shorter hair.

(A) 他覺得女子的頭髮太短。

(B) 他覺得女子留長頭髮比較好看。

(C) 他覺得女子留短頭髮比較好看。

解析 由男子對話的第二句 "You look better with short hair." 知道他覺得女子留短髮比較好看，選 C。

A 17. M: Where to, ma'am?

W: The airport, please. I have a flight to catch.

M: When does it leave?

W: In two hours.

M: Well, the traffic is usually terrible this time of day.

Question: What does the taxi driver mean?

男子：女士，妳要去哪裡？

女子：請到機場。我需要趕飛機。

男子：它什麼時候起飛？

女子：兩小時後。

男子：喔！這個時間路況通常很差。

問題：計程車司機的意思是什麼？

(A) They will probably be caught in the traffic jam.

(B) They will arrive at the airport in two hours.

(C) His taxi isn't available today.

(A) 他們可能會被塞在車陣。

(B) 他們會在兩小時內抵達機場。

(C) 計程車今天無法載客。

解析 從計程車司機最後一句回應的關鍵詞 traffic（交通）和 terrible（差勁的）可以推測計程車司機的意思是會遇到塞車，選 A。

A 18. W: Do you know where Mark is?

M: Mark? I haven't seen him all morning.

W: Where could he be? He promised to go to the performance with me.

M: Why don't you call Kevin? He might know where Mark is.

Question: What is the woman's problem?

女子：你知道馬克在哪裡嗎？

男子：馬克？我整個早上都沒看到他。

女子：他會去哪裡？他答應我今天會一起去看表演。

男子：你要不要打電話給凱文？他可能知道馬克在哪裡。

問題：女子遇到的問題是什麼？

(A) She can't find Mark.

(B) She's late to the performance.

(C) She doesn't know Kevin's number.

(A) 她找不到凱文。

(B) 她看表演遲到。

(C) 她不知道凱文的電話號碼。

解析 對話中女子的兩句話都是在找凱文，由此可知答案為 A。

A 19. B: The box is so big. What's inside?

W: The new coats I bought for you and your brother.

B: Wow! Thanks, Mom. Can I open it now?

W: Your brother gets back at 5:00. You can open it together.

Question: What will the boy do next?

男孩：這盒子好大。裡面是什麼？

女子：我幫你跟你哥哥買的新外套。

男孩：哇！謝謝媽。我現在可以打開嗎？

女子：你哥五點回來，你們到時可以一起開。

問題：男孩接著會做什麼？

(A) Wait for his brother.

(B) Try on the coat.

(C) Open the box.

(A) 等他哥哥。

(B) 試穿外套。

(C) 打開盒子。

解析 由女子最後一句 "You can open it together." 得知答案為選項 A。

A 20. W: I've decided to go to the UK for my last year of high school.

M: Really? I thought you gave up on that idea.

W: Well, I did. But then I had second thoughts.

M: So that means we can't graduate together next year?

W: I'm afraid so. I'll miss you for sure.

Question: What did the woman mean when she said she had second thoughts?

女子：我已經決定高中最後一年去英國了。

男子：真的嗎？我以為妳已經放棄這個想法了。

女子：我是，但後來我又改變主義。

男子：所以意思是我們明年不能一起畢業嗎？

女子：恐怕是這樣。我一定會想你的。

問題：女子說她改變主義是什麼意思？

(A) She changed her mind.

(B) She would think about the man.

(C) She didn't want to go after all.

(A) 她改變了心意。

(B) 她會想念男子。

(C) 她最後不想去。

解析 從男子與女子的前三句對話可以知道女子原本不去英國，後來又決定要去，由此可以推測答案是選項 A。

___A___ 21. M: Wow, that was a great performance! I didn't know you could sing so well.

W: I've been taking singing lessons for six months.

M: What made you want to take lessons?

W: Actually, I've always wanted to be a singer.

M: That's cool.

Question: Why is the woman taking singing lessons?

男子：哇！真是一場精彩的演出！我不知道妳唱歌唱得這麼好。

女子：我上歌唱課上六個月了。

男子：妳怎麼會想到要學唱歌？

女子：其實，我一直都很想當歌手。

男子：酷耶！

問題：女子為什麼去上歌唱課？

(A) To make her dream come true.

(B) To make a lot of money.

(C) To sing at a party.

(A) 讓自己的夢想成真。

(B) 賺很多錢。

(C) 在派對上唱歌。

解析 選項 A 的 "dream come true" 指的是「夢想成真、達成目標」，對話中女子提到 "I've always wanted to be a singer." 得知答案為選項 A。

C 22. W: I feel like having some coffee.

M: OK, let's see if we can find any coffee shops around here.

W: There's one! But I don't have any cash on me.

M: Me, neither. Don't worry. Most shops have more than one way to pay now.

Question: What does the man mean?

女子：我想要喝咖啡。

男子：好啊！我們來看看這附近有沒有什麼咖啡館。

女子：這邊有一家！可是我身上沒有現金。

男子：我也沒有。別擔心，現在很多店家都有一種以上的支付方式。

問題：男子的意思是什麼？

(A) He can buy the woman some coffee.

(B) He doesn't want to pay.

(C) They can pay without using cash.

(A) 他可以請女子喝咖啡。

(B) 他不想付錢。

(C) 他們沒有現金也能付款。

解析 男子提到 "Most shops have more than one way to pay"「現在很多店家都有一種以上的支付方式。」表示除了現金之外還會有其他支付的方式，因此得知答案為選項 C。

C 23. W: Wow, is this the self-driving car?

M: Isn't it cool? My dad just got it last month.

W: It's amazing. Does this mean you can take a nap in the car on the highway?

M: You don't want to try that. Drivers still need to keep their eyes on the road in case something goes wrong.

Question: What does the man mean when he says "you don't want to try that"?

女子：哇！這是無人車嗎？

男子：很酷吧！我爸上個月才新買的。

女子：很神奇。所以意思是說你在高速公路上可以小睡嗎？

男子：你不會想這麼做。駕駛還是需要看路，以防萬一。

問題：男子說「你不會想這麼做」是什麼意思？

(A) Don't do it if you don't want to.

(B) Do it only if you are able to.

(C) You had better not do it.

(A) 如果不想做可以不用做。

(B) 如果可以才做。

(C) 最好不要這麼做。

解析 從男子在 "You don't want to try that." 後面的說明，可以知道男子覺得駕駛在無人車行進時睡覺不是好主意，因此可以推測答案為選項 C。

B 24. M: Would you like to go to Kenting with us next weekend?

W: Who else is going?

M: Mike, Jack, Rose, and Terry.

W: Oh, I'd really like to go, but I've spent too much money lately. I don't think I can go.

Question: Will the woman go to Kenting with the man?

男子：你下週末想和我們一起去墾丁嗎？

女子：還有誰要去？

男子：麥克、傑克、蘿絲和泰瑞。

女子：喔！我很想去，但是我最近花太多錢了。我覺得我不能去。

問題：女子會跟男子一起去墾丁嗎？

(A) Yes, she will.

(B) No, she won't.

(C) She will, but she'll be late.

(A) 是，她會去。

(B) 不，她不會去。

(C) 她會去，但會比較晚到。

解析 婉拒邀約時常用 "I'd like to, but..." 的句型，因此由女子最後一句的回答得知女子不會去墾丁，選 B。

A 25. W: I think I left my wallet on the bus.

M: No, not again! There's nothing we can do now.

W: Well, I can call the bus company and ask if they found it.

M: That's a good idea.

W: Well, I guess I've learned from experience.

Question: Why did the man say "not again"?

女子：我想我把錢包忘在公車上了。

男子：不會又來一次吧！我們現在無法做任何事。

女子：嗯 ... 我可以打電話給公車公司，問問他們有沒有找到。

男子：好主意。

女子：嗯！我猜我還是有學到經驗。

問題：為什麼男子說"not again"?（不會又發生了吧！）

(A) It has happened before.

(B) He asked the woman not to do it again.

(C) He doesn't know what to do.

(A) 這件事之前發生過。

(B) 他請那名女子不要再做一次。

(C) 他不知道怎麼辦。

解析　"not again" 常在對反覆出現的問題表達不滿情緒時使用。如果男子是想請女子不要再做一次的話，會用"Don't do it again." 因此答案選 A，表示女子常把錢包忘在公車上。

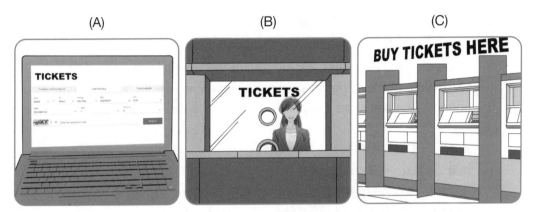

_A_ 26. For Question Number 26, please look at the three pictures.

Listen to the following announcement. Where can the people purchase tickets?

We have three baseball games coming up next week. One on Monday, another on Wednesday and the other on Friday. Also, we'll be holding a dance contest this Saturday. If you want to purchase tickets, they're available on our website. See you next week.

第 26 題，請看三張圖片。

請聽以下廣播。大家可以到哪裡買票？

下週將有三場棒球比賽。一場在週一，另一場在週三，還有一場在週五。另外我們將在這週六舉辦跳舞比賽。如果您想買票，可以在我們的網站上購買。下週見。

解析 由關鍵詞"our website"（我們的網站）可以得知答案為選項 A。

C 27. For Question Number 27, please look at the three pictures.

Listen to the following talk. Where do you think the speaker is?

Good morning everyone. It's my turn to talk about my best friend today. I brought a photo of her to show you. Her name is Polly. She is a little chubby. She has short curly hair. She is very cute.

第 27 題,請看三張圖片。

請聽以下談話。你覺得說話者是誰?

大家早安。今天輪到我聊聊我最好的朋友。我帶了一張照片來給大家看。她的名字是波莉。她有點胖胖的。她留短髮。她很可愛。

解析 由第二句「我帶了一張照片來給大家看」,表示女子可能在做報告,可推測答案為 C 選項。

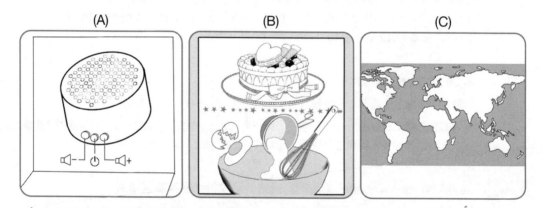

(A)　　　　　　　　(B)　　　　　　　　(C)

A 28. For Question Number 28, please look at the three pictures.

Listen to the following talk. Which is the speaker talking about?

First, you push the middle button to turn it on. When you see the light, that means it's on. Then you can press the button on the right to turn up the volume and the one on the left to turn it down.

第 28 題,請看三張圖片。

請聽以下談話。說話者提到的是哪張圖?

首先,按下中間的按鍵把它打開。當你看到燈亮時,表示已經開了。接著按右邊的按鍵將音量調大,按左邊的按鍵將聲音調小。

解析 從關鍵字 "middle button"（中間的按鍵）、volume（音量）可以知道說話者在 講音響或喇叭，答案為選項 A。

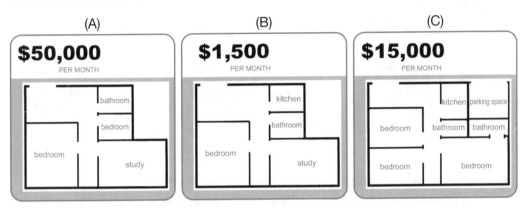

  C   29. For Question Number 29, please look at the three pictures.

Listen to the following talk. Which picture best matches the description?

This apartment has three bedrooms, two bathrooms and a kitchen. It's available for lease. The rent is fifteen thousand per month. By the way, it also comes with parking. This apartment is a great deal, so you'd better hurry if you're interested.

第 29 題，請看三張圖片。

請聽以下談話。那張圖最符合文字描述？

這間公寓有三個房間，兩間衛浴和一個廚房。這間公寓可以出租，租金為一個月 15,000 元。另外，這間房也有附停車位。這間公寓非常划算，有興趣的人最好動作快。

解析 由關鍵字 "fifteen thousand"（15,000）以及房間數量有三個，可得知答案為選 項 C。

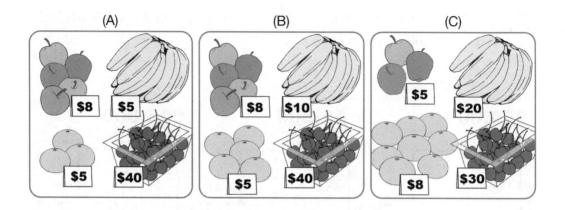

__A__ 30. For question number 30, please look at the three pictures.

Listen to the following announcement. Which picture best matches it?

Good afternoon, shoppers. We're having a sale on fruit today. You can get 5 apples for only 8 dollars, 3 oranges for 5 dollars, and a bunch of bananas for only 5 dollars. And for cherry lovers, one box is just 40 dollars, and you can get a second box for 50% off.

第 30 題，請看三張圖片。

請聽以下廣播。哪張圖片最符合廣播內容？

各位前來購物的賓客午安。今日水果特價。蘋果 5 顆 8 元，橘子 3 顆 5 元，香蕉一堆 5 元。喜愛櫻桃的賓客，一盒櫻桃只要 40 元，第二盒半價。

解析 由蘋果、橘子和香蕉的價錢可以知道答案為選項 A。

第一部分 詞彙

共 **10** 題，每個題目裡有一個空格。請從四個選項中選出一個最適合題意的字或詞作答。

___D___ 1. Please _____ me to send the document next Monday so that Miss Lin can receive it on time.

請在下週一提醒我寄出文件，這樣林小姐才能準時收到。

(A) hope 希望　　　　　　　　(B) allow 允許

(C) expect 期待　　　　　　　(D) remind 提醒

___B___ 2. Jacob needs to take Friday off because he has to _____ a test that day.

雅各需要在周五請假，因為他當天要參加考試。

(A) post 發佈　　　　　　　　(B) take 參加

(C) delay 延遲　　　　　　　 (D) cancel 取消

___A___ 3. The hotel was _____ , and the room was not even cleaned.

這家飯店很糟糕，甚至連房間都沒有打掃。

(A) terrible 糟糕的　　　　　 (B) amazing 驚人的

(C) ordinary 普通的　　　　　(D) marvelous 精彩的

___A___ 4. Mr. Lee, a very _____ teacher, doesn't let students in if they're late.

李先生是一位非常嚴格的老師，若學生們遲到，他就不讓他們進來。

(A) strict 嚴格的　　　　　　 (B) patient 有耐心的

(C) talkative 愛說話的　　　　(D) effective 有效的

___B___ 5. I'm pretty hungry, so can I have two _____ of pizza?

我蠻餓的，所以我可以拿兩片披薩嗎？

(A) bags 袋　　　　　　　　　(B) slices 片

(C) loaves 條　　　　　　　　(D) glasses 杯

___A___ 6. I had a great time on the trip, but I was so _____ after the 12-hour flight back home.

我這次旅行玩得很開心，但在 12 小時的飛行到家後，我非常的疲累。

(A) tired 感到疲累　　　　　　(B) excited 感到興奮

(C) satisfied 感到滿意　　　　(D) interested 感興趣

> **解析** 句首提到旅程玩得愉快，但由 but 推測，其後的句義應是有相反的轉折；再加上搭乘了 12 小時的飛機，所以應是跟愉快相反的負面意思，因此感到疲累的選項 A 正確。

___A___ 7. After many years of hard work, Jenny finally _____ her goal.
經過多年的努力工作，珍妮終於實現了她的目標。

(A) realized 實現
(B) imagined 想像
(C) appreciated 欣賞
(D) understood 理解

___A___ 8. Ray hasn't cleaned his room in months, so it's _____ garbage.
瑞好幾個月都沒有打掃他的房間，所以房間裡充滿垃圾。

(A) full of 充滿
(B) made of 由…製成
(C) covered with 被…覆蓋
(D) crowded with 被…擠滿

> **解析** 沒有打掃房間，合理推測就是充滿垃圾的狀態，選項 A 正確。垃圾是在房間的內部，而不是蓋在房間的頂層，因此房間不會被垃圾「覆蓋」。再者，選項 D 的 be crowded with 字面上雖合理，但嚴格來說只會形容人擠滿某個空間，而非物品。

___C___ 9. Christopher ate all the cookies; _____ , we had none left for dessert.
克里斯多福把所有的餅乾都吃了；因此我們沒有剩下任何作為甜點了。

(A) besides 此外
(B) however 然而
(C) therefore 因此
(D) no wonder 難怪

> **解析** 空格前提到餅乾被吃光，空格後描述甜點沒有剩下，是吃光的「結果」。因此空格中需填入承接因果關係的 therefore，選項 C 正確。

___B___ 10. Bob _____ Mary to do his homework for him.
鮑伯請求瑪麗幫他做作業。

(A) said 說
(B) asked 要求
(C) made 使
(D) pleased 滿足

Part 2 段落填空

共 8 題，包括二個段落，每個段落含四個空格。每格均有四個選項，請依照文意選出最適合的答案。

Questions 11-14

Hey Sylvia,

Just wanted to say thank you for taking me and my family out to dinner while I was in L.A. It was such a pleasant ___(11)___ to run into you there. We hadn't ___(12)___ each other since you moved away five years ago. I really enjoyed the food at the restaurant that you ___(13)___ us to, especially the brownie I had for dessert. I liked it so much that I tried to make some when I ___(14)___ back home. Now I'm really into baking and I can't wait for you to visit and try my desserts. Anyway, thanks again and keep in touch!

Best,

Emma

嘿希爾薇亞：

只想向你說謝謝，感謝在洛杉磯時，你帶我和家人去吃晚餐。在那裡和你偶遇，真是愉快的 **(11) 驚喜**。自從五年前你搬走後，我們就不曾 **(12) 見過面了**。

我真的很喜歡你 **(13) 帶**我們去的那家餐廳的食物，特別是我所點的甜點布朗尼。我太喜歡了，我甚至在 **(14) 回到**家後還自己嘗試製作。現在我對烘焙真的很入迷，等不及要你來我這拜訪，試試我的甜點了。

無論如何，再次感謝你，保持聯繫！

祝好，

艾瑪

  D   11. (A) event 事件   (B) matter 事項

            (C) chance 機會   (D) surprise 驚喜

解析 可由空格後的 run into（巧遇）得知，兩方相遇是意外發生的，算是驚喜，因此選項 D 最適合。

__D__ 12. (A) saw 看見了　　　　　　(B) see 看
　　　　(C) seeing 正看著　　　　(D) seen 看到過

__C__ 13. (A) visited 參觀　　　　　(B) shared 分享
　　　　(C) took 帶　　　　　　　(D) paid 付款

__B__ 14. (A) get 到達　　　　　　(B) got 到達了
　　　　(C) will get 將到達　　　(D) have got 已經到達

解析 空格前描述喜歡甜點，並在家裡自己做，都是用過去式動詞來描述過去的事情，因此「到家」這件事也是使用過去簡單式，選項 B 正確。

Questions 15-18

_____(15)_____ you heard of EVs? EV stands for electric vehicle. These are cars that have electric motors rather than gas engines. One of the biggest advantages of EVs _____(16)_____ that they cause no air pollution when running. An EV can even drive _____(17)_____ . However, there have been some major accidents caused by EVs. In one case, an EV caught on fire, and the people inside couldn't open the doors. In _____(18)_____ , the EV's computer failed, causing the car to crash. People are still worried whether EVs are safe to drive, but one thing we know for sure is that there will be more and more electric cars in the future.

你 (15) 曾經聽說電動車嗎？"EV"是電動車的縮寫。這些是使用電動馬達而非汽油引擎的汽車。電動車最大優點之一 (16) 就是它們在運行時不會造成空氣污染。一輛電動車甚至可以 (17) 自行駕駛。然而，有些重大事故也是電動車造成的。在一個案例中，一輛電動車著了火，而且車內的人無法打開門。在 (18) 另一個案例中，電動車的電腦故障，導致車輛撞車。人們仍然擔心電動車是否安全，但我們確定的一件事是未來會有越來越多的電動車。

__C__ 15. (A) Do 做　　　　　　　(B) Can 能
　　　　(C) Have 曾經　　　　　(D) Are 是

___A___ 16. (A) is 是   (B) are 是
       (C) will be 將是   (D) have been 一直是

> **解析** 此句的主詞是 one of the biggest advantages，是眾多好處的其中「之一」，因此為單數。此外，此句的時態可由意思判斷，是和前句一樣在介紹電動車，為客觀的事實，因此採用描述事實的「現在簡單式」，選項 A 正確。

___B___ 17. (A) it 它   (B) itself 它自己
       (C) themselves 他們自己   (D) yourself 你自己

___B___ 18. (A) other 其他的   (B) another 另一個
       (C) the other 剩下的那個 (D) one more 再多一個

> **解析** 空格前的一句，用 in one case 描述一個案例，而空格後描述另一案例時，選項 B 的 another 可代表眾多之中的「另一個」。Other 後應該加複數名詞。the other 是用於剩下的最後一個。One more 代表再多一個，與句意不符。

共 12 題，包括 4 個題組，每個題組含 1 至 2 篇短文，與數個相關的四選一的選擇題。請由試題上的選項中選出最適合的答案。

Questions 19-21

Picnic Day!

- 11:00 am, Saturday, June 22, 2024
- Lakeshore Park
- Wear your most comfortable t-shirt and shorts.
- Bring your family and friends along with your favorite snacks
- Enjoy the sandwiches and mini burgers that we've prepared for you!
- The park has tennis and badminton courts, so if you'd like to play, don't forget to bring your own equipment.

Let's have fun together!

Email Ashley three days before the picnic at ashley.davis@citygovernment.com if you plan to come. In case of rain, the picnic will be cancelled, so be sure to watch the weather report the evening before the event.

野餐日！

- (21) 2024 年 6 月 22 日，週六上午 11:00
- 湖畔公園
- 穿上你最舒服的 T 恤和短褲。
- (19) 帶你的家人和朋友，再加上你最喜歡的點心一起來
- 享受我們為你準備的三明治和迷你漢堡！
- 公園有網球場和羽毛球場，所以如果你想打球，別忘了帶你自己的裝備來。

一起來開心的玩吧！

如果你計劃要來參加，(21) 請在野餐前三天寄電子郵件給 (20) Ashley，ashley.davis@citygovernment.com。若遇到下雨，野餐將會取消，所以務必要在活動前一晚關注天氣預報。

A 19. What can people do at Lakeshore Park on June 22?

(A) Spend time with their friends and family.

(B) Have fun while wearing their finest clothes.

(C) Prepare snacks for all the people at the picnic.

(D) Learn how to make sandwiches and mini burgers.

人們在 6 月 22 日能在湖畔公園做什麼？

(A) 與他們的朋友和家人共度時光。

(B) 穿上他們最華麗的衣服享樂。

(C) 為所有參加野餐的人準備點心。

(D) 學習如何製作三明治和迷你漢堡。

解析 可由第四項得知，參加者可以攜帶家人朋友和喜愛的點心，因此選項 A 正確。穿著是以休閒短褲為主，而漢堡三明治是主辦方會準備。

__B__ 20. Who was the event likely planned by?

(A) Lakeshore Park

(B) The city government

(C) A food product company

(D) A maker of sports equipment

這項活動很可能是由誰策劃的？

(A) 湖畔公園

(B) 市政府

(C) 食品公司

(D) 運動器材製造商

解析　文中唯一的線索是聯絡資訊裡承辦人的電子郵件地址，在 @ 符號後有提到 city government，因此選項 B 正確。

__A__ 21. What is the last possible day to make a decision about going to the picnic?

(A) June 19

(B) June 20

(C) June 21

(D) June 22

參加野餐的最後決定日是哪一天？

(A) 6 月 19 日

(B) 6 月 20 日

(C) 6 月 21 日

(D) 6 月 22 日

解析　由第一段的第一項得知，野餐是在 6 月 22 日，再由最後一段第一行推知，要在活動三天前聯絡主辦方，因此為 6 月 19 日，選項 A 正確。

Questions 22-24

Are you struggling with weight loss? Have you tried different methods but still haven't achieved the body you always wanted? Here is some advice from Dr. Ramies.

1. Eat Right → Eat more meat like chicken, beef and fish.
Have less rice, noodles and bread.
Stay away from snacks.

2. Stay Active → Do exercise that brings your heartbeats up to 130 bpm. (beats per minute)
Exercise for at least 30 minutes, three times a week.

3. Make exercise a habit → Exercising 30 minutes at a time isn't difficult. Most people fail to lose weight not because they can't do it, but because they struggle to continue doing it.

你遇到了減重困難嗎？ **(22) 你有嘗試過了不同方法，但仍未達到一直想要的身材嗎？**這裡有一些拉米斯醫師的建議。

1. 正確飲食 → 多吃肉，如雞肉、牛肉和魚類。
少吃米飯、麵條和麵包。
遠離零食點心。

2. 保持活躍 → 做能讓你心跳達到每分鐘 130 次的運動。（每分鐘次數）
(23) (24) 運動至少 30 分鐘，每週三次。

3. **(23) 將運動變成習慣** → 每次運動 30 分鐘並不困難，大多數人減重失敗，不是因為他們做不到，而是因為他們難以持續做下去。

__D__ 22. Who would be interested in this article?

(A) Someone who is sick or injured.

(B) Someone who is experiencing hunger.

(C) Someone who is dealing with a heart condition.

(D) Someone who is worried about their body shape.

誰會對這篇文章感興趣？

(A) 生病或受傷的人。

(B) 正在經歷饑餓的人。

(C) 正處理心臟問題的人。

(D) 擔心自己身材的人。

> **解析** 文章第一段第二句在詢問讀者減重所碰到的困難，接下來就給出意見，因此是給有身材困擾的人看的。

__B__ 23. Which of the following is suggested for losing weight?

(A) Getting 8 hours of sleep.

(B) Getting regular exercise.

(C) Not eating meat or bread.

(D) Taking a weight loss class.

下列哪一項是對減重的建議？

(A) 擁有八小時的睡眠。

(B) 進行規律運動。

(C) 不吃肉或麵包。

(D) 參加減肥課程。

> **解析** 文中第二項和第三項建議都是跟運動有關，而且第二項說明運動一週三次，即為規律運動的意思，選項 B 正確。

__C__ 24. How many minutes should people exercise each week?

(A) At least 30 minutes

(B) At least 60 minutes

(C) 90 minutes or more

(D) Three times a week

人們每週應該運動多少分鐘？

(A) 至少 30 分鐘

(B) 至少 60 分鐘

(C) 90 分鐘或更多

(D) 每週三次

> **解析** 由文中第二項建議的第二句得知，一次 30 分鐘的運動每週要進行三次，因此共 90 分鐘，選項 C 正確，選項 D 是頻率，因此不符合題目問到的分鐘數 how many minutes。

Question 25-27

When visiting or staying with friends in other countries, it's always polite to bring gifts to show your appreciation. But before you give a gift, you should make an effort to learn about the gift giving customs in that country.

Flowers are a common gift, but in many European countries, red roses are a symbol of love, and thus wouldn't be a <u>suitable</u> gift for your host. In Japan, your host will appreciate a gift that is carefully wrapped. But don't use white paper, because white is the color of death. And in the Middle East, be careful about praising things in your host's house. They may offer it to you as a present, and it would be impolite to refuse it!

After all, no matter where you're going, it's always a good idea to spend some time learning about the culture. Not only because it's fun to do so, but also because it's a good way to improve your travel experience.

(25) <u>當在其他國家拜訪或與朋友同住時，帶禮物表達你的感激，永遠是很有禮貌的。</u>但在你送禮物之前，你應該費心了解那個國家的送禮習俗。

(26) <u>花朵是常見的禮物，但在許多歐洲國家，紅玫瑰是愛情的象徵，因此不是個適合給主人的禮物。</u>

(25) <u>在日本，你的主人會很感激精心包裝的禮物。但不要使用白色包裝紙，因為白色是死亡的顏色。</u>

(27) <u>而在中東，在主人家裡稱讚任何東西時要小心。他們可能會把它當作禮物送給你，而拒絕是不禮貌的！</u>

畢竟，無論你去哪裡，花時間了解當地文化總是個好主意。這樣做不僅因為是很有趣，也因為這是提升你旅游體驗的好方法。

A 25. What's the main theme of the article?

(A) Gift giving around the world.

(B) Flowers make good presents.

(C) Say "No" to the gifts people give.

(D) Every country has a different culture.

這篇文章的主題是什麼？

(A) 世界各地的送禮習俗。

(B) 花朵是好禮物。

(C) 對人們給的禮物說「不」。

(D) 每個國家都有不同文化。

解析 文章第一段提到不同國家的交友，第二段提到了歐洲、日本、中東的送禮文化，可推知全篇文章主旨為世界各地的送禮習俗，選項 A 正確。

B 26. What does the word "suitable" mean in the article?

(A) useful

(B) appropriate

(C) fashionable

(D) send

文章中 "suitable" 這個詞是什麼意思？

(A) 有用的

(B) 適當的

(C) 時髦的

(D) 寄送

解析 由第二段第一行的描述得知，花朵在歐洲很常見，但接下來的 but 就表示文意有轉折，意指花被誤用的情景。紅玫瑰象徵愛情，不應是給主人的花。而由 suitable 這個字前的 wouldn't 判斷，要選一個和否定意思相符的字，因此選項的 B 的 appropriate 正確。

B 27. According to the article, which of the following would be rude?

(A) Giving your host red roses as a gift.

(B) Not accepting a gift from your host.

(C) Admiring things in your host's house.

(D) Not wrapping your gift in white paper.

根據文章，下列何者會是失禮的？

(A) 給主人紅玫瑰作為禮物。

(B) 不接受主人的禮物。

(C) 稱讚你主人家中的東西。

(D) 不用白色紙包裝你的禮物。

解析 題目中的 rude 意味失禮或魯莽，跟此字最相關的是第二段最後一句話所提到的 impolite。失禮的行為是拒絕中東主人的禮物，因此選項 B 正確。送主人紅玫瑰只是不適當，而非失禮或魯莽，因此 A 選項不適合。

Questions 28-30

My name is Jane and I moved to the U.S. with my family last year. At first, I was both excited and nervous about attending high school here. But guess what? It's been a cool experience so far!

I have a different schedule at school each day, and I have to take a lot of required classes, like math, science, and English—just like in Taiwan. I also get to choose more fun classes, like art, music, cooking, and even bowling! The best thing is that my school offers a lot of activities, such as sports teams and clubs. I joined the soccer team, and I'm in great shape now. I'm also a member of the chess club, which has helped me make new friends from different grades.

Overall, I'm enjoying my new life here in the U.S., even though I sometimes miss my friends back in Taiwan. I know how lucky I am, and I'm doing my best to learn and grow.

我的名字叫作珍，去年和家人一起搬到了美國。剛開始，我對於在這裡上高中感到既興奮又緊張。但你猜怎們樣？到目前為止，這個經驗都很酷！

我每天在學校的課表都不一樣，而且我必須修很多必修課，像是數學、自然和英文—就像在台灣一樣。但我也可以選更多有趣的課，像是藝術、音樂、烹飪，甚至是保齡球！**(30) 最棒的是，我的學校提供很多活動，如校隊和社團。**我加入了足球隊，而且我現在狀態超好。**(28) 我也是棋藝社的社員，這讓我交了不同年級的新朋友。**

(29) 總的來說，雖然我有時會想念在台灣的朋友，但我正享受著我在美國的新生活。我知道我很幸運，而且我正盡全力去學習和成長。

___C___ 28. What has helped Jane make friends at her new school?

    (A) Taking lots of fun classes.

    (B) Playing on the soccer team.

    (C) Joining activities outside of class.

    (D) Missing her friends back in Taiwan.

什麼幫助珍在新學校交到朋友？

    (A) 上很多有趣的課程。

    (B) 參加足球隊。

    (C) 參加課外的活動。

    (D) 想念她在台灣的朋友。

解析 第二段最後一句提到參加了棋藝社，接下來提到就是社團這件事，讓她交了很多不同年級的朋友。社團活動就是課外的活動，因此選項 C 正確。

___A___ 29. How does Jane feel about her life in the U.S.?

    (A) Lucky

    (B) Nervous

    (C) Unhappy

    (D) Homesick

珍對她在美國的生活感覺如何？

    (A) 幸運的

    (B) 緊張的

    (C) 不開心的

    (D) 思鄉的

解析 由最後一段的第一句可定位是在談美國的生活，第二句就提到她知道自己有多幸運，因此選項 A 正確。

___A___ 30. What does Jane like most at her new school?

    (A) Many activates that the school offered.

    (B) Making friends from different grades.

    (C) Required classes like math and science.

    (D) Taking fun classes like cooking and bowling.

珍最喜歡她新學校的那一部分？

    (A) 學校所提供的許多活動。

    (B) 交不同年級的朋友。

    (C) 必修課程，如數學和自然。

    (D) 修有趣的課程，如烹飪和保齡球。

解析 由第二段第三句的 the best thing 得知，最棒的事就是有各種活動，而這也就是珍最喜歡的事情，因此選項 A 正確。

GEPT
初級模擬試題
第 4 回
解答、翻譯與詳解

第 4 回解答

 聽力測驗解答

1. C	2. A	3. B	4. B	5. C
6. A	7. C	8. A	9. A	10. B
11. C	12. B	13. C	14. C	15. B
16. C	17. B	18. C	19. C	20. C
21. A	22. C	23. C	24. C	25. C
26. A	27. C	28. B	29. A	30. B

閱讀測驗解答

1. B	2. A	3. B	4. D	5. C
6. D	7. D	8. C	9. A	10. D
11. B	12. C	13. D	14. A	15. A
16. B	17. C	18. C	19. C	20. D
21. C	22. C	23. C	24. B	25. C
26. D	27. A	28. D	29. C	30. C

第 4 回聽力

第一部分 **看圖辨義**

___C___ 1. For Question Number 1, please look at the picture. What is this?

(A) A sign

(B) A report

(C) An invitation

A Party at
Irene's new house.

Date & Time : July 30, 6:00 PM

第一題，請看此圖片。

這是什麼？

(A) 一個標誌

(B) 一份報告

(C) 一張邀請函

解析 由關鍵字 party（派對），以及 date & time（日期與時間）可以看出這是一張派對的邀請函，答案選 C。

___A___ 2. For Question Number 2, please look at the picture.

Who is cutting out some stars?

(A) A boy with curly hair.

(B) A girl with short hair.

(C) Some students with glue.

第二題，請看此圖片。

誰在剪星星？

(A) 捲頭髮的男孩。

(B) 短髮的女孩。

(C) 拿著膠水的學生。

解析 圖中正在剪星星者頭髮微捲，手上拿著剪刀（scissors），符合題意，因此答案選 A。

__B__ 3. For Question Number 3, please look at the picture.

What are the students doing?

(A) They are sorting the trash.

(B) They are typing on computers.

(C) They are playing a card game.

第三題，請看此圖片。

這些學生在做什麼？

(A) 他們正在做垃圾分類。

(B) 他們正在電腦上打字。

(C) 他們正在玩撲克牌遊戲。

解析 從電腦上的字 (table) 和下面的空格可看出，圖片上的學生正在使用電腦和鍵盤打字，答案為選項 B。

__B__ 4. For Question Number 4, please look at the picture.

What are the workers wearing?

(A) coats

(B) pants

(C) shorts

第四題，請看此圖片。

工人們穿著什麼？

(A) 大衣

(B) 長褲

(C) 短褲

解析 圖片中的工人穿著短袖上衣 (T-shirts) 和長褲 (pants)，因此答案為選項 B。

C 5. For Question Number 5, please look at the picture.

What will happen next?

(A) There will be a car crash.

(B) The ambulance will take the boy home.

(C) The kid will be taken to the hospital.

第五題，請看此圖片。

接下來會發生什麼事？

(A) 將會有車禍。

(B) 救護車將把男孩載回家。

(C) 孩子將被送往醫院。

解析　圖片中可以看到小孩躺在地上，還有救護人員跟救護車，因此可以知道接下來圖片中的小孩應該會被送往醫院，答案選 C。

__A__ 6. Is that the school you went to when you were eight?

   (A) No, it's the building on your right.

   (B) I'm not sure if this is a good choice.

   (C) Yes, I go there every morning at eight.

那是你八歲時就讀的學校嗎？

(A) 不是，你右手邊那棟建築物才是。

(B) 我不確定這是不是一個好的選擇。

(C) 是的，我每天早上八點去那裡。

解析 選項 B 答非所問，選項 C 重複題目中的 eight 試圖誤導，不過題目的 eight 指的是八歲，而選項 C 的 eight 指的是八點，所以也答非所問。答案為選項 A。

__C__ 7. Can I pay with a credit card?

   (A) Thank you for this card.

   (B) Sorry, we don't sell cars.

   (C) Sorry, we only take cash.

我可以用信用卡付款嗎？

(A) 謝謝你送我這張卡。

(B) 抱歉，我們不賣汽車。

(C) 抱歉，我們只收現金。

解析 題目詢問可否使用信用卡付款，選項 A 和選項 B 皆答非所問，選項 C 在致歉後回覆可接受的付款方式，有回答到問題。因此答案選 C。

__A__ 8. Who is in the bathroom?

   (A) I think it's Mary.

   (B) It must have been locked.

   (C) Go straight then turn right.

誰在浴室裡？

(A) 我想是瑪麗。

(B) 它一定是被鎖住了。

(C) 往前走然後右轉。

解析 Who 的中文是「誰」，選項 A 針對「誰」回答了問題，其餘兩個選項皆答非所問。因此答案選 A。

__A__ 9. This shrimp spaghetti tastes bad.

    (A) I don't like it, either.

    (B) I spent hours preparing for the exam.

    (C) I'm sure you'll do better on the next test.

這份鮮蝦義大利麵不好吃。

(A) 我也不喜歡。

(B) 我花了幾個小時準備考試。

(C) 我相信你下次的考試會考得更好。

解析 "taste" 的發音為長音 [e]，"test" 則為短音 [ɛ]，兩者發音易混淆請注意。題目中的說話者提到麵不好吃 (taste bad)，選項 A 回應說話者的意見，表示自己也不喜歡，符合說話邏輯，其餘兩個選項答非所問，因此答案選 A。

__B__ 10. Where did you get this book?

    (A) I want to buy it, too.

    (B) My brother gave it to me.

    (C) It's on the shelf over there.

你從哪裡取得這本書？

(A) 我也想買。

(B) 我弟弟送我的。

(C) 它在那邊的書架上。

解析 get 的意思有很多，在這邊為「取得」的意思。選項 A 答非所問，選項 C 需要將 on the shelf 改成 from the shelf（從那邊的書架），因此答案選 B。

__C__ 11. I can't think of anything to do.

    (A) So do I.

    (B) It's exciting, isn't it?

    (C) I have an idea. Let's go jogging.

我想不到事情可做。

(A) 我也是。

(B) 真刺激，不是嗎？

(C) 我有個主意。我們去慢跑。

解析 因為題目為否定句，所以選項 A 的附和句需要改成 "Neither can I."（我也是），選項 B 沒有針對題目的句子回應，因此答案為選項 C。

__B__ 12. Would you like me to help you with the math assignment?

    (A) No, not at all.

    (B) That would be nice.

    (C) Yes, you are so forgiving.

你想要我幫你寫數學作業嗎？

(A) 別客氣。

(B) 那會很好。

(C) 要，你真寬容。

解析　"Would you like...?"（你想要⋯嗎？）為提案時有禮貌的說法。接受提案時可以回答 "That would be great!" 或 "That would be nice." 因此答案為選項 B。其餘兩個選項皆答非所問。另外 "Not at all." 也有強烈拒絕「一點也不」的意思。「一點也不」在這邊雖然語意邏輯可接受，但禮貌上並不合適。

___C___ 13. I lent Robert my bike last night.
(A) He's such a kind person.
(B) I didn't know he owned a bike.
(C) Did he say when he'll return it?

我昨天晚上把自行車借給了羅伯特。
(A) 他真是個好心的人。
(B) 我不知道他有自行車。
(C) 他有說他什麼時候會還嗎？

解析　腳踏車是由說話者出借給羅伯特，因此選項 A 需將 "He" 改成 "You" 才符合對話邏輯。而選項 B 沒有針對題目回應，因此答案為選項 C。

___C___ 14. Sophie, don't stay up late.
(A) I'll be downstairs right away.
(B) No problem. I'll stay right here.
(C) Ok. I'll go to bed in ten minutes.

蘇菲，不要熬夜了。
(A) 我馬上就下樓。
(B) 沒問題。我會一直在這裡。
(C) 好的。我十分鐘後會去睡覺。

解析　"stay up" 為一個片語，「熬夜」的意思，跟 stay（留在原地）或是 up（上面）完全不相關，因此選項 A 和選項 B 都不正確。答案為選項 C。

___B___ 15. Is it more convenient to take the MRT there?
(A) Yes, there's a convenience store on the corner.
(B) Yes, it is. Also, it's much cheaper than taking a taxi.
(C) The MRT is considered the best form of public transportation.

坐捷運去那裡會比較方便嗎？
(A) 是的，轉角處有一間便利商店。
(B) 是的，而且比坐計程車便宜得多。
(C) 捷運被認為是最好的大眾運輸工具。

解析　選項 A 沒有針對交通方式的便利性做回應，選項 C 的回應則是一個概況，沒有針對題目的問題回應，因此答案選 B。

__C__ 16. W: We're going to have dinner with our cousins tomorrow.

M: Nice. What are we going to have?

W: Steak! We haven't had it for a while.

M: You're right. I can't wait.

Question: Why did the man say "I can't wait"?

女子：明天我們要和我們的堂兄弟姐妹一起吃晚飯。
男子：太好了。我們要吃什麼？
女子：牛排！我們有一段時間沒吃了。
男子：你說得對。我等不及了。
問題：男子為什麼說「我等不及了？」

(A) He is in a hurry.
(B) He is on the way.
(C) He is excited about dinner.

(A) 他在趕時間。
(B) 他正在路上。
(C) 他對晚餐感到興奮。

解析 "I can't wait!" 常在為未來即將到來的活動感到興奮時使用。從對話可以知道他們隔天晚餐會有聚餐，因此答案為 C。選項 A 和選項 B 都不是會使用 "I can't wait!" 的情況。

__B__ 17. W: What are you going to get Mindy for her birthday?

M: Maybe a pair of earrings or a nice watch.

W: I got her earrings last year, and a nice watch can be really expensive.

M: You're right. What about getting her some notebooks and pens?

W: I'm sure she'd like that.

Question: What are they going to buy for Mindy?

女子：敏蒂生日你打算送什麼？
男子：可能是一對耳環或者一支好錶。
女子：我去年已經送她耳環了，而且好的手錶可能很貴。
男子：說得對。送她一些筆記本和筆怎麼樣？
女子：我確定她會喜歡。
問題：他們打算買什麼給敏蒂？

(A) A nice watch

(B) School supplies

(C) A pair of earrings

(A) 一支好錶。

(B) 學校用品。

(C) 一對耳環。

解析 school supplies（學校用品）包含筆、紙、書包、鉛筆盒等在學校用得到的東西。由對話最後男子提議送筆記本和筆，女子表示贊同可得知他們會送敏蒂學校用品。

C 18. B: Mom, I'm sorry. I got in a fight with Albert at school today.

W: Tell me what happened.

B: He pushed me on the playground, and I pushed him back.

W: Don't worry. Let me talk to your teacher.

Question: What will the mother do later?

男孩：媽媽，對不起。我今天在學校和艾伯特打了一架。

女子：告訴我發生了什麼事。

男孩：他在操場上推我，我也推了他一把。

女子：別擔心。讓我去和你的老師談談。

問題：之後母親會做什麼？

(A) She will talk to Albert.

(B) She will punish her son.

(C) She will call the teacher.

(A) 她會和艾伯特談話。

(B) 她會處罰她的兒子。

(C) 她會打電話給老師。

解析 從對話中女子說 "Let me talk to your teacher."（讓我去和你的老師談談。）可以知道答案為選項 C。

C 19. W: Rose and Jim are twenty minutes late.

M: I'm not surprised.

W: Let me call them.

M: Do you know when they left home?

W: An hour ago, I think.

Question: Why did the man say "I'm not surprised"?

女子：羅斯和吉姆遲到二十分鐘了。

男子：我一點都不驚訝。

女子：我打個電話給他們。

男子：你知道他們是什麼時候從家裡出發的嗎？

女子：我想大約一小時前吧。

問題：男子為什麼說「我一點都不驚訝？」

(A) He is very angry.	(A) 他很生氣。
(B) It's rude to be late.	(B) 遲到是不禮貌的。
(C) They are often late.	(C) 他們經常遲到。

解析　"I'm not surprised." 表示事情的發生在意料之內。因此可以推測羅斯和吉姆應該經常遲到，答案選 C。

C 20. W: It's freezing today.

M: I know. And I left my coat at the office.

W: You can wear mine if you like.

M: It's probably too small. I'll just get mine.

Question: What will probably happen next?

女子：今天真冷。

男子：我知道。而且我把大衣忘在辦公室了。

女子：如果你願意的話可以穿我的。

男子：可能太小了。我還是去拿我的吧。

問題：接下來可能會發生什麼事？

(A) The man will try to lose weight.

(B) The woman will lend her coat to the man.

(C) The man will go to the office to get his coat.

(A) 男子會試圖減肥。

(B) 女子會把她的大衣借給男子。

(C) 男子會去辦公室拿他的大衣。

解析 從對話中可以知道男子將大衣忘在辦公室，而從男子的回覆 "I'll just get mine." 可以知道答案是 C，他會回辦公室拿大衣。這裡的 "mine" 是 "my coat" 的意思。

A 21. M: We had a new English teacher today.

W: What's the teacher like?

M: Actually, you know her. It's Ms. Winston.

W: Oh. She's really strict and gives a lot of tests. Good luck.

Question: What is the English class going to be like?

男子：我們今天有位新的英文老師。

女子：老師怎麼樣？

男子：其實你認識她。是溫斯頓老師。

女子：哦。她很嚴格，而且常常考試。祝你好運。

問題：這堂英文課會是怎麼樣的？

(A) It's not going to be easy.

(B) The tests won't be difficult.

(C) The man won't have to study hard.

(A) 不會很容易。

(B) 考試不會很難。

(C) 男子不需要用功念書。

解析 從女子的回應 "She's really strict and gives a lot of tests." 可以知道這堂課老師很嚴格，考試很多，因此答案為 A，這堂課不會很容易。

___C___ 22. M: I bought a new bike.

W: I didn't know you like to go biking.

M: I just started not long ago and it's really fun.

W: How far can you ride? Like 20 kilometers?

M: Way more than that!

Question: Which is true about the man?

男子：我買了一輛新的自行車。

女子：我不知道你喜歡騎自行車。

男子：我才剛開始不久，而且真的很好玩。

女子：你能騎多遠？ 20 公里嗎？

男子：比那還遠！

問題：關於男子的敘述，以下何者正確？

(A) He is lying.　　　　　　　　　　(A) 他在撒謊。

(B) He spent a lot of money.　　　　(B) 他花了很多錢。

(C) He enjoys his new hobby.　　　　(C) 他很喜歡他的新嗜好。

解析　從對話中看不出男子在撒謊，所以選項 A 不正確。對話中也沒有提到自行車的價錢，所以選項 B 也不正確。正確答案選 C。

___C___ 23. M: Would you like some bread?

W: No, thank you. I seldom eat bread, rice, or noodles in the morning.

M: What do you eat then?

W: I don't. I usually don't eat anything until noon.

Question: What's true about the woman?

男子：你要吃一點麵包嗎？

女子：不，謝謝。我很少在早上吃麵包、飯或麵條。

男子：那你吃什麼？

女子：我不吃。我通常中午前不吃任何東西。

問題：關於女子的敘述，以下何者正確？

(A) She can't make bread.

(B) She just had a big lunch.

(C) She doesn't eat breakfast.

(A) 她不會做麵包。

(B) 她剛吃了一頓豐盛的午餐。

(C) 她不吃早餐。

解析 從女子的回應 "I usually don't eat anything until noon."（我通常中午前不吃任何東西。）知道答案為 C。

<u>C</u> 24. G: Dad! All my fish are dead.

M: Why? What did you do?

G: I didn't do anything.

M: What do you mean? When was the last time you fed them?

G: A few weeks ago, after I cleaned the tank.

Question: Why did the fish die?

女孩：爸爸！我所有的魚都死了。

男子：為什麼？你做了什麼？

女孩：我什麼也沒做。

男子：什麼意思？你上次餵牠們是什麼時候？

女孩：幾個星期前，在我清洗了魚缸之後。

問題：這些魚為什麼死了？

(A) The fish tank was too dirty.

(B) The girl gave them too much food.

(C) The girl didn't give them enough food.

(A) 魚缸太骯髒了。

(B) 女孩給了牠們太多食物。

(C) 女孩沒有給牠們足夠的食物。

解析 從對話中得知女孩上次餵魚是幾個星期前的事情，所以可以推測答案為選項 C。

__C__ 25. W: Do you have any tissue paper?

M: Sorry, I don't. You can get some from the vending machine over there.

W: But I don't have any change on me.

M: No problem. Here you go.

Question: What will happen next?

女子：你有衛生紙嗎？

男子：對不起，沒有。你可以去那邊的自動販賣機買。

女子：但是我身上沒有零錢。

男子：沒問題，這些拿去。

問題：接下來會發生什麼事？

(A) The man will repair the vending machine.

(B) The woman will borrow tissue paper from the man.

(C) The woman will buy tissue paper from the machine.

(A) 男子會修理自動販賣機。

(B) 女子會向男子借衛生紙。

(C) 女子會從自動販賣機購買衛生紙。

解析　從對話中知道男子沒有衛生紙，提議女子去販賣機購買並把身上的零錢給她，可以知道接下來女子會去販賣機買衛生紙，答案選 C。

__A__ 26. For question number 26, please look at the three pictures.

Listen to the following advertisement. What kind of medicine is this?

Do you often get sick when you ride in a car, especially in the mountains? Take Dramamine thirty minutes before you get in your car and you can finally enjoy your trip! Come to Mark's Drug Store this week and get Dramamine for five dollars off.

第 26 題，請看三張圖片。

請聽以下廣告。廣告中賣的藥品是哪一個？

您在乘車時，尤其是在山區，常感到不適嗎？在乘車前 30 分鐘服用卓瑪明（Dramamine）您便能享受整趟旅程！於本週至馬克藥房購買卓瑪明即可享有 5 元折扣。

解析 暈車為 car sick，從廣告中的關鍵詞 sick（不適）與 car（車），可以知道答案為選項 A。

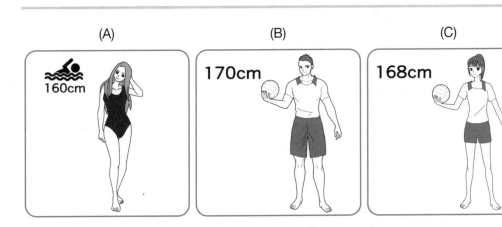

 C 27. For question number 27, please look at the three pictures.

Listen to the following hiring ad. Who is the best choice for the job?

Sunny Sports Club is looking for a female teammate to join our staff--someone who's outgoing and loves to work with others. If you're 165 to 170 centimeters tall, fit and healthy, and also good at playing volleyball, you're the right fit for this position. If you want to apply for the job, call us at 715-4264 to set up an interview.

第 27 題,請看三張圖片。

請聽以下的徵人廣告,哪一個人最適合這份工作?

陽光運動俱樂部正在尋找外向及熱愛團隊合作的女性夥伴。如果妳的身高在 165 到 170 公分之間,勻稱、身體健康,並擅長打排球,妳就是我們要找的人。應徵這份工作請撥打 715-4264 與我們聯絡,安排面試。

解析 由關鍵資訊:身高 165~170 公分、女性、擅長打排球,可以知道答案為 C。

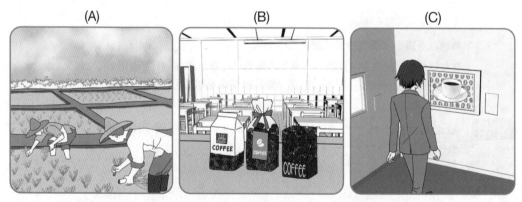

(A)　　　　　　　　(B)　　　　　　　　(C)

 B 28. For question number 28, please look at the three pictures.

Listen to the following statement. Which picture best describes the class?

There are so many different kinds of coffee beans. Some are sour, some are bitter and some have a fruity flavor. If you're interested in learning more about coffee, we have the perfect class for you. Please fill out the form and send it to us for more information.

第 28 題,請看三張圖片。

請聽以下這段話。哪張圖片最貼近這堂課程的敘述?

咖啡豆種類多元,有的酸,有的苦,有的帶有果香。如果您有興趣學習更多咖啡相關知識,這堂課是完美的選擇。請填好表格後寄給我們,以索取更多資訊。

解析　從關鍵詞 coffee（咖啡）、coffee beans（咖啡豆）以及 class（課）可以知道這段敘述為咖啡相關課程介紹，答案為 B。選項 C 雖然也有咖啡的圖畫，但背景為畫廊的展示，與敘述內容不符。

(A)　　　　　　　　(B)　　　　　　　　(C)

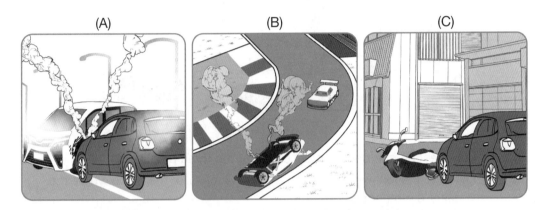

___A___ 29. For Question Number 29, please look at the three pictures.

Listen to the following news. Which best matches the description?

Good evening, everyone! This is "NOW" news. And now for the traffic report. Because of heavy fog today, a lot of people are saying they can't see well while driving. For this reason, there were several car accidents on the highway today. Fortunately, no one was injured.

第 29 題，請看三張圖片。

請聽以下新聞。哪張圖最符合敘述？

各位晚安，這裡是現代新聞，請聽交通報導。由於今日濃霧，許多民眾指出駕車時視線不清。因此今日在高速公路上發生多起車禍，所幸無人受傷。

解析　由關鍵詞 heavy fog（濃霧）以及 highway（高速公路）可以知道答案為選項 A，只有 A 的畫面中有濃霧，選項 B 為賽車場。

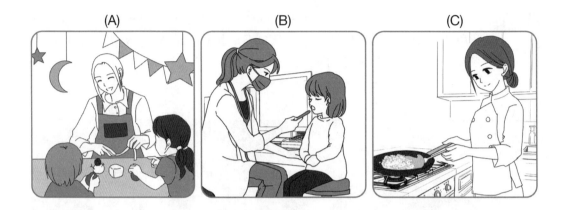

___B___ 30. For question number 30, please look at the three pictures.

Listen to the following statement. Which looks like the place where the speaker's mother works?

My mom is a doctor who takes care of young children. She is very kind and gentle. Since she has many patients, she has to work long hours. Still, I'm very proud of her because I know she always does her best to help others.

第 30 題，請看三張圖片。

請聽以下這段話。哪一張圖片看起來最像說話者母親工作的地方？

我的母親是一名照顧年幼兒童的醫生。她很溫柔和善。因為她有很多病人，所以工作時間很長。但是我還是很以她為榮，因為我知道她總是盡全力幫助別人。

解析　由關鍵詞 doctor（醫生）和 patient（病人）可以知道答案為 B。

第一部分　詞彙

__B__ 1. Alex was _____ to work for several months after the car accident.

車禍之後，艾力克斯有好幾個月都無法工作。

(A) willing 願意的　　　　　　(B) unable 無法的

(C) difficult 困難的　　　　　(D) painful 痛苦的

> **解析** 句子最後的部分有提到車禍，而空格後是接工作，因此可推知是車禍後無法工作，選項 B 正確。difficult 若形容人，是指這個人很難取悅的意思。而 painful 是用來形容令人痛苦的經驗或事件，不是指人本身。

__A__ 2. Jerry has a _____ for art and hopes to become a painter in the future.

傑瑞對藝術有天分，並且希望以後能成為一名畫家。

(A) talent 天分　　　　　　　(B) interest 興趣

(C) degree 學位　　　　　　　(D) expert 專家

__B__ 3. Tim, the most _____ guy I know, never lies.

提姆是我認識最誠實的人，從來不說謊。

(A) bitter 苦的　　　　　　　(B) honest 誠實的

(C) curious 好奇的　　　　　(D) childish 幼稚的

__D__ 4. I've lost one of the _____ from my shirt.

我的襯衫掉了一顆鈕扣。

(A) colors 顏色　　　　　　　(B) clothes 衣服

(C) irons 熨斗　　　　　　　(D) buttons 鈕扣

__C__ 5. Give me your _____ on which job offer I should accept.

告訴我你的意見，我該接受哪個工作。

(A) record 紀錄　　　　　　　(B) belief 信仰

(C) opinion 意見　　　　　　(D) result 結果

__D__ 6. Can you pick Mr. Chen up when his _____ arrives?

當陳先生的班機抵達時，你能去載他一程嗎？

(A) television 電視機　　　　(B) napkin 餐巾紙

(C) package 包裹　　　　　　(D) flight 班機

__D__ 7. We need to buy some new chairs and desks, so where is the nearest
_____ store?

我們要買新的椅子和書桌，所以最近的家具店在哪裡？

(A) grocery 食品雜貨   (B) clothing 衣服

(C) sports 運動   (D) furniture 家具

__C__ 8. Benjamin asked me if I can _____ him my bike.

班傑明問我是否可以借給他我的腳踏車。

(A) race 賽跑   (B) borrow 借入

(C) lend 借給   (D) repair 修理

> **解析** 空格後接的是 him，可得知是借腳踏車給班傑明用，因此「lend ＋人＋物」的用法適合，選項 C 正確。lend 另外一個用法是「lend 物 to 人」。相反的，borrow 是向別人借東西來用，用法是「borrow 物 from 人」。

__A__ 9. Please get the first ten items on the _____ , and I'll get the rest.

請拿清單上的前十樣東西，然後我會去拿剩下的。

(A) list 清單   (B) wrist 手腕

(C) ink 墨水   (D) mall 購物中心

__D__ 10. All the new buildings and the convenient MRT system have turned this into
a _____ city.

所有新建築和便利的捷運系統把這裡變成了一個現代城市。

(A) novel 新穎的   (B) ordinary 普通的

(C) traditional 傳統的   (D) modern 現代的

Part 2 段落填空

第二部分　段落填空

共 8 題，包括二個段落，每個段落含四個空格。每格均有四個選項，請依照文意選出最適合的答案。

Questions 11-14

Uncle Jerry is ___(11)___ I greatly admire. He was raised by his grandparents in a family that lacked money. From a young age, he ___(12)___ working to help support his family. Because of his humble background, he has always ___(13)___ fight for the things he desires. ___(14)___ he has faced many difficulties in his work and life, he never gives up. Uncle Jerry really inspires me with his strong will and desire to succeed.

傑瑞叔叔是 (11) 某位我非常敬佩的人。他是由祖父母撫養長大，在一個缺乏金錢的家庭中長大。從小，他就 (12) 開始工作來幫忙養家。因為他卑微的出身背景，他總是 (13) 必須要為他渴望的事物而奮鬥。(14) 雖然他在工作和生活中面臨許多困難，他從不放棄。傑瑞叔叔用他的堅強意志和對成功的渴望，著實地激勵了我。

__B__ 11. (A) person 人物　　　　　(B) someone 某人
　　　　(C) adult 成人　　　　　(D) character 角色

> **解析** 空格前並沒有冠詞 a 或是 the，因此 person、adult、和 character 都不符合。唯一前面可以不加冠詞的就是不定代名詞 someone，選項 B 正確。

__C__ 12. (A) starts 開始　　　　　(B) will start 將開始
　　　　(C) started 開始了　　　　(D) has started 已經開始

> **解析** 由空格前的 From a young age 可得知，這是在敘述小時候的事，因此用過去式的選項 C。

__D__ 13. (A) has to 必須　　　　　(B) having to 必須要
　　　　(C) have to 必須　　　　　(D) had to 必須要

解析　可由空格前的 has always 得知，always 是表示頻率的副詞，而 has 代表的是現在完成式，後面要用過去分詞，因此選項 D 正確。

___A___ 14. (A) Although 雖然 　　　　　(B) Besides 除此之外
　　　　　(C) Even 即使 　　　　　　　(D) However 然而

解析　句首的空格後接的是兩個子句，也就是兩個主詞動詞的結構，可推知空格應填連接詞。四個選項中 although 為唯一的連接詞，而語意也正確，因此選 A。其他選項都是副詞，無法有連接兩句的功能。Besides 和 However 放在句首後都會接逗點。

Questions 15-18

Clocks can not only tell time ____(15)____ beautiful sounds. A cuckoo clock is a type of clock that makes sounds like a cuckoo call when it strikes the hours. It is unknown who ____(16)____ the first cuckoo clock, but it is widely believed that the first cuckoo clocks came from the Black Forest region in southwestern Germany. Cuckoo clocks are made ____(17)____ wood and are usually decorated with leaves and animals. They come in many different designs and sizes, but they have one thing in ____(18)____ —a cuckoo bird, which sings every hour on the hour. It is one of the most popular souvenirs for people who travel to Germany.

鐘不僅能報時，(15) 也能製造美妙的聲音。布穀鳥鐘是一種在報時的時候，會發出像布穀鳥叫聲的鐘。關於誰 (16) 發明第一個布穀鳥鐘，尚未得知，但普遍認為第一個布穀鳥鐘來自德國西南部的黑森林區。布穀鳥鐘是用 (17) 由木頭製成，通常用葉子和動物裝飾。它們有許多不同的設計和大小尺寸，但它們有個 (18) 共同之處—內部皆有一隻布穀鳥，每到整點都會唱歌。這是去德國的旅客最喜歡購買的紀念品之一。

___A___ 15. (A) but also produce 也能製造 　　(B) and produce 並製造
　　　　　(C) and it produces 而且它製造 　(D) but producing 但製造

解析　由空格前的 not only 得知，這組相關連接詞後缺少的是 but also，因此選項 A 正確。

__B__ 16. (A) creates 創造   (B) invented 發明

        (C) has developed 已開發   (D) had made 曾製造

__C__ 17. (A) in 在裡面   (B) for 為了

        (C) of 由   (D) from 從

> **解析** 有空格後的 wood 得知，是在陳述鐘的製造材質為木頭，因此選項 C 正確。
> "Be made of" 後面必須接「本質不變的材質」，如木頭製成桌椅。Be made
> from 後面必須接「本質改變的材質」，如葡萄變成葡萄酒。

__C__ 18. (A) similar 相似   (B) same 相同

        (C) common 共同   (D) general 一般

> **解析** 可由空格前提到，各式鐘的設計雖有不同，但都 have one thing 推知，這裡
> 是 have... in common 的用法，意思是「和…有共通之處」，因此選項 C 正
> 確。

共 12 題，包括 4 個題組，每個題組含 1 至 2 篇短文，與數個相關的四選一的選擇題。請由試題上的選項中選出最適合的答案。

Questions 19-21

Dear students,

As you all know, we're going to have a hot pot party at school this Saturday. As you can see on the list below, the food has been divided into different types. I'd like everyone to bring one food item of each type to the party. Your parents should be able to find all of these items at the supermarket or wet market.

Please use the list to tell me what you'd like to bring. Just sign your name next to the items you've chosen. Be sure to return the list to me by e-mail tomorrow. If there are too many of some items and not enough of others, we can make changes as needed. I'll provide you with the final list of what everyone should bring on Friday. Sauces will be available at the party, but you can also bring your own if you like.

親愛的同學們：

大家都知道，本週六我們要在學校舉辦火鍋聚會。如各位在下方的列表所見，食材分成了幾類。**(19) 希望每位同學能夠依照清單，從每一類中選擇一項食材帶來參加。** 各位的父母應該能在超市或是傳統市場都找得到全部的食材。

(20) 請根據這份列表回覆我你們想要帶什麼，只要在你選擇的項目旁邊簽名即可。 請務必在明天結束前用電子郵件將列表回傳給我。如果某些項目選擇過多，而有些不足，我們可以依需求做調整。**(21) 我將在週五提供各位最終版的列表，列出每個人都應該帶的食材。** 聚會上會準備各種醬料，但若您有特別偏好，也歡迎自行攜帶。

Meat	Vegetables	Others
chicken slices _____	cabbage _____	pork balls _____
pork slices _____	lettuce _____	dumplings _____
beef slices _____	broccoli _____	shrimp _____
lamb slices _____	mushrooms _____	tofu _____
	corn _____	noodles _____

(19) 肉類	**(19) 蔬菜**	**(19) 其他**
雞肉片 _____	高麗菜 _____	豬肉丸 _____
豬肉片 _____	萵苣 _____	餃子 _____
牛肉片 _____	花椰菜 _____	蝦子 _____
羊肉片 _____	蘑菇 _____	豆腐 _____
	玉米 _____	麵條 _____

___C___ 19. How many food items should each student bring to the party?

(A) one

(B) two

(C) three

(D) four

每位學生應該帶多少種食材到派對？

(A) 一種

(B) 兩種

(C) 三種

(D) 四種

解析 由第一段第三句得知，每一種類的食物要帶一項。而列表裡總共有肉、菜、以及其他，總共三類，因此選項 C 正確。

__D__ 20. What are the students asked to do?

    (A) Have their parents sign the list and return it to the teacher by e-mail.

    (B) Write a number next to each item to show how much they're bringing.

    (C) Complete the list and hand it in to the teacher on Friday.

    (D) Write their name on the list next to the food they want to bring.

學生們被要求做什麼？

    (A) 請他們的家長在列表上簽名，並使用電子郵件將其交給老師。

    (B) 在每項食材旁邊寫上數字，顯示他們會帶多少來。

    (C) 完成列表並在星期五交給老師。

    (D) 在列表上他們想帶的食物旁寫上自己的名字。

解析 由第二段第一句得知，老師要求學生在想要帶的食材旁簽名，因此選項 D 正確。

__C__ 21. Which of the following is true?

    (A) The teacher asks the students to buy food at the supermarket.

    (B) A hot pot party will be held at the school next Sunday.

    (C) The students won't know for sure what to bring until Friday.

    (D) The students are required to bring their own hot pot sauces.

下列何者正確？

    (A) 老師要求學生們在超市購買食物。

    (B) 下週日學校將舉辦火鍋聚會。

    (C) 直到星期五，學生們才會確定要帶什麼。

    (D) 學生被要求帶自己的火鍋醬料。

解析 由第二段倒數第二句得知，老師會在週五提供最終的購買清單，因此選項 C 正確。此外，這些食物可以在超市或是傳統市場購買，但老師並無要求學生一定要在超市購買才行。

Tired of taking the bus? Do you want a scooter, but can't afford to purchase a new one? We have all kinds of second hand scooters for you to choose from. You'll find our shop on the first floor of Metro Mall. Come have a look and take your pick! Our mechanics make sure all the scooters we sell are in good condition. We're having a special Chinese New Year sale, so now is the perfect time. Buy any used scooter and get $1,000 off. And you can get another $500 off if you spend over $20,000. This offer is only available on the two weekends before the Chinese New Year holiday.

(24) 厭倦了坐公車嗎？想要一輛機車，但買不起新的嗎？我們有各種二手機車供您選擇。我們的店在地鐵購物中心的一樓。來看看，並且挑選你的愛車！我們的技師確保我們賣的所有機車都有良好的狀況。我們正在舉行農曆新年特賣，所以現在是最佳時機。(22) 購買任何二手機車，立刻折扣 1,000 元。如果您消費超過 20,000 元，還可以再減 500 元。(23) 此優惠只在農曆新年假期前的兩個週末提供。

___C___ 22. If you purchase a $25,000 scooter during the sale, how much can you save?

(A) $500
(B) $1,000
(C) $1,500
(D) $2,000

如果你在特賣期間購入一輛 25,000 元的機車，可以省下多少錢？

(A) 500 元
(B) 1,000 元
(C) 1,500 元
(D) 2,000 元

解析 由倒數第二句和第三句得知，25,000 元的車符合兩個折扣的條件，因此可以總共減掉 1,500 元，選項 C 正確。

__C__ 23. How long will the sale last?

(A) One day

(B) Two days

(C) Four days

(D) The whole Chinese New Year holiday

特賣會持續多久？

(A) 一天

(B) 兩天

(C) 四天

(D) 整個農曆新年假期

解析 由最後一句得知，新年前的 "two weekends" 才有特價。兩個週末總共是四天，因此選項 C 正確。

__B__ 24. Who would be interested in this advertisement?

(A) A person who is interested in buying a new scooter.

(B) Someone who doesn't like taking public transportation.

(C) A person who wants to trade in their old scooter for a new one.

(D) Someone who purchased a scooter and needs it repaired.

誰會對這個廣告感興趣？

(A) 一個有興趣買新機車的人。

(B) 不喜歡乘坐大眾交通工具的人。

(C) 想要用舊機車換新機車的人。

(D) 購買了機車且需要維修的人。

解析 由文章前兩句得知，此文是寫給厭倦搭公車，但又買不起新機車的人，因此選項 B 正確。

Questions 25-27

Let's have salad!

Salad makes a perfect lunch for a hot summer day. If you're tired of meat, rice, and noodles, and would like to have something a little lighter, why not try this healthy vegetarian **recipe**?

Ingredients:

¼ cup olive oil

½ teaspoon salt

1 ¼ cups chopped lettuce

½ cup chopped red cabbage

1 cup sliced tomatoes

¼ cup mozzarella cheese

fresh basil leaves

balsamic vinegar to taste

Time to make your salad! Put the oil, vinegar, and salt in a large bowl and mix well with a fork. Add the cabbage, tomatoes, mozzarella cheese, some basil leaves to it. Viola! Now you have a wonderful summer salad to enjoy.

來吃沙拉吧！

沙拉是炎炎夏日的完美午餐。如果你吃膩了肉、米飯和麵條，想吃點更清淡的東西，何不試試這個健康的素食沙拉食譜？

(25) 食材：¼ 杯橄欖油、 (27) ½ 茶匙鹽 、1 ¼ 杯切碎的萵苣 、½ 杯切碎的紅甘藍 1 杯切片番茄、 ¼ 杯莫札瑞拉起司、新鮮的羅勒葉、適量的巴薩米克醋

(25) 做沙拉的時候到了！在大碗中放入油、巴薩米克醋和鹽，(26) (27) 用叉子充分攪拌。加入甘藍、番茄、莫札瑞拉起司和一些羅勒葉。你看！現在你有美妙的夏日沙拉可以享用了。

__C__ 25. What is a recipe?

(A) Something that tells you how to eat healthy.

(B) A list telling you what to buy at the supermarket.

(C) A set of steps showing you how to prepare food.

(D) Information about how you can lose weight.

recipe 是什麼？

(A) 告訴你如何吃得健康的東西。

(B) 告訴你在超市要買什麼的清單。

(C) 展示如何準備食物的一系列步驟。

(D) 有關你能如何減肥的資訊。

解析 由 recipe 這個字的下兩段得知，其內容描述了沙拉的說明成分和作法，因此選項 C 正確。

__D__ 26. Which of the following is true about the salad?

(A) It will be satisfying to meat lovers.

(B) It is for someone who likes sweets.

(C) It will take people an hour to make.

(D) It can be made without a stove.

關於此沙拉，下列何者正確？

(A) 它將滿足肉類愛好者的口味。

(B) 它是為喜歡甜食的人所準備的。

(C) 要花一小時製作。

(D) 製作時不需要使用爐子。

解析 可由第一段第二句以及食材內容判斷，這份沙拉是給吃膩肉類、想吃輕食的人。
而由第三段得知，製作時只需要把食材切碎並且攪拌，沒有提到爐具，因此選項
D 正確。此外，無法從文中判定需多少時間製作此沙拉，因此時間選項不列入考
慮。

__A__ 27. What is probably required to make the salad but not mentioned?

(A) a knife

(B) a spoon

(C) a fork

(D) a mixer

製作沙拉可能需要，但未提到的是什麼？

(A) 一把刀

(B) 一把湯匙

(C) 一把叉子

(D) 一個攪拌器

解析 可由 ingredient 的段落以及下一段內容得知，需要用湯匙來測量橄欖油，並用叉
子攪拌。唯一沒有提到的是 chopped lettuce 和 chopped red cabbage 所需要
的刀子，選項 A 正確。

Questions 28-30

Do your eyes feel tired after using your phone or computer? If you're looking for something that can improve your eye health, lutein may be just the thing you need. What is lutein? Many people have never heard of it. Lutein is a natural part of the human diet and is best known for its ability to improve and maintain eye health. It can be found in yellow and green fruits and vegetables. It's easier for your body to use when it's taken with a healthy fat like olive oil. As for the amount, most doctors would suggest taking 3 to 20 mg daily. According to some research, it can be good not only for eye health but also your heart and even your brain. Lutein is sold in bottles, but you can also get enough of it by eating plenty of fruits and vegetables. So next time when you see some "greens and yellows" on the dining table, be sure to eat more!

在使用手機或電腦後，你會感到眼睛疲勞嗎？ **(28) 如果你正在尋找能促進眼睛健康的東西，葉黃素可能正是你需要的。(28) 葉黃素是什麼？** 很多人都沒有聽過。**(29) 葉黃素是人類飲食中的天然成分，最知名的功能是可以促進和維持眼睛健康。** 它可以在黃色和綠色的水果和蔬菜中找到。當它和健康的脂肪，如橄欖油一起攝取時，你的身體更容易利用它。至於用量，大多數醫生會建議每天攝取 3 到 20 毫克。根據一些研究指出，葉黃素不僅對眼睛健康有好處，對心臟甚至大腦也有益。**(30) 葉黃素是以瓶裝銷售，但你也可以透過吃很多水果和蔬菜來獲取足夠的量。** 所以下次當你在餐桌上看到一些「綠色和黃色」的時候，務必多吃一些！

__D__ 28. Which of the following is the best title for this article?

(A) *The Right Amount of Lutein*

(B) *The Key to a Healthy Diet*

(C) *Stay Away from Your Screens*

(D) *A Secret for Your Eye Health*

這篇文章最適合的標題是什麼？

(A) 葉黃素的正確用量

(B) 健康飲食的關鍵

(C) 遠離你的螢幕

(D) 你眼睛健康的祕密

> **解析** 全篇文章都在介紹葉黃素，包含其與眼睛健康、攝取來源和攝取量的細節。最適合包含全篇內容的標題，即為使用葉黃素促進眼睛健康，因此選項 D 正確。

__C__ 29. What is "lutein"?

(A) A kind of green and yellow vegetable.

(B) A type of fat that's good for your health.

(C) Something found in certain vegetables.

(D) Something that can help us lose weight.

lutein 是什麼？

(A) 一種綠色和黃色的蔬菜。

(B) 一種對健康有益的脂肪。

(C) 某樣可在蔬菜中找到的物質。

(D) 一個可以幫助我們減重的物質。

> **解析** 由第六句的 found in yellow and green fruits and vegetables 得知，葉黃素存在於蔬菜水果中，選項 C 正確。葉黃素不是脂肪，而是要和脂肪一起吃，吸收效果最佳。

__C__ 30. Which of the following is true about lutein?

    (A) Doctors say it's still not clear what lutein can do for our health.

    (B) Some doctors don't believe it's a good idea to take it every day.

    (C) Eating fruits and vegetables isn't the only way to get enough of it.

    (D) Lutein can work better when it's taken with a lot of warm water.

關於葉黃素，何者正確？

(A) 醫生指出它對我們健康的影響還不清楚。

(B) 一些醫生不覺得每天攝取葉黃素是好的。

(C) 吃水果和蔬菜不是唯一獲得足夠量的方式。

(D) 葉黃素與大量溫水服用時，可以發揮更好的作用。

解析 由倒數第二句 Lutein is sold in bottles 得知，葉黃素也有瓶裝販售，因此不一定要吃蔬菜水果才可攝取，選項 C 正確。

GEPT
初級模擬試題
第5回
解答、翻譯與詳解

第 5 回解答

 聽力測驗解答

1. C	2. B	3. A	4. B	5. B
6. C	7. A	8. C	9. B	10. B
11. C	12. C	13. A	14. B	15. C
16. B	17. B	18. A	19. B	20. B
21. A	22. A	23. A	24. C	25. C
26. C	27. A	28. B	29. C	30. B

 閱讀測驗解答

1. A	2. D	3. C	4. C	5. D
6. A	7. B	8. C	9. A	10. C
11. D	12. A	13. B	14. B	15. C
16. A	17. D	18. B	19. D	20. C
21. B	22. B	23. C	24. A	25. C
26. B	27. A	28. A	29. B	30. D

第 5 回聽力

第一部分　看圖辨義

C　1. For Question Number 1, please look at the picture.
What happened to the old man?

(A) The old man is sick.

(B) The old man is excited.

(C) The old man drank too much.

這名老人怎麼了？

(A) 老人生病了。

(B) 老人很興奮。

(C) 老人喝酒喝太多了。

解析　drink 有「喝」或「喝酒」的意思，從老人手上的酒瓶可以推測老人喝太多酒，喝醉了，答案選 C。

B　2. For Question Number 2, please look at the picture.
What is happening?

(A) They are going on vacation together.

(B) They are saying goodbye to each other.

(C) They are going to study in the United States.

第二題，請看此圖片。

圖片中正在發生什麼事？

(A) 他們一起去度假。

(B) 他們在向彼此道別。

(C) 他們要去美國讀書。

解析　圖片背景看起來像是車站或是機場，圖片裡的人相擁，並看起來很傷心，所以可以推測他們正在道別，答案為選項 B。

358

__A__ 3. For Question Number 3, please look at the picture.
Where is this place?

(A) It's a bakery.

(B) It's a food stand.

(C) It's a grocery store.

第三題，請看此圖片。

這是哪裡？

(A) 麵包店。

(B) 食物攤販。

(C) 雜貨店。

解析　圖片中的女子正在夾麵包，可以知道她是在麵包店，選 A。麵包店的英文是 bakery（烘焙坊），字面上沒有 bread（麵包）比較難記，請多注意。

__B__ 4. For Question Number 4, please look at the picture.
What is the child doing?

(A) The girl is wearing a suit.

(B) The boy is putting on his uniform.

(C) The student is taking off his jacket.

第四題，請看此圖片。

這個孩子在做什麼？

(A) 這名女孩正在穿套裝。

(B) 這名男孩正在穿制服。

(C) 這名學生正在脫外套。

解析　圖片中的男孩正在穿襯衫，並非在脫外套，所以選項 C 不正確。圖片中沒有看到套裝，因此選項 A 也不正確。正確答案選 B，男孩正在穿制服的襯衫。

B 5. For Question Number 5, please look at the picture.

What happened at school?

(A) The athlete is sad about losing the game.

(B) The boy is embarrassed about his weight.

(C) The student feels bad about his test score.

第五題，請看此圖片。

在學校發生什麼事？

(A) 運動員因為比賽輸了很傷心。

(B) 男孩因為自己的體重感到尷尬。

(C) 學生因為考試成績覺得不開心。

解析 從圖片上可以看出學生們正在排隊量體重，而站在體重機上的男孩面露尷尬笑容，因此答案為選項 B。

__C__ 6. I still have a headache.
  (A) Is it better now?
  (B) Really? I am, too.
  (C) Did you take the pill I gave you?

我頭還是會痛。
(A) 現在好些了嗎？
(B) 真的嗎？我也是。
(C) 我給你的藥吃了嗎？

解析 選項 A 明知故問，不是適合的回應。選項 B 的 "I am" 需要改成 "I do" 才符合文法。因此答案選 C。

__A__ 7. Hello, who is this?
  (A) Hi, this is Tina.
  (B) That's my cousin.
  (C) Hmm, let me guess.

你好，請問你是哪位？
(A) 你好，我是提娜。
(B) 這是我表妹。
(C) 嗯，讓我猜看看。

解析 "who is this?" 為講電話時請問對方的名字時使用的句型，而在電話上介紹自己的名字時則是用 "this is..." 的句型。因此選項 A 為最適合的回應，其他兩個選項皆不正確。

__C__ 8. I don't think I can do this by myself.
  (A) I am still thinking about it.
  (B) You can do it alone, then?
  (C) You won't know unless you try.

我覺得我一個人做不來。
(A) 我還在考慮。
(B) 那你一個人做，好嗎？
(C) 不試試怎麼知道呢。

解析 選項 C 回應了題目中講話者「一個人做不來」的擔憂，鼓勵講話者做嘗試，其餘兩個選項沒有直接回應題目，因此選 C。

__B__ 9. I need someone to take me to the airport.
  (A) I missed my flight.
  (B) When are you leaving?
  (C) I'm really sorry about that.

我需要有人接送我去機場。
(A) 我錯過了我的航班。
(B) 你什麼時候要去？
(C) 對此我真的很抱歉。

解析 選項 B 詢問題目中的講話者 "When are you leaving?" 表示可能願意幫忙接送他到機場，因此需要詢問更多資訊，最符合對話邏輯，因此這題選 B。

B　10. Which do you want, the chocolate one or the strawberry one?
(A) Yes, I want this one.
(B) I'd like the strawberry one.
(C) Chocolate and strawberry are tasty.

你想要哪個，巧克力口味的還是草莓口味的？
(A) 是的，我想要這個。
(B) 我想要草莓口味的。
(C) 巧克力和草莓都很好吃。

解析 回答別人對 Which 的問句時，你需要說出自己選擇。選項 B 說自己想要草莓口味，直接回答了問題，其餘兩個選項都沒有回答問題，因此選 B。

C　11. How may I help you?
(A) I don't need it.
(B) Help would be nice.
(C) I'm looking for a jacket.

我能幫您什麼嗎？
(A) 我不需要。
(B) 來點幫助會很好。
(C) 我在找一件外套。

解析 對話中 "How may I help you?" 是服務人員待客時常用的句子。婉拒幫忙時可以說 "No, I'm good. Thank you." 需要幫忙時則可以直接說出自己的需求，因此選項 A 和選項 B 都不合適，答案為選項 C。

C　12. Have you been to the zoo before?
(A) So have I. It was lots of fun.
(B) No, I haven't. I used to work there.
(C) Yes, I have. I went there last month.

你去過動物園嗎？
(A) 我也是。那裡非常好玩。
(B) 不，我沒有。我以前在那裡工作。
(C) 是的，我去過。我上個月去的。

解析 回答 "Have you..." 開頭的問句時，簡答為 Yes, I have. 或是 No, I haven't。選項 A 的回答不正確，選項 B 後面解釋 "I used to work there" 和簡答 "No, I haven't" 意思相反，也不正確，因此答案為 C。

A 13. What is this for?
(A) It's used to hold water.
(B) We use it in the morning.
(C) I used to cook for myself.

這是用來做什麼的？
(A) 它是用來盛水的。
(B) 我們早上會用它。
(C) 我以前會自己做飯。

解析 "What is... for?" 的句型常使用來詢問東西的用途。三個選項中只有選項 A 回答了用途，其餘兩個選項答非所問，因此選 A。

B 14. Excuse me, you're not allowed in there.
(A) I wouldn't do that.
(B) Sorry, I didn't know.
(C) No, thank you. I'm fine.

不好意思，你不能進去那裡。
(A) 我不會那樣做的。
(B) 抱歉，我不知道。
(C) 不，謝謝。我沒事。

解析 題目為阻止他人進入特定區域時的用語。選項 B 在道歉後，用過去式 "I didn't know" 說明自己事前不知道規定，最符合情境，因此選 B。

C 15. The car is making strange noises.
(A) Don't let the stranger in.
(B) Could you please keep quiet?
(C) You should take it to the repair shop.

車子正在發出奇怪的聲音。
(A) 不要讓陌生人進來。
(B) 你能保持安靜嗎？
(C) 你應該把它送修車廠。

解析 題目說明車子出了問題，選項 C 建議解決方案為送修車廠，其餘兩個選項和題目無關，因此答案為選項 C。

B　16. M: Would you like to go camping?

W: Well, I don't know how to set up a tent.

M: You don't have to. There are places you can go where the staff takes care of that.

W: Really? Can you show me a website?

Question: What does the man mean by "You don't have to"?

男子：你想去露營嗎？

女子：嗯，我不知道怎麼搭帳篷。

男子：你不用會搭帳篷。有些地方會有工作人員幫忙處理。

女子：真的嗎？你可以給我看那裡的網站嗎？

問題：男子說的 "You don't have to" 是什麼意思？

(A) She doesn't have to go.

(B) Someone else sets up the tents.

(C) Learning to set up a tent is difficult.

(A) 她不必去。

(B) 有其他人會搭帳篷。

(C) 學搭帳篷很難。

解析　從 "You don't have to." 後面補充的說明可以知道這裡是將前一句 "know how to set up a tent" 省略，而原因是因為其他人會幫忙搭帳篷，因此答案選 B。

B　17. M: Do you like this song?

W: Not really. I mostly listen to Korean pop music.

M: I usually listen to rock, but I'd love to hear something new.

W: Great! I think you'll like my favorite station.

M: OK. Let's check it out.

Question: What are they probably going to do next?

男子：你喜歡這首歌嗎？

女子：不太喜歡。我大多聽韓國流行音樂。

男子：我通常聽搖滾樂，但我很想聽點新的。

女子：太好了！我覺得你會喜歡我最愛的廣播電台。

男子：好喔！我們一起收聽。

問題：他們接下來可能要做什麼？

(A) Learn how to sing.

(B) Listen to the radio.

(C) Listen to rock music.

(A) 學唱歌。

(B) 聽廣播。

(C) 聽搖滾音樂。

解析 女子提到自己最愛的廣播電台之後,男子說 "Let's check it out."(我們一起收聽)因此知道他們接下來會一起收聽女子提到的廣播電台。

A 18. W: My face is so dry. What should I do?

M: Let me see if I can find the skin cream I bought at the drugstore last month.

W: When did you last see it?

M: I left it on the table in my room. But now it's nowhere to be found.

Question: Where is the skin cream now?

女子:我的臉好乾喔。該怎麼辦?

男子:我看看我找不找得到上個月從藥妝店買的護膚霜。

女子:你上次看到它是什麼時候?

男子:我把它放在房間的桌子上,但現在找不到了。

問題:那罐護膚霜現在在哪裡?

(A) We don't know.

(B) It's on the table.

(C) It's in the drugstore.

(A) 我們不知道。

(B) 它在桌子上。

(C) 它在藥妝店裡。

解析 由男子的回答知道護膚霜原本被放在桌上,但現在沒看到。對話中沒有提到護膚霜現在在哪裡,因此答案選 A。

B 19. B: Mom, Spot doesn't look well.

W: And he hasn't eaten anything since last night.

B: He's just lying there on the floor. I tried to take him for a walk, but he didn't want to go.

W: Maybe we should have him examined.

Question: Who is "Spot"?

男孩：媽媽，斑斑 (Spot) 看起來不太舒服。

女子：而且他從昨晚開始就沒吃東西。

男孩：他就只是躺在地板上。我有試著帶他出去散步，但他不想去。

女子：也許我們應該帶他去診察。

問題：請問斑斑 (Spot) 是誰？

(A) He's a goldfish.

(B) He's a pet dog.

(C) He's the woman's brother.

(A) 他是一隻金魚。

(B) 他是一隻寵物狗。

(C) 他是女子的兄弟。

解析 從對話中男孩提到 "I tried to take him for a walk..."（我有試著帶他出去散步）可推測斑斑是一隻寵物狗。

B 20. G: Oh, no! I broke Mom's favorite glass.

M: That was a gift from grandpa. She's had it for years.

G: I didn't mean to. What should I do now?

M: Tell her the truth when she gets home. I think she'll forgive you.

Question: What will the girl probably do later?

女孩：哎呀，糟了！我打破了媽媽最喜歡的玻璃杯。

男子：那是外公送的禮物。她已經用了很多年了。

女孩：我不是故意的。現在我該怎麼辦？

男子：等她回來時告訴她實情。我想她會原諒你的。

問題：女孩接下來可能會怎麼做？

(A) She will forgive her mom.

(B) She will be honest with her mom.

(C) She will call her mom and tell her everything.

(A) 她會原諒她媽媽。

(B) 她會對她媽媽說實話。

(C) 她會打電話給媽媽，和她說明清楚。

解析 從男子回應 "Tell her the truth when she gets home." 可以推測女孩接下來會等媽媽到家後，對媽媽說實話，答案選 B。

A 21. M: Do you know if there are any good restaurants around here?

W: Yes, I know of a few. Why?

M: Some of my friends from elementary school are going to visit me next week.

W: Then you can take them to the new American restaurant across from the library.

Question: What will the man probably do next week?

男子：你知道這附近有沒有什麼好餐廳嗎？

女子：有的，我知道幾家。為什麼這樣問？

男子：一些小學時的朋友下週要來拜訪我。

女子：那你可以帶他們去圖書館對面新開的美式餐廳。

問題：男子下週可能會做什麼？

(A) See his old friends.

(B) Look for good restaurants.

(C) Take his friends to America.

(A) 與老朋友見面。

(B) 尋找好餐廳。

(C) 帶他的朋友去美國。

解析 從男子提到自己小學時的朋友下週即將來訪，因此可以知道答案是選項 A。

A 22. M: Have you bought the tickets yet?

W: Not yet. I've been so busy.

M: You'd better hurry. Plane tickets are expensive during the high season and sometimes hard to find.

W: OK, I'll take care of it this week.

Question: What are they planning to do?

男子：你買票了嗎？

女子：還沒。我一直在忙。

男子：你最好快一點。旺季的機票貴，且有時很難找。

女子：好的，我會在這週內處理。

問題：他們計劃做什麼？

(A) Take a trip.	(A) 去旅行。
(B) Buy a ticket	(B) 買票。
(C) See a concert.	(C) 去看演唱會。

解析 由對話可知男子和女子計畫要搭飛機出遊。選項 B "buy a ticket"（買票）意思雖然可通，但對話中使用複數 tickets，選項 B 為單數所以不正確。正確答案選 A。

A 23. M: You have to try this!

W: Why?

M: It's so creamy. And I really like the peanut powder on it.

W: OK, let's see. Wow! I usually don't like night market food, but this is really good.

Question: What are they doing?

男子：妳一定要試試看這個！

女子：為什麼？

男子：它很濃郁，而且我真的很喜歡上面的花生粉。

女子：好吧，我嚐一點。哇！我通常不喜歡夜市小吃，但這個真的很好吃。

問題：他們正在做什麼？

(A) They're eating.

(B) They're cooking a meal.

(C) They're looking at a menu.

(A) 他們在吃東西。

(B) 他們在煮菜。

(C) 他們在看菜單。

解析 從女子在 "let's see"（我嚐一點）之後提到的關鍵字，"night market food"（夜市小吃）還有 "this is really good"（真的很好吃。）可以知道他們正在吃東西。

C 24. M: I heard that you can speak German and Japanese.

W: Yes. And French too.

M: Wow. What's your secret?

W: I watch a lot of videos and try to repeat whatever the speakers say.

Question: What is the woman good at doing?

男子：我聽說你會說德語和日語。

女子：是的，還有法語。

男子：哇。你的祕訣是什麼？

女子：我看很多影片，試著模仿說話者的發音。

問題：女子擅長做什麼？

(A) Sharing secrets.

(B) Watching videos.

(C) Learning languages.

(A) 分享祕密。

(B) 觀看影片。

(C) 學習語言。

解析 「be good at + 事物」表示擅長某項事物。對話中的女子會說多種語言，並分享了自己學習的祕訣，所以可以知道女子擅長的事物為學習語言，答案選 C。

C 25. M: I signed up for a marathon for fall.

W: Really? You know that you have to run over 26 miles, right?

M: Of course! I've been training every day.

W: Wow! I didn't know you were such an athlete.

Question: What are the speakers talking about?

男子：我報名參加了秋季馬拉松。

女子：真的嗎？你知道你得要跑超過 26 英里，對吧？

男子：當然！我每天都在做訓練。

女子：哇！我不知道你那麼喜愛運動。

問題：對話中的說話者在談論什麼？

(A) An exercise class.

(B) A swimming event.

(C) A long-distance race.

(A) 一個運動課程。

(B) 一個游泳比賽。

(C) 一場長程賽跑。

解析　由關鍵字 marathon（馬拉松）和 run over 26 miles（跑超過 26 英里）可以知道說話者在討論長程賽跑，答案選 C。

(A)　　　　　　　　　(B)　　　　　　　　　(C)

<u>C</u>　26. For question number 26, please look at the three pictures.

Listen to the talk. What is the speaker talking about?

Preparing a wedding is a lot of work. You have to figure out how many guests you want to invite and where you are going to hold the event. You also have to find the right wedding dress for the bride. But it's a once in a lifetime experience so be sure to enjoy it!

第 26 題，請看三張圖片。

請聽對話。說話者在談論什麼？

籌備婚禮要處理很多事。你必須弄清楚要邀請多少客人，以及婚禮地點會辦在哪裡。你還得找到適合新娘的婚紗。但這是一生一次的經歷，所以一定要好好享受這段過程！

解析　從關鍵詞 wedding（婚禮）和 bride（新娘）可以知道談話的內容和婚禮有關，選 C。

(A)　　　　　　　　　(B)　　　　　　　　　(C)

A 27. For question number 27, please look at the three pictures.

A woman is talking to a group of people. What does she ask the people to do?

It is necessary to pass a riding test before riding a scooter. It's not legal to ride without it. If you're stopped by the police, you could get a fine of at least six thousand dollars and up to twelve thousand dollars.

第 27 題，請看三張圖片。

一位女子正在對一群人講話。她要這些人做什麼？

騎機車之前一定要通過駕照考試。沒有駕照騎乘機車是違法的。如果被警察攔下會有最低六千元至最高一萬二千元的罰款。

解析　由關鍵詞 riding test（駕照考試）和 scooter（機車）可以知道女子說話的內容和圖片 A 最接近，提醒大家不可無照騎機車。

(A)　　　(B)　　　(C)

B 28. For question number 28, please look at the three pictures.

Listen to the ad. What company probably made the ad?

Have you ever traveled around Taiwan? There are so many ways to do it. You can take a bus or a train, or you can drive a car. To have a good trip, you need to plan ahead. But you can leave the hard work to us by calling 0812-345-6782. Then all you have to do is relax and enjoy your trip.

第 28 題，請看三張圖片。

聽廣告。請問這則廣告可能是哪家公司製作的？

你曾經環島旅行過嗎？環島方式有很多。你可以搭乘巴士或火車，或者自己開車。為了有個愉快的旅程，你需要提前規劃。但是你可以把這份辛苦的工作交給我們，只需撥打 0812-345-6782。接著，你只需要放鬆和享受旅程了。

Part 4 短文聽解

解析 廣告中提到的 traveled around Taiwan（環島旅行）以及 plan（規劃）可以知道這則廣告是由旅遊公司所製作，因此答案選 B。

(A)　　　　　　(B)　　　　　　(C)

C　29. For question number 29, please look at the three pictures.

Listen to the movie information. Which picture fits the description?

The movie is about an Asian teenager who moves to Europe and must learn how to survive in a new environment. Everything is hard in the beginning. She doesn't even have enough food to eat. She starts as a humble hotel maid, and in the end becomes the owner of a large company. Tickets are available now on our website!

第 29 題，請看三張圖片。

請聽以下電影訊息，哪張圖片符合描述？

這部電影講述一名亞洲少女移居歐洲，必須學習如何在新環境中生存。開始時一切都很困難，她甚至沒有足夠的食物可吃。她從一位謙卑的飯店女傭開始，最後成為大公司的老闆。門票現在可在我們的網站上購買！

解析 由關鍵詞 hotel maid（飯店女傭）和 owner of a large company（大公司的老闆）可以知道答案為選項 C。

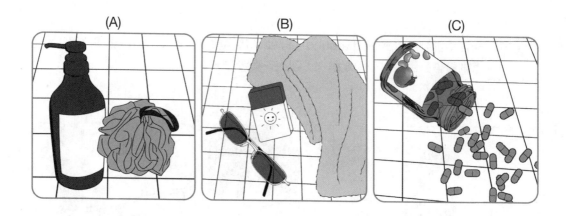

(A)   (B)   (C)

__B__ 30. For question number 30, please look at the three pictures.

Listen to the ad. What is the product?

Using our product is the best way to keep your skin from burning. Apply it before you go to the beach, or play sports outdoors. Don't forget to bring it with you when you have to spend time in the sun. Just apply it every two hours for the best protection.

第 30 題，請看三張圖片。

請聽廣告，廣告的產品是什麼？

使用我們的產品是保護皮膚、免於曬傷的最佳方法。在去海灘或戶外運動前塗上它。當你必須在陽光下曝曬時，不要忘記攜帶它。每兩小時塗抹一次，以得到最佳保護。

解析 由關鍵詞 skin（皮膚）、beach（海灘）、sun（陽光）、protection（保護）可以知道這是防曬產品的廣告，答案為選項 B。

第一部分 詞彙

共 10 題，每個題目裡有一個空格。請從四個選項中選出一個最適合題意的字或詞作答。

___A___ 1. I don't want to be late for my exam tomorrow, so can I borrow your _____ ?

我不想明天考試遲到，所以我能借你的摩托車嗎？

(A) scooter 摩托車   (B) balloon 氣球

(C) wallet 錢包   (D) textbook 教科書

___D___ 2. I think we're lost; let's ask someone for _____ .

我想我們是迷路了；我們來問人方向。

(A) advice 建議   (B) money 錢

(C) information 訊息   (D) directions 方向指引

___C___ 3. Miss Fisher often buys us ice cream after PE class; she's very _____ .

費雪老師常在體育課下課後買冰淇淋後給我們；她非常慷慨。

(A) confident 有信心的   (B) hungry 飢餓的

(C) generous 慷慨的   (D) natural 自然的

___C___ 4. I haven't _____ Betty today yet.

我今天還沒看見貝蒂。

(A) looked 看   (B) watched 觀看

(C) seen 看見   (D) heard 聽

解析 look 為不及物動詞，意思是後需要加介系詞才行，如 look at 看著，look for 尋找。watch 表示長時間觀看，比如是看電視 watch TV。see 即為看到，因此選項 C 正確。

___D___ 5. Are you Jack or Jason? Sorry, I have a poor _____ for names.

你是傑克還是傑森？抱歉，我對名字的記憶力很差。

(A) sight 視力   (B) speech 演說

(C) brain 大腦   (D) memory 記憶力

__A__ 6. I hate driving to work in bad weather, so luckily it _____ snows here.

我討厭在天氣不好的時候開車上班,所以幸運的是這裡很少下雪。

(A) seldom 很少　　　　　　(B) sometimes 有時

(C) suddenly 突然　　　　　(D) usually 通常

解析 由空格前的 luckily 可推知,這裡的天氣應該「並非」不好,因此要選一個不常下雪的選項。由發生頻率多到少排列為:usually>sometimes>seldom,因此選項 A 正確。選項 C 不描述頻率,只是描述動作的快慢。

__B__ 7. I _____ chocolate ice cream, but they only had vanilla at the grocery store.

我偏好巧克力冰淇淋,但是食品雜貨店只有香草口味的。

(A) choose 選擇　　　　　　(B) prefer 偏好

(C) admire 讚賞　　　　　　(D) purchase 購買

__C__ 8. My parents punished me after I got in _____ at school.

我在學校惹上麻煩後,我的父母懲罰了我。

(A) touch 接觸　　　　　　(B) shape 形狀

(C) trouble 麻煩　　　　　(D) line 隊伍

解析 get in touch 意思是「聯繫」;get in shape 是「變得健康」或「身材變好」,而 get in line 意思是「排隊」,語意不合,選項 C 的「惹上麻煩」正確。

__A__ 9. Do you have anything in _____ for next week's science project?

你對下週的科學計畫有什麼任何打算嗎?

(A) mind 心智　　　　　　(B) head 頭腦

(C) thought 想法　　　　　(D) idea 點子

解析 mind 在此題做名詞,指人的理智或意識。have... in mind 是片語,意思是「心裡想著…」,或「打算…」。

__C__ 10. During the _____ season, people celebrate by giving each other gifts.

在佳節季節,人們通過互贈禮物來慶祝。

(A) vacation 假期　　　　　(B) sports 體育

(C) holiday 節日　　　　　(D) business 商務

Part 2 段落填空

第二部分　段落填空

共 8 題，包括二個段落，每個段落含四個空格。每格均有四個選項，請依照文意選出最適合的答案。

Questions 11-14

Come visit Nature's Wonderland, our exciting wild animal park! See lions, tigers, bears, monkeys, and more up close from your car as you _____(11)_____ slowly through the park. Learn fun facts about the animals from signs along the trail. Picnic areas are available _____(12)_____ you can eat lunch while watching the active animals play. Nature's Wonderland is open every day _____(13)_____ 9 am to 5 pm. Tickets are $12 for adults and $8 for children under 12. A wonderful experience is waiting for nature lovers of _____(14)_____ ages at Nature's Wonderland wild animal park!

來探訪「大自然奇觀」，我們刺激的野生動物園！當你慢慢地 **(11) 開車** 穿越園區時，可以從車子裡近距離觀賞獅子、老虎、熊、猴子等更多動物。從沿途的標示來學習和動物相關的有趣事實。野餐區可供使用，**(12) 因此**你可以一邊吃午餐，一邊觀賞活潑的動物玩耍。「大自然奇觀」的開放時間 **(13) 從**每天上午 9 點到下午 5 點。門票成人 12 元，12 歲以下兒童 8 元。美妙的體驗在大自然奇觀野生動物園等待 **(14) 所有**年齡的自然愛好者！

__D__ 11. (A) drives 駕車　　　　　　(B) driven 被駕駛、驅動
　　　　 (C) driving 駕駛中　　　　 (D) drive 駕車

__A__ 12. (A) so 因此　　　　　　　　(B) and 並且
　　　　 (C) thus 因此　　　　　　　(D) even 甚至

> **解析** 空格前提到野餐區，之後提到可邊吃午餐邊欣賞動物，可推測「有提供野餐區」是原因，而「可以在野餐區欣賞」是結果。選項 A 的 so 為連接詞，可連接子句，為正確答案。Thus 雖然也是表因果的「因此」，但其為副詞，並無連接功能，而且其後也要接逗點，無法連接前後兩子句。

__B__ 13. (A) until 直到　　　　　　　(B) from 從
　　　　 (C) at 在　　　　　　　　　(D) for 為了

> **解析** 空格後 9 am 和 5 pm 中間有 to，可得知是從早上到下午，因此可和 to 相配的
> 介系詞為 from，意味「從…到…」，選項 B 正確。

____B____ 14. (A) every 每一個　　　　　　(B) all 所有
　　　　　(C) each 每個　　　　　　　(D) many 許多

> **解析** 空格後的 ages 字尾有 s 為複數，因此和複數名詞符合的為選項 B 的 all。雖
> 然 many 後也可加複數，但並沒有 "many ages" 來修飾的表達法。Every 和
> each 之後都需要加單數名詞。

Questions 15-18

What do you do when you have free time? Some people exercise to stay healthy
when they have the time, and ____(15)____ like learning new things. It doesn't really
matter what you do ____(16)____ you plan your time well and find activities you really
enjoy. If you aren't effective in planning your time, ____(17)____ , having a lot of time
on your hands isn't necessarily a good thing. A good example is summer vacation,
which last two months. If you don't use this time wisely, it's easy to become bored.
In short, if you want to enjoy your free time, it's a good idea ____(18)____ a plan.

當你有空時，你會做什麼？有些人在有空時運動保持健康，**(15) 其他人**喜歡學習新事物。真正重要的
不是你做什麼，**(16) 只要**你能好好規劃你的時間，並找到你真正喜愛的活動。如果你在規劃時間上不
夠有效時，**(17) 然而**，手邊有滿滿的時間，並不一定是好事。兩個月長的暑假就是很好的例子。如果
你沒有聰明一點地利用這段時間，很快就會覺得無聊了。簡而言之，若想要享受你的空閒時間，**(18)**
有計畫是很好的。

____C____ 15. (A) another 任何人　　　　　(B) the other 特定剩下的人
　　　　　(C) others 其他人　　　　　　(D) together 一起

> **解析** 空格句子裡的句首提到 some people 為複數，因此和其相配的就是選項 C 的
> others，意味「一方…另一方」。

____A____ 16. (A) as long as 只要　　　　　(B) even though 即使
　　　　　(C) in order to 為了　　　　　(D) because of 因為

解析 空格前為結果:「不論做什麼事都不重要」,而空格後是表達「條件」:好好利用時間和享受活動,因此選項 A 的 as long as 即為連接條件和其結果的連接詞。

__D__ 17. (A) then 然後　　　　　　　　(B) therefore 因此
　　　　　(C) but 但是　　　　　　　　(D) however 但是、然而

解析 空格前一句是描述好好利用時間的狀況,而本題的句子則是描述無法有效利用時間的狀況,因此表轉折的選項 C 和 D 符合。可由句首的 if 判斷此句已經有連接詞,因此不用再選 but。選項 D 的 however 正確。

__B__ 18. (A) for having 為了擁有　　　　(B) to have 擁有
　　　　　(C) will have 將會擁有　　　　(D) that one has 那個人擁有

共 12 題，包括 4 個題組，每個題組含 1 至 2 篇短文，與數個相關的四選一的選擇題。請由試題上的選項中選出最適合的答案。

Questions 19-21

Hi Helen,

I'm writing this email to ask if you can do me a favor. As you know, we're having a party at the office this Sunday (Jan. 26). I'm inviting some of our biggest and most important customers, so I want to have the office cleaned this Saturday. And because Irene and Sophie said that they saw a mouse in the kitchen, I want to have the job done by a cleaning company. Could you make the arrangements for me?

At the end of this email is a list of the prices charged by different cleaning services. Please have a look and choose the company that has the lowest prices and is available when we need them. We have two floors that need cleaning with three rooms and one bathroom each. Most importantly, all the companies require that you contact them at least two days before cleaning, so be sure to make the arrangements before you leave the office today. This way, the cleaners can come the day after tomorrow. Thanks in advance!

Yours,

Jim

嗨海倫，

我寫這封電子郵件是想問你能否幫我一個忙。**(20) (21) 如你所知，我們這個星期日（1月26日）要在辦公室辦派對。我要邀請一些我們最大且最重要的客戶，所以我想要在這個星期六讓辦公室清潔乾淨。**而且因為艾琳和蘇菲說他們在廚房看到有老鼠，我想要請清潔公司來做這件事。你能幫我安排一下嗎？

在這封電子郵件的最後，有一些不同清潔服務的收費表。請你看一下，**(20) 然後選擇一家價格最低，在我們需要時有空的公司。**我們有兩層樓需要清潔，每層有三個房間和一間浴室。**(19) (21) 最重要的是，所有的公司都要你至少在清潔前兩天聯絡他們，所以請務必在今天離開辦公室前安排好，這樣清潔工可以後天來。**先謝謝你了！

誠摯的，

吉姆

List of cleaning service prices

Company	Per room	Per bathroom	Notes
EZ Cleaning	$1,800	$400	
Acme Cleaners	$1,500	$500	Not available until February 20, 2025
Jiffy Clean	$1,600	$600	
Honest Cleaning	$1,700	$500	

清潔服務價目表

公司名稱	每間房間	每間浴室	備註
易潔清潔	$1,800	$400	
高點清潔	$1,500	$500	2025 年 2 月 20 日 之前無法提供服務
(20) 快捷清潔	**$1,600**	**$600**	
誠信清潔	$1,700	$500	

__D__ 19. What will Helen have to do after receiving the email?

(A) She will send out invitation cards.

(B) She will start cleaning the office.

(C) She will call Jim about the service.

(D) She will arrange a cleaning service.

海倫收到郵件後必須做什麼？

(A) 她將寄出邀請卡。

(B) 她將開始清潔辦公室。

(C) 她將詢問吉姆關於服務的事。

(D) 她將安排清潔服務。

解析　由第二段倒數第二句 "so be sure to make the arrangements before you leave the office today" 得知，海倫被要求要安排清潔公司服務，選項 D 正確。

__C__ 20. Which company will be hired for the job?

(A) EZ Cleaning

(B) Acme Cleaners

(C) Jiffy Clean

(D) Honest Cleaning

哪家公司將被聘請來做這項工作？

(A) 易潔清潔

(B) 高點清潔

(C) 快捷清潔

(D) 誠信清潔

解析　由第一段第二句得知，此公司需要的清潔服務是要在 1/26 日前做好，而由第二段第二句得知要找最便宜的公司，再加上第四句描述有要在 1/26 兩天前通知，因此高點清潔雖然是最便宜的，但是日期不符合條件。第二便宜的快捷清潔即為最適合選擇，選項 C 正確。

__B__ 21. What day was the email sent on?

(A) Wednesday

(B) Thursday

(C) Friday

(D) Saturday

郵件是什麼時候被發送的？

(A) 週三

(B) 週四

(C) 週五

(D) 週六

解析　由第一段第一句得知派對是在週日，因此應該是要在週六清理乾淨。由第二段倒數第二句得知，清潔公司需要在至少兩天前聯絡到，即為週四。寫信時應為週四，因為海倫要求在下班前要辦好這件事。

Questions 22-24

Smiling is a simple way to express happiness, and it benefits not only the people who smile, but also the people around them. People always wonder what they can do to improve their lives. Why not start by smiling?

People smile when they feel happy. However, many people aren't aware that smiling can actually make them feel better or help them stay calm in stressful situations. **Believe it or not**, scientists have found that even a fake smile can have a positive effect on people's mood. This is because smiling causes muscles in the face to send signals to the brain that tell people to be happy. Smiling may seem like an easy thing to do, but it can make a big difference. So don't forget to smile!

(22) 微笑是表達快樂的簡單方法,它不僅對微笑的人有益,也對周遭的人有益。人們總想知道能做什麼來改善生活,為什麼不從微笑開始呢?

人們在感到快樂時會微笑。然而,許多人並不知道,(22) 微笑事實上可以讓他們感覺更好,或是幫他們在壓力大的情況下保持冷靜。(24) 信不信由你,科學家們發現,即使是假微笑也能對人們的心情有正面影響。這是因為微笑讓臉部肌肉發出傳達信訊號到大腦,告訴人們要快樂。(23) 微笑可能看來很容易,但它能帶來很大的改變。所以,別不要忘了微笑!

__B__ 22. What is the best title for the article?

(A) *Laughing at Others*

(B) *The Power of Smiles*

(C) *How to Smile Better*

(D) *Don't Give a Fake Smile*

本篇文章最適合的標題為何?

(A) 嘲笑別人

(B) 微笑的力量

(C) 如何更好地微笑

(D) 不要假笑

解析 根據第一段第一句 "Smiling is a simple way... around them." 以及第二段第二句 "smiling can actually make them feel better or help them stay calm in stressful situations." 可看出微笑的好處與力量,最符合的選項為 B,微笑的力量。

__C__ 23. According to the article, what should we do to make a difference?

(A) Tell people to be happy.

(B) Make people feel better.

(C) Remember to smile more.

(D) Stay calm in stressful situations.

根據文章，我們應該做什麼來產生改變？

(A) 告訴人們要快樂。

(B) 使人們感覺更好。

(C) 記得要多微笑。

(D) 在壓力大的情況下保持冷靜。

解析 第二段倒數第二句 "Smiling may seem like an easy thing to do, but it can make a big difference." 提到微笑可以帶來改變，因此選項 C 最符合。

__A__ 24. When do we use "believe it or not"?

(A) When we say something surprising.

(B) When someone is telling a lie.

(C) When a person doesn't believe you.

(D) When someone is being fooled.

我們何時會用「信不信由你」？

(A) 當我們說出令人驚訝的事情。

(B) 當有人在說謊時。

(C) 當一個人不相信你的時候。

(D) 當有人被愚弄的時候。

解析 believe it or not 後面接的是科學家的新發現 "scientists have found that even a fake smile can have a positive effect on people's mood"，意味著點出某個真實陳述，雖然聽起來不太可能，因此選項 A 符合。

Part 3 閱讀理解

Questions 25-27

Suzie's Garden Reopening!

After closing for three months, we're back with a new café that serves delicious drinks and **one-of-a-kind** desserts. We're celebrating our reopening with special offers only available this weekend. If you've visited us before, you'll be excited to see all the changes we've made. And if you've never been here before, you'll be surprised how happy and relaxed flowers can make you. According to research, plants are not only able to calm people down, but also bring feelings of peace. So come to Suzie's Garden, where you can spend a relaxing afternoon enjoying the beauty of flowers. We now even offer potted flowers for sale so you can enjoy them at home. If you don't want to take flowers home in a pot, how about in your stomach? We're now offering special desserts made with flowers!

Tickets
Adults: $200

Students: $120

Children 6 and under: free of charge

Potted Flowers
Lilies: $120

White roses: $200, Roses in other colors: $300

Tulips: $320

Sunflowers: $100

*With every $500 spent on tickets, receive $100 off on potted flowers

Desserts
Rose Jelly: $70

Lily cake: $120

Sunflower ice cream: $90

Tulip cookies: $60/bag $180/box

蘇茜的花園重新開幕！

在歇業三個月之後，我們回來了，全新的咖啡館，提供美味的飲品和獨一無二的甜點。為慶祝重新開幕，我們提供只限週末的特別優惠。如果您之前來過我們這裡，您一定會對我們所做的各種變化感到興奮。如果您從未來過，您會驚訝於花朵能讓你多麼地快樂和放鬆。根據研究，植物不僅能夠讓人平靜下來，還能帶來和平的感覺。所以，來蘇茜的花園吧，您可以在這裡度過一個輕鬆的下午，享受花朵的美麗。**(25) 我們現在甚至販賣盆栽花卉，因此您可以把它們帶回家中享受。** 如果您不想帶盆栽花回家，那麼試試帶回肚子裡如何？ **(27) 我們現在提供花朵製作成的特別甜點！**

(26) 門票

成人：200 元

學生：120 元

6 歲及以下兒童：免費

盆栽花卉

百合：120 元

白玫瑰：200 元，**(26) 其他色玫瑰：300 元**

鬱金香：320 元

向日葵：100 元

(26) * 每消費 500 元門票，可在盆栽花卉上獲得 100 元折扣

甜點

玫瑰果凍：70 元

百合蛋糕：120 元

向日葵冰淇淋：90 元

鬱金香餅乾：60 元 / 袋 180 元 / 盒

__C__ 25. Who would be interested in this ad?

(A) Someone who wants to have a full meal at a café.

(B) People who want to learn to cook with flowers.

(C) Someone who wants to bring some flowers home.

(D) People who are interested in planting a garden.

這則廣告會吸引誰的興趣？

(A) 想在咖啡館享用一頓豐盛餐點的人。

(B) 想學習如何用花烹飪的人。

(C) 想帶一些花回家的人。

(D) 對在花園中種植花草感興趣的人。

解析 由第一段倒數第三句 We now even offer potted flowers for sale so you can enjoy them at home 得知，花園現在可以讓人買花回家，因此最吸引的是想在家裡賞花的人，選項 C 正確。

__B__ 26. Richard is going to take his wife, his son, who is 13, and his 5-year-old nephew to Susi's garden and bring two pots of pink roses home. How much money does he need to spend?

(A) $920

(B) $1,020

(C) $1,220

(D) $1,240

理查打算帶他的妻子、13 歲的兒子和 5 歲的侄子去蘇茜的花園，並帶兩盆粉紅玫瑰回家。他需要花多少錢？

(A) 920 元

(B) 1,020 元

(C) 1,220 元

(D) 1,240 元

解析 理查夫妻兩個大人，成人票花費 400 元，13 歲的兒子算學生票，120 元。5 歲的姪子依花園規定六歲以下，不用錢。粉紅玫瑰算在 "roses in other colors" 每盆 300 元，有兩盆共 600。最後因為 With every $500 spent on tickets, receive $100 off on potted flowers，有優惠，盆栽可減 100，只要 500 元。400＋120＋500 總共 1020，選項 B 正確。

A 27. What does "one-of-a-kind" likely
mean?
(A) unique
(B) common
(C) fancy
(D) different

「獨一無二」很可能意味著什麼？
(A) 獨特的
(B) 普通的
(C) 拉風的
(D) 不同的

解析 one-of-a-kind 修飾的是後面的 desserts 甜點，而隨著文章鋪陳，可由第一段的最後一句提到 special desserts made with flowers 推知，甜點是特別的，還有跟花卉有關，因此和特別最符合的就是選項 A 的 unique。

Questions 28-30

There are many wonderful places in the world worth visiting, and Cappadocia in central Turkey is certainly one of them. It's nothing like anywhere you've ever been before. We have a day tour planned for you, and we promise the sights will amaze you.

You will be picked up in front of the hotel by our tour bus after breakfast. The first stop is Devrent Valley, which is known for its many giant rocks shaped like animals. You can see rocks that look like snakes, seals, birds, and even camels! Next stop is an art center, where you can see how traditional art and jewelry in the Cappadocia region was made. Then, you're going to dine at a fine restaurant which offers traditional Turkish food.

After the lunch break, you'll be going to Goreme Valley to see the Open Air Museum, which has ancient churches in caves with colorful paintings. Finally, you will visit the largest and deepest underground city in Cappadocia. Our tour guide will help you discover the wonders and history of this amazing place.

世界上有許多值得一遊的奇妙地方，位於土耳其中部的卡帕多西亞肯定是其中之一。這裡與你以往任何去過的地方都不同。我們為你安排了一天的旅遊，而且我們承諾這些景點會讓你讚歎。

(28) 早餐後，我們的旅遊巴士將在飯店前接您。(29) (30) 第一站是德芙倫特谷，這裡以其許多形狀如動物的巨石而聞名。您可以看到像蛇、海豹、鳥類、甚至駱駝的岩石！下一站是藝術中心，您將有機會了解卡帕多西亞地區傳統藝術和珠寶是如何製作的。接著，您將在一家傳統土耳其美食的高級餐廳用餐。

(28) (30) 午餐休息後，您將前往格雷梅谷參觀露天博物館，那裡有彩繪的古老洞穴教堂。最後，您將參觀卡帕多西亞最大最深的地下城市。我們的導遊將協助您探索這個驚人之地的奇觀和歷史。

___A___ 28. Who is most likely the author?　誰最有可能是作者？

    (A) a tour guide　(A) 導遊

    (B) a hotel manager　(B) 飯店經理

    (C) a history teacher　(C) 歷史老師

    (D) a restaurant chef　(D) 餐廳廚師

> **解析** 全篇文章在介紹土耳其旅遊，而由第二段和第三段得知是在描述行程，因此最符合的就是選項 A 的導遊。

___B___ 29. What is Devrent Valley famous for?　德文特谷以什麼聞名？

    (A) wild animals　(A) 野生動物

    (B) giant rocks　(B) 巨石

    (C) art and jewelry　(C) 藝術和珠寶

    (D) fine dining　(D) 精緻餐飲

> **解析** 由第二段第二句 The first stop is Devrent Valley, which is known for its many giant rocks shaped like animals. 得知，其聞名是因為像動物的石頭，因此選項 B 正確。

__D__ 30. According to the text, which is true about Cappadocia?

(A) It is a large ancient city in Turkey.

(B) It has been discovered quite recently.

(C) It is famous for its many wild animals.

(D) It has both natural and historic sights.

根據文本，關於卡帕多西亞的描述，何者正確？

(A) 它是土耳其的一個大型古城。

(B) 它最近才被發現。

(C) 它以其許多野生動物而聞名。

(D) 它既有自然又有歷史景點。

解析 由第二段第二句得知此地有巨石，屬於自然景觀。第三段的第一句描述了此地有博物館和古老教堂，因此選項 D 正確。

GEPT
初級模擬試題
第6回
解答、翻譯與詳解

第 6 回解答

🔊 聽力測驗解答

1. C	2. B	3. A	4. B	5. C
6. C	7. B	8. C	9. B	10. A
11. C	12. C	13. B	14. B	15. A
16. A	17. A	18. A	19. B	20. B
21. B	22. C	23. A	24. C	25. B
26. B	27. B	28. B	29. A	30. A

閱讀測驗解答

1. C	2. D	3. D	4. A	5. B
6. C	7. D	8. A	9. A	10. B
11. C	12. C	13. B	14. D	15. A
16. B	17. B	18. C	19. D	20. C
21. C	22. B	23. C	24. B	25. D
26. B	27. B	28. D	29. A	30. D

第一部分 看圖辨義

__C__ 1. For Question Number 1, please look at the picture.
What is happening?

(A) The dog is in great danger.

(B) A dog is being chased by a kid.

(C) A kid is being chased by a dog.

第一題，請看此圖片。

發生什麼事？

(A) 狗正陷入危險的情況中。

(B) 狗被小孩追。

(C) 小孩被狗追。

解析　"A be chased by B" 是 A 被 B 追的意思。圖片中可以看到是小孩被狗追，所以答案為 C。

__B__ 2. For Question Number 2, please look at the picture.
What is the girl going to do?

(A) The girl is going to take a shower.

(B) The girl is going to get some more water.

(C) She will go to a store to buy a new bottle.

第二題，請看此圖片。

女孩要做什麼？

(A) 女孩要去沖澡。

(B) 女孩要去多裝一點水。

(C) 她要去店裡買一個新的水壺。

解析　圖片中女孩流了很多汗，水壺裡的水喝完了，並想著水的事情，可以知道女孩是想多裝一點水補充水分，答案選 B。

<u>A</u>　3. For Question Number 3, please look at the picture.
How do the people feel?

(A) The kids in the classroom are scared.

(B) The children are excited about the pet.

(C) Everyone is interested in the insect.

第三題，請看此圖片。

這圖片中的人有什麼感覺？

(A) 教室裡的孩子們很害怕。

(B) 小孩們對寵物感到興奮。

(C) 大家對這隻昆蟲感到有興趣。

解析　圖片中的背景是教室，兩位穿著制服的學生因為蟑螂而露出害怕的表情，答案選 A。

<u>B</u>　4. For Question Number 4, please look at the picture.
How would you describe the room?

(A) The room looks very dirty.

(B) The room has been cleaned.

(C) The room has good natural light.

第四題，請看此圖片。

你會怎麼形容這個房間？

(A) 房間看起來很髒。

(B) 房間被整理乾淨了。

(C) 房間有很棒的自然光。

解析　圖片中沒有看到對外窗，無法推論是不是有很棒的自然光，因此選項 C 不正確。可以看出來房間乾淨得發亮，所以 A 也不正確。答案選 B。

_C_ 5. For Question Number 5, please look at the picture.

What is the woman doing?

(A) She is playing a video game.

(B) She is recording a football match.

(C) She is watching the weather forecast.

第五題,請看此圖片。

這名女子在做什麼?

(A) 她在打電動。

(B) 她在錄足球比賽。

(C) 她在看氣象預報。

解析　圖片上 FRI、SAT、SUN 分別為週五、週六、週日的英文縮寫,可以看出是這三天的天氣和氣溫的預報,答案選 C。

__C__ 6. Roy doesn't eat beef.

    (A) Yes, he eats a lot of it.

    (B) Let's get some for him.

    (C) I seldom have it either.

羅伊不吃牛肉。

(A) 是，他吃很多。

(B) 我們幫他買一點。

(C) 我也很少吃。

解析 選項 A 和 B 皆不符合對話邏輯，選項 A 的 Yes 需要改成 No 才合理，因此答案為 C。

__B__ 7. Would you mind opening the door for me?

    (A) Sure. Let me help.

    (B) No. It's my pleasure.

    (C) Yes, I opened the door.

你介意幫我開一下門嗎？

(A) 當然。我來幫你。

(B) 不。我很樂意。

(C) 是，我開門了。

解析 回應 "Would you mind…?"（你介意 ...?）的句子時，要用 "No" 來表示自己不介意；"Yes"、"Sure" 則代表自己介意，不願意幫忙。選項 A 和選項 C 的句子前後邏輯相反，因此正確答案選 B。

__C__ 8. Do you know where I can find a post office?

    (A) It takes around five minutes.

    (B) How many letters do you have?

    (C) It's across from the train station.

你知道我去哪裡可以找到郵局嗎？

(A) 大約要花費 5 分鐘。

(B) 你有幾封信？

(C) 在火車站對面。

解析 題目中「Do you know where I can find + 名詞？」的句型常用來問路或是詢問物品擺放的位置。除了選項 C 在告知位置，其餘的選項皆答非所問，答案選 C。

__B__ 9. Have you seen Jonathan around lately?

    (A) Jonathan is my cousin.

    (B) He's on a trip to Japan.

    (C) Yes, he often arrives late.

你最近有看到強納森嗎？

(A) 強納森是我的表弟。

(B) 他正在日本旅遊。

(C) 是，他常常遲到。

解析　選項 A 和 C 答非所問。選項 B 省略 "No," 表示沒看到，而直接說明強納森目前的所在地為正確答案，選 B。

A　10. Do you have any hobbies?　　　　你有什麼嗜好嗎？
    (A) Yes, I enjoy playing tennis.　　　　(A) 有，我喜歡打網球。
    (B) I'm not used to getting up early.　　(B) 我不習慣早起。
    (C) Having good habits is important.　　(C) 養成好習慣很重要。

解析　habit（習慣）和 hobby（嗜好）的發音類似，請注意。三個選項中只有選項 A 有回答到問題，其餘兩個答非所問。正確答案選 A。

C　11. Will you be able to come tomorrow morning?　　你明天早上能來嗎？
    (A) I can get back home before you do.　　(A) 我可以在你之前到家。
    (B) I'll leave everything at my mom's office.　(B) 我會把東西都放在我媽的辦公室。
    (C) What time do you want me to be there?　(C) 你想要我幾點到？

解析　問題中沒說明到達的地點，但因為回家（come home）中的 home 不能省略，所以可以知道不是在討論回家，選項 A 不正確。選項 B 答非所問。正確答案選 C，詢問對方希望自己在幾點到達。

C　12. Wow! Look at the stars!　　　　哇！你看那些星星！
    (A) When are we going to start?　　(A) 我們什麼時候開始？
    (B) All right, I'll stop doing it now.　(B) 好。我會停下來。
    (C) I've never seen them in the city.　(C) 我從來沒有在都市看到過。

解析　選項 A start（開始）和題目中 stars（星星）的發音相似，為陷阱，回應不符合對話邏輯，選項 B 也不合理，不需要停止 (stop) 做某事。正確答案為 C，表示自己在都市未曾見過。

__B__ 13. I'm not feeling well today.

(A) Why do you like it?

(B) Do you have a fever?

(C) Let me call the police.

我今天不大舒服。

(A) 你為什麼喜歡？

(B) 你有發燒嗎？

(C) 我來報警。

解析 "not feeling well" 表示身體不舒服，選項 B 追問對方身體狀況最符合對話邏輯，其餘兩個選項皆不合理，正確答案選 B。

__B__ 14. The pork at that restaurant tastes bad.

(A) I got a bad score too.

(B) The fish isn't fresh either.

(C) Yes, the restroom is dirty.

那間餐廳的豬肉很難吃。

(A) 我也考得不好。

(B) 魚也不新鮮。

(C) 是的，廁所很髒。

解析 由於題目是說 the pork tastes bad，在評論餐廳的餐點，但選項 A 和成績有關，taste（嚐起來）和 test（考試）的發音類似，為陷阱，不能選。選項 C 提到 restroom（廁所），和題目的 restaurant（餐廳）發音相似，但不合對話邏輯，只有選項 B 為相關評論，選 B。

__A__ 15. Is studying abroad a good idea?

(A) Why? Are you thinking of going?

(B) It's good to spend time with family.

(C) I have no idea what the test is about.

你覺得出國讀書是個好主意嗎？

(A) 為什麼這麼問？你考慮出國讀書嗎？

(B) 跟家人一起共度時間是很好的事。

(C) 我不知道這個測驗是關於什麼的。

解析 idea 有幾種用法，「想法／主意」，或「明白／了解」。選項 C 的 "have no idea" 表示「不知道」，和題目中的用法不同，也不符合對話邏輯，因此不正確。選項 B 答非所問。正確答案為 A，反問對方問問題的原因。

A 16. W: Have you tried the new Italian place on the corner?

M: I have. Actually, I went there yesterday.

W: You did?! My sister and I spent almost an hour waiting in line there. And we finally gave up because we were too hungry.

M: You should've called me. I had a table for four and it was just Mary and me.

Question: What did they do yesterday?

女子：你有去過轉角那間新開的義大利餐廳了嗎？

男子：有。其實我是昨天去的。

女子：你去了嗎！？我姐姐和我排隊排了快一個小時，最後因為太餓所以就放棄了！

男子：你應該要打電話給我的。我那時候是坐四人桌，但是只有我跟瑪麗兩個人。

問題：他們昨天做了什麼？

(A) They went to the same restaurant.

(B) They met each other at a coffee shop.

(C) They both spent an hour waiting in line.

(A) 他們去了一樣的餐廳。

(B) 他們在咖啡廳見面。

(C) 他們兩個都排隊排了一個小時。

解析　女子聽到男子表明自己是在昨天去義大利餐廳時，非常驚訝；而男子也提到女子應該打電話給他，可能可以一起坐。由此可知男子和女子都在昨天去了那間義大利餐廳，答案選 A。

A 17. M: Miss Wu said that the test won't be as easy next time. Now I'm worried.

W: Don't worry. As long as you take notes in class, it won't be too difficult.

M: I didn't take any this week. By the way, you took her class last year, didn't you?

W: Yes, I did. And I still have the notes I took.

Question: What will the man probably do next?

男子：吳老師說下次的考試不會那麼容易。現在我有點擔心。

女子：別擔心。只要你上課好好抄筆記，不會太難的。

男子：我這個禮拜什麼都沒抄。對了，妳去年修了她的課，對嗎？

女子：對。我那時抄的筆記還有留著。

問題：男子接下來可能會做什麼？

(A) Ask the woman to lend him her notes.

(B) Ask the woman to take the test for him.

(C) Ask the woman to take the class with him.

(A) 請女子借他筆記。

(B) 請女子幫他代考。

(C) 請女子跟他一起修同一堂課。

解析 整段對話的重點為上課筆記，順著邏輯往下推可以知道男子接下來可能會請女子借他筆記，答案選 A。

A　18. M: The elevator is too crowded. Let's take the stairs.

W: I can't! My ankle still hurts.

M: Come on! It's been a month since your car accident.

W: But my ankle was badly injured.

M: Then why did I see you playing volleyball with Jenny yesterday?

Question: Which of the following is likely true?

男子：電梯太擠了。我們走樓梯吧！

女子：不行！我的腳踝還在痛。

男子：拜託！距離妳出車禍已經過了一個月了。

女子：但我的腳踝傷得很嚴重。

男子：那為什麼我昨天還看到妳跟珍妮在打排球？

問題：以下何者可能為真？

(A) The woman is lying.

(B) The man is being funny.

(C) The woman has to see a doctor.

(A) 女子在說謊。

(B) 男子在開玩笑。

(C) 女子需要看醫生。

解析 從對話中男子提到女子昨天還在打排球，女子卻說自己腳踝受傷嚴重，所以不能走樓梯，可以推測女子可能在說謊。答案選 A。

B　19. W: Please wait here.

　　M: How long will I have to wait to see the doctor?

　　W: At least an hour. There are a lot of patients today.

　　M: OK, I'll go have lunch first.

　　Question: What will the man do next?

　　女子：請在這邊稍等。

　　男子：我要等多久才能看到醫生？

　　女子：至少一個小時。今天病人很多。

　　男子：好，那我先去吃午餐。

　　問題：男子接下來會做什麼？

(A) See a doctor.　　　　　　　　(A) 看醫生。

(B) Get some food.　　　　　　　(B) 買些食物。

(C) Go to the hospital.　　　　　(C) 去醫院。

解析 從男子最後一句回應 "I'll go have lunch first." 可以知道男子接下來會去買一些食物，答案選 B。

B　20. W: I had a fight with Jenny.

　　M: Why?

　　W: She asked me to help her cheat on an English test, and I refused. Jenny told me good friends should help each other no matter what.

　　M: That's just not true.

　　Question: What does the man mean?

　　女子：我和珍妮吵架了。

　　男子：為什麼？

　　女子：她請我英文考試時幫她作弊，我拒絕了。珍妮說好朋友不管什麼事都應該互相幫忙。

　　男子：那不正確。

　　問題：男子的意思是什麼？

(A) The man believes Jenny's opinion is correct.

(B) The man doesn't agree with what Jenny said.

(C) He doesn't think the women should have fought.

(A) 男子覺得珍妮的想法是對的。

(B) 男子不同意珍妮的說法。

(C) 他覺得兩名女子不應該吵架。

解析 男子所說的 "That's just not true." 中的 "That" 指的是珍妮的說法；"not true" 則是「不正確」的意思。因此答案選 B。

B 21. W: Why didn't you pick up the phone last night?

M: What? Did you call? I didn't hear the phone ring.

W: Yes, I did. Look! I called five times!

M: My ring volume was probably too low. Sorry!

Question: What likely happened?

女子：你昨天為什麼沒接電話？

男子：什麼？妳有打給我嗎？我沒聽到電話響。

女子：我有。你看！我打了五次！

男子：我的電話鈴聲音量可能太小聲了。對不起！

問題：可能發生了什麼事？

(A) The man's telephone was broken.

(B) The phone's volume was turned down.

(C) The man and woman talked on the phone.

(A) 男子的電話壞了。

(B) 電話的音量被調小聲了。

(C) 男子和女子講電話。

解析 音量大小在英文使用 high 和 low，調整音量大小則是用 turn up 和 turn down。對話中男子說因為鈴聲音量太小聲所以沒接到電話，由此可以推測電話音量可能被轉小聲了，答案選 B。

C 22. W: I really want to go outside. It's been raining for a week.

M: Me, too. I wonder when the rain will stop.

W: Probably in another week.

M: I guess the only way to cheer us up is to watch the travel channel so we know where to visit next time.

Question: What will they probably do next?

女子：我真的很想出門。雨已經下了一個星期了。

男子：我也是。我在想不知道雨什麼時候才會停。

女子：大概還要一個禮拜吧！

男子：我想唯一一個可以提振我們精神的方式是看旅遊頻道，這樣我們就知道下次可以去哪裡玩。

問題：他們接著可能要做什麼？

(A) Go on a trip.

(B) Check the weather.

(C) Watch some TV shows.

(A) 去旅遊。

(B) 看天氣。

(C) 看電視。

解析 對話中男子最後提到要看旅遊頻道來提振精神。由此可知他們接下來要看電視，答案選 C。

A 23. W: This cake is for you.

M: Wow, how nice! But you didn't have to spend money on a cake.

W: I didn't. I made it myself. I've been taking lessons recently.

M: No wonder I couldn't reach you for the past two weeks.

Question: What has the woman been doing?

女子：這個蛋糕是要給你的。

男子：哇！這麼好！你不用花錢買蛋糕的。

女子：我沒有花錢。我自己做的。我最近都在上課。

男子：難怪我過去兩週都找不到妳。

問題：女子最近在做什麼？

(A) Learning to bake.

(B) Shopping for a cake.

(C) Looking for the man.

(A) 學習怎麼烘培。

(B) 買蛋糕。

(C) 找這名男子。

解析　從對話中女子說到蛋糕是自己做的，而且最近都在上課，可以知道女子最近在學烘培，答案選 A。

C　24. M: I don't like Chinese New Year.

W: Why? It's fun! You get lucky money from your parents.

M: Yeah, I know. I just don't like my relatives asking me all those questions.

W: I'm OK with that. They're just showing their concern.

Question: Which of the following is true?

男子：我不喜歡過農曆年。

女子：為什麼？過年很好玩。還能跟你爸媽拿紅包。

男子：對啊！我知道。我只是不喜歡我親戚問我一堆問題。

女子：我還好。他們只是在表達他們的關心而已。

問題：以下何者為真？

(A) They enjoy chatting with relatives.

(B) Both of them like Chinese New Year.

(C) Receiving lucky money is the fun part.

(A) 他們喜歡和親戚聊天。

(B) 他們兩個都喜歡農曆年。

(C) 拿紅包是過年好玩的地方。

解析　男子不喜歡過年，也不喜歡回答親戚的問題，因此選項 A 和 B 皆不正確。女子提到可以跟爸媽拿紅包很好玩，男子也用 "Yeah, I know." 表示認同，答案選 C。

B 25. W: Oh, no! I've put on 3 kilos.

M: It's not a big deal.

W: It IS! I've had too many snacks lately.

M: Me too. That's why I've been jogging.

Question: What is the man's point?

女子：喔，不！我胖了三公斤。

男子：那沒什麼大不了的。

女子：有！我最近吃太多零食了。

男子：我也是。所以我最近都在慢跑。

問題：男子說話的重點是什麼？

(A) He doesn't like eating snacks.

(B) Exercising regularly is important.

(C) The woman needs to lose weight.

(A) 他不喜歡吃零食。

(B) 保持規律運動很重要。

(C) 女子需要減肥。

解析 由於本題詢問「男子說話的重點」，所以要特別注意男子回應的熱切程度。對話顯示，男子也覺得自己吃太多零食，所以選項 A 不正確。當女子提到自己胖了三公斤的時候，男子覺得沒什麼大不了，表示女子增加體重對男子也無關緊要，所以選項 C 也可以排除。男子表示，自己也吃了很多零食，而這也是他最近在慢跑的原因，表示保持規律運動很重要，正確答案為 B。

B 26. For question number 26, please look at the three pictures.

A man is telling the audience about a class. What kind of class is he talking about?

Do you know how to cook? Would you be interested in learning how to make Chinese food? If so, this class is for you. You'll learn how to make delicious pan fried pork dumplings. We'll start with preparing the pork. Don't worry if you're a beginner. We'll teach you step by step. And the best part is you can bring the food home to share with your family.

第 26 題，請看三張圖片。

男子正在和聽眾說明一堂課的內容。請問他提到的是什麼課？

你知道怎麼烹飪嗎？有興趣學習如何烹調中式料理嗎？如果有的話，這堂課會非常適合你。你會學習到如何做好吃的豬肉煎餃。我們會從準備豬肉餡料開始。就算是初學者也不用擔心。我們會一步一步的教導你。最棒的地方是你可以把食物帶回家和家人一起分享！

解析 從關鍵字 "cook" 和 "Chinese food" 可以知道這堂課與烹飪有關。圖片 B 最符合短文內容，答案選 B。

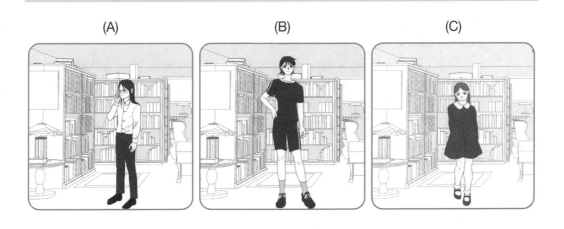

_B_ 27. For question number 27, please look at the three pictures.

A teacher is telling her students about the new student, Kathy. What does Kathy look like?

Good morning, everyone. There will be a new student joining us next Monday. Her name is Kathy. She has short hair. She loves sports and she's quite tall. She used to play for the school basketball team. Anyway, you'll meet her next week. Remember to be nice, everyone!

第 27 題，請看三張圖片。

一名老師正在跟她的學生介紹新學生凱西。請問凱西長什麼樣子？

各位早安。下週一會有一名新學生加入我們。她的名字是凱西。她的頭髮短短的。她喜歡運動，而且個子很高。她以前是籃球校隊的隊員。你們下週就會見到她了。大家要記得保持和善。

解析 由關鍵字 "short hair," "tall" 以及 "sports" 可以知道選項 B 中個子高，穿著運動服裝的短髮女生最符合凱西外表的敘述，答案選 B。

| (A) | (B) | (C) |

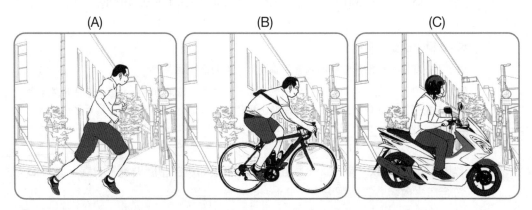

_B_ 28. For question number 28, please look at the three pictures.

A speaker is talking about an event. How are the people going to experience the city?

Have you tried cycling around the city before? You won't know how fun it is unless you try it. We're inviting all of you to experience the beauty of the city on a bike. We'll be meeting at the main gate of Central Park this Saturday at 7 a.m. Hope to see you there!

第 28 題，請看三張圖片。

說話者正在談論一個活動。大家會用什麼方式做城市體驗？

Part 4 短文聽解

你試過在城市中騎乘腳踏車嗎？除非你試過，不然你不會知道這有多有趣。我們誠摯邀請大家一同用腳踏車來體驗這個城市的美麗。我們會在這星期六早上七點在中央公園的正門集合。希望能見到大家！

解析 由關鍵詞 "cycling"（騎乘腳踏車）以及 "bike"（腳踏車）可以知道這項活動是邀請大家用騎腳踏車的方式體驗城市，答案選 B。

(A) 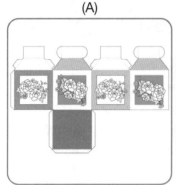 (B)  (C)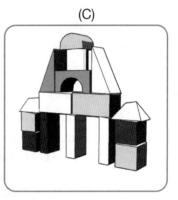

__A__ 29. For question number 29, please look at the three pictures.

A teacher is giving a lesson. What is the lesson about?

First, arrange all the parts in front of you. Second, use the glue to join the white parts together to form a cube. Third, put the light bulb in the center. And there you go! A beautiful lantern.

第 29 題，請看三張圖片。

一名老師正在講課。這堂課是什麼課？

首先，把所有的配件都放到自己的前面。第二步，用膠水把白色的部分黏起來，做成一個正方體。第三步，把燈泡放在中間。漂亮的燈籠就做好了！

解析 從關鍵字 "glue"（膠水）可以知道選項 B 修車不正確，最後的關鍵字 "lantern"（燈籠）可以知道選項 C 的積木也不正確。正確答案為 A，這堂課在教如何做紙燈籠。

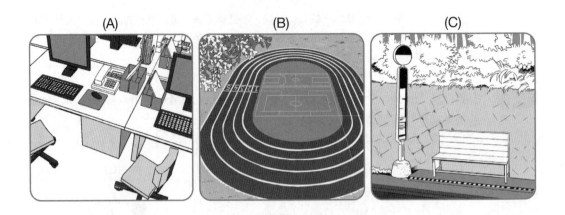

(A)　　　　　　(B)　　　　　　(C)

__A__ 30. For question number 30, please look at the three pictures.

Listen to the following announcement. Where is the speaker?

Can I have your attention, everyone? Mrs. Lee is going to visit our office today. However, she's caught in traffic at the moment. We may have to wait for her another twenty minutes. Food and drinks are available in the meeting room. Please help yourselves. The meeting will start when Mrs. Lee arrives.

第 30 題，請看三張圖片。

請聽以下公告。說話者在哪裡？

大家可以注意一下我這邊嗎？李女士將在今天拜訪我們公司。不過她現在正塞在車陣中。我們可能需要再等 20 分鐘。會議室裡有飲料和食物，請大家自由享用。等李女士一到，會議就會馬上開始。

解析 由關鍵詞 "visit our office" 以及 "meeting room" 可以知道講話的人在室內辦公的場所，答案選 A。

第一部分 **詞彙**

共 **10** 題，每個題目裡有一個空格。請從四個選項中選出一個最適合題意的字或詞作答。

__C__ 1. You should always look both ways before you _____ the street.

在你穿越街道之前，應該要左右看。

(A) drive 駕駛　　　　　(B) turn 轉彎

(C) cross 越過　　　　　(D) walk 步行

> **解析** 空格前提到要先看兩邊，可推知是要過馬路，因此 C 選項的 cross 是正確用法。若要用 walk，則是要再加上介系詞 across，成為 walk across the street。

__D__ 2. Roger is very _____ . He doesn't care about his friends and family.

羅傑非常自私。他不在乎他的朋友和家人。

(A) greedy 貪婪　　　　(B) warm 溫暖

(C) jealous 嫉妒　　　　(D) selfish 自私

__D__ 3. I marked my doctor's visit on the _____ so I wouldn't forget to go.

我在日曆上註記了醫生看診的時間，以免忘記。

(A) memory 記憶　　　　(B) program 節目

(C) notebook 筆記本　　(D) calendar 日曆

__A__ 4. I have no _____ after cleaning the whole house from top to bottom.

從頭到尾打掃整個房子之後，我已經沒有力氣了。

(A) energy 精力　　　　(B) motion 運動

(C) youth 青春　　　　(D) waste 浪費

> **解析** 由後半部 whole house「整棟房子」與 from top to bottom「從頭到尾」，可得知是全部清理乾淨，所以沒力氣，選項 A 正確。

__B__ 5. Please put the flowers in a _____ and don't forget to add some water.

請把花放在花瓶裡，別忘了加點水。

(A) lamp 燈　　　　　　(B) vase 花瓶

(C) course 課程　　　　(D) napkin 餐巾

__C__ 6. My dad always drinks black coffee, but it's too _____ for me.

我爸爸總是喝黑咖啡，但對我來說太苦了。

(A) sweet 甜

(B) spicy 辣

(C) bitter 苦

(D) thick 濃

__D__ 7. Jane said she would _____ for my birthday party, but she never came.

珍說她會出現在我的生日派對，但她最後卻沒有來。

(A) wake up 醒來

(B) get up 起床

(C) dress up 打扮

(D) show up 出現

__A__ 8. The swimming pool is only available for use by club _____ .

游泳池只對俱樂部的會員開放。

(A) members 會員

(B) passengers 乘客

(C) servants 僕人

(D) individuals 個人

__A__ 9. Traffic was heavy this morning, so it took me _____ to get to work than usual.

今天早上交通壅塞，所以我花了比平常更久的時間才到達工作地點。

(A) longer 更長

(B) slower 更慢

(C) quicker 更快

(D) faster 更快速

> **解析** 花時間的用法為「It takes 人 + 時間長度 + to V...」。而由句首得知交通壅塞，因此是花了更長的時間，選項 A 正確。

__B__ 10. My parents are going to Thailand for vacation this year, but I won't be _____ them.

我的父母今年要去泰國度假，但我不會和他們一起去。

(A) inventing 發明

(B) joining 加入

(C) booking 預定

(D) reminding 提醒

Part 2 段落填空

第二部分　段落填空

共 8 題，包括二個段落，每個段落含四個空格。每格均有四個選項，請依照文意選出最適合的答案。

Questions 11-14

When I was a high school student, I always struggled with math. It was my ____(11)____ subject in school, and I always had trouble understanding it. However, I never gave up and kept ____(12)____. Miss Miller was very patient and always encouraged me. She ____(13)____ me that it's all right to make mistakes and that's how we learn. She helped me become more confident and I slowly started to improve. Miss Miller was the first person ____(14)____ my interest in math.

當我是高中生時，我總是在數學上遇到困難。這是我在學校裡 **(11) 最弱**的科目，我總是很難理解它。然而，我從未放棄，並持續 **(12) 練習**。米勒老師非常有耐心，總是鼓勵我。她 **(13) 告訴**我，犯錯是正常的，而我們就是這樣學習的。她幫助我變得更有自信，我慢慢開始進步。米勒老師是第一個 **(14) 啟發**我對數學的興趣的人。

____C____ 11. (A) strongest 最強　　　　(B) hardest 最難
　　　　　(C) weakest 最弱　　　　(D) easiest 最容易

> **解析** 由第一句 struggle with math 在數學上掙扎學習，還有空格後 had trouble understanding 理解有問題，可得知是最弱的科目，選項 C 正確。Hardest 只能表達門科目很難，但未必是成績差。

____C____ 12. (A) considering 考慮　　　(B) solving 解決
　　　　　(C) practicing 練習　　　(D) swallowing 吞嚥

____B____ 13. (A) talked 談論　　　　　(B) told 告訴
　　　　　(C) said 說　　　　　　(D) spoke 說話

> **解析** Tell 後可以直接加人做受詞。Talk, say, speak 後都要加 to 再加受詞。

__D__ 14. (A) inspired 啟發了　　　　　　(B) that inspire 啟發

(C) would inspire 將要啟發　　　(D) to inspire 啟發

> **解析** 空格前的 first person 表示了第一的順序，因此要用 to V 不定詞來說明序數詞後的主要動作。

Questions 15-18

Karen was so ____(15)____ with her cousin, Eric. She asked him to take care of her cat while she was away ____(16)____ a trip, but he forgot to feed it. When she came back, her cat was very skinny and sick. Karen was so angry ____(17)____ she didn't want to talk to Eric. However, Eric felt really bad and decided to do ____(18)____ to make up for it. So he bought Karen a new bed for her cat. Karen was very surprised and happy. She forgave Eric and thanked him for the gift.

凱倫對她的表哥艾瑞克感到非常 **(15) 生氣**。她請他在她外出 **(16) 旅途中**照顧她的貓，但他忘了餵貓。當她回來時，她的貓非常瘦弱而且病懨懨。凱倫非常生氣 **(17) 因此**她不想和艾瑞克說話。然而，艾瑞克感到非常難過，決定做 **(18) 某事**來彌補這件事。所以他為凱倫的貓買了一個新床。凱倫非常驚訝和高興。她原諒了艾瑞克，並感謝他的禮物。

__A__ 15. (A) angry 生氣　　　　　　　(B) happy 高興

(C) sad 傷心　　　　　　　　(D) surprised 驚訝

__B__ 16. (A) in 在內　　　　　　　　(B) on 在上

(C) at 在　　　　　　　　　　(D) by 藉由

> **解析** 與 trip 共用的介系詞是 on a trip，意為在旅途中，選項 B 正確。

__B__ 17. (A) when 當　　　　　　　　(B) that 因此

(C) then 然後　　　　　　　(D) while 在…期間

> **解析** 空格前有 "so angry"，後有 S+V 結構 "she didn't want..."，可推知是用 "so adj./adv that S+V" 作為強調句型，選項 B 正確。

__C__ 18. (A) nothing 什麼都沒有　　(B) everything 一切
　　　　(C) something 某事　　　　(D) anything 任何事情

解析 空格後的 make up for 是補償…之意，可推知艾瑞克是要做些事情來讓凱倫原諒他。而下一句提到買了貓床，為一件補償的作法，因此 C 選項的 something 正確。

共 12 題，包括 4 個題組，每個題組含 1 至 2 篇短文，與數個相關的四選一的選擇題。請由試題上的選項中選出最適合的答案。

Questions 19-21

Read the following department store directory.

Subject: Welcome to Our New Factory!

Dec 10, 2024

Dear Team,

Exciting news! Our new factory opened on December 9, 2024!

I know you can't wait to work in the newly-completed sports equipment factory. I can't either, and I will give you a tour of our new factory at 2 p.m. tomorrow. However, before the tour, please read the warning notice that is posted outside of the factory entrance. Be sure to obey all the safety rules when inside the factory. Thank you for your attention.

Let's make our new factory safe and successful!

Best regards,

Frank Smith

Factory Manager

主題：歡迎來到我們的新工廠！

2024 年 12 月 10 日

親愛的團隊，

令人振奮的消息！我們的新工廠已於 2024 年 12 月 9 日啟動！

(20) 我知道你們迫不及待地想在新建好的運動器材工廠工作。我也是，我會在明天下午 2 點帶各位參觀我們的新工廠。(19) 不過，在參觀之前，請閱讀工廠入口處張貼的警告通知。請確保在工廠內遵守所有安全規則。感謝你的關注。

我們一起來讓新工廠安全又成功！

最好的祝福，

法蘭克·史密斯

工廠經理

Warning Notice

*No running inside the factory.

*Always wear a helmet and gloves for protection.

*Read the handbook before operating any machine, and make sure you follow each step in the handbook.

*Don't touch any machine you don't know how to operate.

*Press the emergency button if anything goes wrong.

警告通知

* 工廠內禁止跑步。

* 請務必隨時戴著頭盔和手套保護安全。

* 在操作任何機器之前，請閱讀說明手冊，並確定遵循手冊中的每一步。

(21) * 不要觸碰任何你不知如何操作的機器。

* 如果發生任何問題，按下緊急按鈕。

D   19. What's the main purpose of Frank Smith's email?

(A) To introduce the team's new members.

(B) To share the launch date with his team.

(C) To tell the workers about a factory tour.

(D) To ask team members to read a notice.

法蘭克・史密斯的電子郵件主要目的為何？

(A) 介紹團隊的新成員。

(B) 與團隊分享推出日期。

(C) 告知工人有參觀工廠的活動。

(D) 要求團隊成員閱讀通知。

解析　由第一篇內文的第六、七句得知，在告知新工廠資訊後，重點在於要工廠從業人員閱讀通知，目的是要他們遵守規範，因此選項 D 正確。

C   20. Who is the email for?

(A) Other managers

(B) All office workers

(C) New factory workers

(D) Sports team members

這封電子郵件是寫給誰的？

(A) 其他經理

(B) 所有辦公室員工

(C) 新工廠工人

(D) 運動隊成員

解析　由第一篇內文的第四句得知，人們會迫不及待的在新工廠裡工作，可推知他們應是工廠工人，選項 C 正確。

C   21. According to the warning notice, what is true about working in the factory?

(A) Workers can skip a few steps in order to speed things up.

(B) Helmets and gloves can keep workers from all dangers.

(C) People can only operate machines they know how to use.

(D) Experienced workers aren't required to read the handbook.

根據警告通知，有關在工廠工作，以下哪一項是正確的？

(A) 工人可以跳過幾個步驟以加快速度。

(B) 頭盔和手套可以保護工人免於所有危險。

(C) 人們只能操作他們知道如何使用的機器。

(D) 有經驗的工人不需要閱讀手冊。

解析　由第二篇的倒數第二項得知，不要碰不懂的操作的機器，因此選項 C 正確。第二項雖提到要戴頭盔和手套來保護，但並無提到如此可以預防所有的危險，因此不符合。

Questions 22-24

Westminster, a busy area in London, is home to Buckingham Palace. Another famous sight is the Palace of Westminster, where you'll find Elizabeth Tower, better known as **Big Ben**. The chime of the bells in this clock tower can be heard from miles away. Just west of the palace is Westminster Abbey, a historic church where many English kings and queens have been crowned. In addition to sights like the Abbey, Westminster also has many museums, theaters, art galleries and restaurants for visitors to enjoy. It truly has something for everyone. And to the north, not far from Westminster, is Oxford Street, which is known as Europe's busiest shopping street. If you ever come to London, make sure to pay a visit to Westminster!

倫敦的繁忙地區西敏市，是白金漢宮的所在地。另一個著名景點是西敏宮，你可以在那裡找到伊麗莎白塔，其更廣為人知的名字是大笨鐘。**(22) 這座塔樓的鐘聲可以從數英里外聽到。(23) 宮殿西邊就是西敏寺，這是一座歷史悠久的教堂，許多英國國王和王后都在此加冕。**除了像教堂這樣的景點外，西敏市還有許多博物館、劇院、藝術畫廊和餐廳供遊客享受。**(24) 在那裡每個人都有可以從事的活動。**離西敏市北邊不遠處是牛津街，這是歐洲最繁忙的購物街。如果你來到倫敦，一定要去西敏市旅遊！

____B____ 22. What is Big Ben?

(A) A clock

(B) A tower

(C) A church

(D) A chime

大笨鐘是什麼？

(A) 一個鐘錶

(B) 一座塔樓

(C) 一間教堂

(D) 一個鐘聲

解析　根據第三句 "The chime of the bells in this clock tower can be heard from miles away." 可得知大笨鐘是個 tower（塔樓）。

C 23. What can visitors do at Westminster Abby?

(A) Have a nice dinner.

(B) Watch a play.

(C) Learn about history.

(D) Do some shopping.

遊客在西敏寺可以做什麼？

(A) 享用美味晚餐。

(B) 觀看戲劇。

(C) 了解歷史。

(D) 購物。

解析 第四句得知，西敏寺歷史悠久，許多英國國王和王后都在這裡加冕，因此遊客可以在那裡學習歷史。選項 C 正確。

B 24. Which would be the best title for this article?

(A) *Westminster, Europe's Busiest Shopping*

(B) *Westminster, Something for Everyone*

(C) *The Historic Palace of Westminster*

(D) *Westminster, Home of Kings and Queens*

這篇文章最適合哪個標題？

(A) 西敏市，歐洲最繁忙的購物城市

(B) 西敏市，人人都能樂在其中

(C) 歷史悠久的西敏宮

(D) 西敏市，國王和王后的家

解析 文章討論了各種景點，包括白金漢宮、西敏寺、博物館、劇院、畫廊和餐廳，再由倒數第三句 "It truly has something for everyone." 得知，在那裡每個人都有可以從事的活動，因此選項 B 正確。

Questions 25-27

Do you know that the liver, one of our body's most important organs, has an amazing ability to regrow? When the liver gets hurt or a part of it is taken out, it can repair itself and grow back. This ability is called liver regrowth.

The liver is made up of tiny cells called hepatocytes. These cells are like little factories that can produce new liver tissue. When the liver gets damaged, these cells start working hard to fix it. They divide and grow, gradually making the liver whole again.

The fact that our livers can regrow provides hope for people with liver disease. Understanding how the liver repairs itself could **lead to** new treatments, and possibly even the ability to create whole new livers.

(25) 你知道肝臟是我們身體中最重要的器官之一，它有著驚人的再生能力嗎？當肝臟受傷或部分被切除時，它能夠自我修復並重新生長。這種能力被稱為肝臟再生。

肝臟由稱為肝細胞的小細胞組成。**(26)** 這些細胞就像小工廠，可以生產新的肝組織。當肝臟受損時，這些細胞會努力工作來修復它。**(26)** 它們分裂然後增生，逐漸使肝臟恢復完整。

我們的肝臟能夠再生這一事實，為患有肝病的人們帶來了希望。**(26) (27)** 理解肝臟如何自我修復可能可以引領新的治療方法，甚至有可能創造出全新的肝臟。

D 25. According to the article, which is true?

(A) Everything in our body can regrow.

(B) You can get a new liver at the hospital.

(C) There are factories that can make livers.

(D) A liver can grow back when it's damaged.

根據文章，哪一項正確？

(A) 我們身體的一切都能再生。

(B) 你可以在醫院獲得新的肝臟。

(C) 有工廠可以製造肝臟。

(D) 肝臟在受損時可以再生。

解析 第一段第一和二句提到肝臟可以在受損時再生。因此選項 D 正確。

B 26. What function of hepatocytes is mentioned?

(A) Removing waste from the blood

(B) Producing new liver tissue

(C) Creating whole new livers

(D) Curing liver disease

文章提到肝細胞的哪項功能？

(A) 從血液中去除廢物

(B) 產生新的肝組織

(C) 創造全新的肝臟

(D) 治療肝病

解析 第二段第二句提到小細胞可以生產新的肝組織。第二段最後一句提到小細胞能使逐漸使肝臟恢復完整，但沒有提到可以創造全新的肝臟。最後一段最後一句也是指未來有可能發生的事，並非現在就會發生。所以選項 B 最符合。

__B__ 27. Which is closest in meaning to the phrase "lead to"?
(A) start
(B) cause
(C) solve
(D) depend

"lead to"一詞最接近的意思是？
(A) 開始
(B) 導致
(C) 解決
(D) 依賴

解析 lead to 之前提到了解肝臟修復，之後提及新的療法，兩個應是因果關係。所以選項 B 的「造成」，「導致」最符合。

Questions 28-30

My name is Connie and I'm from Korea. I came to England to study English. I'm staying with a host family in London. I share a room with my roommate, Giorgia, who is from Italy. Giorgia makes **panna cotta** every weekend, and thanks to her, I've started to fall in love with desserts. Although Giorgia and I go to the same English language school, we're in different classes. I was placed in a higher level class because I've been studying English for over ten years. Giorgia wasn't really serious about learning English until recently.

I only have classes in the morning, but Giorgia has to stay at school until three o'clock in the afternoon. While waiting for her, I usually go to the library or the campus café. Once Giorgia finishes, we head back home together, often stopping by Tesco to buy breakfast food for the next day. We spend a lot of time together even though we don't always understand each other. I really enjoy having her as a friend. She makes this place feel like a home away from home.

我叫康妮，來自韓國。我來英格蘭學習英文。我在倫敦住在寄宿家庭。我和我的室友喬琪亞共用一個房間，她來自義大利。**(28) 喬琪亞每個週末都會做奶油糖凍，多虧了她，我開始愛上了甜點。**雖然喬琪亞和我都在同一間英語學校學習，但我們卻不同班。因為我學英文超過十年，所以我被安排在更高級的班級。喬琪亞直到最近才真正認真學習英文。

我只在早上有課，但喬琪亞要在學校待到下午三點。在等她的時候，我通常會去圖書館或校園咖啡館。**(29) 喬琪亞下課後，我們一起回家，經常會順路去特易購買第二天的早餐食品。**雖然我們不能總是能了解對方，但我們花了很多時間相處。**(30) 我真的很高興和她做朋友。她讓這個地方像家一樣舒適。**

<table>
<tr><td>_D_</td><td>28. What is "panna cotta"?</td><td>奶油糖凍是什麼？</td></tr>
</table>

D 28. What is "panna cotta"?

    (A) A drink

    (B) A pasta

    (C) A snack

    (D) A dessert

奶油糖凍是什麼？

    (A) 一種飲料

    (B) 一種義大利麵

    (C) 一種小吃

    (D) 一種甜點

解析 文章第一段第五句提到因為喬琪亞，康妮開始愛上甜點，可得知這是一種甜點，選項 D 正確。

A 29. What do Connie and Giorgia do in the afternoon?

    (A) They go shopping at a supermarket.

    (B) They spend time studying at the library.

    (C) They both have classes in the afternoon.

    (D) They have coffee together at a coffee shop.

康妮和喬琪亞下午做什麼？

    (A) 他們在超市購物。

    (B) 他們在圖書館學習。

    (C) 他們下午都有課。

    (D) 他們在咖啡店一起喝咖啡。

解析 由第二段第三句 Once Giorgia finishes, we head back home together, often stopping by Tesco to buy breakfast food for the next day. 得知，他們會一起去購買食物，其他選項不正確，故選 A。

D 30. How does Connie feel about staying in England?

(A) She misses her family and friends back in Korea.

(B) She likes her host family and her classmates a lot.

(C) She is happy because she has made lots of friends.

(D) She enjoys her time there because of her roommate.

康妮對在英格蘭的生活感受如何？

(A) 她想念在韓國的家人和朋友。

(B) 她非常喜歡她的寄宿家庭和同學。

(C) 她很高興因為她交了很多朋友。

(D) 因為她的室友，她享受在那裡的時光。

解析 文章第二段倒數兩句可得知她喜歡和室友相處，並且有回家的感覺，因此是享受在那裡的時光。因此選項 D 正確。

GEPT
初級模擬試題
第7回
解答、翻譯與詳解

第 7 回解答

🔊 聽力測驗解答

1. A	2. B	3. C	4. A	5. B
6. A	7. B	8. B	9. A	10. C
11. C	12. B	13. C	14. B	15. A
16. A	17. C	18. A	19. B	20. B
21. C	22. A	23. C	24. A	25. C
26. A	27. B	28. A	29. A	30. C

閱讀測驗解答

1. C	2. D	3. A	4. C	5. B
6. D	7. A	8. B	9. B	10. C
11. B	12. B	13. A	14. D	15. B
16. D	17. C	18. C	19. C	20. A
21. B	22. A	23. D	24. C	25. B
26. D	27. C	28. A	29. D	30. D

第一部分　看圖辨義

__A__ 1. For Question Number 1, please look at the picture.

What is the woman doing?

(A) The woman is making the bed.

(B) The woman is mopping the floor.

(C) The woman is cleaning the window.

第一題，請看此圖片。

女子正在做什麼？

(A) 女子正在鋪床。

(B) 女子正在拖地。

(C) 女子正在清潔窗戶。

解析　片語："make the bed" 是「整理床鋪」「鋪床」的意思。圖片中的女子正在鋪床，因此答案為 A。

__B__ 2. For Question Number 2, please look at the picture.

What's going on?

(A) The child is sleeping deeply.

(B) There's a mosquito flying around.

(C) The child is dreaming about a mosquito.

第二題，請看此圖片。

發生什麼事？

(A) 小孩正在熟睡。

(B) 有一隻蚊子在飛來飛去。

(C) 小孩做了蚊子的夢。

解析　圖片中的小孩雖然在床上，但眼睛是睜開的，所以選項 A 和選項 C 皆不正確。圖片中有蚊子和飛來飛去的圖示，因此答案為選項 B。

__C__ 3. For Question Number 3, please look at the picture.
What can we learn from the sign?

(A) The machine is out of oil.

(B) The machine needs to be repaired.

(C) The machine must be used carefully.

第三題，請看此圖片。

從這個標誌我們可以知道什麼？

(A) 機器沒油了。

(B) 機器需要修理。

(C) 機器必須小心使用。

解析 從標誌上的英文字 "Danger"（危險）可以知道這台機器比較危險，使用時要小心，因此選 C。

__A__ 4. For Question Number 4, please look at the picture.
What are the students doing?

(A) They are building a fire.

(B) They are visiting a castle.

(C) They are setting up a tent.

第四題，請看此圖片。

這兩個學生在做什麼？

(A) 他們在生火。

(B) 他們在參觀城堡。

(C) 他們在搭帳篷。

解析 圖片中可以看到帳篷 (tent) 和火堆 (fire)，帳篷已經搭好，兩個人正在放木頭進入火堆，因此知道答案為 A。

__B__ 5. For Question Number 5, please look at the picture.

What is this?

(A) It's a menu.

(B) It's a notice.

(C) It's a calendar.

Lost and Found

Did you lose something important?
Please tell the lost and found office.
We will try to give lost things
back to their owners.

第五題，請看此圖片。

這是什麼？

(A) 菜單。

(B) 公告。

(C) 月曆。

解析 圖片上沒有價格也沒有告知日期的數字，因此選項 A 和選項 C 皆不正確。圖片上英文中譯如下：「失物招領：你有遺失重要的東西嗎？請洽失物招領辦公室。我們會將失物歸還原主。」答案為選項 B。

__A__ 6. Have you read this book before?

(A) Yes, a long time ago.

(B) Yes, I'll read it tomorrow.

(C) No, but I did last semester.

你讀過這本書嗎？

(A) 有，很久之前。

(B) 會，我明天會讀。

(C) 沒有，不過我上學期讀過。

解析 完成式 (Have/Has...) 開頭的問句可用來問過去經驗。選項 B 答案為未來式，所以不正確，選項 C 簡答和詳答的內容相互矛盾也不正確，因此答案為選項 A。

__B__ 7. When will the next train come?

(A) On platform 2.

(B) In five minutes.

(C) Yes, it's coming soon.

下一班火車什麼時候來？

(A) 2 號月台。

(B) 5 分鐘後。

(C) 是的，快要來了。

解析 用 When（何時）開頭的問句回答時要回答時間。只有選項 B 的答案是時間，其餘兩選項皆不正確。

__B__ 8. How would you like your steak?

(A) It was delicious.

(B) Medium, please.

(C) I enjoyed my stay.

你的牛排要幾分熟？

(A) 很好吃。

(B) 五分熟。

(C) 我住得很開心。

解析 詢問牛排幾分熟時的固定問法為題目的 "How would you like your steak?" 答案可以是 rare（三分熟）、medium（五分熟）或是 well done（全熟）。steak 和 stay 的發音相近，請注意尾音。

__A__ 9. How much coffee do we have left?

(A) Two bags.

(B) Twenty-five dollars.

(C) It's expensive.

我們還剩多少咖啡？

(A) 兩包。

(B) 二十五元。

(C) 很貴。

解析 coffee（咖啡）為不可數名詞，詢問「數量」時使用 "How much...?" 的句型。詢問價錢也是用 "How much...?" 但句子會是 "How much is the coffee?" 三個選項中只有選項 A 有針對「數量」回答到問題，其餘皆答非所問。

__C__ 10. I don't know if we can be there on time.

(A) As soon as they arrive.

(B) It's OK. Just take turns.

(C) Don't worry. The people can wait.

我不知道我們能不能準時到達。

(A) 他們一到的時候。

(B) 沒關係。輪流就好。

(C) 別擔心。大家會等。

解析 說話者擔心無法準時到達，選項 C 針對說話者的擔心做出回應，為正確答案。其餘兩個選項皆答非所問。

__C__ 11. Do you know what we're doing in class today?

(A) The teacher will be late.

(B) We watched a short film.

(C) I think we're having a quiz.

你知道我們今天上課要做什麼嗎？

(A) 老師會遲到。

(B) 我們看了一部短片。

(C) 我想我們會有小考。

解析 針對題目中「要做什麼…」回答的只有選項 C，選項 B 為過去式所以答非所問，選項 A 和要做的事情無關，因此答案選 C。

__B__ 12. I'll finish my report before Nancy visits next month.

(A) I didn't know she was writing a report.

(B) Good. She'll need it right when she arrives.

(C) Yes. It took her a month to finish the report.

我會在南西下個月來訪前完成我的報告。

(A) 我不知道她在寫報告。

(B) 很好。她到達的時候會需要它。

(C) 是的。她花了一個月的時間完成報告。

解析 寫報告的人為題目中的說話者，而非南西，因此選項 A 和選項 C 皆不正確，答案為選項 B。

__C__ 13. All of us love your work.

(A) Yes, I love to work very much.

(B) Congratulations. It's such an honor.

(C) Thanks. It took me three months to finish.

我們所有人都很喜歡你的作品。

(A) 是的，我非常喜歡工作。

(B) 恭喜。這真是一份榮譽。

(C) 謝謝。我花了三個月的時間才完成。

解析 選項 A 答非所問，選項 B 的「恭喜」不符合對話邏輯，只有選項 C 針對說話者的稱讚表達感謝，並提供更多的相關資訊，因此為正確答案。

__B__ 14. It's time for math class.

(A) I don't know what time it is.

(B) Oh, no. It's my worst subject.

(C) Math class is at eleven o'clock.

數學課的時間到囉！

(A) 我不知道現在是幾點。

(B) 噢，不。這是我最不擅長的科目。

(C) 數學課是在十一點。

解析 "It's time for..." 常用來宣布「…的時間到了」像是 "It's time for lunch."（吃午餐囉！）跟幾點沒有關係，因此選項 A 和選項 C 皆不正確。只有選項 B 的回應符合對話邏輯。

__A__ 15. Can I keep a pet, Mom?

(A) Well, it's a lot of work.

(B) Sure, you can use my pen.

(C) I told you not to pet the dog.

媽媽，我可以養寵物嗎？

(A) 嗯，那很費工夫。

(B) 當然可以，你可以用我的筆。

(C) 跟你說過不要摸狗。

解析 注意 "pen" 跟 "pet" 字尾的發音。選項 B 的 "pen" 為誤導。選項 C 的 "pet" 為動詞，有輕拍的意思，和題目中養寵物的問題無關，因此也不正確。正確答案為選項 A。

__A__ 16. W: Did you eat the sandwich in the refrigerator?

M: No, it wasn't me. I think it was Jessie.

W: Oh, no! I forgot to tell you guys not to eat it, because I ate the other half and got a stomachache.

M: Good thing I didn't eat it then.

Question: What probably happened?

女子：冰箱裡的三明治你吃掉了嗎？

男子：沒有，不是我。我想是潔西吧。

女子：喔，不好了！我忘了告訴你們不要吃，因為我吃了另一半結果肚子痛。

男子：還好我沒吃。

問題：可能發生了什麼事？

(A) Jessie had a stomachache.

(B) The woman made the sandwich.

(C) The man told Jessie to eat it.

(A) 潔西胃痛。

(B) 女子製作了三明治。

(C) 男子告訴潔西不要吃。

解析 因為女子說明自己吃了一半的三明治後胃痛，而傑西吃了另外一半，因此可以推測傑西可能也有因為吃了三明治後胃痛，答案為選項 A。

__C__ 17. G: Dad, I'm terrible at learning languages.

M: Why do you say that?

G: I can't speak Spanish well. And I've studied it for three years.

M: Ha-ha. Don't feel bad. I've studied Japanese my whole life and I still can't speak it.

Question: Which is true?

女孩：爸爸，我很不擅長學習語言。

男子：為什麼這麼說？

女孩：我西班牙語說得不好。我都已經學了三年了。

男子：哈哈，別難過。我一輩子都在學日語，但還是不會說。

問題：以下何者為真？

(A) Spanish is more difficult than Japanese.

(B) The father lived in Japan for many years.

(C) The father and daughter have the same problem.

(A) 西班牙語比日語難。

(B) 男子在日本住了很多年。

(C) 父親和女兒有相同的問題。

解析 對話中的父親和女兒討論的是學習外語時遇到的難處，對日文與西班牙語的難度沒有做比較，父親也沒有提到自己住在日本，因此只有選項 C 符合對話內容，為正確答案。

A 18. W: I really like our teacher, Miss Ou.

M: So do I. What do you like about her?

W: She really cares about us. Not only our studies but also our lives.

M: I think so too. We're so lucky to have her as a teacher.

Question: What are the students talking about?

女子：我真的很喜歡我們的老師，歐老師。

男子：我也是。你喜歡她的哪些地方？

女子：她很關心我們。不只是學業，還有我們的生活。

男子：我也這麼覺得。我們真幸運能有她當老師。

問題：學生們在談論什麼？

(A) The reason they like their teacher.

(B) The teaching methods Miss Ou uses.

(C) How much they like their former teacher.

(A) 他們喜歡老師的原因。

(B) 歐老師使用的教學方法。

(C) 他們有多喜歡以前的老師。

解析 從男子的提問 "What do you like about her?" 可以知道兩人在討論喜歡老師的原因。因為整段對話為現在式，所以知道是現在的老師。答案為選項 A。

B 19. W: What's your favorite film?

M: My favorite film? I'd have to say Titanic.

W: What's that? I've never heard of it.

M: What? You must be kidding. It's a classic. Let me lend you the DVD.

Question: What does the man want the woman to do?

女子：你最喜歡的電影是什麼？

男子：我最喜歡的電影？我得說是《鐵達尼號》。

女子：那是什麼？我從來沒聽說過。

男子：什麼？你一定在開玩笑。這部可是經典。我借你 DVD。

問題：男子想要女子做什麼？

(A) Read a story.

(B) Watch a movie.

(C) Go to a movie theater

(A) 讀個故事。

(B) 看電影。

(C) 去電影院。

解析 對話從討論最喜歡的電影開始，從男子 "Let me lend you the DVD." 可以知道他想要女子看他提到的那部電影，選 B。

B 20. W: Is Tina OK?

M: What do you mean? We haven't talked for days.

W: You don't know? Her grandmother passed away.

M: Oh, really? I feel so bad for her.

Question: What happened to Tina?

女子：提娜還好嗎？

男子：什麼意思？我們已經好幾天沒說話了。

女子：你不知道嗎？她奶奶過世了。

男子：哦，真的嗎？我為她感到難過。

問題：提娜發生了什麼事？

(A) Her grandma visited her.

(B) A member of her family died.

(C) Tina doesn't like the man anymore.

(A) 她奶奶來探望她。

(B) 她家人去世了。

(C) 提娜不再喜歡這名男子。

解析 過世可以直接說 die（死去）或是 pass away（去世），由女子對話中提到 "Her grandmother passed away." 可以知道答案為選項 B。

C 21. M: Hey, don't sit on that chair.

W: Why not?

M: One of the legs is broken. Look!

W: Oh, thanks. I could've hurt myself.

Question: What did the man do?

男子：嘿，別坐那把椅子。

女子：為什麼？

男子：其中一個椅腳斷了。你看！

女子：哦，謝謝。我差點就害自己受傷了。

問題：男子做了什麼？

(A) He fixed the broken chair leg.

(B) He broke his leg on the chair.

(C) He told the woman about a danger.

(A) 他修好了斷裂的椅腳。

(B) 他在坐椅子時摔斷腿。

(C) 他告知女子有危險。

解析 男子提醒女子椅腳斷裂不要坐在椅子上，男子並沒有將椅腳修好，自己也沒有因此受傷，因此答案為 C。

A 22. W: Oh, no! My phone isn't working.

M: What happened?

W: I dropped it on the street when I was running to catch the bus.

M: Hmm, there's a big crack here, and the screen is dead. You could try to get it fixed, but it'll probably be cheaper to get a new one.

Question: What will the woman likely do?

女子：哦，不好了！我的手機壞了。

男子：怎麼了？

女子：我在追公車的時候，把它摔在路上了。

男子：嗯，這裡有一個大裂縫，螢幕也沒反應了。你可以試著修修看，但買一支新的可能會比較便宜。

問題：女子可能會做什麼？

(A) Buy a new phone.　　　　　　　　(A) 買一支新手機。

(B) Keep using her phone.　　　　　　(B) 繼續使用她的手機。

(C) Have a cheap repair done.　　　　(C) 以便宜的價格維修。

解析　由對話內容可以知道手機已經壞掉，所以不可能是選項 B，而男子的對話
"...it'll probably be cheaper to get a new one." 知道維修應該不便宜，買新手
機比較划算，所以知道選項 C 也不可能，答案為選項 A。

C　23. M: This is my favorite restaurant in the neighborhood.

W: Really? I went there last month. I wouldn't say it's great, but it's not bad either.

M: What did you order?

W: My husband ordered the salmon, and I got a tuna sandwich.

M: Oh, you should try their special--fried chicken.

Question: What does the man think?

男子：這是我在附近最喜歡的餐廳。

女子：真的嗎？我上個月去過。我不會說它很棒，但也不差。

男子：你點了什麼？

女子：我丈夫點了鮭魚，我點了一個鮪魚三明治。

男子：哦，你應該試試他們的拿手菜──炸雞。

問題：男子怎麼想？

(A) The fish dishes are better than the chicken dishes.

(B) He thinks the woman is right about the restaurant.

(C) The woman should give the restaurant another chance.

(A) 魚的料理比雞肉料理好吃。

(B) 他認為女子對餐廳的看法是正確的。

(C) 女子應該再給餐廳一個機會。

解析　女子對餐廳的評價還好，不像男子那麼喜歡這間餐廳。從男子最後一句話 "You
should try their special--fried chicken." 可以知道答案為選項 C。

A 24. W: Could you hold the door open for me?

M: Oh, Kelly. It's you! What happened to your leg?

W: Long story short. I had a car accident and broke my leg.

M: Does it still hurt?

W: No, I feel much better now. The doctor said I'll recover fully within four months.

Question: What will happen to Kelly?

女子：你能幫我把門撐住嗎？

男子：哦，凱莉。是你啊！妳的腿怎麼了？

女子：長話短說，我出車禍把腿摔斷了。

男子：還痛嗎？

女子：不痛了，現在好多了。醫生說我會在四個月內完全康復。

問題：凱莉會怎麼樣？

(A) She'll be able to walk again.	(A) 她會能夠再次行走。
(B) She'll be in pain for months.	(B) 她會痛好幾個月。
(C) Her leg will never get better.	(C) 她的腿永遠不會好轉。

解析 從對話中可以知道凱莉的腿已經不痛，而且四個月後會完全康復，因此答案為選項 A。

C 25. G: Dad said that he'll be home late today. So we have to make our own dinner.

B: Does that mean I'll have to eat the food you cook again?

G: I'm afraid so. I guess I'll make boiled vegetables again.

B: Can we just order something from a restaurant?

Question: Why did the girl say "I'm afraid so"?

女孩：爸爸說他今天會晚回家。所以我們必須自己做晚餐。

男孩：意思是我得吃妳煮的菜？

女孩：恐怕是的。我應該還是會煮水煮蔬菜。

男孩：我們能不能直接從餐廳訂餐點？

問題：女孩為什麼說「恐怕是的」？

(A) She's afraid to cook dinner.

(B) She's scared of her brother.

(C) She isn't a good cook.

(A) 她怕做菜。

(B) 她怕她的兄弟。

(C) 她不是很會做菜。

解析 "I'm afraid so." 表示 "Yes." 但帶有抱歉或遺憾，不是真的「害怕」，所以選項 A 和選項 B 都不正確，答案為選項 C。

(A)　　　　　　　(B)　　　　　　　(C)

__A__ 26. For question number 26, please look at the three pictures.

A teacher is speaking about a rule. What are the students required to do?

Remember to wash your hands before you eat. Your hands may look clean, but there are bacteria that we can't see. When you eat a meal without washing your hands, the bacteria on your hands can get in your mouth and give you a stomachache.

第 26 題，請看三張圖片。

一位老師正在說明規定。學生們需要做什麼？

記得在用餐前洗手。你的手或許看起來很乾淨，但細菌是我們看不見的。如果你在飯前不洗手，手上的細菌可能會進入你的嘴裡，讓你肚子痛。

解析　談話主要在說明飯前洗手的重要性，因此答案為選項 A。

(A)　　　　　　　(B)　　　　　　　(C)

__B__ 27. For question number 27, please look at the three pictures.

Listen to the radio ad. What tickets are being sold?

Tickets to the Korean Pop Music Concert are available now. You'll get to hear all the popular K-pop songs and see all your favorite Korean pop stars live. Visit our website and get your tickets while they last. Don't miss this chance to join us for a night to remember!

第 27 題，請看三張圖片。

請聽廣播廣告。正在販售什麼門票？

韓國流行音樂演唱會的門票已經開始販售。您將聽到所有熱門的韓流歌曲，並現場欣賞您喜愛的韓國流行歌手。請上我們的網站，即時購票。不要錯過這個難得的機會，與我們一同度過難忘的夜晚！

解析　由關鍵詞 K-pop songs（韓國流行歌曲）、Korean pop stars（韓國流行歌手）可以知道答案為選項 B。

(A)　　　　　　(B)　　　　　　(C)

__A__ 28. For question number 28, please look at the three pictures.

Listen to the talk. Who do you think is the speaker?

Which hand do you use more often? Your left or your right? According to a study, about 90 percent of the people are right-handers, which means only 10 percent of the people prefer using their left hand. There is no right or wrong about it. What people should do is respect those who are different from them.

第 28 題，請看三張圖片。

請聽以下演說。你認為講話者是哪位？

Part 4 短文聽解

你比較常使用哪隻手？你的左手還是右手？根據研究表示，大約有 90% 的人是右撇子，這意味著只有 10% 的人比較喜歡使用左手。這沒有對錯。大家應該尊重那些與自己不同的人。

解析 雖然談話中有提及研究，讓人感覺選項 B 醫生也有可能。但因為談話最後提及彼此尊重，所以選項 A 的老師是更好的選項。答案為 A。

(A)　　　　　　　(B)　　　　　　　(C)

__A__ 29. For question number 29, please look at the three pictures.

Listen to the talk. Where would you most likely hear it?

On the right is a famous museum. Around seven to eight million people visit it each year. On the left is a well-known bridge where you can find a lot of locks. They're put there by couples wishing for their love to last forever.

第 29 題，請看三張圖片。

請聽以下談話。在哪裡最有可能聽到這段談話？

右邊是一家著名的博物館。每年大約有七到八百萬人到訪。左邊是一座知名的橋樑，您可以在上面看到很多的鎖。這些鎖是由希望他們的愛情永恆的情侶們所放置的。

解析 這段談話內容為觀光導覽。選項 B 的場景在森林，選項 C 在大海中央，表示可能在船上，兩者的周圍都不會出現 museum（博物館）或是 bridge（橋），所以答案選 A，在觀光巴士上。

(A)　　　　　　(B)　　　　　　(C)

__C__ 30. For question number 30, please look at the three pictures.

Listen to the ad. What kind of store is it?

Now you don't have to travel far to do your grocery shopping. We have everything you need for your kitchen, home and personal care. We're having an opening day sale this Saturday. Come shop with us!

第 30 題，請看三張圖片。

請聽廣告。這是什麼類型的商店？

現在您不必遠行就能採購日常用品。我們有您廚房、家居和個人護理所需的一切用品。本週六我們將舉行開幕日促銷活動。歡迎前來與我們一同購物！

解析　圖片 A 為家電行，圖片 B 為服飾店，由關鍵詞 kitchen（廚房）、home（家居）、personal care（個人護理）可以看出來圖片 C 最符合描述，答案選 C。

第一部分　詞彙

___C___ 1. Small backpacks count as _____ items on most flights.
小型後背包在大多數航班上被當作個人物品。
(A) foreign 外國的　　　　　(B) regular 規律的
(C) personal 個人的　　　　 (D) dangerous 危險的

___D___ 2. Terry never _____ fault, nor does he apologize.
泰瑞從不承認錯誤，也不會道歉。
(A) receives 接受　　　　　 (B) obeys 服從
(C) believes 相信　　　　　 (D) admits 承認

___A___ 3. If you send the letter today, it should be _____ on Wednesday.
如果你今天把信寄出去，應該會在星期三送達。
(A) delivered 送達　　　　　(B) canceled 取消
(C) measured 測量　　　　　(D) forced 強制

___C___ 4. The team celebrated their _____ after winning the basketball game.
隊伍在贏得籃球比賽後慶祝他們的勝利。
(A) influence 影響力　　　　(B) opportunity 機會
(C) victory 勝利　　　　　　(D) freedom 自由

___B___ 5. The _____ president was very popular, but the current president isn't.
那位前任總統非常受歡迎，但現任總統卻不是。
(A) primary 主要的　　　　　(B) former 前任的
(C) local 當地的　　　　　　(D) national 國家的

___D___ 6. I don't feel like climbing to the top of the tower because I'm afraid of
_____ .
我不想爬到塔頂，因為我害怕高處。
(A) buildings 建築物　　　　(B) animals 動物
(C) planes 飛機　　　　　　(D) heights 高處

__A__ 7. Can you _____ why you're almost two hours late?

你能解釋為什麼你遲到了將近兩小時嗎？

(A) explain 解釋　　　　(B) accept 接受

(C) notice 注意　　　　(D) discuss 討論

__B__ 8. The movie was so _____ that both Eric and I fell asleep.

這部電影太無聊了，以至於我和艾瑞克都睡著了。

(A) exciting 刺激的　　(B) boring 無聊的

(C) scary 可怕的　　　(D) funny 有趣的

__B__ 9. Dora has a toothache. Would you mind taking her to see a _____ ?

朵拉牙痛。你介意帶她去看牙醫嗎？

(A) vet 獸醫　　　　　(B) dentist 牙醫

(C) lawyer 律師　　　(D) doctor 醫生

__C__ 10. After a long day at work, _____ of us had the energy to go out for dinner.

工作了一整天後，我們都沒有精力出去吃晚餐。

(A) all 所有人　　　　(B) both 兩者都

(C) none 沒人　　　　(D) either 二者之一

解析　空格前提到「在工作了一整天之後」可推知是暗示大家都很累，「沒有人」有精力，選項 C 正確。

Part 2 段落填空

第二部分　段落填空

共 8 題，包括二個段落，每個段落含四個空格。每格均有四個選項，請依照文意選出最適合的答案。

Questions 11-14

Last weekend, my parents took me camping for my sixteenth birthday. It was my ____(11)____ first camping trip. We drove a few hours from our city to a national park with a beautiful lake. When we got to our campsite, my dad ____(12)____ the new tent he had bought for the trip, while my mom rolled out our sleeping bags. I helped by collecting sticks for our campfire later that night. My favorite part was when we cooked hot dogs over the fire and told stories under the stars. Even ____(13)____ I was tired, I had trouble falling asleep on the bumpy ground. After a fun weekend of fishing, hiking, and exploring the outdoors, I ____(14)____ wait for our next camping trip!

上週末，我父母帶我去露營，慶祝我十六歲生日。這是我 **(11) 有生以來**第一次露營。我們從所處的城市出發，開了幾個小時的車，來到了一個有美麗湖泊的國家公園。當我們到達營地時，我爸爸 **(12) 設置**了他為這次旅行買的新帳篷，而我媽媽鋪好我們的睡袋。我幫忙收集木柴，為當晚的營火做準備。我最喜歡的部分是我們用火烤熱狗，並在星空下講故事。**(13) 雖然**我很累，但我在顛簸的地面上很難入睡。在有釣魚、徒步旅行、還有探索戶外的愉快週末後，我對我們的下一次露營旅行，真是 **(14) 迫不及待**了！

___B___ 11. (A) only 只有　　　　　　(B) very 非常
　　　　　(C) single 單一　　　　　(D) really 真正

> **解析**　由空格前後得知是要強調「我第一次」露營，因此適合強調的是選項 B 的 very。這樣的詞性結構為「副詞 very+ 形容詞 first+ 名詞 trip」。

___B___ 12. (A) set out 出發　　　　(B) set up 設置
　　　　　(C) put in 放進　　　　　(D) put down 放下

> **解析**　空格後加的受詞是「新帳篷」，因此適合搭配的片語為 set up，選項 B 正確。

__A__ 13. (A) though 雖然　　　　　　(B) although 儘管

　　　　　(C) then 然後　　　　　　(D) when 當

> **解析** 空格後提到累，但是卻睡不好，可推知有前後子句反差的意思。因此 even 後應加的是 though，為「雖然…但是…」。而 even though 的同義字為 although 和 though。句型為 "even though S+V, S+V." 或 "S+V even though S+V"。

__D__ 14. (A) don't 不　　　　　　　(B) won't 不會

　　　　　(C) can 能　　　　　　　(D) can't 不能

> **解析** 表達迫不及待，因此答案是 "can't wait to V" 或 "can't wait for N"。因此選項 D 正確。

Questions 15-18

In order to prepare for a swimming contest, Lisa decided to practice swimming every morning. She ____(15)____ finding a swimming pool in her neighborhood. She then ____(16)____ her swimsuit and a towel and walked to the swimming pool. When she got there, the pool appeared to be closed. She ____(17)____ the lifeguard and asked, "Excuse me, when does the pool open?" The lifeguard looked at her and said, "It's already open! You're just at the wrong entrance. This is the entrance for people who work here. Don't worry, I'll take you to the right entrance." ____(18)____ the lifeguard, Lisa found a good place to practice for the swimming contest.

為了準備游泳比賽，麗莎決定每天早上練習游泳。她 **(15) 從**在她的社區找到了游泳池**開始** 。然後她 **(16) 打包了**她的泳衣和毛巾，走到游泳池。當她到達了那裡時，游泳池似乎關了。她 **(17) 走向了**救生員並問道，「不好意思，游泳池什麼時候開放？救生員看著她說：「已經開了！你只是在錯誤的入口。這是給工作人員的入口。別擔心，我會帶你去對的入口。」 **(18) 多虧了**救生員，麗莎找到了練習游泳比賽的好地方。

__B__ 15. (A) started to 開始去　　　　(B) started by 從…開始

　　　　　(C) started up 創立　　　　(D) started on 著手進行

Part 2 段落填空

> **解析** 空格前一句提到要決定練習游泳，空格後接的是要找游泳池，可推知找游泳池是手段，因此用「by+ 方法 / 手段」，選項 B 正確。Start to 不符合是因為其後必須接原形動詞才行。

___D___ 16. (A) rented 租了　　　　　　(B) bought 買了
　　　　　(C) wore 穿了　　　　　　(D) packed 打包了

___C___ 17. (A) got back to 回到了　　　(B) came up with 想到了
　　　　　(C) walked up to 走向了　(D) ran out of 用完了

___C___ 18. (A) Next to 在…旁邊　　　　(B) Along with 與…一起
　　　　　(C) Thanks to 多虧了　　　(D) Except for 除了

> **解析** 空格後接救生員的幫助，再來是麗莎找到地方練習，可推知救生員是原因，因此選項 C 正確。

共 12 題，包括 4 個題組，每個題組含 1 至 2 篇短文，與數個相關的四選一的選擇題。請由試題上的選項中選出最適合的答案。

Questions 19-21

22-year-old Ivana was one of the best athletes at her school. She used to be good at all kinds of sports, including swimming, tennis, basketball and bicycle racing. However, everything changed after she fell off her bike.

Ivana's right leg was seriously hurt in the accident, and she thought she may never be able to play her favorite sports again. After a month recovering in the hospital, she still wasn't able to walk. She told her doctor she'd do anything to be able to walk again, so her doctor gave her exercises to do to improve her strength. At first, she fell down every time she tried to get up, but she didn't give up. After two weeks, she started walking again. A month later, she left the hospital, and she was back on her bike again.

This is all because she believes in herself.

22 歲的伊凡娜是她學校裡頂尖的運動員之一。她以前曾擅長各項運動，包括游泳、網球、籃球和自行車賽。(20) 儘管如此，自從她從自行車上跌落之後，一切都變了。

伊凡娜的右腿在那場意外中受了重傷，而她以為自己可能再也無法從事她最愛的運動。(21) 在醫院一個月的復原之後，她依然無法走路。(19) 她告訴醫生，為了能再走路，她願意做任何事，所以醫生給了她一些運動練習來增強體力。剛開始，每次她試圖站起來時都會跌倒。但她沒有放棄，(21) 兩週後她重新開始走路了。離開醫院一個月後，她再次騎上了自行車。

這一切都是因為她相信自己能夠做任何她想做的事。

___C___ 19. Which is the best title for the reading?

(A) *Women Are Good at Sports*

(B) *Swimming Is the Best Exercise*

(C) *A Woman Who Never Gives up*

(D) *The Smartest Woman in the World.*

這篇文章的最佳標題是什麼？

(A) 女性擅長運動

(B) 游泳是最佳運動

(C) 從不放棄的女子

(D) 世界上最聰明的女子

解析 本文從第一段伊凡娜受傷開始，到第二段第三句的堅持走路，結論提到她相信自己可以做到想做的事。全篇都在敘述她的韌性與堅持，因此選項 C 正確。

___A___ 20. Where did Ivana most likely get hurt?

(A) In a race track.

(B) On a tennis court.

(C) In a swimming pool.

(D) On a basketball court.

伊凡娜最有可能在哪裡受傷？

(A) 在賽車車道上

(B) 在網球場。

(C) 在游泳池。

(D) 在籃球場。

解析 由第一段最後一句得知，她從腳踏車上跌下來後生活就變了，因此和腳踏車最有關的是選項 A。

___B___ 21. After the accident, how long was it before Ivana could walk again?

(A) Four weeks

(B) Six weeks

(C) Eight weeks

(D) Ten weeks

事故發生後，伊凡娜多久才能再次行走？

(A) 四週

(B) 六週

(C) 八週

(D) 十週

解析 由第二段第二句得知伊凡娜花了一個月在醫院康復，一個月即四週的時間；第五句指出兩週後開始走路，因此總共是六週，選項 B 正確。

Questions 22-24

Have you ever returned something you bought? People often return items because they are damaged, the wrong size, or the wrong color, or sometimes they simply change their minds.

If the product is damaged, you can either get your money back or get a new one. If the size or color is wrong, you can return the item and exchange it for the one you want. If you simply don't want the item, you can usually get your money back if you return it within 7 days and it's unused. You'll need to show the receipt though, so be sure to keep it.

Remember to check the store's return policy before you shop. Some stores have special rules or fees for returns. Knowing these rules can make it easier to return things.

(24) 你有沒有把你買的東西拿去退貨的經驗？人們常常因為物品損壞、尺寸不對或顏色不對而退貨。有時候他們只是改變了心意。

如果商品損壞了，你可以選擇退款或換新的。如果尺寸或顏色不對，你可以退貨並換成你想要的。(23) 如果你單純只是不要這個物品，只要在未使用的狀態下 7 天內退回，你通常可以拿回退款。不過你需要出示收據，所以一定要保留收據。

(22) 記得在購物前查看商店的退貨政策。有些商店對退貨有特別的規定或收費。了解這些規定可以讓退貨更容易。

A 22. Why is it important to check the store's return policy before making a purchase?

(A) To know if there's a fee for returns.

(B) To find out the different ways to pay.

(C) To know what's available at the store.

(D) To get the best price on sale items.

為什麼在購物前查看商店的退貨政策很重要？

(A) 了解退貨是否需要付費。

(B) 了解不同的支付方式。

(C) 了解商店有哪些商品。

(D) 獲得特價商品的最佳價格。

解析 由最後一段第一句定位題目所問之關鍵字，再由第二句得知 "have special rules or fees for returns" 推斷，可得知應該了解退貨是否有特殊規定或費用，選項 A 正確。

__D__ 23. According to the article, which is NOT true?

(A) People can get a refund for a damaged item.

(B) People should keep their receipts when shopping.

(C) People can get a refund for items they don't want.

(D) People can get a refund for returns within 10 days.

根據文章，哪一項不正確？

(A) 人們可以對損壞的物品要求退款。

(B) 人們購物時應該保留收據。

(C) 人們可以對不想要的物品要求退款。

(D) 人們可以在 10 天內退貨並要求退款。

解析 由第二段倒數第二句得知，退貨必須在七天內退回，因此錯誤的是選項 D。

__C__ 24. Which of the following is the best title for this article?

(A) *The Art of Successful Shopping*

(B) *The Best Online Shopping Tips*

(C) *A Guide to Returning Purchases*

(D) *Think Twice Before You Shop*

以下哪一項是這篇文章的最佳標題？

(A) 成功購物的藝術

(B) 最佳網購小技巧

(C) 退貨指南

(D) 購物前須謹慎考慮

解析 本文全篇都在說明退貨的原因、退貨的情況，和最後退貨需注意的事項，因此選項 C 最適合。

Questions 25-27

Shadow play is the ancient art of telling stories with shadows. The history of shadow play goes back more than 2,000 years, and probably started in China. The art uses flat figures made from materials like leather, and sometimes painted in bright colors. The figures are placed between a light source and a thin white screen, which creates shadows on the screen. When the figures are moved, the shadows the audience sees move along with them. In this way, storytellers can tell interesting stories using only shadows.

Over the centuries, shadow play spread to many countries around the world. In Turkey, a form of shadow play called Karagöz began hundreds of years ago. Often held in coffee houses, the plays have funny stories with lots of singing and dancing. However, shadow play is not just for fun; it's also an important way to keep old stories and traditions alive. It's a magical way to tell stories that everyone can enjoy!

皮影戲是一種用影子講故事的古老藝術。皮影戲的歷史可以追溯到兩千多年前，可能起源於中國。這種藝術使用皮革等材料製成的扁平人偶，有時會塗上鮮豔的顏色。**(25) (26) 這些人偶被放置在光源和薄屏幕之間，就產生了屏幕上的影子。**當人偶移動時，觀眾看到的影子也隨之移動。這樣，說書人可以只用影子來講述有趣的故事。

幾百年來，皮影戲流傳到世界許多國家。在土耳其，一種叫做卡拉格茲的皮影戲在幾百年前開始形成。這些表演經常在咖啡館舉行，故事幽默，也有很多歌唱和舞蹈。**(27) 儘管如此，皮影戲不僅僅是娛樂；它也是保存古老故事和傳統的重要方式。**這是一種神奇的講故事的方法，人人都喜愛！

B 25. Which is NOT required for shadow play?
(A) Moving shadows
(B) Natural light
(C) Flat figures
(D) A thin screen

皮影戲不需要什麼？
(A) 移動的影子
(B) 自然光
(C) 扁平的人偶
(D) 薄屏幕

解析 第一段第四句提到，皮影戲需要光源來造出影子，但此光源並非是自然光，因此選項 B 不是皮影戲所需的。

__D__ 26. In shadow play, what happens when light shines on the figures?

(A) They disappear from the screen.

(B) They change to a different color.

(C) They move on the screen.

(D) They appear on the screen.

在皮影戲中，當光照在人偶上時會發生什麼事？

(A) 它們從屏幕上消失。

(B) 它們變成不同的顏色。

(C) 它們在屏幕上移動。

(D) 它們出現在屏幕上。

解析 由第一段第四句得知，光照在人偶上，就意味著人偶被放置在光源和薄屏幕之間，因此屏幕上就會出現影子，選項 D 正確。

__C__ 27. Why does shadow play have value as an art form?

(A) It uses figures to make shadows.

(B) It has many colorful characters.

(C) It passes on stories from the past.

(D) It comes from all over the world.

為什麼皮影戲作為一種藝術形式具有價值？

(A) 它使用人偶來製造影子。

(B) 它有許多色彩繽紛的角色。

(C) 它傳承過去的故事。

(D) 它來自世界各地。

解析 由第二段倒數第二句得知，皮影戲不只是娛樂，而是在保留故事方面有重要性，因此選項 C 正確。

Questions 28-30

Maglev trains, or magnetic levitation trains, are a very advanced type of train system. Strong magnets on the bottom of the train and along the tracks allow these special trains to travel above the tracks instead of on them. This provides a very smooth and quiet experience for passengers.

Unlike normal trains with metal wheels that roll on tracks, maglev trains move without touching the track. This allows maglevs to reach much higher speeds—over 500 km per hour, which is faster than some airplanes. However, they do have wheels that can be used when required for safety purposes. Faster speeding up and slowing down is also possible. These advanced trains also save power and need repairs less often.

Countries including Japan, Germany and China have already introduced maglev train lines. In Japan, a maglev train reached the record speed of 603 km per hour in 2015. A number of new maglev rail lines are still being built around the world. Those who support maglev trains believe they will be the future of train travel.

磁浮列車，或稱磁懸浮列車，是一種非常先進的列車系統。列車底部和軌道上的強力磁鐵，讓這些特殊的列車可以懸浮在軌道上方行駛，而不是在軌道上行駛。**(28) 這為乘客提供了一個非常平穩且安靜的乘坐體驗。**

(29) 不同於普通列車的金屬輪子在軌道上滾動，磁浮列車在行駛時並不接觸軌道。這使得磁浮列車能夠達到更高的速度——超過每小時 500 公里，比一些飛機還快。然而，為了安全起見，列車確實也配備了配合安全目的時需使用的輪子。更快加速和減速也是可能的。這些先進的列車還能節省能源，並且需要較少的維修頻率。

包括日本、德國和中國在內的一些國家已經引進了磁浮列車線路。2015 年，在日本，磁浮列車達到了每小時 603 公里創紀錄的速度。**(30) 世界各地仍在建造許多新的磁浮鐵路線。支持磁浮列車的人相信它們將成為未來的列車旅行方式。**

A 28. What can we expect when riding on a maglev train?

(A) We can enjoy a more pleasant ride.

(B) We should allow more time to travel.

(C) It offers great service and bigger seats.

(D) We can travel faster than airplanes.

乘坐磁浮列車時，我們可以期待什麼？

(A) 我們可以享受更愉快的乘車體驗。

(B) 我們應該預留更多的旅行時間。

(C) 它提供優質服務和更大的座位。

(D) 我們的速度比飛機更快。

解析 第一段最後一句提到搭乘體驗是平穩和安靜的,因此可推知選項 A 正確。第二段第二句雖有提到磁浮列車比飛機快,但只是比某些飛機快,而非每輛列車都是如此,因此選項 D 的陳述並非完全正確。

D 29. How are maglev trains different than regular trains?

   (A) They travel on wheels just like a car.

   (B) They have an electric power source.

   (C) They make use of a high speed engine.

   (D) They don't make contact with the track.

磁浮列車與普通列車有什麼不同?

(A) 它們像汽車一樣在輪子上行駛。

(B) 它們以電力為動力來源。

(C) 它們使用高速引擎。

(D) 它們不與軌道接觸。

解析 由第二段第一句得知,磁浮列車和普通列車的最大的不同是輪子並不會接觸軌道,因此選項 D 正確。

D 30. What do we know about the future of maglev trains?

   (A) They will be able to travel faster in a few years.

   (B) They will be made of even lighter materials.

   (C) The ticket prices can be expected to drop.

   (D) They will become more common in the world.

我們對磁浮列車的未來有何了解?

(A) 它們在幾年內會變得更快。

(B) 它們將由更輕的材料製成。

(C) 車票價格可以預期會下降。

(D) 它們將在世界上變得更加普遍。

解析 由第三段最後兩句得知,還有正在建設的磁浮列車系統,也有人相信磁浮列車會成為未來的列車旅行方式,可由此推知會更加普遍,因此選項 D 正確。

GEPT
初級模擬試題
第8回
解答、翻譯與詳解

第 8 回解答

 聽力測驗解答

1. C	2. B	3. B	4. A	5. B
6. C	7. A	8. B	9. C	10. C
11. B	12. C	13. C	14. B	15. C
16. A	17. C	18. B	19. B	20. A
21. A	22. A	23. C	24. A	25. C
26. C	27. B	28. B	29. A	30. B

📖 閱讀測驗解答

1. B	2. C	3. C	4. D	5. A
6. A	7. C	8. B	9. D	10. C
11. B	12. D	13. C	14. A	15. C
16. D	17. D	18. A	19. C	20. B
21. B	22. D	23. C	24. A	25. B
26. A	27. D	28. C	29. C	30. A

第 8 回聽力

第一部分 看圖辨義

<u>C</u> 1. For Question Number 1, please look at the picture.
What are the people doing?

(A) The family is going for a walk in the park.

(B) The students are going to the junior high school.

(C) The parents are taking their kids to the kindergarten.

第一題，請看此圖片。

圖片上的人正在做什麼？

(A) 一家人正在公園散步。

(B) 學生正要去中學上學。

(C) 一對父母正帶著他們的孩子上幼兒園。

解析 圖片上可以看到一對父母帶著女孩朝校舍前進，不在公園裡，也沒有看到中學生，因此知道答案為選項 C。

<u>B</u> 2. For Question Number 2, please look at the picture.
Where is this place most likely to be?

(A) At a nice beach.

(B) In the countryside.

(C) By a modern building.

第二題，請看此圖片。

這個地方最有可能在哪裡？

(A) 在美麗的海邊。

(B) 在鄉間。

(C) 在現代建築旁。

解析　圖片上可以看到農夫正在插秧，沒有看到海景或是現代建築，所以知道答案為選項 B。

__B__ 3. For Question Number 3, please look at the picture.
What are the people doing?

(A) They're making phone calls.

(B) They're trying new computers.

(C) They're shopping for groceries.

第三題，請看此圖片。

圖片上的人正在做什麼？

(A) 他們正在打電話。

(B) 他們在試用新電腦。

(C) 他們在買日常用品。

解析　圖片的場景在電器行，兩個人正在使用電腦，因此可以知道答案為選項 B。

__A__ 4. For Question Number 4, please look at the picture.
What is the man doing?

(A) He's getting into a taxi.

(B) He's trying to get a taxi.

(C) He's learning to drive a car.

第四題，請看此圖片。

男子正在做什麼？

(A) 他正要上計程車。

(B) 他在招計程車。

(C) 他在學開車。

解析　圖片上的男子正伸手開計程車的門，所以知道他已經招到計程車正要上車，因此答案為選項 A。

B 5. For Question Number 5, please look at the picture.
What kind of restaurant is this?

(A) It's a steak house.

(B) It's a Chinese restaurant.

(C) It's a fast food restaurant.

第五題，請看此圖片。
這是什麼樣的餐廳？

(A) 牛排館。

(B) 中式餐廳。

(C) 速食餐廳。

解析　由圖片上的圓桌，以及桌上的炒飯跟炒麵可以看得出來這是在中式餐廳，答案選 B。

__C__ 6. Look. There's a hole in my T-shirt.

(A) Stay away. It's deep.

(B) You should see a doctor.

(C) Let me sew it up for you.

你看，我的短袖運動衫上有一個洞。

(A) 離遠一點。那很深。

(B) 你應該要看醫生。

(C) 讓我幫你縫起來。

解析 句尾的 "in my T-shirt" 表示破洞的位置在衣服上。只有選項 C 的答案為合理的回覆，其餘皆答非所問。

__A__ 7. Does anyone know why Ivan isn't here yet?

(A) He's stuck in traffic.

(B) He's always on time.

(C) That's a good excuse.

有人知道為什麼艾文還沒到嗎？

(A) 他被困在車陣中了。

(B) 他總是準時。

(C) 那是很好的藉口。

解析 這題的題目為間接問句，主要的提問在後半 "Why Ivan isn't here yet"，詢問艾文尚未到場的原因。只有選項 A 有針對問題作答。

__B__ 8. What's that box for?

(A) It's for you.

(B) I keep coins in it.

(C) The box is empty.

這個盒子是拿來做什麼用的？

(A) 是給你的。

(B) 我拿來放零錢的。

(C) 這個盒子是空的。

解析 "What is...for?" 常用來詢問事物的用途。只有選項 B 有說明盒子是放零錢用的，其餘兩個選項沒有回答到問題，因此選 B。

__C__ 9. The floor is so cold.

(A) Yes. It's very old.

(B) How did you do it?

(C) Go put some socks on.

地板好冰。

(A) 對啊！它很舊了。

(B) 你怎麼辦到的？

(C) 去把襪子穿上吧！

解析 old 跟 cold 的發音相近，聽的時候請注意。針對地板很冰提出解決方案的只有選項 C，其餘兩個選項和問題不相關，因此選 C。

___C___ 10. Could you press eight for me?

      (A) Not at all.

      (B) It's OK for me.

      (C) Sure. No problem.

你可以幫我按 8 嗎？

(A) 不客氣。

(B) 我沒問題。

(C) 當然，沒問題。

解析 選項 A 的 "Not at all." 常用來回應對方的道謝，選項 B "It's OK for me." 則是用來表達自己的意見或意願，但這裡的問句其實是請求，並非詢問對方意願，所以 B 不正確。只有選項 C 是用來回覆對方請求時的用語，因此選 C。

___B___ 11. Did you take out the trash?

      (A) I haven't seen the brush.

      (B) Would you mind doing that?

      (C) The waste will be collected today.

你去丟垃圾了嗎？

(A) 我沒有看到梳子。

(B) 可以麻煩你幫我做嗎？

(C) 今天會來收垃圾。

解析 題目 "take out the trash" 表示「把垃圾拿出去」，trash 跟 brush（梳子）的發音相近，但語意無關，所以選項 A 是陷阱。選項 C 雖然和垃圾相關，但和問題無關，且答非所問，選 B。

___C___ 12. Why is your desk so messy?

      (A) It's mine, not Max's.

      (B) Your desk is fancy, too.

      (C) Because I'm really lazy.

你的桌子為什麼那麼亂？

(A) 是我的，不是馬克斯的。

(B) 你的桌子也很華麗。

(C) 因為我很懶。

解析 題目中的 messy（亂）和選項 B 的 fancy（華麗）的發音類似，但意思完全不同，請仔細聽。三個選項中只有選項 C 針對桌子雜亂的原因做出說明，其他皆答非所問，因此答案選 C。

___C___ 13. Is this the wallet you want?

      (A) Where can I find it?

      (B) The wallet belongs to Irene.

      (C) Yes, but it's not the color I want.

這是你想要的皮夾嗎？

(A) 我要去哪裡才能找到？

(B) 這是艾琳的皮夾。

(C) 是，但這不是我要的顏色。

解析 be 動詞開頭的問句答題時使用 Yes 或是 No 來回答。只有選項 C 使用了 Yes，並補充說明皮夾的顏色和自己想要的不同，最符合對話邏輯，所以選 C。

__B__ 14. Will you pick me up today?
(A) All right. Stand up!
(B) Of course. What time?
(C) You can pick up the trash.

你今天會來接我嗎？
(A) 好的。請起立！
(B) 當然會。幾點？
(C) 你可以把垃圾撿起來。

解析 這題的題目和選項都有出現 "pick up"。題目中的「pick 人 up」是「接（某人）」的意思，而選項 C「pick up+ 物」則是把東西撿起來。所以儘管選項 C 有出現 "pick up"，但卻不是同樣的意思，選項 A 也答非所問。只有選項 B 針對問題回答，並加問時間細節，因此正確答案為 B。

___

__C__ 15. I don't feel like going to school today.
(A) You can ride a bike there.
(B) I thought I saw you there.
(C) Come on. You still have to go.

我今天不想要去上學。
(A) 你可以騎腳踏車去。
(B) 我以為我在那裡有看到你。
(C) 快點！你還是得去！

解析 "don't feel like going to school"（不想去上學）和通學方式無關，因此選項 A 不正確。選項 B 使用過去式，不符合題目中「今天不想上學」的對話邏輯，答案為 C。

A 16. G: I don't want to take piano lessons anymore. I'm not making any progress.

M: Be patient. I'm sure you'll get better with more practice.

G: No, I give up. That's it. No more lessons.

M: OK. I'll call the teacher and tell her.

Question: How does the girl feel?

女孩：我不想要再上鋼琴課了。我都沒有進步。
男子：多點耐心。我相信妳多練習就會進步了。
女孩：不，我放棄。就這樣。我不上課了。
男子：好吧！我會打電話給老師跟她說。
問題：女孩覺得怎麼樣？

(A) She is upset.
(B) She is curious.
(C) She is confident.

(A) 她很不開心。
(B) 她很好奇。
(C) 她很有信心。

解析　對話中的女孩因為鋼琴沒有進步而感到不開心，想要停止上課。從 "I give up." "That's it." 也可以感受到女孩有負面情緒，三個選項中只有選項 A 的屬性較為負面，因此答案選 A。

C 17. W: I want to buy some flowers to decorate the living room.

M: Good idea. We can buy some plants for the yard, too.

W: OK. How far away is the flower shop?

M: It's a ten minute drive.

Question: What are they going to do?

女子：我想買一些鮮花來裝飾客廳。
男子：好主意。我們也可以買一些盆栽放在院子。
女子：好的。花店離這裡多遠？
男子：開車十分鐘。
問題：他們要做什麼？

(A) They're going to work in the yard.

(B) They're going to plant some trees.

(C) They're going to do some shopping.

(A) 他們要進行園藝工作。

(B) 他們要種一些樹。

(C) 他們要去買東西。

解析 雖然對話中有出現 yard（院子）和 plants（盆栽、種植）但討論的主題是要購買盆栽以及鮮花。從關鍵字 buy（購買）可以知道他們正要去購物 "do some shopping"。

B 18. G: This story book is really fun.

B: What's it about?

G: It's about a group of animals who help each other get out of the zoo.

B: That's interesting. Can I borrow it?

Question: What does the boy want to do?

女孩：這本故事書很好玩。

男孩：是關於什麼的故事？

女孩：是一群動物合力逃離動物園的故事。

男孩：蠻有趣的！我可以跟妳借嗎？

問題：男孩想要做什麼？

(A) Lend the book to the girl.

(B) Read the girl's story book.

(C) Return the book to the girl.

(A) 把書借給女孩。

(B) 讀女孩的故事書。

(C) 把書還給女孩。

解析 從男孩最後說的 "Can I borrow it?" 可以知道男孩想跟女孩把書借來閱讀。因此答案選 B。

B 19. W: Can I get a new plate, please? This one is dirty.

M: Sure. Let me get you a clean one.

W: Also, can I have some more water?

M: Of course. I'll be right back.

Question: Where does the conversation take place?

女子：我可以有一個新的盤子嗎？這個是髒的。

男子：當然。我幫妳拿一個新的。

女子：還有，可以給我一點水嗎？

男子：當然。我馬上回來。

問題：這段對話發生的場所在哪裡？

(A) In a shop.

(B) At a restaurant.

(C) In a hotel room.

(A) 在一間店。

(B) 在餐廳。

(C) 在飯店房間。

解析　"Can I have...?" 是和服務人員索取東西時常用的句型，由女子向男子要求更換
盤子和索取飲用水的對話內容可以推測這段對話在餐廳，答案為選項 B。

A 20. W: Are you busy right now?

M: No, Mom.

W: Could you take this box to Janet's house for me? I made some cookies for her.

M: Sure. Let me get my car keys.

Question: What was the woman doing?

女子：你現在在忙嗎？

男子：不忙啊，媽。

女子：那你可以幫我把這個盒子拿去珍娜的家嗎？我做了一些餅乾給她。

男子：當然。我拿一下車鑰匙。

問題：女子剛剛在做什麼？

(A) Baking some food.

(B) Taking something to Janet.

(C) Driving her son somewhere.

(A) 烘焙。

(B) 把東西拿給珍娜。

(C) 載他兒子出門。

解析 由對話中 "I made some cookies for her." 可以猜測女子剛才可能正在烤餅乾。烤餅乾的動詞可以用 make（做）或是 bake（烘焙）。

A 21. W: Mmm, hot chocolate. Wait... it's salty!

M: Salty? But I used sugar from this jar.

W: That's the salt jar. See, it says "salt" on the lid.

M: Oh, sorry! I'll make you another cup.

Question: What happened?

女子：嗯…熱巧克力。等一下，這是鹹的。

男子：鹹的？可是我是用這個罐子裡面的糖啊！

女子：那是鹽罐。看，蓋子上面寫「鹽」。

男子：喔！對不起。我再幫你做一杯。

問題：發生什麼事？

(A) The man made a mistake.
(B) The woman enjoyed her drink.
(C) The man used too much sugar.

(A) 男子犯了一個錯誤。
(B) 女子很喜歡她的飲料。
(C) 男子用了太多糖。

解析 男子把鹽罐和糖罐搞混，所以做了鹹的熱巧克力。女子被鹹的熱巧克力嚇了一跳，因此選項 B 不正確，男子用了鹽沒有用糖，因此選項 C 也不正確。正確答案為 A。

A 22. M: This is your desk. It's where you'll be working.

W: OK. Should I answer all the phone calls?

M: Yes, that's part of your job. And you should take messages, too.

W: OK. I can't wait to get started.

Question: Which is true?

男子：這是妳的桌子。妳就會這邊工作。

女子：好。全部的電話我都要接嗎？

男子：對，這是妳工作的一部份。妳也要把留言記錄下來。

女子：好的！我等不及要開始了。

問題：以下何者正確？

(A) The woman is new to the company.

(B) Making calls is part of the woman's job.

(C) The man will buy a new desk for the woman.

(A) 女子是公司的新進員工。

(B) 打電話是女子工作的一部份。

(C) 男子會幫女子買一張新桌子。

解析 對話內容為男子向女子介紹工作職責，因此可以推測答案為選項 A。選項 B 需要把 "making calls"（打電話）改成 "answering calls"（接電話）才會正確。

C 23. W: Can you please slow down? I'm getting tired.

M: It sounds like you didn't practice enough.

W: I did. I went jogging three times last month.

M: I went three times a week.

Question: Which is true about the man and woman?

女子：你可以慢一點嗎？我開始有點累了。

男子：聽起來妳好像練習得不夠。

女子：我有。我上個月慢跑了三次。

男子：我一週就跑了三次。

問題：請問關於男子和女子以下何者正確？

(A) The man practiced less than the woman.

(B) The woman jogged faster than the man.

(C) The man jogged more often than the woman.

(A) 男子比女子練習得少。

(B) 女子跑得比男子快。

(C) 男子比女子常慢跑。

解析 從對話中女子提到的 "three times last month" 與男子的 "three times a week"，可以知道男子慢跑的頻率比女子多，因此答案選 C。

A 24. W: Billy, can you come downstairs?

B: I'm busy helping Dad fix his phone.

W: I need help in the kitchen.

B: Fine. I'll be down in five minutes.

Question: Where is the boy?

女子：比利，你可以下樓嗎？

男孩：我在忙著幫爸爸修理他的電話。

女子：我在廚房裡需要幫忙。

男孩：好。我五分鐘內下去。

問題：請問男孩在哪裡？

(A) Upstairs

(B) In the yard

(C) In the basement

(A) 樓上

(B) 院子裡

(C) 地下室

解析 從女子要求男孩 "Can you come downstairs?" 的請求中可以推測男孩的所在位置在 "upstairs"（樓上），答案為選項 A。

C 25. W: Winnie won the best worker prize again.

M: It's always her. I don't understand.

W: Me neither. I never see her working hard.

M: Let me ask her what her secret is.

Question: What is the man going to do?

女子：維妮又贏得最佳員工獎了。

男子：總是她得獎。我真不明白！

女子：我也不知道為什麼。我從來沒看過她認真工作。

男子：我來問問她得獎的祕訣是什麼。

問題：男子要做什麼？

(A) He is going to win the prize.

(B) He will tell the woman a secret.

(C) He is going to talk to the woman.

(A) 他將獲得獎項。

(B) 他會告訴女子一個祕密。

(C) 他將會和女子說話。

解析 由男子的最後一句話 "Let me ask her what her secret is." 可以得知他會去請教維妮得獎的祕訣，因此選項 C 為正解。男子想要得獎，但從對話中無法得知他會不會得獎，因此選項 A 不正確。

(A)   (B)   (C)

__C__ 26. For question number 26, please look at the three pictures.

Listen to the following talk. What kind of event will be held?

We're going to have a yard sale on the first of May. We have lots of furniture to sell, and things like lamps, carpets and paintings. We also have an exercise machine, two bicycles, and all kinds of board games. The sale will start at nine o'clock in the morning and end at five in the afternoon.

第 26 題，請看三張圖片。

請聽以下談話，即將要舉行哪種活動？

我們將在五月一日舉辦跳蚤市場拍賣。我們會賣很多的家具，以及像是檯燈、地毯、畫作等物品。我們也有一台運動器材、兩台腳踏車、和各式各樣的桌遊。跳蚤市場會從早上九點開始，到下午五點結束。

解析　從關鍵字 yard sale（跳蚤市場）、lamps（檯燈）、carpet（地毯）等可以知道答案為選項 C。

(A)   (B)   (C)

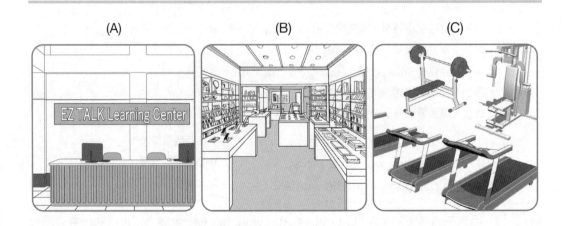

B　27. For question number 27, please look at the three pictures.

Listen to the following talk. Where would you most likely hear this?

This is the cheapest plan you can get. You get sixty minutes of free phone calls and unlimited data for just 20 dollars a month. You can also send as many text messages as you like. The offer is only for this month.

第 27 題，請看三張圖片。

請聽以下談話。在哪裡最可能聽到以下的談話。

這是最便宜的方案。每個月 20 美金，你可以有 60 分鐘的免費通話和無限上網。簡訊量也沒有限制。這個促銷方案只到這個月為止。

解析　limited 意思為「有限的」，加上否定字首 un-，變成 unlimited，意思為「不受限的」、「無限的」，說明網路、電話、線上影音平台方案時常見這個字。從關鍵字 phone calls（電話）、unlimited data（上網吃到飽）、text messages（簡訊）可以知道答案為 B，在電信行。

(A)　　　　　(B)　　　　　(C)

B　28. For question number 28, please look at the three pictures.

Listen to the woman. Who do you think she is talking to?

You have to be very careful when operating this machine. First, turn on the power, and then press "start." Be sure to keep your hands and feet away from the machine while it's running. Also, always wear eye protection when you're using it. When you're finished, press the "stop" button here.

第 28 題，請看三張圖片。

請聽這名女子的談話。你覺得她正在和誰說話？

你在操作機器的時候需要非常小心。首先，先把電源打開，然後按下「開始」鍵。注意機器運作時手腳不要靠近。另外，使用時一定要戴護目鏡。結束的時候請按下這裡的「停止」按鍵。

解析 談話內容為操作機器的注意事項，對話中也可以重複聽到 "machine"（機器）這個關鍵詞，因此答案選 B。

(A)   (B)   (C)

___A___ 29. For question number 29, please look at the three pictures.

Listen to the radio ad. Who are the items for?

Do you have clothes that you don't wear anymore? You can donate them to children who need them. You may not need them anymore, but the children will be happy to have them. We also accept pencils, crayons and story books. You can send these items to the following address.

第 29 題，請看三張圖片。

請聽以下廣播廣告。物品是要給誰的？

你有不穿的衣服嗎？你可以將它們捐給需要的孩童。你可能不再需要那些衣物，但孩子們會很樂意收下這些衣服。我們也接受鉛筆、蠟筆和故事書的捐贈。你可以將捐贈物寄到以下地址。

解析 donate（捐贈）將物品捐贈給某人使用的句型為「donate 物 to 人」，由談話中的關鍵詞 to children（孩童）可以知道捐贈的物品是要給小朋友的，因此答案選 A。

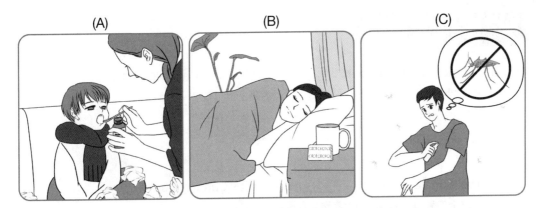

(A)　　　　　　　(B)　　　　　　　(C)

_B_ 30. For question number 30, please look at the three pictures.

Listen to the short talk. What kind of medicine is the woman talking about?

Take this medicine when you have trouble sleeping. Please take it with water and not with coffee or tea. Don't take more than two pills a day. Also, don't take it before you drive or operate machines.

第三十題，請看三張圖片。

請聽以下簡短談話。女子提到的藥物是哪一種？

如果你有睡眠障礙請服用此藥。請配水服用，不要喝咖啡或茶。一天不可服用兩粒以上。開車或是操作機械前請勿服用。

解析　　由談話中的 "have trouble sleeping" 可以推測這個藥品是針對失眠的藥物。圖片 A 是感冒糖漿，圖片 C 是防蚊的外用藥品，答案為選項 B。

第一部分　詞彙

__B__ 1. My mom told me not to _____ my time on video games.

我媽媽告訴我不要把我的時間浪費在電動遊戲上。

(A) select 選擇　　　　　　(B) waste 浪費

(C) divide 切分　　　　　　(D) pass 經過

__C__ 2. The sign says wet _____ , so don't sit on the bench.

標誌上寫著油漆未乾，所以不要坐在長凳上。

(A) wood 木頭　　　　　　(B) metal 金屬

(C) paint 油漆　　　　　　(D) steam 蒸汽

__C__ 3. You'll have to buy some stamps if you want to _____ this letter.

你必須要買些郵票，如果你想寄這封信的話。

(A) write 寫　　　　　　　(B) receive 接收

(C) mail 寄　　　　　　　(D) deliver 送達

__D__ 4. Make sure that you get the car _____ before we go on our road trip.

在我們出發自駕旅行之前，要確認你已經把車子修理好了。

(A) swept 清掃　　　　　　(B) parked 停車

(C) driven 駕駛　　　　　　(D) fixed 修理

__A__ 5. There have been a lot of _____ between Alexander and his father.

亞歷山大和他父親之間一直有很多衝突。

(A) conflicts 衝突　　　　　(B) questions 問題

(C) mistakes 錯誤　　　　　(D) faults 缺點

__A__ 6. If you can hit the _____ , you are the winner.

如果你能擊中目標，你就是贏家。

(A) target 目標　　　　　　(B) focus 焦點

(C) launch 發射　　　　　　(D) meter 計量器

> 解析　target 意指要達到或擊中的目標，因此選項 A 正確。Focus 為「專注或集中注意力」，而不是具體的目標，而其他選項語意不符。

__C__ 7. Kenny _____ cheating on the test. He promised not to do it again.

肯尼對於在考試中作弊感到後悔。他承諾不會再這樣做。

(A) planned 計劃   (B) forgot 忘記

(C) regretted 後悔   (D) enjoyed 享受

__B__ 8. Before speaking in front of others, it's good to _____ your thoughts.

在眾人面前講話之前,最好組織一下你的思緒。

(A) underline 劃線   (B) organize 組織

(C) separate 分開   (D) realize 意識到

__D__ 9. He'd _____ listen to music than watch TV because he finds it more relaxing.

他寧願聽音樂也不願看電視,因為他覺得聽音樂更放鬆。

(A) whether 是否   (B) better 更好

(C) instead 代替   (D) rather 寧願

解析 would rather 是「寧願做…」句型為:「would rather + 原形動詞」,或「would rather + 原形動詞 than 動詞」,意思為「寧願做…,而不願…」

__C__ 10. You have so few friends because you are _____ to people.

你朋友這麼少,是因為你對人很無禮。

(A) frank 坦白的   (B) polite 有禮貌的

(C) rude 無禮的   (D) generous 慷慨的

第二部分　段落填空

共 8 題，包括二個段落，每個段落含四個空格。每格均有四個選項，請依照文意選出最適合的答案。

Questions 11-14

Samantha was very excited to start her new job as a secretary. On her first day, her manager gave her a _____(11)_____ of the office and introduced her to the other employees. Samantha was surprised to see that there were so many different _____(12)_____ in the company. Her manager then showed her how to use the phone and computer. Samantha paid careful _____(13)_____ , taking notes as he spoke. As the day went on, she began to answer phone calls and greet visitors. At the end of the day, Samantha's manager called her into his office. "You did a great job today," he said. "Keep up the good work!" It was a long, hard day, but Samantha felt proud _____(14)_____ .

莎曼姍非常興奮地開始她的新工作，擔任秘書。她工作的第一天，她的經理帶她 **(11) 參觀**辦公室，並介紹她給其他員工認識。莎曼姍驚訝地發現公司裡有這麼多不同的 **(12) 部門**。經理接著向她示範如何使用電話和電腦。莎曼姍特別 **(13) 專注**，並在他說話的同時做了筆記。隨著一天的進展，她開始接聽電話和接待訪客。一天結束時，莎曼姍的經理叫她到辦公室。「你今天做得很好。」他說。「繼續保持！」這是漫長而辛苦的一天，但莎曼姍對 **(14) 自己**感到自豪。

__B__ 11. (A) desk 書桌　　　　　　　(B) tour 參觀
　　　　 (C) key 鑰匙　　　　　　　(D) view 視野

解析　空格前提到了上班第一天，空格後有提到和其他員工見面，可推測新員工在第一天通常會參觀辦公室，因此選項 B 最適合。

__D__ 12. (A) instruments 儀器　　　　(B) basements 地下室
　　　　 (C) apartments 公寓　　　　(D) departments 部門

__C__ 13. (A) advice 建議　　　　　　(B) concern 擔心
　　　　 (C) attention 專注　　　　　(D) respect 尊重

> **解析** 空格前要選一個字跟 careful（仔細的）做搭配，空格後又要跟做筆記的情景
> 有關聯，因此選項 C 正確。

__A__ 14. (A) of herself 自己　　　　　(B) of her 她
　　　　(C) in herself 自己　　　　　(D) about her 關於她

> **解析** 空格前一句提到受到經理的誇獎，可推知莎曼珊應該是對自己第一天的表現感
> 到驕傲。句子中若主詞和受詞為同一人，受詞就用反身代名詞，如：herself,
> himself, myself, yourself, themselves, yourselves, itself。而 proud 後面是
> 接介系詞的 of，因此選項 A 正確。

Questions 15-18

Hiking in the mountains can be a fun experience for anyone ___(15)___ enjoys outdoor activities. However, it's important to get everything ready before you go to make sure your hike is safe and enjoyable. There are things that you need to prepare, including hiking boots, a backpack, extra clothing, and plenty of water and snacks. You should also bring a map ___(16)___ you get lost. In addition, you should always check the weather before you go. You may be run into trouble in the mountains if the weather turns bad. Finally, do not leave any trash on the trail and avoid ___(17)___ plants and wildlife. Everyone is ___(18)___ for protecting the environment.

在登山健行對於任何喜歡戶外活動 **(15) 的人**，都是一個有趣的經驗。然而，重要的是在出發前準備好一切，以確保徒登山健行的安全和愉快。有一些必需品需要準備，包括登山靴、背包、額外衣物以及充足的水和點心。你還應該帶上一張地圖 **(16) 以防**迷路。此外，出發前一定要檢查天氣。如果天氣變壞，你可能會在山裡遇到麻煩。最後，不要在步道上留下任何垃圾，避免 **(17) 危害**植物和野生動物。每個人都有 **(18) 責任**保護環境。

__C__ 15. (A) whom 誰　　　　　(B) which 哪個
　　　　(C) who 誰　　　　　　(D) whose 誰的

> **解析** 空格前是 anyone 任何人，為名詞，空格後為動詞 enjoys。由此判斷，需在空
> 格裡面填上「代替人的關係代名詞」，並且需要做「主詞」，選項 C 正確。

__D__ 16. (A) even though 儘管　　　　(B) after 在…之後
　　　　 (C) until 直到　　　　　　(D) in case 以防

> **解析**　空格後面接的是迷路，可得知帶地圖應該是要避免迷路的情況，因此選項 D
> 正確。

__D__ 17. (A) damaged 被危害的　　　(B) damage 危害
　　　　 (C) to damage 危害　　　　(D) damaging 正在危害

> **解析**　空格前是 avoid，其後面的動詞需改成動名詞 Ving，因此選項 D 正確。

__A__ 18. (A) responsible 負責的　　　(B) possible 可能的
　　　　 (C) available 有空的　　　　(D) comfortable 舒適的

> **解析**　"be responsible for doing something" 的語意為「應對…承擔責任」。

第三部分　閱讀理解

共 12 題，包括 4 個題組，每個題組含 1 至 2 篇短文，與數個相關的四選一的選擇題。請由試題上的選項中選出最適合的答案。

Questions 22-24

Roy

> Hey, Lisa! I'm planning a birthday party for my girlfriend in September and want to get her something special.

Lisa

> Cool. Do you have anything in mind?

Roy

> I mentioned shoes, but she didn't seem interested. I'm thinking jewelry. Something that will go with her red dress or her favorite earrings. Are you free this afternoon?

Lisa

> I'm having lunch with my dad. We'll be done by 2:00. We can meet somewhere after that.

Roy

> Great! How about Metro Mall? They're having a summer sale that just started this week.

Lisa

> Sounds good. I'll go there after lunch. It'll take me about an hour to get there. See you then!

羅伊

嘿,麗莎!我正在為我女友計劃九月的生日派對,想給她買點特別的禮物。

麗莎

酷。你有什麼想法嗎?

羅伊

我提到了鞋子,但她似乎不感興趣。**(20) 我在想買珠寶。一件能搭配她的紅色洋裝或她最喜歡的耳環的東西。**你今天下午有空嗎?

麗莎

(19) 我要和我爸一起吃午餐。我們兩點會吃完。之後我們可以約個地方見面。

羅伊

太好了!去捷運購物中心如何?**(21) 他們的夏季特賣這週才剛開始。**

麗莎

聽起來不錯。**(19) 我午餐後會到那裡去。大概需要一個小時到達。**到時見!

Summer Sale Metro Mall July 20 - August 10		
1F	Shoes	Designer shoes: NT$5000 → NT$3000
2F	Women's clothing	Dresses: NT$5000 → NT$4000 Earrings: NT$2000 → NT$1000 Necklaces: NT$4000 → NT$3000
3F	Men's clothes	Jackets: NT$4000 → NT$3000 Pants: NT$3000 → NT$2400
4F	Sporting Goods	Baseball bat: NT$1800 → NT$1400 Basketball: NT$1500 → NT$1200

夏季特賣 捷運購物中心 (21) 7 月 20 日 - 8 月 10 日		
1 樓	鞋子	設計師鞋子：NT$5000 → NT$3000
2 樓	女裝	洋裝：NT$5000 → NT$4000 耳環：NT$2000 → NT$1000 **(20) 項鍊：NT$4000 → NT$3000**
3 樓	男裝	夾克：NT$4000 → NT$3000 褲子：NT$3000 → NT$2400
4 樓	運動用品	棒球棒：T$1800 → NT$1400 籃球：NT$1500 → NT$1200

C 19. When are Roy and Lisa going to meet?

(A) 12:00

(B) 14:00

(C) 15:00

(D) 17:00

羅伊和麗莎將在什麼時候見面？

(A) 12:00

(B) 14:00

(C) 15:00

(D) 17:00

解析 麗莎的第二回對話中提到吃完午飯時是 2:00，而麗莎的最後一回對話提到要花一個小時到達，因此到的時間是下午三點。選項 C 正確。

B 20. How much will Roy likely save on his girlfriend's gift?

(A) 20%

(B) 25%

(C) 40%

(D) 50%

羅伊購買女友的禮物可能可以省下多少？

(A) 20%

(B) 25%

(C) 40%

(D) 50%

解析 由對話中羅伊的第二回提到要買一件搭配洋裝和耳環的珠寶，以及特賣折扣價表格第二項 Women's clothing 得知，可以買來搭配的特價品是項鍊，而 4000 到 3000 的降幅是 25％，選項 B 正確。

___B___ 21. What month is it now?
    (A) June
    (B) July
    (C) August
    (D) September

現在是哪個月份？
(A) 六月
(B) 七月
(C) 八月
(D) 九月

解析 由對話中羅伊的最後一回最後一句 "They're having a summer sale that just started this week." 得知，現在正是特賣開始的第一週。再由特賣折扣價表格的特賣起始時間 "July 20" 推斷，選項 B 的七月正確。

Questions 22-24

Countries around the world all have their own unique cultures, and with different cultures come different <u>superstitions</u>. In America, for example, it is believed by many that breaking a mirror will bring seven years of bad luck. There is also a saying in the U.S., "Step on a crack, break your mother's back." It means one should avoid stepping on cracks in the sidewalk, or it may bring bad luck for one's mother. In Thailand, there's a superstition that if a woman sings in the kitchen, she will end up marrying an old man. In Taiwan, some believe that if you point at the moon, your ear will be cut off. Another common Taiwanese superstition is that whistling late at night will bring evil spirits. Considering how big the world is, it's no surprise that people in different places have different beliefs. Many superstitions may seem silly to us, but it's best to show respect for other cultures and appreciate the differences.

世界各國都有自己獨特的文化，而不同的文化伴隨著不同的迷信。**(23) 例如在美國，許多人相信打破鏡子會帶來七年的壞運氣。**美國還有一句話說：「踩到裂縫，媽媽就會摔斷背。」這意味著人們應該避免踩到人行道上的裂縫，否則可能會給媽媽帶來壞運氣。在泰國有一種迷信認為，如果女人在廚房裡唱歌，她最後會嫁給一個老男人。在台灣，有些人相信，如果你指著月亮，你的耳朵會被割掉。另一個常見的台灣迷信是，晚上吹口哨會引來惡靈。**(22) 考慮到世界如此之大，人們在不同地方有不同的信仰並不奇怪。(24) 許多迷信可能對我們來說很愚蠢，但最好尊重其他文化並欣賞這些差異。**

__D__ 22. What does the word "superstition" mean?

(A) Things you shouldn't do because they're not legal.

(B) Nice things to do if you want to live a happy life.

(C) A lie that is told to make people feel scared.

(D) Widely held beliefs that are not based on facts.

「迷信」這個詞的意思是什麼？

(A) 你不應該做的事情，因為它們是非法的。

(B) 想過著幸福生活時應該做的好事。

(C) 為了讓人們感到害怕而說的謊言。

(D) 沒有基於事實的普遍信仰。

解析 由最後一兩句得知，不同國家的人有不同的信念，而迷信有時對不同文化的人看來是愚蠢的，因此可推知，迷信只是一些沒有根據的信念，因此選項 D 正確。

__C__ 23. What is believed to happen if people break a mirror in the United States?

(A) It will bring evil spirits or ghosts.

(B) They'll step on cracks in the sidewalk.

(C) They'll experience years of bad luck.

(D) Bad things will happen to their mothers.

在美國，如果人們打破鏡子，據說會發生什麼事情？

(A) 會帶來惡靈或鬼魂。

(B) 他們會踩到人行道上的裂縫。

(C) 他們會經歷幾年的壞運氣。

(D) 壞事會發生在他們的母親身上。

解析 由第二句得知，打破鏡子會帶來七年的厄運，因此選項 C 正確。

__A__ 24. What do we learn from the article?

(A) We should respect different cultures.

(B) Being superstitious is a good thing.

(C) We shouldn't believe superstitions.

(D) Superstitions are common in Thailand.

我們從文章中學到了什麼？

(A) 我們應該尊重不同的文化。

(B) 迷信是一件好事。

(C) 我們不應該相信迷信。

(D) 迷信在泰國很普遍。

解析 由最後一句得知，我們應該尊重不同文化，因此選項 A 正確。

Questions 25-27

I want to share my recent experience visiting my father at the hospital. My dad had to go to the hospital for a minor operation, and I went to visit him the following day. I was a little nervous because I don't like going to hospitals. But a kind volunteer helped me find my dad's room.

When I entered the room, my dad was resting, and he looked quite tired. I sat down next to him and asked him how he was feeling. He told me that he was in a lot of pain but was happy to see me. We talked about various things, and I tried to make him laugh to take his mind off the pain.

Before leaving, I talked to the nurse. I asked her how we could help my dad recover after he returned home. She gave me some helpful tips. I hugged my dad and told him I would be back soon. Even though it was tough seeing him in pain, I was glad I could be there for him and offer my support.

我想分享我最近去醫院探望父親的經歷。**(25) 我爸爸必須去醫院動個小手術，而我在第二天去探望他。**我有點緊張，因為我不喜歡去醫院，但醫院的一名義工非常親切，幫我找到了爸爸的病房。

當我進入病房時，爸爸正在休息，他看起來很疲倦。我坐在他旁邊，問他感覺怎麼樣。**(26) 他告訴我他很疼，但很高興見到我。我們聊了很多事情，我試圖讓他笑，以減輕他的痛苦。**

(27) 在離開之前，我問護理師我們能做些什麼來幫助爸爸回家後康復，她給了我一些有用的訣竅。我擁抱了爸爸，告訴他我會很快回來。雖然看到他疼痛很難受，但我很高興能夠在他身邊，給予支持。

___B___ 25. Why did the author visit the hospital?
- (A) Because he is a student of medicine.
- (B) His father was receiving treatment there.
- (C) The nurse asked him to be a volunteer.
- (D) His father had to perform an operation.

作者為什麼去醫院？
- (A) 因為他是醫學生。
- (B) 他的父親正在接受治療。
- (C) 護士請他當義工。
- (D) 他的父親要執行手術。

解析 由第一段第二句得知，作者的父親要在醫院接受一個小手術，即為治療之意，因此選項 B 正確。

___A___ 26. What did the author do at the hospital?

(A) He tried to cheer his father up.

(B) He gave his father medicine.

(C) He helped his father do his work.

(D) He took care of his dad's wound.

作者在醫院做了什麼？

(A) 他試圖讓父親高興起來。

(B) 他給父親吃藥。

(C) 他幫父親做工作。

(D) 他照顧了父親的傷口。

解析 由第二段第三句和第四句得知，作者試圖讓父親開心，轉移他的注意力，因此選項 A 正確。

___D___ 27. According to the article, which is true?

(A) The author's dad is too sick to leave the hospital anytime soon.

(B) The author got a lot of help from strangers at the hospital.

(C) The author's father is recovering well and is able to walk around.

(D) The author learned something useful before leaving the hospital.

根據文章，哪一項正確？

(A) 作者的父親病得很重，暫時無法出院。

(B) 作者在醫院得到了陌生人的很多幫助。

(C) 作者的父親恢復得很好，能夠四處走動。

(D) 作者在離開前學到了有用的東西。

解析 由第三段第一句得知，作者在離開前從護理師那裡學到了一些有用的訣竅，因此選項 D 正確。

Questions 28-30

Have you ever taken a ride on a hot air balloon? It's an incredible experience! You'll float high above the ground and feel like you're flying with the birds. The view from the balloon is amazing, and you can see for miles in every direction.

Before the balloon goes up, you'll receive information on safely entering the basket. Once you're in the air, the ride is smooth and peaceful. You'll feel the warmth from the burner, which is what keeps the balloon in the air.

The whole ride lasts about an hour, but it will feel like no time at all. It's a great activity to do with friends or family. If you're looking for a new experience, taking a hot air balloon ride is a must-try!

你曾經乘坐過熱氣球嗎？這是個令人難以置信的經驗！你會在空中高高漂浮，感覺像是在和鳥兒們一起飛翔。從氣球上看到的景色令人驚嘆，而且可以看到四面八方幾英哩外的遠處。

(29) 在氣球升空之前，你會收到有關如何安全進入籃子的資訊。一旦你在空中，旅程是穩當而平和的。你會感受到燃燒器的熱度，這是保持氣球升空的原因。

(28) 整個旅程大約持續一個小時，但感覺就像一瞬間一樣。這是一項很適合與朋友或家人一起做的活動。(30) 如果你在尋找新的體驗，乘坐熱氣球是一個必定要嘗試的活動！

_C_ 28. According to the article, what does the author believe about hot air balloon rides?
   (A) They allow you to fly with birds.
   (B) It's best to go in warm weather.
   (C) It feels like time passes quickly.
   (D) They're convenient transportation.

根據文章，作者認為乘坐熱氣球怎麼樣？
   (A) 它們讓你能和鳥一起飛翔。
   (B) 最好在溫暖的天氣裡進行。
   (C) 感覺時間過得很快。
   (D) 它們是便捷的交通工具。

> **解析** 由第三段第一句得知，整個旅程大約持續一個小時，但會感覺時間過得很快，因此選項 C 正確。乘坐熱氣球會有和鳥飛翔一樣的感覺，但並非是真正飛起來，因此選項 A 不符合。

__C__ 29. What kind of information will the passengers be given before the balloon takes off?

(A) The things they are about to see.

(B) The science behind hot air balloons.

(C) Tips on how to board the balloon.

(D) Tips on taking beautiful photos.

乘客在氣球升空之前，會收到什麼資訊？

(A) 他們即將看到的東西。

(B) 熱氣球背後的科學知識。

(C) 如何登上氣球的提示。

(D) 拍攝美麗照片的提示。

> **解析** 由第二段第一句得知，乘客會收到安全進入籃子的資訊，即為登上熱氣球的意思，因此選項 C 正確。

__A__ 30. Where is this article most likely to appear?

(A) On the website of a travel agency.

(B) On a sign in front of a historical site.

(C) In a story about a pilot school.

(D) In a magazine for photographers.

這篇文章最有可能出現在什麼地方？

(A) 旅行社的網站上。

(B) 歷史遺址前的標誌上。

(C) 關於飛行學校的故事中。

(D) 攝影師雜誌中。

> **解析** 由最後一段推知，本文建議可以利用熱氣球搭乘來豐富人生的經驗，因此這篇文章最可能出現在旅行社的網站上，因此選項 A 正確。

GEPT
初級模擬試題
第 9 回
解答、翻譯與詳解

第 9 回解答

 聽力測驗解答

1. A	2. A	3. B	4. C	5. C
6. C	7. B	8. A	9. A	10. B
11. A	12. C	13. A	14. C	15. C
16. A	17. A	18. B	19. B	20. B
21. A	22. A	23. A	24. A	25. C
26. B	27. A	28. B	29. C	30. C

 閱讀測驗解答

1. B	2. B	3. D	4. A	5. B
6. C	7. A	8. D	9. D	10. D
11. C	12. D	13. D	14. C	15. D
16. C	17. B	18. A	19. D	20. C
21. C	22. B	23. C	24. A	25. A
26. C	27. C	28. D	29. A	30. A

第一部分　看圖辨義

___A___ 1. For Question Number 1, please look at the picture.

Where is the student?

(A) At a library

(B) At a bookstore.

(C) At a computer store.

第一題，請看此圖片。

這名學生在哪裡？

(A) 在圖書館。

(B) 在書店。

(C) 在電腦店。

解析　圖片背景有很多書架和書籍，書桌上除了書本還有電腦，可以知道學生正在讀書，因此可以排除選項 B 和選項 C。正確答案選 A。

___A___ 2. For Question Number 2, please look at the picture.

How does the girl feel?

(A) The girl is happy sitting next to the boy.

(B) She's sad because the boy doesn't like her.

(C) She's angry because the boy is ignoring her.

第二題、請看此圖片。這個女孩的感覺如何？

(A) 女孩坐在男孩旁邊很開心。

(B) 她很傷心因為男孩不喜歡她。

(C) 她很生氣因為男孩不理她。

解析　圖片上女孩坐在男孩旁邊，帶著微笑的表情，所以可以知道她很開心，答案選 A。

B 3. For Question Number 3, please look at the picture.
What did the man do?

(A) The man sold a lot of things.

(B) The man bought a lot of things.

(C) The man gave away a lot of things.

第三題，請看此圖片。

男子做了什麼？

(A) 男子賣了很多東西。

(B) 男子買了很多東西。

(C) 男子送出去很多東西。

解析 圖片中的男子在超市 (supermarket) 前把東西從購物車中搬到車上，因此可以推測他買了很多東西，答案選 B。

C 4. For Question Number 4, please look at the picture.
What is the girl doing in the classroom?

(A) The girl is sleeping.

(B) The girl is taking a test.

(C) The girl is taking notes.

第四題，請看此圖片。

女孩正在教室裡做什麼？

(A) 女孩正在睡覺。

(B) 女孩正在考試。

(C) 女孩正在做筆記。

解析 女孩視線朝下，拿著筆在筆記本上書寫，因此可以知道女孩正在抄筆記，選 C。

_C_ 5. For Question Number 5, please look at the picture.

What is happening?

(A) The woman is playing a game with the boy.

(B) The mother is having fun together with her son.

(C) The mother is angry at the boy for not studying.

第五題，請看此圖片。

發生什麼事？

(A) 女子正和男孩一起打電動。

(B) 媽媽正和她的兒子共享歡樂時光。

(C) 媽媽因為男孩不讀書，所以很生氣。

解析 圖片上可以看到女子生氣的拿著一本書，男孩正在專注打電動，可以推測女子因為男孩只打電動不讀書而生氣，答案選 C。

___C___ 6. Can you tell me how to get to the nearest gas station?

(A) I don't work at the gas station anymore.

(B) There's a train station in the city center.

(C) There's one two blocks away on the left.

你能告訴我離這裡最近的加油站怎麼去嗎？

(A) 我已經不在加油站工作了。

(B) 市中心有一個火車站。

(C) 兩個街區外，左手邊有一個加油站。

解析 「Can you tell me how to get to + 地方」常用來問路。三個選項中只有 C 是在報路，其餘兩個答非所問，因此答案選 C。

___B___ 7. Would you like to join us for dinner at Miss Lee's place tonight?

(A) I'd like to, but I can't cook.

(B) Sure. What time should I be there?

(C) Yes, we hope you can come to dinner.

你今天晚上想要和我們一起到李小姐家吃晚餐嗎？

(A) 我很想，可是我不會煮飯。

(B) 當然。我應該幾點到？

(C) 是的，我們希望你能一起用晚餐。

解析 「Would you like to join us for + 事物？」是邀請對方一起做某件事情的常用句型。B 選項答應邀約後，詢問應該到達的時間最符合情境，其餘兩個選項答非所問，答案選 B。

___A___ 8. What's your favorite sport to play?

(A) I love playing soccer.

(B) I enjoy watching golf.

(C) Playing sports can be fun.

你最喜歡從事什麼運動？

(A) 我喜歡踢足球。

(B) 我喜歡看高爾夫球。

(C) 做運動很好玩。

解析 題目在 "sports" 後加上 "to play" 來強調是喜歡從事的運動，選項 B 的回答是觀看而非從事，所以不正確。選項 C 則答非所問，因此答案選 A。

__A__ 9. I need to borrow your car.

（A) OK. When do you need it?

（B) I'm afraid my cart is broken.

（C) Sorry, I don't have any money.

我需要跟你借車。

（A) 好，你什麼時候需要？

（B) 很抱歉我的推車壞了。

（C) 對不起，我沒錢。

解析 選項 B 的 cart（推車／購物車）和題目中的 car（車）的發音相似容易搞混，請小心。題目是要借車，選項 C 答非所問。正確答案為 A，回答可以之後詢問對方需要用車的時間。

__B__ 10. Have you seen the new movie that just came out?

（A) Yes, I'm going to see the movie on Friday.

（B) No, I haven't had the chance to see it yet.

（C) He came out of the movie theater at 8:30.

剛上映的那部電影你已經看了嗎？

（A) 是，我週五要去看。

（B) 不，我還沒有機會去看。

（C) 他 8:30 的時候從戲院出來。

解析 選項 A 必須把 Yes 改成 No，表示還沒看過，再提供更多的訊息才合理。選項 C 答非所問，因此正確答案為 B。

__A__ 11. Do you like French food?

（A) Yes, it's really delicious.

（B) No, I've never been to France.

（C) French is my favorite language.

你喜歡法國料理嗎？

（A) 是，法國料理很好吃。

（B) 不，我沒去過法國。

（C) 法文是我最喜歡的語言。

解析 選項 B，回答沒去過法國，但不需要去過法國才能吃到法國料理，因此不正確。選項 C 答非所問。正確答案為 A。答案的 "It" 指的是題目中的 "French food"。

__C__ 12. How do you like your coffee?

(A) I need only one.

(B) Yes, I like it very much.

(C) With cream and sugar.

你咖啡想要怎麼喝？

(A) 我只需要一杯。

(B) 是，我很喜歡。

(C) 加奶精和糖。

解析　"How do you like...?" 可用來詢問他人意見，「想如何吃某種食物或飲料」。How 開頭的問句不使用 Yes/No 回答，所以選項 B 不正確。選項 A 答非所問。正確答案為 C。

__A__ 13. What do you do for a living?

(A) I'm a secretary.

(B) I live in Chicago.

(C) It's in my living room.

你靠什麼謀生？

(A) 我是祕書。

(B) 我住芝加哥。

(C) 在我的客廳。

解析　"What do you do for a living?" 用來詢問對方工作。這邊的 "living" 指的是「收入、生計」，只有選項 A 有回答到問題，選項 B、C 答非所問，因此答案選 A。

__C__ 14. Have you ever traveled abroad?

(A) I can speak five languages.

(B) I've only taken an airplane once.

(C) Yes, I've been to several countries.

你出國旅遊過嗎？

(A) 我可以講五種語言。

(B) 我只搭過一次飛機。

(C) 是的，我去過幾個國家。

解析　雖然從台灣出國旅遊大多要搭飛機，但搭飛機不見得是出國旅遊，也可能是國內航線，因此選項 B 不正確，選項 A 答非所問。正確答案為選項 C。

__C__ 15. Do you know where Mommy went?

(A) She's listening to music.

(B) She'll be back tomorrow.

(C) She's picking your sister up.

你知道媽媽去哪裡嗎？

(A) 她在聽音樂。

(B) 她明天回來。

(C) 她去接妳妹妹回家。

解析　"where" 是詢問地方的疑問詞，三個選項中只有 C 是針對媽媽去的地方回答，A 和 B 皆答非所問，因此答案選 C。

_A_ 16. W: I'm planning a trip to Italy this summer. Do you have any tips?

M: You should definitely visit Rome and Florence. The food there is amazing.

W: Sounds great. What about places to stay?

M: There are lots of nice hotels and apartments you can rent.

Question: What is the woman doing this summer?

女子：我正在規劃今年夏天去義大利的行程。你有什麼建議嗎？

男子：妳一定要去羅馬跟佛羅倫斯。那邊的美食很令人驚豔。

女子：聽起來很棒。住的地方呢？

男子：那裏有很多不錯的飯店以及出租公寓。

問題：女子這個夏天要做什麼？

(A) Going traveling.	(A) 去旅遊。
(B) Trying some food.	(B) 嘗試一些食物。
(C) Planning a project.	(C) 規劃一個專案。

解析 旅遊的英文有兩種說法：trip 和 travel。由對話中女子的第一句話可以得知女子正在規劃旅遊行程 (planning a trip)，因此知道答案為 A：女子夏天要去旅遊 (travel)。

_A_ 17. W: I'm really tired today. I think I need a break.

M: Yeah, you do seem tired. Maybe you should take a day off tomorrow.

W: But there's so much work to do.

M: Don't worry. I can help you with some of it.

Question: What does the man offer to do for the woman?

女子：我今天很累。我想我需要休息一下。

男子：是啊！妳的確看起來很累。妳明天應該請一天假。

女子：但是我還有好多工作。

男子：不用擔心。我可以幫妳做一點。

問題：男子提議幫女子做什麼？

(A) Do some of her work.	(A) 幫她做一點工作
(B) Give her a break later.	(B) 之後給她一點時間休息
(C) Take a day off with her.	(C) 和她一起請一天假

解析 問題中 offer 的意思為「提議、主動提出」。對話中男子說了 "I can help you with some of it.",這裡的 it 指的是上一句的 work(工作),因此選項 A 為正確答案。

B 18. W: I'm really interested in learning a new language. Any ideas?

M: You should try Spanish or French. They're both useful and widely spoken.

W: They both sound interesting. Where can I learn them?

M: There are many language schools and online courses available.

Question: What is the man doing?

女子:我對學一種新的語言很感興趣。有什麼想法嗎?

男子:妳應該試試看西班牙文或法文。兩種都很有用而且廣泛使用。

女子:兩種聽起來都很有趣。我可以去哪裡學?

男子:有很多語言學校和線上課程,你都可以參加。

問題:男子在做什麼?

(A) He's learning a language.
(B) He's giving her some advice.
(C) He's taking an online course.

(A) 他在學一種語言。
(B) 他在給她一點建議。
(C) 他在上線上課程。

解析 對話中男子給了女子學新語言的建議,但沒有提到自己在上線上課程或是也在學新的語言,因此答案為選項 B。

B 19. W: I'm sorry, but I'm afraid I can't make it to the meeting tomorrow.

M: That's all right. We can change it to next week.

W: Thank you for understanding.

Question: What will they do about the meeting?

女子:對不起,我恐怕無法出席明天的會議。

男子:沒關係。我們可以改到下週。

女子:謝謝你的體諒。

問題:他們這次的會議會怎麼做?

(A) Cancel it completely.

(B) Hold it next week instead.

(C) Hold it without the woman.

(A) 完全取消。

(B) 改成下週舉行。

(C) 女子不出席的情況下照常舉行。

解析 舉辦會議的英文可以是 have a meeting 或是 hold a meeting。對話中男子提到可以將會議改到下週，因此得知答案為 B。

B 20. W: I can't decide what to wear to the party tonight. Maybe the red dress I wore last time?

M: How about that new dress you bought last week? It looks great on you.

W: Really? I wasn't sure if it was too formal.

M: Not at all. I think it's the perfect choice.

Question: What does the man suggest the woman wear to the party?

女子：我不能決定晚上的派對要穿什麼衣服。可能穿上次穿過的紅色禮服？

男子：你上週買的新禮服如何？妳穿起來很好看。

女子：真的嗎？我不確定會不會太正式。

男子：完全不會。我覺得那會是個完美的選擇。

問題：男子建議女子穿什麼去派對？

(A) Something less formal.

(B) The new dress she bought.

(C) The dress she wore last time.

(A) 比較不那麼正式的服裝。

(B) 她買的新禮服。

(C) 她上次穿的禮服。

解析 "How about...?" 是在給予提議時常用的句型。從對話中 "How about that new dress you bought last week?" 得知男子提議女子穿上週買的新禮服，因此答案為 B。

A 21. W: I'm having trouble with this question. Can you help me?

M: Sure, let me take a look. OK, I see where your problem is. You need to add these two numbers together before you multiply.

W: Oh, now it makes sense. Thank you so much.

M: It's not a big deal. I love to help.

Question: What does the woman need help with?

女子：這題我有點不懂。你能幫我嗎？

男子：當然，我看一下。好，我知道你的問題出在哪裡了。你需要把這兩個數字加起來後再相乘。

女子：喔，現在說得通了。真謝謝你。

男子：這沒什麼。我很樂意幫忙。

問題：女子什麼地方需要幫忙？

(A) A math problem.
(B) An English story.
(C) A history question.

(A) 數學題。
(B) 英文故事。
(C) 歷史題。

解析 數學題在英文的說法是 "math problem"，從對話中的關鍵詞 add（相加）和 multiply（相乘），可以得知女子需要幫忙的地方是數學題，答案為 A。

A 22. W: I'm applying for a position at a bank next week.

M: That's great. Have you worked at a bank before?

W: No, but I have experience working with money. I hope I don't get nervous when I meet with the manager.

M: I'm sure you'll do fine. Just be confident and tell them about your experience.

Question: What will the woman do next week?

女子：我下禮拜要應徵一個銀行的職位。

男子：太棒了。你之前有在銀行工作過嗎？

女子：沒有，不過我有做過和錢相關的工作。希望我到時和經理見面時不會緊張。

男子：我相信你會做得很好。只要保持自信並且告訴他們你的經驗。

問題：女子下週要做什麼？

(A) Go to a job interview.

(B) Put money in the bank.

(C) Attend a work meeting.

(A) 參加工作面試。

(B) 把錢存進銀行。

(C) 參加工作上的會議。

解析 從對話中女子提到要應徵一個職位 (applying for a position)，以及會和經理見面 (meet with the manager)，可以推論女子下禮拜要做的事情是參加工作面試，答案選 A。

A 23. W: I think I left my phone at the restaurant we went to earlier. Can you help me look for it?

M: Of course. Let's go back and ask the staff if they found it.

W: I wonder if someone may have taken it. It's an expensive phone.

M: Don't be so negative. Let's hurry and see if we can find it.

Question: What does the woman think?

女子：我想我把手機忘在我們先前去的餐廳了。你可以幫我一起找嗎？

男子：當然。我們回去問問那邊的員工有沒有看到。

女子：我在想會不會被人拿走了。那支電話很貴。

男子：不要想得那麼負面。我們快去看看找不找得到。

問題：女子的想法是什麼？

(A) She may not find her phone.

(B) The staff took away her phone.

(C) She will find her phone for sure.

(A) 她可能會找不到她的手機。

(B) 員工把她的手機拿走了。

(C) 她一定能找到她的手機。

解析 女子提到覺得自己的手機可能已經被人拿走了 (someone may have taken it)，所以選項 C 不正確。女子使用 "someone" 表示沒有特定對象，所以選項 B 也不正確。正確答案為 A。

A 24. W: I'm so excited to start college next semester.

M: That's great. Have you decided your major yet?

W: I'm not sure yet. I'm good at math, so maybe science or technology.

Question: What are the people talking about?

女子：下學期就要開始上大學了，我好興奮。

男子：太好了。你決定好妳的主修了嗎？

女子：我還不確定。我對數學很在行，所以大概是科學或是科技。

問題：這兩個人在討論什麼？

(A) The woman's future studies.

(B) Their memories from college.

(C) Science and technology problems.

(A) 女子將來的攻讀的領域。

(B) 他們大學時期的回憶。

(C) 科學和科技問題。

解析 從男子的提問 "Have you decided...?"（…決定好了嗎？）可以知道兩個人討論的是未來的事情，加上關鍵詞 college（大學）和 major（主修），可以知道正確答案為 A。

C 25. W: I feel terrible. I think I may have the flu.

M: Do you have a fever? You should check your temperature.

W: I did. It's normal. But I have a headache and a cough.

M: Well, it sounds like you should see a doctor. Let's go.

Question: What is wrong with the woman?

女子：我很不舒服。我想我可能得到流感了。

男子：妳有發燒嗎？妳應該量一下體溫。

女子：我量了，體溫正常。不過我頭痛而且咳嗽。

男子：聽起來妳需要看醫生。走吧！

問題：女子怎麼了？

(A) She has the flu.

(B) She has a fever.

(C) She isn't feeling well.

(A) 她得流感了。

(B) 她發燒了。

(C) 她不舒服。

解析 從對話中女子用 may（可能）來說明自己覺得可能得流感，但還不確定，因此選項 A 不正確。女子體溫正常，所以選項 B 也不正確。正確答案為 C。

(A)　　　　　　　　　(B)　　　　　　　　　(C)

___B___ 26. For question number 26, please look at the three pictures.

A teacher is talking to her students about a field trip. Where will they visit in the afternoon on that day?

As you all know, we're going on a field trip next Tuesday. We'll leave school at nine a.m. and be back at four p.m. We'll spend two hours at the National Museum, take an hour for lunch, and then spend two hours at Wonderland Amusement Park.

第 26 題，請看三張圖片。

一名老師正和學生說明校外教學。他們那天下午會去哪裡？

大家都知道我們下週二要校外教學了。我們會在早上九點離開學校，並在下午四點回來。我們會在國立博物館逛兩個小時，花一小時吃午餐，然後在奇妙世界遊樂園停留兩個小時。

解析 　午餐後的行程為遊樂園。圖片 B 可以看到摩天輪、旋轉木馬等遊樂設施，所以知道答案為 B。

(A)　　　　　　　　　(B)　　　　　　　　　(C)

Cinema Timetable

MOVIE	Showing Dates
Toy Story	June 30th-July 20th
Spider-Man	July 14th-July 20th
The Tiger King	July 28th-August 3rd
Car Racing	June 30th-July 6th
Tomorrow Land	July 7th-July 13th

$120　TICKET　TICKET

$180　TICKET

A 27. For question number 27, please look at the three pictures.

Listen to the radio ad. Which is true about the movie theater?

The Grand Palace movie theater is showing five movies this weekend. Tickets cost 120 dollars each. We also have a snack special that includes a large popcorn and a soft drink for an extra 80 dollars.

第 27 題，請看三張圖片。

請聽收音機廣告，和電影院相關的資訊何者為真？

這個週末皇宮電影院將播放五部電影。每張電影票要價 120 元，再加 80 元可升級為零食套餐，包括大杯爆米花和一杯無酒精的飲料。

解析 每張電影票 120 元，但選項 B 有兩張票，所以不正確。選項 C 套餐的內容雖然正確，但金額不正確，因此也不是正確答案。正確答案為 A，共播五部電影。

(A)

(B)

(C)

B 28. For question number 28, please look at the three pictures.

A man is talking about a book. Which is the cover for the book?

This book is about a girl who goes on an exciting journey to a secret kingdom. Along the way, she meets a talking cat and a group of little people who help her find the fairy castle. But will she be able to find the magic shoes that can take her home?

第 28 題，請看三張圖片。

男子正在談論一本書。哪一個是這本書的封面？

這本書是關於一個女孩在祕密王國裡的刺激旅程。在旅途中，她遇見了一隻會說話的貓和一群小矮人幫忙她找到仙女城堡。但她能找到可以帶她回家的魔法鞋嗎？

解析 從關鍵詞 cat（貓）和 secret kingdom（祕密王國）可以推論這本書的背景非選項 A 顯示的日常生活，也和選項 C 的獲獎無關。答案為選項 B。

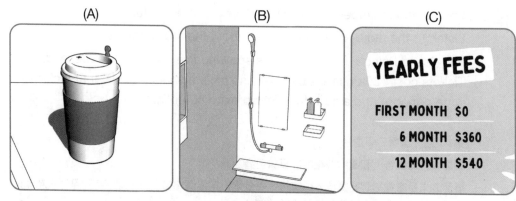

(A)   (B)   (C)

YEARLY FEES

FIRST MONTH	$0
6 MONTH	$360
12 MONTH	$540

__C__ 29. For Question Number 29, please look at the three pictures.

A man is talking about an offer. What will new members receive when they sign up this month?

Sport Power gym is offering a special deal for new members. If you sign up this month, you'll get a whole month for free. The gym has all kinds of weights and machines for you to use, and offers sports and exercise classes for both men and women. We even have a coffee shop for you to enjoy after you exercise.

第 29 題，請看三張圖片。

男子正在談論一項折扣。本月報名的新會員可以得到什麼？

運動力健身中心正推出給新會員的特別折扣。於本月報名可享有整個月免費的優惠。本健身中心有各式重物和健身機器供您使用，並且有提供給男女會員的運動課程。我們甚至有咖啡館可以讓您在運動後前往。

解析 談話內容中雖然有提到咖啡，但不限本月報名的新會員，因此選項 A 不正確。選項 B 的淋浴設備沒有出現於談話，因此也不正確。新會員能得到的折扣是一個月免費，答案為選項 C。

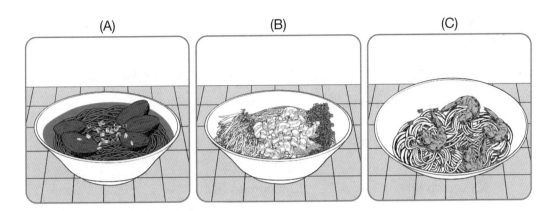

(A)   (B)   (C)

___C___ 30. For question number 30, please look at the three pictures.

A waiter is talking about a new dish. Which fits his description?

Our restaurant is serving a new dish called red hot shrimp pasta. The dish is made with giant shrimp, spaghetti noodles, and a rich tomato sauce with lots of pepper. Fresh vegetables and Italian cheese give the dish extra flavor. The price is just 15 dollars.

第 30 題，請看三張圖片。

服務生在談論新菜色。哪個最符合他的敘述？

我們餐廳現在供應名為赤辣鮮蝦義大利麵的新菜色。這道菜由大蝦、義大利麵條、濃郁的番茄醬和大量辣椒所製成。新鮮蔬菜和義大利起司為這道菜增添不少風味。只要 15 元。

解析 由關鍵詞鮮蝦 (shrimp) 和義大利麵 (spaghetti) 可以得知答案為選項 C。

共 10 題，每個題目裡有一個空格。請從四個選項中選出一個最適合題意的字或詞作答。

__B__ 1. The teacher asked me to _____ my paper because there were some errors in it.

老師要求我修改我的文章，因為裡面有一些錯誤。

(A) finish 完成　　　　　　　(B) revise 修改

(C) search 搜尋　　　　　　　(D) upgrade 升級

> 解析　空格後提到文章中有些錯誤，可推知是需要對文章做些修改，因此選項 B 正確。

__B__ 2. Please let me know _____ you decide on a date for the meeting.

一旦你決定會議日期，請讓我知道。

(A) while 當…同時　　　　　　(B) once 一旦

(C) until 直到　　　　　　　　(D) though 雖然

> 解析　空格後提到決定日期，可推知是「一旦」決定了之後，就要通知別人，選項 B 正確。選項 A 的 while 後的子句通常會用進行式，為「正在」的意思，與題意不符。

__D__ 3. _____ on the birth of your beautiful baby girl!

恭喜你美麗的女兒出生！

(A) Best wishes 最佳祝福　　　(B) Appreciation 感謝

(C) Compliments 讚美　　　　　(D) Congratulations 恭喜

__A__ 4. I counted the money, and the _____ amount in the jar was $562.

我算好了錢，罐子裡總計的總量是 562 元。

(A) total 總計　　　　　　　　(B) least 最少

(C) equal 平等　　　　　　　　(D) enough 足夠

__B__ 5. You should wear a hat to _____ your face from the sun.

你應該戴帽子來保護你的臉以阻擋陽光。

(A) avoid 避免　　　　　　　　(B) protect 保護

(C) increase 增加　　　　　　　(D) improve 改善

> 解析　空格後的受詞是「你的臉」，得知戴帽子是要來「保護」臉，因此選項 B 正確。選項 A 不符合，是因為戴帽子並不是要「避免」臉，而是要避免陽光。

___C___ 6. We're ready for dessert. May I see the _____ , please?

我們準備好要吃甜點了。請給我菜單。

(A) price 價格　　　　　　　(B) check 帳單

(C) menu 菜單　　　　　　　(D) order 訂單

___A___ 7. Pink diamonds are more expensive than white diamonds because they are so _____ .

粉紅鑽比白鑽昂貴，因為它們非常稀有。

(A) rare 稀有　　　　　　　(B) useful 有用

(C) perfect 完美　　　　　　(D) ordinary 普通

解析 空格中要填鑽石價格昂貴的原因，而選項 A 的「稀有」最符合。選項 C 的「完美」並不盡然代表價格昂貴。

___D___ 8. Everyone cheered when our team achieved a narrow _____ at the last second.

當我們的隊伍在最後一秒險勝時，每個人都歡呼起來。

(A) score 得分　　　　　　　(B) effort 努力

(C) finish 完成　　　　　　　(D) victory 勝利

解析 句子一開頭就提到歡呼，可推知是隊伍「獲勝」。此外，空格後提到是最後一秒才達成勝利，所以是隊伍是「險勝」，選項 D 正確。選項 A 的 score 要用 "close" score 來做搭配詞。

___D___ 9. The toothache was so _____ that I couldn't sleep all night.

我的牙痛非常疼痛，以至於整夜都無法入睡。

(A) sour 酸痛的　　　　　　(B) hurt 傷害

(C) unfair 不公平的　　　　　(D) painful 痛苦的

___D___ 10. When Rosalyn tells stories, she uses _____ to make them more interesting.

當羅莎琳講故事時，她使用手勢讓故事更有趣。

(A) languages 語言　　　　　(B) speeches 演講

(C) practices 練習　　　　　　(D) gestures 手勢

第二部分 **段落填空**

共 8 題，包括二個段落，每個段落含四個空格。每格均有四個選項，請依照文意選出最適合的答案。

Questions 11-14

In the past, the train station in my neighborhood was never very busy. But since the new sports stadium opened, it's become _____(11)_____ more crowded. Weekends are the worst because that's when they have the big games. I _____(12)_____ the sound of the trains, but the laughing, screaming fans always wake me up. _____(13)_____ local restaurant and store owners are glad to have more customers, others, including me, aren't happy about the new stadium. I wish I _____(14)_____ turn back time and have my quiet and peaceful weekends back.

我家附近的火車站過往都不熱鬧。但自從新體育場開幕後，這裡變得 **(11) 更**擁擠。週末是最糟的，因為那時會有大型比賽。我 **(12) 已經習慣**火車的聲音，但笑聲、尖叫聲的球迷總是把我吵醒。**(13) 雖然**當地的餐館和店主很樂意接納更多顧客，但其他人，包括我在內，對這個新的體育場並不樂見。我希望我 **(14) 能夠**倒轉時光，重拾安寧和平靜的週末。

___C___ 11. (A) very 非常　　　　　　　　(B) many 許多
　　　　　(C) much 更　　　　　　　　(D) such 如此

> **解析** 空格後接比較級形容詞 more crowded，因此需要用能夠修飾比較級的副詞 much 來表示「比…擁擠得多了」，選項 C 正確。

___D___ 12. (A) use 使用　　　　　　　　(B) used to 曾經
　　　　　(C) am using 正在使用　　　　(D) am used to 習慣於…

> **解析** "be V used to + N/Ving" 是「習慣於…」的意思，因此選項 D 正確。選項 B 的「Used to + 原 V」指的是以前曾經發生的事。

___D___ 13. (A) When 當　　　　　　　　(B) Because 因為
　　　　　(C) Therefore 因此　　　　　　(D) Although 雖然

Part 2 段落填空

> **解析** 空格後兩子句提到，一些人樂見車站周邊的變化，但另一群人則非如此。選項 D 的 Although 正可用來表達句子「雖然…但是」的轉折。最符合題意。

<u>C</u> 14. (A) can 可以   (B) will 將會
      (C) could 能夠   (D) should 應該

> **解析** 空格前的 wish 表達的是「不會成真的願望」，因此其後接的字句，需要使用過去式來表達與「現在事實相反的假設」，選項 C 正確。

Questions 15-18

Are you thinking about buying a new house? There are many things to ___(15)___ before you begin your hunt. You need to ___(16)___ on the price range, location, house size, and house type. Do you want a home with a big yard for your children to play in? Would you like to live in a convenient neighborhood close to restaurants and a shopping area? It probably won't be possible to get everything on your wish list, so you may have to make some ___(17)___ choices. By thinking carefully about your wants and needs, you should be ___(18)___ to find the right house at the right price.

你是否在考慮買新房子？在開始找房子之前，有很多事情需要 (15) 思考。你需要 (16) 決定價格範圍、地點、房屋大小和房屋類型。你是否想要一個有大院子的家，讓孩子們玩耍？你是否想住在靠近餐館和購物區的便利社區？實現願望清單上的所有項目，應該不是可能的，因此你可能需要做出一些 (17) 困難的選擇。藉由仔細考慮你的需求和願望，你應該 (18) 能夠 找到以合理價出售的合適房子。

<u>D</u> 15. (A) indicate 指出   (B) provide 提供
      (C) receive 接收   (D) consider 思考

<u>C</u> 16. (A) choose 選擇   (B) guess 猜測
      (C) decide 決定   (D) figure 計算

> **解析** 空格後有介系詞 on，需要選一個動詞可以和它搭配，因此選項 C 的 decide on... 正確，意思為「決定」。Choose 後直接加受詞即可，不需要介系詞 on。

__B__ 17. (A) easy 容易的   (B) hard 困難的
               (C) likely 可能的   (D) strong 強的

__A__ 18. (A) able 能夠   (B) near 接近
               (C) ready 準備好   (D) willing 願意

解析 空格後提到用對的價格，找到對的房子，可推知空格中的意思是「能夠」找到，因此選項 A 的 be able to V 即為「能夠做⋯」，是正確選項。Be ready to V 是「準備好作⋯」。Be willing to V 是「願意做⋯」，都不符合題意。

第三部分 **閱讀理解**

共 12 題，包括 4 個題組，每個題組含 1 至 2 篇短文，與數個相關的四選一的選擇題。請
由試題上的選項中選出最適合的答案。

Questions 19-21

Pacific Ocean Park

We're back with exciting new rides and animal shows!

BUY ONE ticket, GET ONE for FREE!

Bring a friend and share all the fun experiences our park offers.

The Dolphin Aquarium is closed in the evenings

Offer is only for evening hours on weekdays for the next month (17:00-20:00)

Offer is only for students with a student ID

太平洋海洋公園

(20) 我們帶著令人興奮的遊樂設施和動物表演回來了！

買一張門票，再送一張免費門票！

帶一位朋友來，共享我們樂園提供的所有樂趣體驗。

* 海豚水族館晚上關閉 *

(19) (21) * 此優惠僅限於下個月的平日晚上時段 * (17:00-20:00)

* 此優惠僅適用於持有學生證的學生 *

Benson

Hey, did you see the ad for Pacific Ocean Park?

William

Yeah, it sounds like a good deal. We should go this weekend.

Benson

The deal's only good on weekday evenings.

William

Oh, right. That wouldn't give us much time, would it? And after a day of classes, we may be pretty tired.

Benson

True, but we don't have to see everything. And you can't beat the price.

William

OK, you win.

Benson

嘿，你看到太平洋海洋樂園的廣告了嗎？

William

有喔，這優惠聽起來好划算。**(21) 我們這個週末就應該去。**

Benson

這個優惠僅在平日晚上有效。

William

哦，對耶。**(21) 這樣我們就要趕快去了，對吧？** 而且上了一整天的課以後，我們可能會很累。

Benson

這倒沒錯，但我們不必所有的項目都逛。而且這個價格相當實惠。

William

好吧，你贏了。

D 19. Who would be interested in the ad?

(A) Parents with a kindergarten kid who is crazy about sea animals.

(B) High school students who want to go to the park in daytime.

(C) Students who are doing a natural science project on dolphin behavior.

(D) College students looking for something fun to do on a Wednesday night.

誰會對這個廣告感興趣？

(A) 對海洋動物著迷幼兒園小孩的父母。

(B) 想在白天去樂園的高中生。

(C) 正在做有關海豚行為科學計畫的學生。

(D) 正在找週三晚上有趣活動的大學生。

解析 由廣告的最後兩句得知，必須要有學生證才可以享受優惠，且只有平日晚上才能享受優惠，因此選項 D 最符合。無法判斷 A 選項中所提的父母和小孩是否有學生證，因此選項與題意並非完全符合。

C 20. What is true about Pacific Ocean Park?

(A) It's a new park that just opened this year.

(B) Only students are allowed to visit the park.

(C) Some changes have been made to the park.

(D) The park is only open on weekday evenings.

關於太平洋海洋樂園，以下哪一項正確？

(A) 這是今年才剛開幕的新樂園。

(B) 只有學生能參觀此樂園。

(C) 樂園做了一些改變。

(D) 樂園只在平日晚上開放。

解析 由第一篇第一句得知樂園重新開放，而且還有令人興奮的遊樂設施和動物表演，能夠推斷是舊的樂園重新開幕，並多了新的特色，因此選項 C 正確。

__C__ 21. What do you think the two people will do?

(A) Visit the park in the daytime next month.

(B) Visit the park in the evening this weekend.

(C) Visit the park in the evening within a month.

(D) Wait for a better deal before visiting the park.

你認為這兩個人會做什麼？

(A) 下個月的白天去參觀公園。

(B) 這個週末晚上去參觀公園。

(C) 一個月之內，在晚上參觀公園。

(D) 等待更好的優惠後再去參觀公園。

解析 由廣告的倒數第二項得知，優惠只限於下個月。再由威廉對話的第一和第二回可以得知，兩人會使用優惠，因此是在下個月的週間晚上前往。選項 C 正確。

Questions 22-24

I love dumplings, a traditional Chinese dish that has been around for over 1,800 years. They can be served as a main dish or snack and come in a variety of delicious flavors and fillings. However, none of those things are why I love dumplings. I love them for the memories they bring back. The best dumplings that I've ever tried are my grandma's recipe. My grandma made special fillings that I haven't been able to find anywhere else. She always made dumplings for Chinese New Year, my birthday, and sometimes other family holidays. When those days come, I miss my grandma even more than usual. My parents and I often make dumplings when we miss her. Even though we can't make dumplings as tasty as hers, it's a great way to keep her memory alive.

我愛餃子，這是一道超過 1800 年歷史的中華傳統菜餚。餃子可以作為主菜或小吃，並且有各種美味的口味和餡料。然而，這些都不是我愛餃子的原因。我愛餃子是因為它們帶來的許多回憶。**(22) 我吃過的最好的餃子是我奶奶的食譜做的。我的奶奶製作的特別餡料，是我在其他地方都找不到的。**她總是在農曆新年、我的生日，或有時在其他家庭節日包餃子。當這些日子來臨時，我比平時更想念奶奶。**(23) 我和父母常常在想念她的時候包餃子。(24) 雖然我們包的餃子無法像她的那樣美味，但這是一種讓她在我們記憶永存的好方法。**

__B__ 22. What is a "recipe"?

    (A) A way of showing love to family.

    (B) A way to prepare and cook food.

    (C) A way to take care of young children.

    (D) A kind of food that comes from China.

"recipe"是什麼？

    (A) 向家人表達愛的方式。

    (B) 準備和烹飪食物的方法。

    (C) 照顧孩童的方式。

    (D) 來自中國的食物。

解析 由 recipe 這個字的後面那一句得知，奶奶會用特別的餡料包餃子，可推知是和食物有關的意思，因此選項 B 最符合。

__C__ 23. Why does the author's family make dumplings?

    (A) To sell dumplings as a business.

    (B) To attempt to create the best recipe.

    (C) To remember a member of the family.

    (D) To enjoy themselves in their free time.

作者的家人為什麼要包餃子？

    (A) 為了做生意賣餃子。

    (B) 為了嘗試創造最好的食譜。

    (C) 為了懷念一位家族成員。

    (D) 為了在閒暇時間享受樂趣。

解析 由最後兩句得知，當想念奶奶時會包餃子，藉此懷念她，因此選項 C 正確。

__A__ 24. Which is likely true about the author's grandmother.

    (A) She is no longer alive.

    (B) She lives in another city.

    (C) She has a good memory.

    (D) She likes to eat dumplings.

關於作者的奶奶，下列哪一項可能為真？

    (A) 她已經不在人世。

    (B) 她住在另一個城市。

    (C) 她記憶力很好。

    (D) 她喜歡吃餃子。

解析 最後一句提到要把關於奶奶的回憶保留，讓記憶永存，可推知是奶奶已離開人世，才要珍惜回憶懷念奶奶，選項 A 正確。另外，雖然文章提到奶奶的食譜獨特，但無法從文章推知奶奶本人是否喜歡吃餃子。

Questions 25-27

Dear Mr. Lin,

I'm writing this letter to thank you for everything you've done for our son Derek. I haven't seen Derek this happy in a long time. Before you came, Derek didn't like to go to the PE class because he wasn't as good at sports as other students. On the days with the PE class, he was always worried that he couldn't catch up with his classmates.

However, things have really changed ever since you became his PE teacher. You've taken time to encourage and help him. As a result, he's beginning to improve. Last week, Derek told me that he looks forward to PE class. Even though he still gets nervous sometimes, he's proud of himself for making progress.

Derek has become much more confident thanks to you. Therefore, we'd like to invite you to his birthday party next month. It would be a great surprise for Derek, and we would really like to thank you in person. If you can make it, please let us know!

Sincerely,

Ms. DuPont

親愛的林老師：

(25) 我寫這封信是為了感謝您為我們的兒子德瑞克所做的一切。 我很久沒有看到德瑞克這麼開心了。在您來之前，德瑞克不喜歡上體育課，因為他不像其他學生那樣擅長運動。在有體育課的那天，他總是憂心忡忡，擔心自己跟不上同學們。

(26) 然而，自從您成為他的體育老師後，一切都不同。您花了時間鼓勵並幫助他。(27) 因此，他開始有所進步了。上週，德瑞克告訴我他很期待體育課。 雖然他有時仍然會緊張，但他對進步而感到自豪。

德瑞克變得更加自信，這都要感謝您。因此，我們想邀請您參加他下個月的生日派對。這對德瑞克來說將是很大的驚喜，我們也很想親自感謝您。如果您能來，請告訴我們！

真誠的，

度龐女士

A 25. What is one of the purposes of the letter?
    (A) To thank Mr. Lin for doing so much for Derek.
    (B) To tell Mr. Lin about Derek's learning problems.
    (C) To let Mr. Lin know how much Derek has grown.
    (D) To apologize for Derek not practicing hard enough.

這封信的目的之一是什麼？
    (A) 感謝林老師為德瑞克所做的一切。
    (B) 告訴林老師德瑞克的學習問題。
    (C) 讓林老師知道德瑞克的成長。
    (D) 為德瑞克沒有努力學習而道歉。

解析 由第一段第一句得知，這封信是要表達感謝，因此選項 A 正確。

C 26. Which of the following is true about Mr. Lin?

(A) Most students get nervous when they are around Mr. Lin.

(B) Mr. Lin believes that weaker students should work harder.

(C) Mr. Lin is a kind teacher who is willing to help his students.

(D) Mr. Lin always asks students to make more effort to improve.

關於林老師，下列哪一項正確？

(A) 大多數學生在林老師身邊時會感到緊張。

(B) 林老師認為較弱的學生應該更加努力。

(C) 林老師是願意幫助學生的善良老師。

(D) 林老師總是要求學生更加努力改進。

解析 由第二段的第一、二句得知林老師會鼓勵和幫助學生，因此選項 C 正確。雖然德瑞克因為自己的進步而驕傲，但無法從文中判斷老師是否會「總是」要求學生努力。

C 27. Which statement best describes Derek?

(A) He always feels terrible around his friends.

(B) He gets upset when he fails to do something.

(C) He is trying hard and starting to enjoy PE class.

(D) He used to be one of the top students in his class.

下列哪一項最能描述德瑞克？

(A) 他總是在朋友身邊感到糟糕。

(B) 當他失敗時，他會感到難過。

(C) 他正在努力並開始享受體育課。

(D) 他曾經是班上優秀的學生之一。

解析 由第二段的第三和第四句得知，德瑞克開始進步，表示他有努力，也喜歡上體育課了，因此選項 C 正確。

Questions 28-30

Do you often feel sad and lacking in hope for no reason? <u>**Depression**</u>, according to the WHO, is very common, with around 5% of the world's population affected by it. If you or someone you know is experiencing these feelings, it's important to tell to someone you trust. They can offer support and help you find a doctor who can provide you with treatment.

Remember, you are not alone, and there is always help available. There are also things you can do to feel better. Here are some steps you can take:

1. Express your feelings: Sometimes, it helps to express how you feel in a healthy way. You could try talking to a friend or family member, writing in a diary, or even painting.

2. Be more active: Try doing some exercise, even something light. Studies show that exercise can help improve your mood. You can start by walking for just 20 minutes a day.

3. Try a healthy diet: Some people don't feel like eating when they experience depression, and risk becoming loosing too much weight. Others find comfort in food and gain weight. Make sure to eat meals with plenty of meat and vegetables and try to avoid sugar and snacks.

4. Find activities you enjoy: Doing something you like, such as listening to music, reading, or spending time with friends, can help make you happier.

<u>(28) 你是否經常沒來由地感到悲傷和沒有希望？</u>，根據世界衛生組織顯示，憂鬱症是非常普遍的。全世界約有 5% 的人口受其影響。<u>**(28) 如果你或你認識的人正在經歷這些感覺，告知你信任的人是很重要的。**</u>他們可以提供支持，並能幫你找到可以提供治療的醫師。

請記住，你並不孤單，而且隨時都能得到幫助。<u>**(29) 你也可以做一些事情來讓自己感覺好一些。以下是一些可以實踐的步驟：**</u>

1. 表達你的感受：有時候，以健康的方式表達你的感受會有幫助。你可以試著和朋友或家人談談、寫日記，甚至是畫畫。

2. 多活動：嘗試做一些運動，即使是輕微的運動。研究指出，運動可以幫助改善你的情緒。你可以從每天散步 20 分鐘開始。

3. 嘗試健康飲食：一些人在經歷憂鬱時會沒有食慾，風險是會變得過瘦。<u>**(30) 其他人則會在食物中找到安慰，體重會增加。**</u>確保你的飲食中有足夠的肉類和蔬菜，並且儘量避免糖分和零食。

4. 找到你喜歡的活動：做一些你喜歡的事情，比如聽音樂、閱讀或和朋友共度時光，這可以幫助你更快樂。

D 28. According to the article, what is "depression"?
(A) A WHO program to help people who feel sad.
(B) A kind of medicine that keeps your mind healthy.
(C) Someone who can give support to people in need.
(D) A state of mind where people often feel unhappy.

根據文章，什麼是 "depression"？
(A) 一個世界衛生組織的計畫，幫助悲傷的人。
(B) 一種保持你心靈健康的藥物。
(C) 能提供弱勢者支援的人。
(D) 一種人們經常感到不開心的心理狀態。

解析 第一段第一句和第三句都提到「感覺」，因此可推知是心理狀態，選項 D 正確。

A 29. What are the steps in the article for?
(A) Helping people who feel sad and lack hope.
(B) Teaching people to be good a friend to others.
(C) Showing the way to care for family and friends.
(D) Introducing what courses students can choose.

文章中步驟的目的是什麼？
(A) 幫助感到悲傷和缺乏希望的人。
(B) 教導人們如何成為他人的好友。
(C) 示範照顧家人和朋友的方法。
(D) 介紹學生可以選擇的課程。

解析 由第二段的第二和第三句可得知，這些步驟是要幫助人們，讓他們覺得感覺好一些，因此選項 A 正確。

A 30. What is NOT something the author suggests to feel better?
(A) Finding comfort in food.
(B) Trying painting.
(C) Getting some light exercise.
(D) Talking to friends or relatives.

下列哪一項不是作者建議讓自己感覺更好的方法？
(A) 在食物中找安慰。
(B) 嘗試畫畫。
(C) 做一些輕微的運動。
(D) 和朋友或親戚談話。

解析 由第三個步驟中得知，有些人從食物找安慰，結果體重增加。這並非讓自己感覺好的方法，而是要嘗試健康飲食才行，選項 A 正確。

GEPT
初級模擬試題
第 10 回
解答、翻譯與詳解

第 10 回解答

 聽力測驗解答

1. C	2. A	3. A	4. B	5. C
6. B	7. C	8. A	9. A	10. A
11. A	12. B	13. C	14. B	15. B
16. C	17. C	18. B	19. A	20. A
21. B	22. B	23. B	24. C	25. B
26. B	27. A	28. C	29. B	30. A

閱讀測驗解答

1. A	2. C	3. A	4. B	5. C
6. D	7. D	8. C	9. B	10. A
11. A	12. C	13. B	14. B	15. A
16. B	17. D	18. A	19. C	20. B
21. B	22. D	23. B	24. B	25. B
26. C	27. B	28. D	29. D	30. A

第 10 回聽力

第一部分　看圖辨義

C 1. For Question Number 1, please look at the picture.
What is the boy doing?

(A) The boy is cooking dinner.

(B) The boy is setting the table.

(C) The boy is washing the dishes.

第一題，請看此圖片。
男孩正在做什麼？

(A) 男孩正在煮晚餐。

(B) 男孩正在擺碗盤。

(C) 男孩正在洗碗。

解析　圖片中的男孩正在拿著菜瓜布洗碗 (washing the dishes)，其他選項皆不正確，選 C。

A 2. For Question Number 2, please look at the picture.
What is happening in the picture?

(A) Someone is getting married.

(B) Three couples are eating a meal.

(C) People are having fun at a concert.

第二題，請看此圖片。
圖片中正在發生什麼事情？

(A) 有人在結婚。

(B) 有三對情侶／夫妻正在用餐。

(C) 人群正在欣賞演唱會。

解析　圖片中間為穿著禮服的新郎和新娘，可以看出來有人在結婚，沒有人在用餐，也沒有人在聽演唱會，因此答案選 A。

530

A 3. For Question Number 3, please look at the picture.
Who would be interested in this information?

(A) Someone who is ready for food.

(B) People who want to take the MRT.

(C) Those who get lost in the mountains.

第三題，請看此圖片。

什麼人會對這些資訊感興趣？

(A) 準備好要吃東西的人。

(B) 要搭捷運的人。

(C) 在山上迷路的人。

 圖片為菜單 (menu)，因此準備好要吃東西，要點餐的人會對上面的資訊感興趣，答案選 A。

B 4. For Question Number 4, please look at the picture.
What are these people going to do?

(A) They will have to call for an ambulance.

(B) They will wait for the tree to be removed.

(C) They are going to have their cars repaired.

第四題，請看此圖片。

這些人正要做什麼？

(A) 他們需要打電話叫救護車。

(B) 他們要等樹木被移走。

(C) 他們要把車送去修。

解析 從圖片上可以看到樹倒在路中央,但沒有人受傷,所以選項 A 不正確。兩台車只有一台車靠倒下的樹木比較近,可能需要修理,但選項 C 使用複數也不正確。正確答案為 B。

C 5. For Question Number 5, please look at the picture.
Where is the wallet?

(A) Next to the bike.

(B) On the first floor.

(C) Under the scooter.

第五題,請看此圖片。

錢包在哪裡?

(A) 在腳踏車旁邊。

(B) 在一樓。

(C) 在機車下面。

解析 選項 A 的 "bike" 可指摩托車或是腳踏車,圖片中是機車 (scooter) 因此不正確。東西在地上的說法是 "on the floor",選項 B 的 "on the first floor" 為陷阱,也不正確。正確答案為 C。

__B__ 6. Can you pass me the salt?

(A) Yes, it's salty.

(B) There you go.

(C) I don't like salt.

你能把鹽拿給我嗎？

(A) 對，這很鹹。

(B) 給你。

(C) 我不喜歡鹽。

解析 在英語系國家在餐桌上起身拿東西是不禮貌的行為，會用「Can you pass me + 名詞」請人幫忙拿。把東西交給對方時可以說 "Here you are." 或是 "There you go." 表示你要的東西在這邊，正確答案為選項 B。

__C__ 7. What time does the show start?

(A) I'm not sure what time it ends.

(B) The movie is over two hours long.

(C) The ticket says it begins at 7:30 pm.

表演幾點開始？

(A) 我不確定幾點結束。

(B) 電影超過兩個小時。

(C) 票上寫著晚上 7:30 開始。

解析 表演開始可以用 "begin" 或是 "start"。題目問表演開始的時間，選項 A、B 皆答非所問，正確答案選 C。

__A__ 8. Why are you wearing a coat indoors?

(A) I forgot to take it off.

(B) I bought it at the mall.

(C) It's really warm in here.

你為什麼在室內還穿著大衣外套？

(A) 我忘記脫下來了。

(B) 我在購物中心買的。

(C) 這裡很暖。

解析 選項 B 和選項 C 都沒有回答室內穿大衣外套的原因，只有選項 A 符合對話邏輯，說明自己是忘記脫下來。答案選 A。

__A__ 9. How have you been these days?

(A) Busy! I've been studying for a test.

(B) I will visit my friends in Hong Kong.

(C) Tired! I went swimming this morning.

你最近過得怎麼樣？

(A) 很忙！我最近都在準備考試。

(B) 我會去香港探望朋友。

(C) 很累！我今天早上去游泳。

解析　題目使用完成式「have/has+ p.p.」詢問對方「最近」的生活情況，因此回答時也需要使用一樣的時態句型回覆，正確答案選 A。

__A__ 10. I can't turn on my computer.

(A) Let me take a look.

(B) Sorry, I'm busy right now.

(C) Did you try turning it on?

我電腦打不開。

(A) 讓我看看。

(B) 不好意思，我現在很忙。

(C) 你有試著把它打開嗎？

解析　題目說明自己遇到電腦無法開機的困難。因為已經試著打開才知道打不開，選項 C 的回應不合理。選項 B 在對方求助前就回應自己正在忙，回應不恰當。只有選項 A 在聽到對方有困難時主動提出協助，為正確答案。

__A__ 11. Do you have any plans for the weekend?

(A) No, I haven't made any yet.

(B) Yes, I've visited a few places.

(C) I'm trying to fix the problem.

你週末有什麼計畫嗎？

(A) 沒有，我還沒訂任何計畫。

(B) 有，我去了幾個地方玩。

(C) 我正在試著解決問題。

解析　題目問的是即將到來的週末計畫。選項 A 使用 any 來取代 any plans 回應題目問題，為正確答案。選項 B 回答自己在過去到訪了幾個地方，答非所問。選項 C 則完全不合對話邏輯。正確答案選 A。

__B__ 12. Do you know how to change tires?

(A) Of course you can take a rest.

(B) No, I've never done it before.

(C) I don't know what they charge.

你知道怎麼換輪胎嗎？

(A) 你當然能休息一下。

(B) 不會。我從來沒做過。

(C) 我不知道他們收多少錢。

解析　選項 B 簡答 "No" 表示不會後，補充說明自己沒有換過輪胎，為正確答案。A 和 C 皆是利用單字發音雷同衍伸出來的誤導選項。tires（輪胎）和 tired（疲勞）；change（更換）和 charge（收費）。

__C__ 13. I don't think I can finish this hamburger.

(A) No thanks, I'm too full.

(B) You can get another one.

(C) You can eat the rest later.

我不覺得我能吃完這個漢堡。

(A) 不用，謝謝。我太飽了。

(B) 你可以再去拿一個。

(C) 你可以等等再把剩下的吃完。

解析 選項 C 中 "the rest" 為 "the rest of the hamburger"（剩下的漢堡）的簡略說法，提供了題目中「漢堡吃不完」的解決辦法，因此為正確答案。其餘兩個選項答非所問。選 C。

__B__ 14. What's your favorite book?

(A) I got it at the new bookstore.

(B) I can't think of one right now.

(C) You can learn a lot from this book.

你最喜歡的書是哪一本？

(A) 我在新的書店買的。

(B) 我現在想不出來。

(C) 你可以從這本書中學到很多。

解析 選項 A 回答購買的地方，適用於 Where 開頭的問句。選項 C 答非所問。選項 B 中的 one 指的是題目中的 "favorite book"。雖然沒有直接給出書名，但回應了提問，為正確答案。

__B__ 15. Where's the new mug that I just bought?

(A) I keep my cups in that cupboard.

(B) Is this the one you're looking for?

(C) I just brought a new mug last week.

我新買的馬克杯在哪裡？

(A) 我把我的杯子都放在那個碗櫃裡。

(B) 你在找的是這個嗎？

(C) 我上週才帶了一個新馬克杯來。

解析 選項 A 因為有 my（我的），回答的是自己的馬克杯的位置，所以不正確。選項 C 答非所問。只有選項 B 幫忙找馬克杯，並詢問對方是不是在找自己手上的那個杯子，為合理回覆，答案選 B。

C   16. W: I'm really sorry that I broke your vase. I'll buy you a new one.

M: Don't worry about it. It was an accident.

W: How much did you pay for it?

M: I didn't. It was a gift.

Question: Which is true about the vase?

女子：我很抱歉把你的花瓶打破了。我會買一個新的賠你。

男子：沒關係。那是意外。

女子：你花多少錢買那隻花瓶？

男子：我沒有花錢。那是贈品。

問題：以下關於花瓶的敘述何者正確？

(A) The man broke it.	(A) 是男子弄壞的。
(B) It cost a lot of money.	(B) 花瓶價格高昂。
(C) It was a gift to the man.	(C) 那是送給男子的贈品。

解析 花瓶是女子弄壞的，因此選項 A 不正確。由男子最後一句話可以知道花瓶是男子收到的贈品，所以價錢無從得知，選項 B 不正確。正確答案為選項 C。

C   17. W: Do you know what time the singing contest starts?

M: I think Mary said it starts at seven pm.

W: Let's check the notice on the board over there. I don't want to be late.

M: Look! It IS seven. Let's go in now. I can't wait to see if Mary wins.

Question: What are they discussing?

女子：你知道歌唱比賽幾點開始嗎？

男子：我想瑪莉是說晚上七點。

女子：我們去看看那個板子上貼的告示。我不想遲到。

男子：你看！的確是七點。我們現在進去吧！我等不及想看瑪莉是不是能贏得這次的比賽了。

問題：他們在討論什麼？

(A) Whether they are going to sing or not.

(B) Whether they should call Mary for help.

(C) Whether they are on time for the event.

(A) 他們等一下要不要唱歌。

(B) 他們要不要打電話找瑪莉幫忙。

(C) 他們有沒有準時到場。

解析　從對話中女子說的 "I don't want to be late."（我不想遲到。）以及男子和女子去看告示確認比賽時間，可以知道他們在討論自己是不是有準時，答案為 C。

B　18. W: I'm thinking of starting a new hobby, but I'm not sure what to choose.

M: Why don't you try painting or cooking? They can be very interesting and fun.

W: Do you do either of those?

M: Yes, I do both. But I find painting a lot more interesting.

Question: What does the woman want the man to do?

女子：我在想要開始一個新的嗜好，但我不知道要選什麼。

男子：何不試試看畫畫或是烹飪？這兩種都可能很有趣和好玩。

女子：你有從事其中的哪一種嗎？

男子：有啊！我兩種都做。但我覺得畫畫比較有趣。

問題：女子希望男子做什麼？

(A) Start a new hobby.

(B) Give her some advice.

(C) Teach her how to cook.

(A) 開始一個新嗜好。

(B) 給她一點建議。

(C) 教她怎麼烹飪。

解析　女子在對話一開始時說明自己不知道要選哪個嗜好 "I'm not sure what to choose." 雖非直接提問，但透露出希望對方給予建議，因此正確答案選 B。

A 19. W: I can't find my boarding pass.

M: Don't worry! I have it here.

W: OK. When should we board? I feel like doing some shopping.

M: Let's see. Our flight number is BT32, so boarding starts in 40 minutes. If you want to buy something, we'd better head for the shops now.

Question: Where does the conversation take place?

女子：我找不到我的登機證。

男子：不用擔心，在我這邊。

女子：好。我們應該要幾點登機？我想要買點東西。

男子：我看看。我們的班機號碼是 BT32，所以再 40 分鐘就要登機。如果你想要買東西的話，我們最好現在就往商店走。

問題：這段對話發生的地點在哪裡？

(A) An airport.

(B) A train station

(C) A shopping mall

(A) 機場。

(B) 火車站。

(C) 購物中心。

解析 由關鍵詞 "boarding pass"（登機證）和 "flight number"（班機號碼）可以推測這段對話發生的地點是在機場，選 A。

A 20. M: Are you excited about the trip we have planned for next month?

W: Well, it's going to be my first time camping in the mountains and I don't know what to bring.

M: It's going to be my fifth time. I'll take care of everything. You can just relax.

W: That's so sweet of you!

Question: What does the man suggest the woman do?

男子：妳很期待我們已經規劃好、下個月要去的旅遊嗎？

女子：嗯，那會是我第一次在山上露營，我不知道要帶什麼。

男子：那會是我的第五次。我會準備所有的東西。妳放輕鬆就好。

女子：你真貼心。

問題：男子建議女子做什麼？

(A) Not worry about the trip.

(B) Bring everything they need.

(C) Plan the trip for next month.

(A) 不用擔心旅遊的事。

(B) 帶所有他們需要的東西。

(C) 規劃下個月的旅遊。

解析 由男子對話中提到 "I'll take care of everything. You can just relax." 可以知道男子不要女子擔心旅遊的事，答案選 A。

B 21. W: Did you finish the report I asked you to do?

M: Yes, I did. I emailed it to you this morning.

W: I didn't see it when I checked two hours ago.

M: Let me make sure I've got your email right. Is it "jcwu@pc.com.tw?"

Question: What problem are they discussing?

女子：你完成我請你做的報告了嗎？

男子：是，我做完了。今天早上用電子郵件寄給妳了。

女子：我兩個小時前查郵件的時候沒看到。

男子：我確認一下有沒有把妳的電子郵件地址寫對。是 "jcwu@pc.com.tw?" 嗎？

問題：他們在討論什麼？

(A) The man forgot to complete the report.

(B) The women hasn't received the report.

(C) The man didn't send the report by email.

(A) 男子忘記完成報告。

(B) 女子還沒收到報告。

(C) 男子沒有用電子郵件寄出報告。

解析 對話中女子提到自己兩小時前查郵件沒有看到報告："I didn't see it when I checked two hours ago." 可以知道答案為 B，女子還沒收到報告。

B 22. W: Have you ever planned a picnic before?

M: Sure, several times.

W: Great. I could really use your help. I need to plan a picnic for 50 people.

M: No problem. We can start by making a list of food you'd like to serve and possible activities.

Question: What do the people decide to do together?

女子：你有規劃過野餐嗎？

男子：有啊！好幾次。

女子：太好了！我需要你的幫忙。我需要規劃一場 50 人的野餐。

男子：沒問題。我們可以先列出妳想要提供的食物，還有可能舉辦的活動清單。

問題：這兩個人打算一起做什麼？

(A) Pick a restaurant.	(A) 選一間餐廳。
(B) Organize an event.	(B) 規劃一場活動。
(C) Go watch a movie.	(C) 去看電影。

解析　"I could really use your help." 直譯為「我可以利用你的協助」，雖然不是問句，但常用來請求他人協助，因此男子聽到後也馬上回答「沒問題。」並開始幫忙規劃野餐，因此知道正確答案為 B。

B 23. W: Did you remember to buy milk at the grocery store? I need some for my coffee.

M: Yes, I did. Did you look in the refrigerator?

W: Yeah, I didn't see it. Wait, there it is on the table.

M: Oh, I must have forgot to put it away.

Question: Where did the man put the milk?

女子：你記得去雜貨店買牛奶了嗎？我需要加一點牛奶在我的咖啡裡。

男子：有。你看過冰箱了嗎？

女子：有，但我沒看到。等一下，就在餐桌上。

男子：喔！我一定是忘記把它放好了。

問題：男子把牛奶放在哪裡？

(A) In the fridge.
(B) On the table.
(C) In the coffee.

(A) 在冰箱。
(B) 在桌上。
(C) 在咖啡裡。

解析 女子在冰箱裡沒看到牛奶，後來發現是男子忘記收好，還放在餐桌上。由此可知答案為 B。"put away" 字面上看起來是「丟到旁邊去」，但其實是「收好、放好」的意思。

C 24. M: Can you please turn down the music? I like it, but I have a headache.

W: Sorry, I didn't realize it was so loud. Is it better now?

M: A little. Thanks.

W: I'll turn it off completely.

Question: What will the woman do for the man?

男子：妳可以把音樂轉小聲一點嗎？我很喜歡這個音樂，但頭有點痛。

女子：不好意思，我沒有注意到音樂那麼大聲。現在好一點了嗎？

男子：好一點點。謝謝。

女子：我整個關掉好了。

問題：女子會為了男子做什麼？

(A) Lower the volume.
(B) Turn up the music.
(C) Stop playing the music.

(A) 將聲音轉小。
(B) 把音樂轉大聲。
(C) 停止播放音樂。

解析 女子已經幫男子把音樂轉小聲，所以選項 A 不正確。男子頭痛只有略為好轉，所以女子在最後提到自己會將音樂整個關掉，正確答案選 C。

__B__ 25. W: What time is it?

M: It's almost six.

W: Oh no, I have to pick my kids up from baseball practice, but I can't leave on time.

M: I'd help, but I'm having dinner with a customer.

W: My husband's still at work too. I guess they'll just have to wait for me at the park.

Question: Where does the conversation probably take place?

女子：現在幾點？

男子：快要六點。

女子：糟糕，我需要去接小孩棒球練習下課，但我沒辦法準時走。

男子：可以的話我就幫妳，不過我要跟客戶吃飯。

女子：我先生也還在工作。我猜他們只能在公園等我了。

問題：對話可能發生的地點為何？

(A) At a park.

(B) At an office.

(C) At a restaurant.

(A) 在公園。

(B) 在辦公室。

(C) 在餐廳。

解析 從男子提到自己需要跟客戶吃飯，女子提到自己先生「也」還在工作，可以知道男子和女子對話的地點是在工作場合，選 B。

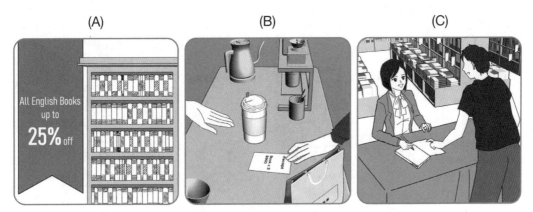

(A)　　　　　　(B)　　　　　　(C)

All English Books
up to
25% off

B　26. For question number 26, please look at the three pictures.

Listen to the ad. What is available to bookstore customers?

Our bookstore is having a special event this week. You can receive a free postcard for every novel you buy. And if you buy three or more history books, you can get a free cup of coffee at the coffee shop next door. The event ends on Sunday, so come in soon if you want to participate. We can't wait to see you.

第 26 題，請看三張圖片。

請聽廣告。書店客人能得到什麼？

本書店在這星期有特別活動。每買一本小說就能免費得到一張明信片。買三本以上的歷史叢書，就能到隔壁的咖啡廳兌換一杯免費咖啡。活動到週日截止。想要參加活動的人請盡快過來！等不及見到你們了。

解析　從題目得知，只要消費，書店客人就可以得到 "postcard"（明信片）或 "coffee"（咖啡）。圖 B 可以看到客人出示 receipt（發票），而獲得一杯咖啡，為正確答案。廣告中沒有提到折扣或是簽書活動，因此 A、C 皆不正確。

(A)　　　　　　　(B)　　　　　　　(C)

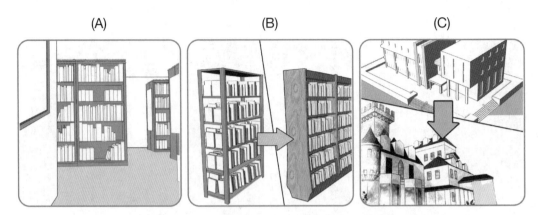

__A__ 27. For question number 27, please look at the three pictures.

Listen to the announcement. What will the new library look like?

The city library has been with us for over 30 years, and it's time for it to get a new look. The library will be closed for a month, during which time all the inside walls will be painted and a new floor will be put in. We'll have a party to celebrate when all the work is done. The party is scheduled for the first Sunday of May, and everyone is invited. See you then!

第 27 題，請看三張圖片。

請聽以下公告。新圖書館會像什麼樣子？

市立圖書館已經成立超過 30 年，也到了該重新整理門面的時候了！圖書館將會關閉一個月，這段期間內，館內的牆壁會重新粉刷，也會鋪上新的地板。完工時會有慶祝派對。派對將在五月的第一個週日舉行，邀請所有的人前往參加。到時見！

解析　從關鍵詞 "walls" 和 "floor" 可以得知圖書館裝修重點在牆壁和地板。只有在圖片 A 可以看到牆壁和地板，為正確答案。

(A)　　　　　　　(B)　　　　　　　(C)

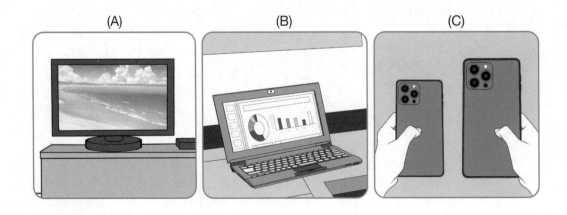

__C__ 28. For question number 28, please look at the three pictures.

A woman is introducing a new product. What is the product?

Besta 7 is very different from our older phone models. It has a bigger screen, a better camera, and takes higher quality pictures. It also has a more modern look and is available in two different sizes. Come to one of our stores and take a look. What are you waiting for?

第 28 題，請看三張圖片。

一名女子正在介紹新產品。請問是哪種產品？

Besta 7 和以前舊的電話機型有很大的不同。它的螢幕比較大，相機功能比較好，可以拍出高畫質的照片。它的設計外觀新穎，並且有兩種尺寸大小。快來我們的店內看看吧！還在等什麼呢？

解析 女子開頭直接說明產品和之前的 "phone models"（電話機型）有很大的不同，加上後面提到的 "two different sizes"（兩種不同尺寸），可以知道圖片 C 最符合廣告內容，女子介紹的產品為電話，正確答案選 C。

(A) Friday 6pm - 7pm (B) Saturday 7pm - 9:30pm (C) Sunday 7pm - 8pm

__B__ 29. For Question Number 29, please look at the three pictures.

Angie is listening to a phone message. When will the concert be held?

Hi, Angie. It's me, Susan. I know Tony Smith is your favorite piano player. You know what? This Saturday at seven pm, he's giving a performance at the concert hall. The concert is free and open to the public. How would you like to go together? It's going to be two and a half hours long. We should arrive early so we can get good seats.

第 29 題，請看三張圖片。

安琪正在聽電話留言。演奏會什麼時候舉辦？

嗨，安琪。是我，蘇珊。我知道東尼史密斯是妳最喜歡的鋼琴演奏家。妳知道嗎？這個週六晚上七點，他要來音樂廳表演。演奏會免費開放給民眾參加。妳要一起去嗎？演奏會長度是兩個半小時。我們最好早一點到才能坐到好的位子。

解析　從關鍵詞 "Saturday," "seven pm" 和 "two and a half hours long" 可以知道演奏會是在週六晚上七點到九點半。選 B。

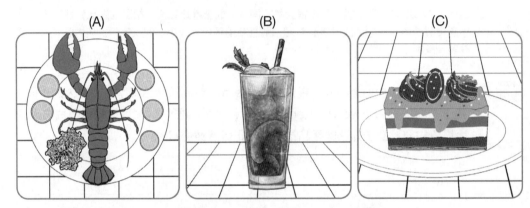

(A)　(B)　(C)

___A___ 30. For question number 30, please look at the three pictures.

Listen to the ad. What kind of store is it?

Rosa's place has been famous for seafood since it opened in 2018. Lately, they've hired a new chef, James Lee, who used to work at a five-star hotel. People who have tried his dishes always come back for more. His dishes not only taste good; they also look good! Rosa's is the perfect place for a family dinner or a date night.

第 30 題，看三張圖片。

請聽廣告。這是間什麼樣的店？

「蘿莎的家」自 2018 年開幕以來就以海鮮馳名。最近他們新聘了一名在五星級飯店任職過的廚師，詹姆士李。吃過他料理的客人都會回流。他的料理不僅美味，也很美觀。不管是家族聚餐或是情侶約會，「蘿莎的家」都是您完美的選擇。

解析　圖片 A 上看得到用心擺放的龍蝦，符合廣告中提到的關鍵詞 "seafood," 以及 "look good," 為正確答案。廣告中沒有提到飲料或是甜點，因此圖片 B、C 皆不正確。

第一部分　詞彙

共 10 題，每個題目裡有一個空格。請從四個選項中選出一個最適合題意的字或詞作答。

__A__ 1. Please fill _____ this form and return it to me by Monday morning.

請填寫此表格並在星期一早上前交還給我。

(A) out 填寫　　　　　　　(B) up 填滿

(C) over 覆蓋　　　　　　(D) on 開啟

> 解析　空格後接「表格」，可得知要選 fill out 來作為「填寫表格」之意。Fill in/out 可用於填寫正式文件。

__C__ 2. Can you _____ the kids off at school on your way to work?

你能在上班的路上順便載孩子們到學校嗎？

(A) take 帶　　　　　　　(B) drive 開車送

(C) drop 載　　　　　　　(D) send 寄送

> 解析　空格後有小孩，還有介系詞 off，可得知是 "drop off"，意為「用車載某人」。用車子載小孩，並把他們放在學校下車。選項 C 正確。

__A__ 3. I'm afraid I can't _____ the meeting on Monday.

我恐怕無法參加星期一的會議。

(A) attend 參加　　　　　(B) support 支持

(C) carry 搬運　　　　　　(D) happen 發生

__B__ 4. Air tickets to Europe can cost as _____ as a thousand dollars.

飛往歐洲的機票可能要花費多達一千美元。

(A) many 很多　　　　　　(B) much 多

(C) high 高　　　　　　　(D) great 大

__C__ 5. All groups must have their projects _____ by the end of the week.

所有小組必須在本週結束前完成他們的專案。

(A) established 建立　　　(B) developed 開發

(C) completed 完成　　　　(D) indicated 表明

__D__ 6. After studying cooking, Vivian got a job at a restaurant and started her
_____ as a chef.

學習烹飪後，維薇安在一家餐廳找到了工作，並開始了她作為廚師的職業生涯。

(A) activity 活動　　　　　(B) target 目標

(C) hire 雇用　　　　　　(D) career 職業生涯

__D__ 7. To see the run rise, we have to get up before _____ .

要看到日出，我們必須在黎明前起床。

(A) dark 黑暗　　　　　　(B) scene 場景

(C) break 破曉　　　　　　(D) dawn 黎明

__C__ 8. When can we expect to _____ a reply from Ms. Wilson?

我們何時候能預計收到威爾遜女士的回覆？

(A) accept 接受　　　　　(B) send 寄送

(C) receive 收到　　　　　(D) gather 收集

__B__ 9. What you need is a _____ . A lot of people have had their bikes stolen
lately.

你需要的是一把鎖。最近很多人的自行車都被偷了。

(A) police 警察　　　　　(B) lock 鎖

(C) host 主人　　　　　　(D) report 報告

__A__ 10. Good table _____ are a way of showing respect for others at the table.

良好的餐桌禮儀是對桌邊其他人的尊重。

(A) manners 禮儀　　　　(B) fashions 時尚

(C) scores 分數　　　　　(D) methods 方法

第二部分　段落填空

共 8 題，包括二個段落，每個段落含四個空格。每格均有四個選項，請依照文意選出最適合的答案。

Questions 11-14

Jenny woke up at seven, got dressed, and went to the office, arriving just before eight. She started her day by drinking coffee when she ____(11)____ her e-mail. Next, Jenny went to a department meeting to discuss future projects. Around noon, Jenny took a quick ____(12)____ to eat a sandwich. In the afternoon, she finished a report that her manager needed ____(13)____ the end of the day. At seven, she ____(14)____ her desk before leaving the office after a long, tiring day.

珍妮七點起床，穿好衣服後去辦公室，在八點前抵達那裡。她一邊喝咖啡，一邊 **(11) 檢查**她的電子郵件，展開她的一天。接著，珍妮參加了一個部門會議，討論未來的計畫。大約中午時，珍妮快速 **(12) 休息**了一下，吃了三明治。下午，她完成了一份報告，需要在一天結束 **(13) 之前**交給她的經理。晚上七點，她 **(14) 整理**了辦公桌，然後結束了漫長而疲憊的一天，離開了辦公室。

__A__ 11. (A) checked 檢查   (B) watched 觀看
        (C) examined 審查   (D) confirmed 確認

> **解析** 檢查電子郵件的動作用選項 A 的 check；而選項 C 的 examine 是檢驗式的檢查，與題意不符。

__C__ 12. (A) meal 餐   (B) period 時段
        (C) break 休息   (D) pause 暫停

__B__ 13. (A) on 在…上   (B) by 之前
        (C) in 在…內   (D) to 到

__B__ 14. (A) investigated 調查   (B) organized 整理
        (C) cooperated 合作   (D) exercised 鍛煉

Questions 15-18

What are the most popular pets today? _____**(15)**_____ people love to have dogs as pets. Dogs are known for being loyal and friendly. They need _____**(16)**_____ walks and enjoy playing with their owners. Cats are also popular pets; they are often more quiet and like to explore on their own. Both dogs and cats need lots of exercise to _____**(17)**_____ healthy. It is important to take them to the doctor for check-ups and shots. Having a pet can bring a lot of joy and happiness to a home. Pets can also teach us about responsibility and _____**(18)**_____ others.

現今最受歡迎的寵物有哪些？ **(15)** 許多人喜愛養狗作為寵物。狗以忠誠和友善著稱，牠們需要 **(16)** 定期的散步，並且喜歡與主人玩耍。貓也很受歡迎；牠們通常比較安靜，喜歡獨自探索。無論是狗還是貓，都需要大量運動才能 **(17)** 保持健康。定期帶牠們去看醫生進行檢查和接種疫苗也很重要。擁有寵物可以為家庭帶來許多歡樂和幸福。寵物還能教會我們責任感以及如何 **(18)** 關心他人。

__A__ 15. (A) Many 許多　　　　　　　　(B) Any 任何
　　　 (C) Much 很多　　　　　　　　(D) Every 每個

> **解析**　people 為複數可數名詞，選項中只有 many 和 much 後面可以接複數名詞，其中又只有 many 後面可以接複數可數名詞。

__B__ 16. (A) often 經常　　　　　　　　(B) regular 規律的
　　　 (C) normal 正常的　　　　　　　(D) usual 通常的

__D__ 17. (A) staying 保持　　　　　　　(B) stays 保持
　　　 (C) to stay 保持　　　　　　　(D) stay 保持

__A__ 18. (A) caring for 照顧　　　　　　(B) care for 照顧
　　　 (C) caring to 關心　　　　　　　(D) care on 關心

> **解析**　"caring for"表示「照顧他人」，符合文意。"care for"也可行，但不如"caring for"順暢，"caring to"和"care on"則語法不正確。

第三部分　閱讀理解

共 12 題，包括 4 個題組，每個題組含 1 至 2 篇短文，與數個相關的四選一的選擇題。請由試題上的選項中選出最適合的答案。

Questions 19-21

To	Olivia Miller
From	Pittsburg Art Museum
Subject	Congratulations! You're a winner!

B *I* U ¶▾ 🖊 A▾ T▾ 🔗 🖼 🏷 ≡ ≡ ≡ ↺ ↻ </>

Dear Olivia,

We are happy to inform you that you are a winner at the 19th Pittsburg Junior Art **Competition**. As winner of the Oil Painting Award, your prize will be a full scholarship for four years at the Pittsburg Art School. This opportunity will provide you with training that will set you on the path towards a successful career in the arts.

We would also like to invite you to attend Awards Night, which will be held on September 30 at City Arena. Please dress formally for the evening. If, for any reason, you are unable to attend Awards Night, please kindly inform us by September 18.

Once again, congratulations on the great work!

If you have any questions or need further information, please call the Pittsburg Junior Art Competition Office. We look forward to celebrating your success and welcoming you to Awards Night.

Pittsburg Junior Art Competition Office

Jennifer Rowling

Send

收件人　奧利維亞·米勒

發件人　匹茲堡藝術博物館

主題　(20) 恭喜！你是優勝者！

B　I　U　¶·　✎　A·　T·　⌖　🖼　🏷　≣　≣　≣　↺　↻　</>

親愛的奧利維亞，

(19) 我們很高興通知你，你是第 19 屆匹茲堡青少年藝術比賽的獲勝者。作為油畫獎的獲獎者，(20) (21) 你的獎項將是匹茲堡藝術學校為期四年的全額獎學金。這個機會將提供你培訓，助你走上通往成功藝術生涯的道路。

(20) 此外，我們邀請你參加頒獎晚會，將於 9 月 30 日在市體育館舉行。請穿著正式服裝。若因任何原因無法參加頒獎晚會，請在 9 月 18 日前通知我們。

再次恭喜你獲得優異的成就！

如果你有任何問題或需要進一步的資訊，請致電匹茲堡青少年藝術比賽辦公室。我們期待與你一起慶祝你的成功，並歡迎你參加頒獎晚會。

匹茲堡青少年藝術比賽辦公室

珍妮弗·羅琳

傳送

_C_　19. What does the word "competition" in the first paragraph mean?

(A) fight

(B) quiz

(C) contest

(D) meeting

第一段中的 "competition" 這個詞是什麼意思？

(A) 戰鬥

(B) 測驗

(C) 比賽

(D) 會議

解析　competition 這個字之前有提到「優勝者」，可推知是跟比賽有關，因此選項 C 正確。

___B___ 20. Based on the content, how will Olivia Miller probably feel when receiving the e-mail?

    (A) upset

    (B) excited

    (C) impressed

    (D) satisfied

根據內容，奧利維亞‧米勒收到這封電子郵件時可能會有什麼感覺？

    (A) 難過

    (B) 興奮

    (C) 印象深刻

    (D) 滿意

解析 由第三行書信主旨表達恭喜的 congratulations 開始，接下來第一段有提到獎學金和訓練，最後還有獲邀去頒獎典禮，一連串的好消息，可推知心情應是興奮，選項 B 正確。

___B___ 21. What can Oliva Miller expect in the near future?

    (A) To be invited to organize an award party.

    (B) To begin study at the Pittsburg Art School.

    (C) To receive an invitation to attend Awards Night.

    (D) To accept a job offer at the Pittsburg Art School.

奧利維亞‧米勒在不久的將來可期待什麼？

    (A) 被邀請去籌劃一個頒獎派對。

    (B) 開始在匹茲堡藝術學校就學。

    (C) 收到參加頒獎晚會的邀請。

    (D) 接受匹茲堡藝術學校的工作邀請。

解析 由第一段的第二句得知有四年的獎學金可推知，收信者將會就學，因此選項 B 正確。

Questions 22-24

Studying at coffee shops is becoming more and more popular among high school students these days. They enjoy studying at coffee shops for many different reasons, including their comfortable seats and convenient locations. They also provide a nice change of environment from home or the library. Another reason is the food and drinks. Students can drink coffee to keep from getting sleepy, and also enjoy a variety of snacks.

However, there are also many students who don't like studying at coffee shops. Loud conversations and music can make it hard to focus. And unlike libraries, there are no available textbooks. Also, the drinks and snacks aren't free like at home. Whether students decide to study at coffee shops or not depends on what kind of environment helps them study best.

(23) 到咖啡館唸書，很受現在的高中生歡迎。他們有喜歡在咖啡館唸書的不同原因，包括那裡的舒適座椅和便利的位置。(22) 咖啡館也提供了一個不同於家裡或圖書館的理想環境轉換。另一個原因是餐點和飲料。學生可以喝咖啡阻止睡意，還可以享受各種點心。

(23) 然而，也有許多學生不喜歡在咖啡館唸書。(24) 大聲的談話和音樂會讓人難以集中注意力。而且，與圖書館不同的是，咖啡館裡沒有可用的教科書。此外，飲料和點心也不像在家裡那樣免費。學生是否決定在咖啡館唸書，取決於什麼樣的環境能幫助他們更好地學習。

___D___ 22. According to the article, why do some students like to study at coffee shops?

(A) Coffee shops have an environment similar to that of a library.

(B) Coffee shops provide a great opportunity to meet new people.

(C) Coffee shops provide better snacks than what's available at home.

(D) Studying there makes a nice change from where they usually study.

根據文章，為什麼有些學生喜歡在咖啡館唸書？

(A) 咖啡館的環境類似於圖書館。

(B) 咖啡館提供了結識新朋友的好機會。

(C) 咖啡館提供的點心比家裡的好。

(D) 在那裡學習是一種很好的環境轉換。

解析 文中第一段第三句開始敘述喜愛在咖啡館唸書的原因，有提到咖啡館提供了環境的轉換，因此選項 D 正確。

B 23. What is the main idea of the article?

(A) Snacks at home may be free, but snacks at coffee shops aren't.

(B) There are reasons to study at coffee shops and reasons not to.

(C) Libraries are better places to study because they are quiet.

(D) Students like studying at coffee shops because they are convenient.

文章的主要觀點是什麼？

(A) 雖然家裡的點心是免費的，但咖啡館的點心不是。

(B) 有在咖啡館學習的理由，也有不在那裡學習的理由。

(C) 圖書館是比較好的學習場所，因為它們很安靜。

(D) 學生喜歡在咖啡館學習，因為那裡的位置很方便。

解析 由這兩段的前兩句可以看出，全篇的主旨在於去咖啡館念書的優點和缺點，因此選項 B 正確。

B 24. What is NOT mentioned as a reason students don't like studying at coffee shops?

(A) No available textbooks

(B) A lack of comfortable seats

(C) The cost of food and drinks

(D) Loud music and conversations

哪一項不是學生不喜歡在咖啡館學習的原因？

(A) 沒有可用的教科書

(B) 缺乏舒適的座椅

(C) 食物和飲料的費用

(D) 大聲的音樂和談話

解析 第二段講述學生不喜歡在咖啡館讀書的原因，但其中並沒有提到椅子是否舒適，因此選項 B 並非不喜歡的原因。

Hearing loss is common in older adults, and it's important to understand the signs. These include trouble with conversations, trouble hearing certain sounds, and asking for repeats often. When older adults have trouble understanding conversations, like missing parts in noisy places, it is often an early sign of hearing loss. Another sign is finding it hard to hear specific sounds, such as the sound of a doorbell ringing. If someone often asks other people to repeat themselves, like saying "What?" a lot, it could mean they are facing hearing difficulties.

Have you seen any of these signs in an older relative? One possible solution is getting them to use hearing aids—small tools that make sounds louder. Other things that help are facing people directly when talking and finding quiet spots. These steps can make a big difference in improving the daily lives of seniors who are experiencing hearing loss.

(25) (27) 聽力喪失在長者中很常見，了解其病徵非常重要。這些病徵包括對話困難、聽不清某些聲音，以及經常要求重複。當長者無法理解對話，比如說在嘈雜的地方聽不到一部分的對話，這通常是聽力喪失的早期跡象。另一個跡象是難以聽到特定的聲音，例如門鈴響的聲音。如果某人經常要求別人重複他們的話，例如經常說「什麼？」這可能意味著他們正面臨聽力問題。

(26) (27) 你是否在年長的親戚身上見過這些徵兆？一個可能的解決方法是讓他們使用助聽器—這是種能放大聲音的小工具。直接面對面交談也有幫助，還有找個安靜的地方。這些步驟可以大大改善經歷聽力喪失長者的日常生活。

__B__ 25. According to the article, which is NOT a sign of hearing loss?

(A) When people can't hear the phone ringing

(B) When people keep hearing sounds in their ears

(C) When people can't hear parts of conversations

(D) When people ask others to say something again

根據文章,哪一項不是聽力喪失的跡象?

(A) 當人們聽不見電話鈴聲時

(B) 當人們一直聽到耳中聲音時

(C) 當人們聽不清對話的部分時

(D) 當人們要求別人重複說話時

解析 第一段第一句和第二句講述了聽力喪失的徵兆,並沒有包含聽到其他聲音,因此選項 B 正確。

__C__ 26. What is a suggested way to talk to an older adult with hearing loss?

(A) Stand very close to that person

(B) Talk to them in a crowded place

(C) Look at the person you're talking to

(D) Turn your back while speaking to them

與有聽力喪失的老年人交談時,建議的方式是什麼?

(A) 站得離那個人非常近

(B) 在擁擠的地方與他們交談

(C) 看著你正在交談的人

(D) 背對著他們說話

解析 第二段第二句開始提供解決方法,其中之一就是第三句的直接面對對方說話,這與看著交談的人狀況相符,因此選項 C 正確。

B　27. What would be the best title for this article?
(A) *Difficulty Hearing in Older People*
(B) *Hearing Loss—Signs and Solutions*
(C) *Ways to Prevent Hearing Problems*
(D) *The Many Causes of Hearing Loss*

這篇文章最適當的標題是什麼？
(A) 年長者的聽力困難
(B) 聽力喪失——跡象與解決方案
(C) 預防聽力問題的方法
(D) 聽力喪失的多種原因

解析　文章第一段提到了年長者的聽力問題癥兆，而第二段提供了解決方法，因此選項 B 最適合。

Questions 28-30

NOTICE
Friday, April 5th

Dear Students,

We would like to inform you that all the computer classrooms in this building will be closed for a week, from April 8th to April 14th. For months, teachers and students have complained about the classrooms being too warm. We have recently found some problems with the air conditioning system. For the sake of a better and more comfortable learning environment during the coming summer, we will have the system checked and repaired during the above dates.

All courses taking place in the computer classrooms will be canceled during those dates. If you need to use a computer while the classrooms are closed, you can talk to your teacher and ask for permission to use the teacher's computer room on the second floor of the office building.

General Affairs Office

Rowland High School

公告

(30) 4 月 5 日，星期五

親愛的學生們，

(28) 我們想通知你們，本棟樓內所有的電腦教室將從 4 月 8 日至 4 月 14 日關閉一周。幾個月來，老師和學生們抱怨教室太熱。我們最近找到了空調系統的一些問題。(30) 為了在接下來的夏季有更優良和更舒適的學習環境，我們將在上述日期之間檢查並維修系統。

這段時間內，所有於電腦教室進行的課程將取消。(29) 如果您在教室關閉時需要使用電腦，可以與您的老師聯繫，要求獲准使用辦公大樓二樓的教師電腦室。

總務處

羅蘭高中

__D__ 28. What is the main purpose of this notice?

(A) To describe issues with the office building

(B) To provide an update on new summer courses

(C) To announce a school event happening in April

(D) To explain why computer classrooms are closing

這個公告的主要目的是什麼？

(A) 描述辦公大樓的問題

(B) 提供新的夏季課程更新

(C) 宣布四月份舉行的校園活動

(D) 解釋為什麼電腦教室將關閉

解析 由第一段第一句提到電腦教室要關閉，接下來講述關閉的原因，最後提供電腦使用的替代方案，因此選項 D 正確。

D 29. What should students do if they need a computer next week?

(A) Wait until after April 14th

(B) Go to the General Affairs Office

(C) Use their own personal laptops

(D) Ask to use the teacher's computer room

如果學生下周需要使用電腦，應該怎麼做？

(A) 等到 4 月 14 日之後

(B) 前往總務處

(C) 用他們自己的筆記型電腦

(D) 請求使用教師電腦室

解析 由第二段第二句得知，可以使用老師的電腦教室，因此選項 D 正確。

A 30. During what season was the notice most likely written?

(A) Spring

(B) Summer

(C) Fall

(D) Winter

這則公告最有可能是在什麼季節寫的？

(A) 春天

(B) 夏天

(C) 秋天

(D) 冬天

解析 由公告的日期 4 月 5 日可得知當時為春天，第一段最後一句也說，為了在接下來的夏季能提供更舒適的環境，表示撰寫公告的季節為春天。